All He Wants

A Blazing Collection

DEBBI RAWLINS

KELLI IRELAND

KIMBERLY RAYE

MILLS & BOON

First Published 2015
Second Australian Paperback Edition 2024
ISBN 978 1 038 91216 9

First Published 2015
Second Australian Paperback Edition 2024
ISBN 978 1 038 91216 9

First Published 2014
Second Australian Paperback Edition 2024
ISBN 978 1 038 91216 9

Published by
Mills & Boon
An imprint of Harlequin Enterprises (Australia) Pty Limited (ABN 47 001 180 918), a subsidiary of HarperCollins Publishers Australia Pty Limited (ABN 36 009 913 517)
Level 19, 201 Elizabeth Street
SYDNEY NSW 2000
AUSTRALIA

Printed and bound in Australia by McPherson's Printing Group

CONTENTS

The Kiss

Debbi Rawlins

Debbi Rawlins grew up in the country and loved Western movies and books. Her first crush was on a cowboy—okay, he was an actor in the role of a cowboy, but she was only eleven, so it counts. It was in Houston, Texas, where she first started writing for Harlequin, and now she has her own ranch...of sorts. Instead of horses, she has four dogs, four cats, a trio of goats and free-range cattle on a few acres in gorgeous rural Utah.

Books by Debbi Rawlins

Made in Montana

Barefoot Blue Jean Night
Own the Night
On a Snowy Christmas Night
You're Still the One
No One Needs to Know
From This Moment On
Alone with You
Need You Now
Behind Closed Doors
Anywhere with You
Come On Over

All backlist available in ebook format.

Visit the Author Profile page at millsandboon.com.au for more titles.

Dear Reader,

I think I'm starting to have a thing for rodeo cowboys. In *This Kiss* you'll meet Ethan Styles, a champion bull rider and the third rodeo hero I've written for the Made in Montana series.

During late spring and throughout the summer, there are a number of rodeos that take place close to my home. I like most of the events—not so much others, which I'll refrain from naming though you'll probably be able to guess from reading this book. But something occurred to me while doing some research, and by that I mean I begin "skimming" one of my rodeo books and forget to put it down. It seems my growing fondness for this true American sport has a lot to do with the cowboys, for whom rodeo is not just a sport or a job but a way of life. These men are a different breed. So much passion and dedication. What's not to love?

The heroine, Sophie, is a bit younger than most of my heroines, but she is so perfect for Ethan, I couldn't resist.

I hope everyone is enjoying their summer!

All my best,

Debbi Rawlins

1

"GOTCHA!" SOPHIE MICHAELS grinned when she saw the motel's address on the computer screen. After a quick sip of morning coffee, she sent the file to her partner, Lola, who was sitting in the next office.

The rush from *getting her man* lasted barely a minute. Sophie sank back in her chair and sighed. Lately, the thrill of success was fleeting and not all that sweet.

Locating the deadbeat dad was rewarding because, well…he had three kids to support. But if he was going to jump bail anyway, couldn't he have done a better job of covering his tracks? For God's sake, a fourth grader could've found him.

After four years the job was finally getting to her. Too much sitting at the computer. Too much of the same old thing every day. Skip traces, lame excuses, shaken or resigned parents putting up collateral for their wayward children or, almost as frequently, the roles being reversed. Here in Wattsville, Wyoming, nothing much exciting happened. Oh, they had bank robberies occasionally and liquor store holdups, but those types of criminals tended to be really stupid and that made her job boring.

Sophie sighed. Working in the bail bond business wouldn't be forever. Mostly she'd signed on to help Lola get the company off the ground. Sophie looked on her cousin more like a sister. And Lola didn't mind that Sophie was sticking around only until she'd figured out what to do with her life.

Rolling her chair away from her dinged-up metal desk, Sophie dropped her chin to her chest and stretched her neck to the side. Feeling the strain of muscles that had been worked too hard earlier at the gym, she tried not to whimper. At least not loud enough for Lola to hear.

The front door to the reception area squeaked open and she glanced at the clock. "Oh, come on," she muttered. How could it be only eight-fifteen? It felt like noon.

They were expecting Mandy, the third member of their team, to return from Jackson Hole sometime this morning. But in case it was a potential client, Sophie got up. When she heard Hawk's voice, she promptly sat back down. And wished her door was closed. Hawk was Lola's sleazy boyfriend of three months. Sophie didn't like him, but so far she'd kept her mouth shut.

Lola hadn't had much luck with men in the past, but two people had never been less suited to each other. Hawk wasn't very bright, was sometimes crude and was under the delusion that riding a Harley and wearing black leather made him a badass.

He was a poser, no doubt in Sophie's mind. She knew something about desperately pretending to be someone you weren't just to fit in. A tiny bit of sympathy for him stopped her from telling Lola that his real name was Floyd and he was a high school dropout.

Sophie smiled. The idiot didn't get that she was really, really good with computers. And she knew a whole lot more about him than she'd let on.

Which she'd keep to herself. Unless Floyd kept pissing her off. She wasn't the quiet, naive young girl she used to be in high school. Unlike Floyd aka Hawk, she had put a great deal of effort into transforming herself.

"Hey, Shorty," Hawk said, lounging against her office door frame. "Missed you at the gym this morning."

She hated the nickname, which he knew. Anyway, five-four wasn't that short. She gave his tall, lanky body a once-over. "Like you've ever seen the inside of a gym."

He laughed. "Gotta admit, you're looking pretty buff," he said, pushing back his straggly hair and eyeing her legs.

"Lola's in her office."

"I know. She's busy."

"So am I." Resisting the urge to tug down the hem of her bike shorts, Sophie swiveled in her chair so that her legs were under the desk, her gaze on the monitor.

"You guys working on something big?"

She noticed that line 2 was lit. Lola was on the phone. "Why are you still here?"

"Chillax, Shorty. Just making conversation while I wait for the old lady."

The front door opened again and Hawk glanced over his shoulder. His look of dread made Sophie smile. It had to be Mandy. She'd been working as a bounty hunter in Colorado before Lola hired her two years ago, and she could be intimidating at times. Plus, she didn't like Hawk any more than Sophie did. Only, Mandy wasn't as circumspect.

A whoop came from Lola's office. "Okay, ladies, we've got a live one. Mandy, are you here?"

Sophie leaped out of her chair and barreled past Hawk, who had enough smarts to get out of her way. "Somebody jumped bail?"

"Oh yeah." Lola walked out of her office waving a piece of paper. "You'll never guess who."

The waiting area was small, with two chairs, a ficus that was alive only because Lola remembered to water it and a rack of magazines, where Mandy stood, tall, beefed-up and calm as could be. She wasn't the excitable type. "Ethan Styles," she said, and dropped her duffel bag.

Lola shoved back her long red hair and sighed. "How did you know?"

"Ethan Styles," Sophie murmured under her breath. She must've heard wrong. If his name was on the list of bonds they'd posted, she would've noticed. She knew him…sort of… "Who did you say?"

Lola's concerned gaze found Sophie. "I'm pretty sure you remember Ethan."

"The rodeo guy, right?" Hawk moved to the circle and sidled up to Lola when Sophie and Mandy gave him butt-out glares. "He's that hotshot bull rider."

Lola nodded and looked at Mandy. "You just get back from Jackson Hole?"

"An hour ago," Mandy said with a curious glance at Sophie. "I turned Jergens over to Deputy Martin."

Sophie couldn't seem to slow down her brain. Too many memories of Ethan revolved like a slide show on speed. She hadn't seen him up close since high school. She'd gone to a few rodeos just to see him, but only from the bleachers and it had been a while. Sometimes she watched him on TV, but not often. She wasn't a kid anymore and there was only so much daydreaming a woman could do without feeling like a dope.

"You get any sleep yet?" Lola asked Mandy, who just smiled.

"I hate to send you out again, but I got a tip that Styles might be headed for northwest Montana. A town called Blackfoot Falls."

"No shit. Pretty boy has an outstanding warrant?" Hawk laughed. "What did he get locked up for? Screwing somebody's wife?"

The expression on Lola's face hinted that Hawk might not be far off the mark.

It wouldn't surprise Sophie if he was in trouble because of a woman. Half the girls in school had had the hots for him. Even now he left female fans across the country panting, but so what? Lola was mistaken if she thought Ethan's reputation with the ladies bothered Sophie. He didn't faze her. Not anymore.

"Why didn't he pay his own bail? Between his winnings and

endorsement deals, he has to have money," Sophie said, mostly thinking out loud.

Lola shrugged. "He wouldn't be the first pro athlete to blow his cash on stupid things," she said. "We have the pink slip for his motor coach as collateral, so I had no problem with posting. I have to say, though, I'm surprised he skipped. He's not due in court until Monday, but he wasn't supposed to leave the state."

"I'll do it." Sophie squared her shoulders when they all stared at her. "I'll go after him."

Lola shook her head. "Not a good idea, Soph."

"You've never worked in the field." Mandy's quiet reminder somehow felt like a betrayal.

Even though Sophie had started kickboxing and tae kwon do back in college, it was Mandy who'd inspired her to go all out, work her body to its full potential. Sophie was in the best physical shape of her life and Mandy knew it. Anyway, Ethan might not come along willingly, but he wasn't the type to get rough.

"I told you guys I wanted to be more involved." She glared first at Lola, and then Mandy. "I know Ethan. I can bring him back with the least amount of fuss."

Hawk snorted. "No way. You don't know Styles."

"Shut up," Mandy said without looking at him. Her gaze stayed on Sophie. "You think you're ready?"

"I know I am." She glanced at Lola, who'd just given Hawk an impatient look. So maybe all wasn't peachy keen with the lovebirds. Good. Her cousin deserved better.

Lola met her gaze. "No, not Ethan. You can have the next one."

"I'm not asking for permission. I own half this company." Flexing her tense shoulders, Sophie ignored the looks of surprise. She and Lola never argued. Not over business, or their personal lives. "Text me the details. I'll go home, grab a few things and leave within the hour."

"Come on, Soph." Lola pinched the bridge of her nose. "Let's talk privately. Please."

"What she says makes sense." Hawk cut Lola short, earning him a warning look, which he obviously didn't like judging by his creepy scowl. "Why not let her go after him?"

"Excuse me—" Sophie stopped. Hawk was defending her? Okay, now, that was weird. She didn't need his help, but hey, bonus points for trying. "This isn't up for discussion," she said. "All we're doing is wasting time."

"Knowing him might not be an advantage," Mandy said. "Surprise is your best weapon. He sees you, he could run."

"Ethan won't remember me." Sophie avoided Lola's gaze. "Even if he does, he won't associate me with Lola's Bail Bonds."

Lola followed Sophie into her office. "We need to talk, kiddo," she said, closing the door behind her.

"You're not changing my mind." Sophie sifted through her cluttered drawer and found her wallet. Now, where were her keys?

She crouched to check under her desk and found them next to a protein bar she'd misplaced yesterday. Grabbing them both, she pushed to her feet.

"Will you at least hear me out?" Her cousin's dark eyes weren't just worried but annoyed.

"Go ahead." Sophie unwrapped the bar and stuck half of it in her mouth, since she wouldn't have time to eat anything else. She had to get on the road fast. No telling how much of a head start Ethan had… "When did he leave for Montana, do you know?"

"Are you going to listen to me at all?"

"Probably not."

"Goddammit, Sophie." Lola paused and lowered her voice. "We can't afford for you to get all goo-goo-eyed over him. He'll sweet-talk you into letting him go and we'll be screwed."

Sophie chewed a bit, then said, "Wow, your faith in me is really touching."

"It's not that. The money's important, but I hate to think of you getting all twisted up over him again."

"Oh, for God's sake, I was never twisted up."

"Yes, you were." Lola smiled. "Don't forget, I was there. Anyway, that was high school, so you were allowed."

"Exactly. It was high school. I was fifteen. We had a fleeting encounter. Don't make a big deal out of it."

"He was your hero," Lola said, her voice softening.

Sophie turned away to pick up her gym bag. "You're only twenty-eight. I'm sure you still remember what it was like to be fifteen."

At the beginning of her freshman year, Sophie and her mom had moved to Wyoming. Lola had been a junior and the only person Sophie knew in her new school. They hadn't become friends quickly. Her cousin had had her own clique, and back then, Sophie had entered a nerdy phase, trying to balance her high IQ and an awkward social life.

That alone hadn't made her the target of bullies. Having had the audacity to wear the *wrong* dress was the line she'd crossed. She found out later that the most popular girl in school had worn the same sundress the week before Sophie even started at Wattsville High. The whole thing was ridiculous, considering that Ashley had huge boobs and Sophie had little more than two mosquito bites. So of course Ashley had looked so much better in the spaghetti-strap dress.

God, Sophie still remembered what it had felt like to have those girls come after her with scissors. They'd cut her dress to ribbons before Ethan had stopped them and put his jacket over her shoulders.

Turned out Ashley was Ethan's girlfriend. But he'd been furious when he stepped in and warned them off. After that, the girls still gave her evil looks, but they kept their distance.

Damn straight he'd been her hero.

"Are you still following his career?" Lola asked.

"No." Sophie set the gym bag on her chair and shut down her laptop, refusing to look up. "I know you saw me at my worst, sneaking around, following him, trying to stay on his radar. Frankly it embarrasses me to even think about it." All while he'd acted as if she hadn't existed. That part she left out, and met Lola's gaze. "Did you and Hawk have a fight?"

Lola's brows went up. "Why?"

"I saw the look you gave him."

"No, it's just..." Lola waved dismissively. "I'd already told him he shouldn't be hanging around here."

Sophie tucked her tablet under her arm. "Look, the thing with Ethan happened a long time ago. I was a kid." She smiled. "I can do this."

Lola studied her for a moment. "Okay," she said with a resigned sigh. "I just don't understand why you'd want to."

"I know," Sophie said softly. She didn't quite get it herself. It wasn't as if she needed closure, but in a weird way, that was exactly how it felt. She stopped halfway to the door. "Don't you think it's odd he jumped bail? Ethan has a reputation for being a stand-up guy."

"I don't know what he's thinking. He certainly doesn't have a low profile."

"Nope. The National Finals Rodeo in Las Vegas starts in about a week. He's going for his second championship title—" She saw the concern in Lola's eyes. "I read something about it online the other day," she murmured. "Try not to worry, okay? I've got this."

She hoped.

THE WATERING HOLE was noisy, crowded with cowboys drinking beer and gorgeous accommodating women dressed to kill. Ethan Styles had frequented hundreds of bars just like this one in the nine years since he turned pro. He knew what it was like the night before a rodeo, especially in a small town like Blackfoot Falls. So why in the hell had he suggested meeting his friend Matt here?

Somehow Ethan had gotten the dumb idea that this rodeo would be different. No prize money was involved or qualifying points. The event was a fund-raiser for Safe Haven, a large animal sanctuary, so all the ticket and concession money went directly to them. But he should've known better. Rodeo fans were a loyal bunch, and having to travel to this remote Montana town obviously hadn't bothered them.

Normally he was up for signing autographs and getting hit on by hot women. But with the finals a week away he'd been on edge since he hit Montana late this morning. After that bogus arrest in Wyoming and then hearing how fellow bull rider Tommy Lunt had busted his knee, foreboding had prickled the back of his neck.

He'd missed the finals himself because of injuries. Twice. Last year broken ribs and a punctured lung had sidelined him. Two seasons before that, it had been an elbow injury. So he had cause to be jumpy.

"Hey, Styles, 'bout time you showed up." Kenny Horton stood at the bar with another bronc rider and three women, who all turned to eyeball Ethan.

He shook his head when Kenny motioned for him to join them. "Maybe later. I'm meeting someone."

"Right behind you."

At the sound of Matt Gunderson's voice, Ethan grinned and turned around to shake his hand. "Glad to see you, buddy."

"Same here. What's it been…a year?"

"About that." Ethan moved aside for a short, curvy blonde who'd just entered the bar. Their gazes met briefly, surprise flickering in her brown eyes. But then she brushed past him. "So, how's retirement?" he asked Matt and shifted so he could watch the blonde walk up to the bar.

The seats were all taken. A cowboy jumped to his feet and offered her his stool. Shaking her head, she dug into her pocket. Her tight jeans didn't leave room for much, but she managed to pull out a cell phone. She wasn't wearing a wedding ring. He always checked, though it hadn't done him any good last week.

Wendy hadn't been wearing one when he met her at the Ponderosa Saloon last Saturday, or when she invited him to her ranch that night. That hadn't made her any less married, and to a mean, rich son of a bitch on top of everything.

"Retirement? Shit, I work twice as hard for half the money," Matt said with a laugh. "But yeah, it was time."

That part Ethan didn't understand. Matt had been the one to beat. Yet out of the blue he'd just quit competing. Talk around the tour was that his new wife might've had something to do with it. "So, no regrets?"

"Not a one." Matt frowned. "You can't be thinking of getting out—"

"Hell no. Now that you're off the circuit, maybe I can finally win another title."

"Right." Matt laughed. "I seem to remember you leaving me in the dust more than a few times."

"Never when it counted."

"Man, you've had some bad luck right before the finals. I should've convinced you to drop out when we changed the date. You're the main draw this weekend. A lot of people are coming to see you ride Twister, but I should've thought this through."

"Come on, you probably figured I wouldn't make it to the finals."

Matt reared his head back, eyes narrowed. "What the hell's the matter with you, Styles?"

Ethan grinned. "Just joking." No way he'd admit that he had considered bailing because he couldn't risk injury. But then he'd only be superstitious about bad karma or some other bullshit. "It's a worthy cause. I'm glad to do it."

Just before Ethan turned to check on the blonde, he caught his friend's sympathetic look. Most rodeo cowboys started young and came from families of die-hard fans. Matt had been a casual fan who'd climbed onto his first bull at a late age, and yet he understood the pressure coming at Ethan from all sides. Winning another gold buckle wasn't just about ego or satisfying a lifelong dream. He came from rodeo royalty. Both his parents held multiple world champion titles. Most of their fans were also his fans. A lot of expectations drove him to succeed.

The woman was still standing at the bar, guys on either side of her vying for her attention, but she didn't seem interested. She slowly sipped a drink, checked her phone and then leaned over the bar to talk to the older woman filling pitchers of beer.

Ethan smirked to himself. Bending over like that sure wouldn't discourage guys from hitting on her. She knew how to wear a pair of plain faded jeans. Her boots were brown, low-heeled, scuffed. And the long-sleeve blue T-shirt was nothing fancy. No, she sure wasn't dressed to be noticed like the other women circling the room. Maybe she lived on a nearby ranch and had just quit work.

Damn, she was hot.

And familiar. Yeah, women were plentiful for a bull rider, and he was no saint. He also wasn't the type to forget a name or face. It sure felt as though he'd run into her before. More than that, he felt this odd pull… The kind of pull that could get him into trouble. Which he did not need, especially not now.

Someone called out to Matt and he waved in acknowledgment. "We're not gonna find a table or a place at the bar. Maybe we should head over to the diner. Unless you're looking to hook up with that blonde."

"What blonde?" Ethan asked, and Matt smiled. "That describes half the women in here."

"I'm talking about the one at the bar you've been eyeing."

"Nah, I'm not looking for company. I'm keeping my nose clean until the finals."

"A whole week? You'll never make it."

"Probably not." Ethan laughed and glanced back at the bar. "Is she local?"

Matt studied her for a moment. "I don't think so."

"Well, I'll be damned if it isn't the twins," a voice boomed from the back room.

Ethan and Matt exchanged glances. They both knew it was

Tex, a bronc rider from Dallas. Though he wasn't the only one who called them *the twins.* They'd joined the pro tour within months of each other, and in the beginning they'd often been mistaken for brothers. Ethan figured it wasn't so much because they shared similar builds, or even because they both had light brown hair and blue eyes. It was their height. Six feet was tall for a bull rider.

"What are you boys doing standing there talking like two old women?" Tex yelled, a pool stick in one hand, an empty mug in the other. "Grab yourselves a pitcher and get on back here."

"Guess he's had a few," Ethan said. Tex was quiet by nature. But after a couple of beers…

"He'd better be able to ride tomorrow," Matt muttered, then turned when someone else shouted his name.

More people had poured into the bar. Ethan was willing to bet the place had reached capacity before the last ten customers had squeezed inside. And now that big-mouthed Tex had called attention to them, fans were approaching him and Matt for autographs.

They each accepted a pen and began scrawling their names. "You check in at The Boarding House yet?" Matt asked under his breath.

"An hour ago."

"It's not too late. You can stay out at the Lone Wolf. We've got a big house, trailer hookups. The inn's overbooked, so the owner won't have any trouble renting out your room. And my wife's dying to meet you."

"Hey, that's right. You're a married man now. Sorry I missed your wedding."

"No problem. I warned Rachel there'd be conflicts no matter which weekend she chose."

Ethan smiled as he passed the Safe Haven flyer he'd just signed to a middle-aged woman wearing a promotional Professional Bull Riders T-shirt from the 2010 finals, the year he wanted wiped from his memory forever. To be kept from the finals because of an injury was one thing, but to make it that far and then get hurt in the third round? Talk about fate landing a sucker punch.

This year nothing was going to keep him from the finals. Or from winning another gold buckle.

Nothing. Period.

2

SOPHIE SURE WISHED she'd known he was here in Blackfoot Falls for a rodeo before she'd left Wyoming. The event was a fund-raiser, so of course it wasn't listed on the PBR tour. The whole town, which wasn't saying much, since it was so small they had no traffic lights, was busting at the seams with rodeo fans. There was only one inn, a dude ranch twenty minutes away and a number of impromptu bed-and-breakfasts scattered around the area, all of which were booked. So was the large trailer park over thirty minutes away, not that a vacancy there would do her any good.

Somehow she had to get him alone. No clue how she was going to do it with so many fans clamoring for his attention. Those crazy people would string her up if they knew she planned to drag their favorite bull rider back to Wyoming.

The buckle bunnies worried her the most. Turning completely around so that her back was against the bar, she sipped her tonic water and watched the women practically line up, just waiting their turns to hit on Ethan.

She didn't care one bit. If he had enough stamina to screw every last one of them, then God bless him. She was twenty-six, not a silly teenager anymore, and he no longer haunted her dreams. Though if he took one of those eager young ladies back to his room for the night, Sophie could have a problem.

It might mean she'd have to wait till morning to bag him. That left her a very narrow window before the rodeo started at noon.

Maybe she'd have to seduce him herself.

The thought sent a bolt of heat zinging through her body. A hurried sip of tonic water barely made it down her throat. He was still hot as hell. She'd be fooling herself if she couldn't admit that much. Tall and lean with the perfect proportion of muscle, and those dreamy blue eyes… Good Lord.

Bumping into him when she first entered the bar had thrown her. She hadn't been prepared at all. But the wig had done its job. Even up close he hadn't recognized her, and now she was ready for him.

In the middle of signing an autograph, he swung a look at her and she shifted her weight to her other foot. Okay, maybe his gaze hadn't landed on her but vaguely in her direction. Unfortunately her female parts couldn't tell the difference.

Seducing him? That might have to take a few steps back to plan Z.

"Now, why are you sittin' here drinkin' alone, darlin'?" The same husky and very tipsy cowboy who'd offered her a beer earlier wove too close, nearly unseating the guy on her left.

She steadied Romeo with a brief hand on his shoulder. Boy, she sure didn't need either of the men making a scene. "Are you here for the rodeo tomorrow?" she asked.

"You bet."

"Fan or rider?"

He frowned, clearly affronted.

Sophie smiled, despite the wave of beer breath that reached her. "Better go easy on the booze if you're competing."

The younger cowboy sitting on the stool twisted around and grinned. "Yeah, Brady, you don't wanna give those calves a leg up."

Ah, they knew each other. Made sense, since they were both

probably here for the rodeo. Sophie relaxed a bit, and while the two men traded barbs, she slid a glance at Ethan, who was still surrounded by women.

Oddly he didn't seem all that interested in any of them. Not even the blondes. According to the articles and blogs she'd read earlier, his past three girlfriends had been blondes. Although it seemed he hadn't stayed with any of them for more than a few months. Probably thought he was too hot for any one woman to handle. Or decided it was his duty to spread the hotness around.

The cowboy, whose name was apparently Brady and who continued to stand too close, said something she didn't catch. Shifting her attention to him, she wondered if a well-placed knee could seem accidental. "Excuse me?"

He turned his head to look at Ethan. "Okay, now I see why you're being so uppity. You've already got your sights set on Styles. Figures." Lifting his beer, he mumbled, "Damn bull riders," before taking a gulp.

Oh, crap. Was she being that obvious? "Who's Styles?"

Brady frowned. "Are you kiddin'?"

She shook her head, the picture of innocence.

"See, Brady?" Grinning, the other cowboy elbowed him. "She's not snubbing you 'cause you're a calf roper. I bet she's got a whole lot more reasons than that."

Sophie ignored the troublemaker. "A calf roper?"

"That's right, darlin'. You're lookin' at a two-time champ."

"So you're one of those guys who chases the poor little calves and then ties them up?"

Brady's boastful grin slipped. "It's all for sport, darlin', don't you understand?"

"No, I don't. Not at all." She faked a shudder. "I always feel so sorry for the calves."

Even the guy sitting on the stool had shut up and swiveled around to face the other way. Brady just stared at her, then shook his head and walked off.

Sophie hid a smile behind a sip of tonic and turned back to

Ethan. He was watching her. This time there was nothing vague about it. He gave her a slow smile and a small nod. She had no idea what that was supposed to mean. Other than she might need something stronger than tonic water.

Her nipples had tightened, and thank God the room was dim, because her entire body blushed. He couldn't have overheard her taunting Brady, not from over twenty feet away and with all the noisy laughter competing with the jukebox. And no way did Ethan recognize her.

He'd been a senior the year she started at Wattsville High, so he hadn't seen her in eleven years. She doubted he'd recognized her even once since the day he rescued her. How many times had she taken great pains to be in the perfect spot, like the cafeteria or near the boys' locker room so he couldn't miss her? Yet he did, and with unflattering consistency.

A fan stuck a piece of paper in his face and only then did he look away from her. Her heart hadn't stopped pounding.

"Sophie?"

She jumped so hard she nearly knocked over the waitress's loaded tray.

The woman moved back. "Sorry, didn't mean to startle you. Sophie, right?"

What the hell? No one here knew her. She nodded.

"Sadie asked me to give you this," she said, inclining her head at the bartender and passing Sophie a piece of paper. "It's a name and phone number. She said you're looking for a place to stay tonight?"

Ah. Sophie smiled. "Yes," she said, accepting the paper. "Thank you."

"It's a long shot. The Meyers have probably rented out their spare rooms by now. But Kalispell is only a forty-five-minute drive from here." The waitress was already pushing through the crowd. "Good luck."

Sophie sighed. She thought she was so smart, but she stank at this covert stuff. Using her real name had been a stupid rookie move. No matter how doubtful it was that Ethan remembered her.

She studied the scribbled phone number, then glanced at Ethan. Fortunately he was too busy being mobbed to pay her any more attention. Both he and the man with him gave her the impression they'd bolt as soon as possible. She'd be a fool to let Ethan out of her sight, but it was too noisy to make a call in the bar. She'd have to step outside and just stay close to the door.

If she were to find a room, she'd be shocked. But she had to at least try in case she was forced to stay till morning. Or, God forbid, until after the rodeo was over in two days.

It would be so much easier to grab him tonight and leave Blackfoot Falls pronto. She didn't need his buddies interfering, because if they did, what could she do, really? And returning to Wyoming empty-handed wasn't an option.

She thought back to her earlier idea. Coaxing him to ask her to his room might be her best bet. But not if she couldn't get the damn jitters under control. Who was she kidding, anyway? There were several gorgeous women waiting for him to say the word. The only guy she'd attracted was one who roped and tied baby cows.

Hoping her half-full glass of tonic would hold her spot at the bar, she squeezed her way toward the door. The standing crowd was truly ridiculous, oblivious of anyone trying to pass, and forcing her in Ethan's direction.

"Boy howdy, was I shocked to hear you'd be riding this weekend, Ethan! Aren't you afraid of getting injured and missing the finals again?"

Sophie stopped. She turned and saw Ethan tighten his jaw. The people closest to him grew quiet and watchful.

The stout, ruddy-faced fan who'd asked the moronic question continued heedlessly. "I told the wife I figured you'd be too superstitious to take the chance, especially for no prize money."

"It's for a good cause," Ethan said quietly.

"Don't get me wrong, son. I'm glad you're here. I'm looking forward to seeing you ride tomorrow." The man rubbed his palms together, ignoring the blushing woman tugging at his arm. "I understand Matt Gunderson has raised some hard-bucking bulls."

"Yep. I heard the same thing." Ethan's jaw clenched again, then he smiled and moved back a little. "I sure hope all you folks are generous to Safe Haven. They take in a lot of animals who otherwise wouldn't have a chance of surviving. Any donation you'd like to add to the price of the ticket would be appreciated."

Unable to listen anymore, she shouldered her way to the door. No, she told herself. *Uh-uh.* She could not, and would not, feel sympathy for Ethan. As he'd said, Safe Haven was a good cause. He'd volunteered to ride. Great. Good for him. He wasn't letting superstition spook him. That didn't mean she wouldn't drag his ass back to Wyoming. He'd broken the condition of his bail by taking off. And clearly he didn't care at all about screwing her and Lola out of the money they'd posted for his bond. Sure, they had his motor coach as collateral. But until they could sell it, they were on the hook for a lot of cash.

Finally she made it outside. The biting cold November air nipped at her heated cheeks. She drew in a deep breath and immediately started coughing from all the cigarette smoke.

She turned to go the other way. Great. Smokers overran the sidewalk. She refused to stray too far from the door in case Ethan left, so she ducked behind a silver truck. No doubt he was anxious to get away from the stupid questions. And who could blame him?

The lighting was poor. She dug out her phone but could barely make out the number on the crumpled paper. Using the Bic app on her cell to see, she memorized the seven digits, then called. And promptly got the no she'd expected. Disconnecting, she sighed.

"No luck, huh?"

Sophie knew that voice. She slanted a look at Ethan, who stood on the sidewalk, his hands stuffed in his jeans pockets.

He wore a tan Western-style shirt, no jacket. His broad shoulders were hunched slightly, against the cold, she imagined.

"You must have me mixed up with someone else," she said, reminding herself to breathe. "I don't believe we've met."

"No?" He studied her a beat longer than she could manage to keep still. Thankfully he stepped back when she slipped between him and the truck to return to the sidewalk. "I thought maybe we had," he said, shrugging.

She shook her head, held her breath. "Nope."

Jeez. Of course he didn't recognize her. Or really think they'd met before. It was a pickup line guys used all the time.

"You're looking for a place to stay tonight," he said. "Aren't you?"

That stopped her again. "How do you know that?"

"The waitress." His intense stare wasn't helping her nerves, so she moved into the shadows. "I asked her."

Sophie huffed a laugh. "And of course she told you, because…" She closed her mouth. Because of that damn sexy smile of his, that was why, but this was what Sophie wanted, to get him alone, so she'd better lose the attitude.

"Because she's my buddy Matt's sister-in-law," he said, and glanced over his shoulder when the door opened and raucous laughter spilled out into the moonlit night. "Hey, how about we go someplace else? Get away from the bar."

"Sure." She tried not to seem too eager. Or irritated. Picking up a woman was this easy for a guy like Ethan. Just a look, a smile, and he was all set. She moved closer to him. The Boarding House Inn, where she knew he was staying, was within walking distance. "What did you have in mind?"

He looked both ways down Main Street. "How about the diner? Shouldn't be too crowded."

"The diner?"

"Is that all right? We can cross after this next truck."

"Um, sure. I guess."

Glancing at her, he asked, "You have somewhere else in mind?"

A diner? Okay, she was officially insulted. "I was thinking someplace more private," she whispered, linking arms with him.

Surprise flashed across his face. His eyes found hers, then he lowered his gaze to her lips. "I'm Ethan."

"I know who you are."

"And you're Sophie?"

So stupid. She nodded, promising herself that after this, she'd stick to her desk job. At least her name hadn't triggered his memory. If he were to remember anything, it would probably be the pesky twerp who'd kept popping up in the weirdest places half his senior year.

The door to the bar opened again and they both turned. A tall brunette and her blonde sidekick walked out, scanning the groups of smokers.

The moment their gazes lit on Ethan, he tensed. "Let's go," he said, and draped his arm across the back of her shoulders. "Mind walking? It's not far."

"Fine." She huddled close, soaking in the warmth of his body and trying to decide if it would be too much to slide her arm around his waist.

He walked at a fast clip, and with her shorter legs she had some trouble keeping up. "Sorry," he said. "I'll slow down."

She saw her green Jeep parked at the curb just ahead, and two things flashed through her mind. She needed the handcuffs she'd left in her glove compartment, but she couldn't stop for them because of her Wyoming plates. If he knew the Jeep was hers, he could easily put two and two together.

"Cold?" he asked, pulling her closer.

"What?" She realized she'd tensed. "A little." Checking random plates, she saw a variety of out-of-state vehicles from Colorado, Utah, even an SUV from Wyoming. It was worth taking the chance. She really, really needed the cuffs. "Could we stop a minute?"

Ethan frowned and glanced back at the Watering Hole. "Am I still walking too fast?"

"No. We just passed my car and I wanted to grab my jacket."

He started to follow her, but she shook her head while inching backward and digging for the key in her pocket.

"It's kind of a mess," she said, relieved that he only smiled and stayed put.

She unlocked the driver's door. And kept an eye on him while she quickly transferred the handcuffs from the glove box to a deep pocket in the puffy down jacket she'd left on the passenger seat. Pausing, she considered scooping up her purse hidden on the floorboard.

Couldn't hurt. She probably could use some lip gloss about now. Jeez. *This is not a date.*

The door was closed and locked, her purse in hand before she considered the incriminating ID and *bail piece* authorizing her to arrest him inside her bag. It didn't matter, since she was going to do this thing quickly. Preferably the minute they were inside his room.

Instead of continuing to walk when she rejoined him, he studied her car. "I've always liked Jeeps. Looks new. Have you had it long?"

"I bought it last year." She drew in a breath. He was staring at her plates.

"You from Wyoming?"

"Not originally, but I've lived there for a few years now."

"What part?"

"Sheridan," she lied, purposely choosing the farthest town from Wattsville that she could think of.

"I'm from outside Casper myself." Either he was a very good actor or the Wyoming coincidence didn't bother him.

"Really? We're not exactly neighbors, but still..."

"Here, let me help you with your jacket."

Sophie thought she heard the handcuffs clink and clutched

the jacket to her chest. Giving him a come-hither smile, she said, "I'd rather have your arm around me."

"Always happy to oblige a beautiful woman." Ethan took her free hand and drew her close. The jacket served as an unwanted buffer. "You aren't a rodeo fan, are you, Sophie?"

"Um, a little..."

He smiled. "It's okay. My ego isn't that fragile."

"I know who you are. That should count for something."

His puzzled frown sent up a warning flag. It lasted only a moment before the smile returned, and he started them walking again. "So you aren't here for the rodeo."

"No." Wrong answer. She wasn't sure why, but it felt wrong. She was missing something. "Well, yes, sort of. Does it matter?"

"I suppose not." He checked for traffic and guided her across the street, his arm tightening around her shoulders.

The Boarding House Inn was just up ahead. They had another half a block to go and she hoped the men standing on the porch steps deep in conversation would hurry up and leave. If she did her job well, by tomorrow morning it would appear that Ethan Styles had disappeared into thin air. And she preferred not to be identified as the last person seen with him.

That was where the wig came in handy. As a blonde, she barely recognized herself.

Luckily the porch cleared just as they approached. The silence that had fallen between her and Ethan was beginning to feel awkward. She slanted him a glance and caught him watching her. The porch light shone in both of their faces and he stopped, right there, several feet from the steps. Turning to face her, he nudged up her chin and studied her mouth.

She held her breath, certain he was about to kiss her.

"I have one question," he said. "Are you a reporter?"

"What? No."

Something in her expression must have made him doubt her. His gaze narrowed, he seemed to be trying hard to remember...

"Why on earth would you think I'm a reporter?" It hit her

then that everything would have been so much easier if she'd just pretended to be one of his buckle bunny fans. The wariness in his face convinced her to fix that situation right now.

"Okay, I lied," she blurted, the words rushing out of her mouth before she could think. "I'm a huge rodeo fan. The biggest. I go to rodeos all the time. I'm a buckle bunny. I didn't want to admit it and I—" She cleared her throat. "I wanted to stand out to get your attention, and that's why I lied. About not being a fan." She held in a sigh. "Does that make sense?"

Ethan looked as if he was going to laugh.

So she threw her arms around his neck and pulled him down into a blazing kiss.

3

ETHAN RECOVERED FROM her sudden burst of enthusiasm, thankful he hadn't landed on his ass. Sophie was small but strong, too. Strong enough that she'd forced him back a step. He put his arms around her and slowed down the kiss, taking the time to explore and sample the sweet taste of her mouth.

They were standing on the porch, under the light, in full view of Main Street where anyone passing the inn could see them. That didn't bother him. He just couldn't figure out what had caused her unexpected display of passion.

Way before he was finished with the kiss she stepped back, only to stare up at him with dazed eyes, and was that regret? Probably not. He wasn't seeing so clearly himself.

Damn, he should've moved them to his room before now. "How about we go inside where it's warm?" he asked.

She jerked a nod, clutched the jacket to her chest and inched farther away from him, as if she was afraid he was going to grab her.

Wondering if she'd ever picked up a guy before, Ethan was careful to give her some space. More practiced women who followed the circuit had a completely different air about them. He opened the door and motioned for her to go inside. The lobby was tiny, furnished with a desk and two wing chairs, a small oak table on which rolls and coffee would be set out in the morning, or so he'd been told.

"Turn right," he said, and she did so without a word or a backward glance. "I'm near the end."

He watched her as she led the way, admiring the view. Sophie claimed they'd never met, but he wasn't so sure that was true. Once he'd seen her up close, he was even more convinced they'd met before. The shape of her pouty lips had given him the first inkling that he knew her from somewhere. Even now, watching the slight sway of her hips tugged at his memory. It wasn't a particularly distinctive walk, so he didn't get it.

Hell, he could've seen her in the crowd at a rodeo. She'd admitted she was a fan. But that didn't feel right, either. If it turned out she'd lied and really was a reporter, man, he was going to be pissed. So far he'd been lucky. The public didn't know about his arrest. But one more media question about the black cloud that seemed to follow him to the finals every year and he'd shut them all out. No more interviews. No more sound bites. Screw 'em.

Sophie stopped to examine the baseboards and then looked up at the ceiling. "I think this place really was a boardinghouse at one time."

"Yep," Ethan said, glad she seemed more relaxed. "It was built around the 1920s. The new owner bought the place last year and kept the renovations as close to the original structure as possible. She even tried to replicate the detail in the moldings."

Sophie grinned at him. "I like that you know all that stuff."

With a laugh, he pulled the key out of his pocket. "It was on the website."

"The halls are awfully narrow. Men couldn't have had very broad shoulders back in the twenties…" Her voice trailed off, her gaze flickering away from his chest.

"Two doors down," he said, staying right where he was, waiting for her to start walking again so he wouldn't crowd her.

He had to decide what to tell her. That kiss kind of ruined

his plan. He hadn't actually been hitting on her. Blackfoot Falls was small, and with all the fans in town, he'd been rethinking Matt's offer to stay at his ranch. Ethan knew some of the guys had parked their motor coaches there instead of at the RV park outside of Kalispell.

Still, it would be quiet out there. He could help Sophie out by giving her his room. And staying at Matt's meant less chance for Ethan to get in any trouble.

He stuck the key in the lock and glanced at Sophie. With those soft brown eyes and that generous mouth, she looked like big trouble to him, tasted like it, too.

Who was he kidding? If he'd really wanted to just give her his room, he would have said something when they were outside. By her Jeep. Now, though, it would be awkward as hell to pack up and leave. He pushed the door open and she went right on inside.

After glancing around at the antique chair and the old armoire, she focused on the queen-size four-poster bed that took up most of the small room. She moved closer to it, stopping a moment to check out the patchwork quilt, and then ran her hand down the oak post close to the wall.

His cock pulsed.

When she wrapped her fingers around the smooth wood and stroked up, Ethan had to turn away. Yeah, he needed to erase that image real fast.

Between her obvious interest in the bed and his dick's growing interest in her, he decided it was time to offer the room as he'd intended, even if it would make him look like an ass.

"It's nice," she said, smiling, walking close enough he could inhale her sweet scent. "Quaint. Too bad the furniture is so small. I bet you can't even sit on the chair."

She laid her jacket over the back of it, sat on the edge and pulled off a boot.

And there went his last good intention. Ethan sighed. If even her red-striped sock turned him on, he wasn't going anywhere. She was already here. He was here. They were consenting adults.

So he couldn't see a reason to deny himself a little recreation before heading to the Lone Wolf. Matt had left the invitation open.

"Need help with your boots?" she asked, mesmerizing him with those eyes the color of melted chocolate.

He pulled both his boots off before she'd finished removing her second one. "Tell me you're over twenty-one," he said, straightening and pausing at the first snap on his shirt.

Sophie laughed. "Are you serious? I don't look that young."

"I just like to be sure."

"Well, you can relax. I'm twenty-six. Anyway, I think the age of consent is sixteen in Montana."

The same as in Wyoming, not that he paid it any mind. Twenty-one was his personal cutoff.

Getting to her feet, she pulled her shirt from her jeans, then stopped and frowned. "Is something wrong?"

His snaps were still intact. "I have one last question."

"Okay," she said, taking a step closer, her sultry smile designed to scramble his brain.

"Are you married?"

Her eyebrows arched and her lips parted. She looked startled, and maybe confused. "No. Of course not." She shook her head, her eyebrows lowering into a delicate frown. "No, I'm not married, nor have I ever been married." She drew in a breath, seemed to calm herself and took over unsnapping his shirt. "Would it really matter?"

"If you have to ask, damn good thing you're still single." He could see he'd irritated her. Too bad. He wasn't about to get into another scrape like the mess he'd narrowly escaped in Wyoming. After discovering Wendy was married, he'd refused to sleep with her. To get back at him, she'd filed a false charge that he'd stolen some jewelry.

Sophie looked torn for a moment and then unfastened his next snap.

He caught her hand and inspected her ring finger. No mark, not even a faded one. "Sorry, but I'm touchy about the issue," he said, staring into her wary eyes and lifting her hand to his lips for a brief kiss before releasing her. "It's nothing personal."

Without another word, she finished unsnapping him, her eyes cast downward, until she parted the front of his shirt and pushed it off his shoulders. Her preoccupation with his bare chest was flattering but somewhat awkward. He finished shrugging out of the shirt, impatient to see what was under hers.

Uncertainty betrayed itself in the soft, hesitant palms she skimmed over his ribs and then his pecs. Her touch was almost reverent, her expression dreamlike. A few buckle bunnies he'd been with had tried to use their phones to sneak pictures of him shirtless, and even buck naked. But this was different. This seemed more…personal.

Jesus, he hoped it didn't turn out she was one of those crazy stalkers.

He captured her hands and gently lowered them from his chest. When he tried to draw up her T-shirt, she tensed, angling in a way that cut him off.

He took half a step back. "You change your mind?" he asked, keeping his tone low and even, letting her know it was all good. She was allowed.

"No," she said, shaking her head. "I haven't."

He tipped her chin up so he could see her face. "It's okay if you have. Tell me to stop and I will."

Sighing, she pulled off her own shirt and tossed it somewhere over her shoulder. He was too busy taking in the pink bra and creamy skin to see where it landed. Her breasts were the perfect size. They'd fit nicely in his hands. Her arms and shoulders were well toned, and her abs…a woman didn't get that kind of definition from casual exercise. Sophie took her workouts seriously. But she hadn't gone overboard, either, which he greatly appreciated.

He drew his thumb across the silky skin mounding above her bra. She had no freckles, just the faint remnant of a summer tan.

Damned if he wasn't the one staring now.

She shivered and shrank back.

"You're beautiful," he said, and looked up to meet eyes filled with disbelief. "I'm sure you get that line a lot, but I mean it."

She let out a short laugh and went for his belt buckle. He wished she wasn't so nervous. But if he brought it up, it would probably spook her into leaving.

Would that be the right thing to do?

Her frenzied movements confused him. It was as if she was racing the clock. Or…maybe she had someplace else she needed to be. Dammit, he couldn't figure her out. Although once they were in bed, he could slow things down. Make her feel real good.

"Hey."

When she looked up, he caught her chin and kissed her, taking his time, enjoying the velvety texture of her lips, trying to show her he was in no hurry. Although his dick wanted to argue.

She opened up for him and he slid his tongue inside, where it found its mate. The funny little tango that followed made them both smile. He'd always liked kissing best when tongues were involved, but simply moving his lips over hers felt more than satisfying. They found their rhythm and he deepened the kiss while pulling her tighter against him.

Sophie made a startled little sound in the back of her throat and stiffened. But she had to know she was making him hard. Thank God she didn't pull away. She pressed even closer, until her breasts pillowed his chest.

He reached behind to unfasten her bra, anxious to see her bare breasts, to watch her nipples harden and beg for his mouth. With his free hand he cupped her nape, slid his fingers into her hair. A sexy moan filled the inside of his mouth with her warm breath.

All of a sudden she froze.

She let out a squeak and wiggled out of his arms, her hand shooting to the top of her head.

"What happened?" Staying on the safe side, he kept his hands in plain sight. "Did I hurt you?"

They just stared at each other.

She didn't strike him as a woman who'd care if a man mussed up her hair. So what the hell?

"Sorry," she said, her cheeks pink. "Really sorry. I'm not freaking out or anything. About being here...you know...in the room with you. I promise I'm not."

Could've fooled him. "Look, we don't have to—"

"Let's get in bed, okay? I'll feel more relaxed then."

After a quick look at her parted lips, he watched the alarm fade from her eyes. "You don't like leaving the light on?" Ethan asked, worried he was missing something that would come back to bite him. "Is that it?"

"I don't care about the light." She smoothed back her hair and smiled as if nothing had happened.

Now that his body had cooled off some, he needed to think before she took another step toward him. This year he faced more pressure than ever to claim another championship title, partly because of his age, and also because of his kid sister. Mostly, though, it was about his left shoulder. It didn't hurt all the time, but he knew his rodeo days were numbered.

Sophie came up flush against him and looped her arms around his neck. Her pink lips parted slightly as she tilted her head back. She was still wearing the damn bra, not that it seemed to matter, since his mind went blank.

He put his hands on her waist, waiting, hoping he wasn't in for another surprise squeal. Her skin was soft and warm above the jeans waistband. The satiny texture made him itch to explore the rest of her. He settled for rubbing the small of her back, then moved his hands over the curve of her firm backside. Squeezing through denim was better than nothing, he supposed.

Screw that.

The jeans and bra both had to come off.

His request was preempted by an urgent tug. Sophie pulled his head down while she lifted herself up to meet his lips. When she leaned into him, moving her hips against his born-again erection, his whole body tightened. He slid his tongue inside her mouth and touched the tip of hers before circling and sampling the sweetness of her.

"Bed," she whispered.

He lifted her in his arms. With a soft gasp, she hung on tight even after he'd laid her down against the pillows. She resumed the kiss, refusing to let go of his neck, even as he followed her down. The fierce way she was clinging to him made things tricky. He stretched out alongside her, keeping his weight off her and on his braced elbow.

He dragged his mouth away from hers and trailed his lips along her jaw to her ear, wondering where she might be sensitive. After a few nips at her earlobe, he cupped a breast and murmured, "How about we get rid of this bra?"

She vaguely nodded, then stiffened. "Wait."

"For?"

She sat up and sighed. "I forgot something."

Ethan fell onto his back. She just wasn't going to make it easy, was she? "What did you forget?" he asked as she crawled over him and got off the bed.

"Just one sec," she said, raising one finger before she headed for the chair with her jacket draped over the back.

Ethan watched her rifle through the pockets and found it in his heart to forgive her for the interruption. Only because she had one helluva nice ass. Which he hoped to see in the flesh, preferably before the next full moon.

Okay. He finally understood the problem. "I have a condom," he said, rolling to the side and reaching into his back pocket. "It's right here. You can stop looking."

She murmured something he couldn't make out, yet managed to give him the impression she hadn't heard him.

"Sophie?"

She turned to face him, holding the jacket against her front. Fortunately not so her breasts were hidden. Yeah, except the bra took care of that. Shit. Not being able to see and touch was driving him crazy.

He took the packet out of his wallet and tossed both on the nightstand. "Did you hear me?" Why the hell was she bringing the jacket with her? "I have a condom."

"What? Oh." She stopped by the side of the bed. "No, we don't need one."

"Uh, yeah, we do." He never broke that rule.

"I changed my mind about the light." She smiled and leaned down to give him a quick kiss and quite a view. "I think I want it off."

Ethan had never met a woman who ran so hot and cold, and at the speed of sound on top of that. He'd ridden a hundred ornery bulls that had given him less trouble. *Trouble* being the keyword here. Maybe this—Sophie—was an omen he needed to take more seriously.

She kissed him again, lingering this time, using her tongue, while trailing her fingers down his chest. She traced a circle around his navel and then rested her hand on his buckle. "I'll be right back."

Jesus. "What now?"

"The light."

Something else that was confusing. He knew she wasn't shy, and she had a killer body. "How about we leave the one in the bathroom on with the door closed partway?"

She straightened, thought for a moment and then nodded. "I think that might work better, actually."

Yep. She was a strange one, all right. But that nice round bottom of hers wasn't easily dismissed. He watched her walk to the bathroom, flip on the light and angle the door just so.

"I doubt you'll need the jacket," he said.

She only smiled and moved to the wall switch that controlled the two lamps.

"Why don't you get rid of those jeans while you're up?" He'd take care of the bra, no problem.

"Okay. Good idea." The room dimmed. "You take off yours, too."

Ethan watched her approach while he unbuckled and unzipped. It was a little too dark for his taste. Once he finally got her naked, he wanted to see her. Staying right where he was, he lifted his ass and pushed down his jeans.

"Here, let me help." She pulled them off his feet and flung the Wranglers at the chair.

He considered asking her to let a little more light into the room, but she dropped her jacket and climbed onto the bed. She got on her knees and steadied herself with a hand on his belly. And then threw a leg over his thighs and straddled him.

His cock seemed determined to test the resilience of his boxer briefs. "Your turn," he said, reaching for her zipper.

With a throaty laugh, she shoved his hand away. "Not when I have you exactly where I want you."

"I'll make it worth your while," he murmured, rubbing the back of his knuckles against her denim-covered crotch.

She gasped and squeezed her thighs together, only his hips were in the way. He already knew she was strong, but how she was gripping him…holy shit. Managing to move his trapped hand, he put more pressure on her crotch.

Sophie made a strangled sound. Shifting her body, she captured his hand. Intertwining her fingers with his, she pulled his arm up over his head as she leaned down to bite his lip. The aggressive move surprised him in a good way. With his free hand he unhooked her bra.

The left strap slid off her shoulder and bared her breast. He could see the rosy tip, though not as clearly as he wanted. The moment she realized what had happened, she released him. She leaned back, cursing, and trying to pull the bra up.

Like hell.

He slid his hand in before she could cover herself. And cupped her exposed breast, rubbing his thumb over the hard nipple while baring the other.

"You're beautiful," he whispered. "Don't hide yourself."

Closing her eyes, she arched slightly, filling his palm. He

kneaded gently and she sighed, a soft breathy sound he wanted to hear again.

"No." She shrank back.

"Please, Sophie. I know you're nervous, but I promise I'll make you feel better."

"Stop," she said, eyes wide but impossible to read in the dimness.

He immediately lowered his hands. "Did I do something wrong?"

An awkward silence fell between them. She hadn't climbed off, so he figured that was a good sign. She also hadn't fixed her bra, but he was afraid to so much as glance anywhere below her neck until he understood what had just happened. He'd never had a woman tell him no or to stop before. This was brand-new territory and he was at a complete loss on how to respond. Ego played no part here. If anything, he felt like shit.

"Whatever I did to upset you, I'm very sorry," he said, resisting the urge to touch her, offer her comfort the only way he knew how. "I really am."

"Don't apologize," she said, shaking her head. "It's me, I shouldn't have let— Oh, shit. I hate this." She leaned over the side of the bed and reached for the jacket on the floor.

"Hate what?" He tried to do the honorable thing and not stare at her breasts. Apparently he had the willpower of a rutting bull, which he wasn't proud of.

She pulled something out of the pocket and hid it behind her back before he dragged his attention away from her breasts. Cosmic justice, he figured.

He barely had time to blink before she was all over him again. Kissing him, playing the aggressor once more, forcing his arm over his head, her warm soft body pressed close, her hard nipples grazing his chest…the feel of cold metal…

The hard band closing around his wrist jerked him from his haze. He heard a click. Confusion still messed with his brain. Sophie drew back, staring down at him, breathing hard.

He looked at his wrist handcuffed to the bedpost.

Sophie was into that kind of stuff? He wasn't, but he didn't mind accommodating her.

4

"YOU COULD'VE JUST told me." Ethan smiled. "This isn't my thing, but I'll play for a while," he said, and touched her breast.

"Oh, brother." She slapped his hand away, jerking back. For God's sake, she'd forgotten she had no top on. "This isn't a game, you idiot." She climbed off, glanced around the room for her shirt. Finding it near the chair, she pulled the tee over her head.

"What the hell is going on?"

The wig got caught and shifted. Boy, was she glad to get rid of that stupid thing. No one had warned her it would itch like crazy. She grabbed a handful of the fake blond locks and yanked it off her head.

"Jesus. What the—"

Pulling pins from her own hair, she shook it loose from the tight bun and glanced at Ethan, lying against the cream-colored sheets, his muscled chest smooth, bare and tanned. A light smattering of dark hair swirled just below his belly button and disappeared into the waistband of his boxer briefs.

Oh no. No looking there for her.

"I know you," he said, narrowing his gaze.

The light from the bathroom washed over his face, the tanned skin bringing out the blue of his eyes, as he studied her with an intensity that made her turn away. Did seeing her as a brunette trigger a memory? Doubtful. He'd barely noticed her after his grand gesture outside the cafeteria right in the middle of lunch period.

She walked into the bathroom and groaned at her image in the mirror. Well, of course her hair was plastered to her head and looking as unattractive as possible. He hadn't been staring because he remembered her. She could've just stepped off the set of some horror movie.

Rubbing her itchy scalp, she bent at the waist and fluffed out her hair. She straightened to look in the mirror again, not expecting much. And that was exactly what she got.

"Are you gonna get out here and explain what the hell is going on?" Ethan sounded angry.

"You jumped bail," she said, strolling back into the room and picking up her phone. Mostly so she didn't have to look at him. "Without giving a thought to the large bond that was posted on your behalf."

"No, I didn't. Jump bail, I mean. The charges were dropped."

"When?" If that was true, Lola would've told her by now. But he sounded so certain she had to look at him. "When?" she repeated.

"I'm not sure."

A lock of sun-streaked brown hair had fallen across his forehead. His face was lean and spare like the rest of him. Same square jaw she remembered, except for the dark stubble. And that perfect straight nose. He was even hotter now than he'd been back in high school.

Some friggin' nerve.

"So, you weren't sure if you had to show up in court or not and decided to take off anyway. Brilliant move."

"No, it's not like that." He jerked his wrist, clanging the handcuffs against the wooden post. "Is this necessary?"

Well, that had to be rhetorical. She checked for texts or voice mails. "If the charges were dropped, my partner would've notified me. So guess you're out of luck."

"Okay, look, my friend Arnie… Can we turn on more lights?"

"No." She sat on the chair and faced him. "Continue."

Ethan's normal, easygoing expression had vanished, replaced by a piercing frown that made her tense. "Who are you?"

"Sophie's my real name."

"You know what I'm asking."

"I'm a fugitive retrieval agent—"

"Fugitive?"

"You asked."

He cut loose a pithy four-letter word. "What's that, a fancy name for a bounty hunter?"

"Yep."

"And that gives you the right to slap handcuffs on me?"

"It sure does. Didn't you read the bail bond contract?" By signing the document, he'd given her and Lola more authority to arrest him than even the police.

She watched him scrub at his face with his free hand and waited out his mumbled curses. Leaving him with an unrestricted hand wasn't a smart move. The bedpost was made from solid wood and plenty sturdy…she'd checked first thing. But Ethan was agile and strong.

The memory of his hands on her body made her shudder.

Dammit, she should've brought two pairs of cuffs. Mandy preferred using zip ties and had given Sophie a few. But they were sitting in the Jeep.

"So that's why you're in such great shape," he murmured.

"Excuse me?"

"I thought maybe you were a personal trainer or something, but that didn't make sense, either," he said, letting his gaze wander over her.

"What are you talking about?"

"Look, if you just let me make a phone call, I can straighten this out in no time."

"I have a better idea. You can do it in person when I take you back to Wyoming."

"Bullshit."

Sophie smiled. "It's late. No sense driving tonight. We'll leave first thing in the morning."

He jerked hard on the cuffs. The whole bed seemed to shake. "You know I won't let you do that."

"Oh?" She rose. "What are you going to do? Scream?"

Wow, that sure pissed him off. His face reddened, and his eyes turned positively frosty. He looked as if he wanted to put his hands around her neck and strangle the life out of her.

It gave her a new respect for what Mandy had to do all the time. Face down criminals who might actually want to hurt her. Ethan was angry, and he'd try to get away if he could, but Sophie wasn't afraid of him. She knew he would never do her harm.

She walked to the window and parted the drapes, just enough so she could take a peek down the street. The Watering Hole wasn't visible from here. Neither was her Jeep. Lots of people were still milling around, though. Another reason she wouldn't try forcing Ethan into her car tonight.

Damn, she wished she'd grabbed her bag along with the jacket. She needed her toothbrush, face cream, a change of clothes, all that stuff… And she hated leaving Ethan alone while she ran to the Jeep. She turned and caught him staring at her butt.

He gave her a lazy smile.

Oh, so he was pulling out the charm again.

"Aren't you gonna ask if I did it?"

"What's the point?" Sophie said. "Unless you have proof, your answer means nothing. And if you had proof, I wouldn't be here."

His face darkened. "I didn't steal a goddamn thing. Wendy lied."

"Hmm, well, that's what you get for sleeping with a married woman."

"You mean, for *not* sleeping with her." Ethan shook his head, briefly closing his eyes. "Wendy lied about that, too. When I found out she was married, I left. She was pissed. I knew that… I just didn't know how bad."

Sophie thought back to earlier when he'd asked if she was married. He'd even inspected her ring finger. Maybe he was telling the truth, or maybe he'd learned an expensive lesson. The thing was, she didn't believe that he'd stolen anything. It made no sense. Even if he did need money, she'd seen the teenage Ethan's moral center, and age didn't change a person that much. But what she believed didn't matter.

"If I'm supposed to have a hundred grand in stolen jewelry, why would I need someone to post my bond?"

"You didn't have enough time to sell it?"

"Get real. I earned a lot more than that in endorsements alone this year. Plus my winnings."

"Okay, so…" What was she doing? Sophie knew better than to get involved. Her job was to take him back to Wyoming, period. "Why not use your own money to post bond?"

"I don't have that kind of cash lying around. My money's invested. I start withdrawing funds and I get questions. The media are already all over my ass about the finals in a week."

"Why?" She hadn't realized that she'd walked closer to him until she bumped her knee on a corner of the bed.

"Because of my track record. Every year I—" He plowed his fingers through his hair, the action drawing attention to the muscles in his arms and shoulders. "It doesn't matter."

"What?" She snapped her gaze back to his face. "I'm sorry, I missed that last bit."

He was staring at her again, with the same intensity as earlier. Trying to decide if she was the girl from school? Maybe. "My friend Arnie, he was supposed to take care of it. He knows the charge is bogus and said it would never make it to court."

"Is he an attorney?"

Ethan sighed. "He dropped out of law school."

She remembered an Arnie, a dopey junior who used to tag

along behind Ethan. If this was the same guy, she sure wouldn't have trusted him with anything important. "Hope he didn't quit before he learned the part that would keep you from getting locked up."

Ethan blew out a breath. It seemed clear he'd had the same thought. "How about we call him? Can I at least do that?"

Sophie wandered toward the window while she tried to think. Talking to Arnie wouldn't help. Only Lola could tell her if Ethan was in the clear and the bond reimbursed. And for some reason Sophie wasn't anxious to admit she'd found him already. Why, she didn't know. She should be ecstatic and gloating.

"Tomorrow's the Safe Haven Benefit Rodeo," Ethan said. "They could really use the money. Since I'm the main attraction, it would be a shame if I missed—"

"Shut up." She glared at him. "I know about the rodeo. And guess what, genius…trying to make me feel bad isn't helping your cause. It's just pissing me off. I didn't create this problem. You did."

He glared back. "You're gonna deny me a goddamn lousy phone call?"

"Where's your cell?"

Frowning, he glanced at the nightstand. "My shirt…where is it?"

"What am I, your maid?" she grumbled, and spotted it on the floor by the chair. She picked up the shirt and then noticed his phone sitting on the armoire. Tempted to toss the cell to him, she moved close enough to drop it on the mattress barely within his reach.

With the most irritating grin, he strained toward the cell and grabbed it. "What are you afraid of? Huh? What did you think I was going to do to you? I've got one wrist cuffed to this post," he said in a taunting tone of voice. "What are you doing to my shirt?"

"What?" She looked down at the garment she was hugging to her chest. "Nothing."

"Were you sniffing it?"

"No. Ew." She flung the shirt toward the chair. *Oh God, oh God, oh God.* Heat stung her cheeks. She kept her face averted, knowing it must be red, and pulled out her own phone.

If he was laughing at her…

If?

Did she really have any doubt?

One word. Just one wrong word out of his mouth, and she'd drag him to her car in front of the whole damn town. Announce to everyone he was a fugitive from justice.

Her sigh ended in a shudder. She hadn't even been aware of smelling his shirt.

He was awfully quiet.

"Arnie?"

Sophie let out a breath and slowly turned to see Ethan holding the cell to his ear and glaring at the ceiling.

"Don't pull that you're-breaking-up bullshit on me," Ethan said, his voice furious. "What the hell, dude? I thought you were taking care of the charges."

Sophie perched on the edge of the chair to send a quick text to Lola.

"That's good, right?" Ethan stacked two pillows behind his back. "If she insists on lying, her husband will know she's been cruising bars and picking up men while he's out of town." He listened for a few seconds. "And I had to call you to find all this out?"

Before hitting Send, she glanced up again.

Ethan looked worried. His chest rose and fell on a sigh. "Jesus, Arnie, you've got to find out by tomorrow. The finals are in a week. You know this year could be it for me…"

The despair in his voice made her stomach clench. Thank God she had her phone to occupy her, because she couldn't stand to look at him right now. This year could be it for him? Why?

"Maybe I should call my agent," he said, his eyes meeting hers when she looked up. "Brian's going to find out anyway.

They think I jumped bail. I've got a damn bounty hunter staring at me right now."

"Fugitive retrieval agent," she muttered.

"She's got me cuffed to the friggin' bed. Plans on dragging me back to Wyoming tomorrow." He paused. "Shut the fu—" He glanced at her. "Just make the damn call and get back to me first thing tomorrow. And, Arnie, this is your last chance." Ethan disconnected and threw the cell down. Hard.

No point in pretending she hadn't been listening. Anyway, the second he'd left her and Lola holding the bond, so to speak, he forfeited his right to privacy. And no, she absolutely would not feel sorry for him. He'd done this to himself.

She watched him inspect the handcuffs and flex his hand. Then he stared up at the ceiling, thumping his head back against the wooden bed rail, working the muscle at his jaw.

"I wouldn't trust Arnie if I were you," Sophie said. "At this point you really do need an attorney."

Ethan brought his chin down, a faint smile tugging at the corners of his mouth. "You know Arnie?"

Oh, crap. This was what she got for being nice. "No, but it sounded like you don't have confidence in him. So I'm saying, you should go with your instinct." She shrugged, carefully keeping her gaze level with his. "Didn't you mention something about calling your agent?"

His eyes continued to bore into hers. He hadn't so much as blinked. All she could think to do was stare back. She doubted that little slip about Arnie had been the thing that convinced Ethan of her identity. Just because she looked familiar didn't mean he remembered they'd gone to the same high school together for seven months, one week and two days.

Yeah, okay, so she'd counted. Down to the minute, actually, but when she'd been… Fifteen. *Jeez.*

"What did he say, anyway?"

"Arnie?"

"Yes, Arnie." Her phone signaled a new text. She glanced

at the brief message. No surprise there. "I texted a friend who works in the sheriff's office to check on whether the charges were dropped. It seems you already know the answer."

He tightened his mouth. "Can you recommend an attorney?"

"Not really. I know a few, but I couldn't say if they're any good." Except for Craig, but she tried to stay clear of him. "What about your agent? Bet he knows one."

"Brian lives in Dallas. I can't call him this late. But yeah, he knows everybody. I trust he'll steer me right."

"You should've called him before you jumped bail."

Ethan sighed. "I didn't realize I'd jumped bail," he said with forced patience. "The charges were supposed to have been dropped."

"What about your parents? I would think they either have someone they use or know of someone."

"It's clear you're not a rodeo fan, yet you know who they are?"

She shrugged. "I think everyone in Beatrice County knows the name Styles. They own that big ranch and rodeo camp near Otter Lake. And didn't your dad win something like five championship titles for calf roping, and a few more for something else?"

Ethan nodded. "All-around cowboy three years in a row."

"Even your mom has four gold buckles for barrel racing, right?"

"You get all that from doing homework on me? Or did you already know this stuff?"

"Half and half."

"So you probably read about my kid sister." His tone stayed noncommittal and his expression blank.

Nevertheless, she'd bet there were a lot of emotions bubbling under the surface. She'd definitely seen pride in his eyes, but she wondered if there might be some jealousy in the mix.

"Last December Cara won her first championship title on her twenty-first birthday," he said. "She'll be competing for her second title next week. She'll be headed to Vegas with me. Assuming I get to go." He jerked on the cuffs so hard the post shook.

"Ah." Sophie nodded.

"Ah?"

"Sibling rivalry. I get it." She didn't have any siblings, but she could imagine the pressure Ethan was feeling. And a kid sister besting him? Ouch. "Well, I know barrel racing is a woman's event, so I'm guessing that's what she won?"

He nodded.

"Your dad won first place for tying up poor little calves—"

Ethan stared as though she'd just grown fangs.

"And your mom and sister got prizes for riding a horse around a few barrels without knocking them over."

Ethan started laughing.

"I'm not finished," she said. "And you're a bull rider. Correct me if I'm wrong, but don't you compete in the hardest, most dangerous event in rodeo?"

"Look," he said, his laughter ending with a sigh, "I don't know what your point is. I just need to make it to the finals." His mood had soured again. "So, what's it gonna take, Sophie? Tell me."

"You have to return to Wyoming and face the judge."

"I can't ride the next two days here, then go back to Wyoming and the unknown, and trust that I can still make it to Vegas for the finals."

She sucked in a deep breath. He wasn't thinking it through. "It's not as if you have a low profile," she reminded him. "If you fail to appear in court on Monday, the judge will issue a warrant and someone will be waiting in Vegas to arrest you."

"No. No, that can't happen. How can they come after me? I didn't do it. Dammit."

She bit down to keep from stating the obvious. Besides, Ethan had to know the legal system was far from perfect. Or maybe his charmed existence had spared him life's injustices. "Look, I know you don't want the publicity, but your folks live in the next county, along with lots of rodeo fans who adore them. You're probably the most popular bull rider in the country. Who do you think people are going to believe? You or what's her name?"

"Wendy." Ethan's mouth curved in a derisive smile. "Wendy Fullerton."

Fullerton? "Any relation to Broderick Fullerton?"

"His wife."

"Oh, shit."

"Exactly what I said." Ethan's sigh sounded a lot like defeat.

"How could you not know who she was?" Fullerton owned half the county. People generally feared him more than they liked him. But the fact remained, he provided over 60 percent of the jobs and his bank owned a ton of mortgages and notes. Including Sophie and Lola's business loan.

"Wendy is wife number four. They've been married for eight months." He shrugged. "How the hell would I know, anyway? I don't read the society pages and I'm rarely home. Jesus. Here I've been keeping my head down. Staying healthy. Staying out of trouble..."

"You picked up a strange woman in a bar," she muttered, really hating this whole mess. No room for sympathy now. Everything had to go by the book. "And instead of learning your lesson you came here and did it again."

"When?"

Sophie got to her feet so she could pace, hoping to loosen up. Maybe she should be more concerned with toughening up. She'd started to soften toward Ethan, wondering how she could help him out. But anything she did would reflect on Lola, too. Their business loan wasn't in jeopardy. They'd been late with their payment only once in four years. It was silly to worry.

Ethan's response from a moment ago finally sank in and she faced him. "*When?* Is that a joke?"

"Do you see me laughing?" he said, his stare unflinching.

"Did you forget how I ended up here with you?"

"Nope. But you obviously did."

She pushed her fingers through her tangled hair. This was good, him being an ass. Made it easier to shove sympathy aside, be more objective. "Okay, I'll bite. Go ahead."

"Nothing. It's just that you hit on me."

She gaped at him. "Are you nuts?" It took a few more seconds to find her voice again. "You're crazy, you know that. You brought me to your room."

"Actually I was going to give it to you."

"What the hell are you talking about?"

"My friend Matt invited me to stay at his ranch. So when I heard you needed a room, I'd decided to give you this one and I would move over to the Lone Wolf," he said slowly, and with exaggerated patience. "Then you hit on me, and I… I went with the flow." He smiled. "I was only trying to be a gentleman."

"Oh, that's right. I forgot. You like to play hero and then move on." She held her breath. She couldn't believe she'd actually said *play hero.*

With a single lifted eyebrow, he held her gaze until she turned away. He didn't seem surprised or curious about what she'd meant, just faintly amused. So he'd probably remembered…

Swallowing, she stalked to the window, shoved the drapes aside and stared at nothing.

The stupid bastard had recognized her from school and hadn't said a word.

5

FINE. SO WHAT if he remembered? It didn't really matter. Sophie stayed at the window, though nothing happening outside was of particular interest. She simply knew better than to look at Ethan while she planned her next move. The inn sat directly on Main Street. And Blackfoot Falls was crawling with out-of-town fans. The only chance for an uneventful exit would be if they left in the middle of the night. Not her first choice, but…

The more she thought about it, the more she liked the idea. Once the Watering Hole closed, there wouldn't be anything for these people to do. They'd return to the trailer parks and dude ranches, or wherever they were staying. She could pull her Jeep up close to the porch and stuff him into the backseat. She'd gag him if she had to. But she doubted that would be necessary. He wouldn't want to call attention to himself.

Later, once they were on the open road, he'd try to make a move. Plenty of lonely stretches of highway between here and Wyoming for him to give it his all. But that was okay because she'd be ready for him. Sure, he could easily overpower her if he somehow broke free of his restraints. That was why she'd brought pepper spray.

Despite wanting to smack him, she hoped he was considering

what she'd said about finding an attorney. With his high profile he'd be arrested sooner rather than later, and she really didn't want that to happen.

"I have a question," Ethan said.

Good for him. She had a million. Like whether he'd honestly intended to give her the room. And when exactly had he recognized her. He might've thought she seemed familiar and figured he'd met her in another bar, another town. Until she'd made the *hero* crack.

None of those things mattered, really. Her job was to take him back to Wyoming. And that was exactly what she was going to do. As long as she stayed focused, avoided looking at him whenever possible. Because she had enough wits about her to know he was dangerous to her self-control, to her ability to reason. If she wasn't careful, she'd revert to that same smitten fifteen-year-old girl who'd finished her freshman year with a bunch of newly awakened hormones and a broken heart.

Even now, ten feet away, she swore she could smell him. His rugged masculine scent drifted over to her, distracting her. Tempting her to forget she had a job to do.

"Why the blond wig?" he asked after she'd refused to so much as glance at him. "You're much prettier with dark hair."

"Oh, please." Sophie rubbed her eyes. This sucked. She was too tired to drive tonight. And she had to get him back as quickly as possible. For her own peace of mind, if nothing else.

"I'm not trying to butter you up. It's the truth. Were you worried I'd recognize you?"

She knew he was playing her. Or maybe he was still fuzzy about her identity and was looking for confirmation. She wasn't about to fill in the blanks for him. "You like blondes, that's why."

"Who told you that?"

"Every one of your girlfriends has been blonde. Think that might've given me a hint?"

"It's been three years since I've had a steady girlfriend. And she was a brunette…who happened to dye her hair blond."

Sophie snorted a laugh. "Do you ever hear yourself?" Without thinking, she spun around…and let out a squeal. "What are you doing?"

The bastard was using something to pick the lock.

"No. Oh no, you don't."

She dove onto the mattress and crawled over to him. She leaned across his chest, trying to pry his free hand away from the handcuffs. Her right breast smooshed his face, startling him. Her, too. But it was probably the only thing that saved her, since she had barely reached his hand in time.

Unable to get a good grip of his wrist, she threw a leg over him. Straddling him hadn't been the objective, but there she was. She didn't know which was worse, sitting on his junk and squeezing his hips with her thighs or having her boob in his face. But she couldn't back down now.

Pulling on his arm was like trying to move a boulder. "Damn you, Styles. Don't you get it? You're going back to Wyoming one way or another. Why are you making this so hard?"

He grinned.

Okay, unfortunate word choice. He didn't have to be a child about it. She ignored him, other than to use all her might to pull his hand away…

He went completely still. Relaxed his arm. Dropped the small pocketknife.

"Would you stop that?" he growled. "I know you're a lunatic, but my dick doesn't, okay? So ease up. Damn."

"What did you say?"

"Stop wiggling."

"Oh." She stayed right where she was but tried not to move. *Holy shit.* There was a bulge under her left butt cheek. "Then stop trying to pick the lock."

"And how am I supposed to go to the bathroom, huh? Answer me that."

"Is that what this is about? You could've said—"

"No. I don't need to go now. But the point is, you can't keep me prisoner like this. You know damn well it isn't practical..." He trailed off and quietly exhaled, his eyes, wary and watchful, meeting hers dead-on.

Sophie couldn't tell if she was breathing or not. Heat coursed slowly through her body as she fought the urge to touch his muscled shoulders and chest.

They just stared at each other. His pupils were so big and dark she hardly saw any blue. She hated to think what she looked like with her wild tangled hair. Though the bulge under her fanny hadn't subsided, so she couldn't be the utter mess she imagined.

She finally shifted her gaze to his hand, still secured to the bedpost, and she picked up the pocketknife. She had no reason to be sitting on him. Or staring at his bare chest.

She gave the cuffs a reassuring tug, mostly for show, then lifted herself off him. Very carefully. No peeking, no unnecessary touching.

One thing was for certain. She didn't want to be tempted by his bare chest all night, so she'd have to figure a way for him to put his shirt on. As for his lower half, the sheet draped over his lap would have to do for now. It sure wasn't lying flat, though.

"So, how do you plan to deal with bathroom trips? Are you going in with me to be my...handler, so to speak?"

Luckily it took very little for him to annoy the hell out of her. "You're despicable."

Ethan laughed. "I'll make a deal with you."

Sophie rolled to the side of the bed and jumped off. "You have nothing I want."

"You sure about that?"

She glanced back at him. "When you get thrown off a bull, you must land on your head a lot."

"Ah, rodeo humor. Not very good, though. Hey, don't lose my pocketknife."

She shoved it deep into her jeans pocket. "Oh, so now I have everything you want, and you have nothing of interest to me."

She swept a pointed gaze over his body. "So, as for making a deal…" She shrugged. "Too bad."

"I'm being serious."

"You should be. You're in a lot of trouble, Ethan." If he made her regret this, she'd save the court time and money and just shoot him. "What is it you want?"

He started to smirk, then gave up the smug act. "Let me ride for Safe Haven," he said, steadily meeting her eyes. "And you have my word I won't run."

"What about the finals?"

"I'll make it to Vegas."

Sophie was on the verge of a colossal headache. He hadn't been a stupid boy in school, and she assumed he hadn't lost any IQ points since then. "I doubt you can do both and still meet your legal obligation."

"Watch me."

"How am I supposed to believe you won't take off on me?"

"Because I gave you my word."

"Right." She rubbed her left temple.

"Just like I gave Matt Gunderson my word I'd ride for Safe Haven." He sure seemed intent on making a mess of his career. His life. "They haven't done one of these benefits before. If it goes well, it'll become an annual event. What do you think will happen if their headliner scratches at the last minute?"

She sighed. Her job would be a lot easier if he was only pretending to be noble. But this wasn't an act. Even back in high school Ethan had had a reputation for stepping in for the underdog, and not just her.

With a small shake of her head, she reached into her pocket for the key. "What time do you ride?"

"I think I'm last."

"Of course you are," she muttered. "So, after that we leave, right?"

"I'm on the lineup for Sunday, too."

"What if you get thrown on your ass before the eight seconds tomorrow?"

With a deadpan expression, he said, "This isn't about qualifying, so it doesn't matter."

Boy, did she hope she'd packed aspirin. "We'll split the difference. You ride tomorrow and then Sunday we drive straight to Wyoming. That way you can—"

He was already shaking his head. "People paid a lot of money for tickets."

"I bet they pay even more for the finals."

"Let me worry about that."

"Oh yeah? Hmm." She frowned at the key, and then at the lock. Anything to avoid those hypnotic eyes. "That should take care of everything."

"Sarcasm? Sure, that helps."

She glared at him then. "Your main problem is that you're not concerned enough."

He had the most annoying habit of looking like the boy next door one minute, and sex wearing a Stetson the next. It had to stop. Being in the same room with him was nerve-racking enough. But this close?

Just as she was about to free him, someone knocked on the door.

"Oh, Ethan… Ethan Styles?" It was a woman's singsong voice. "Are you in there, sugar?"

Sophie stepped back. "You expecting company?"

He shook his head, staring mutely at her.

"Obviously you gave out your room number."

"Nope," he said, keeping his voice low.

Was she being a total idiot? Once Sophie released him, that was it. She could barely stand this close to him without her skin feeling flushed.

There was another knock. At someone else's door.

Sophie strained to hear.

"Oh, Ethan…" Same woman, same question. Trying every door? That was sick.

Kind of like her back in school. Sophie cringed at the memory of hiding under the bleachers to watch him run track. Begging for a transfer to auto shop, of all the dumb things, just so she could be in the same class as Ethan.

Teenagers did lots of crazy stuff. She couldn't let it get to her. And anyway, she'd bet the woman in the hall was a lot older than fifteen.

She held the key poised at the lock. "Wait," she said, and started when he put a shushing finger to her lips.

It was unnecessary. No one in the hall could've heard her low pitch. And she'd bet he knew that. Yet she simply stood there, staring into the vivid blue of his eyes, while he lightly skimmed the pad of his thumb across her bottom lip before lowering his hand. The move was so subtle, she'd be a fool to make anything of it.

Her cousin was right. Lola had worried Sophie would have trouble dealing with Ethan. But she'd honestly thought he no longer had any effect on her. She was wrong. She would just be more cautious, that was all. Ultimately she trusted he'd keep his word.

"We haven't come to terms on Sunday yet," she said, voice low and firm.

Their eyes dueled a moment.

"We'll renegotiate tomorrow," he said with a sexy smile that could get a ninety-year-old woman in trouble. "After the rodeo."

She laughed. "Oh, hell no." Sophie jabbed a finger at him. "You will stick to me like glue until I tell you otherwise. I want your word on *that*."

He grinned as if he was enjoying this. "You've got it."

"And shut up when I tell you to shut up."

"Yes, ma'am."

"Without the smirk," she murmured as she inserted the small

key, narrowing her attention to the task as she gathered her courage. "You think you know me. From where?"

"Wattsville High."

Her heartbeat went bonkers, and heat flooded her face, but she refused to look at him. "Because I used my real name?"

"No. I didn't remember that."

Okay, at least that was settled. The second the lock sprang, she thought of something else. "Dammit."

"What?" He was quick to pull his wrist free.

It was too late but she should've considered leaving him cuffed until she brought the Jeep closer and got her bag. She glanced at the cuffs still clamped to the bedpost. Maybe she'd leave it there for now.

"Don't worry. I'm staying right here," Ethan said. "I'm not even going for that beer I'd wanted at the Watering Hole."

"You're right about that."

He put a hand on her hip, and a soft gasp slipped past her lips.

"Hands off," she warned, as much with a glare as with words.

"Mind moving so I can get up?"

She ignored the subtle undertone of amusement in his voice and headed back to the window. After she saw him grab his jeans, she looked out through the parted drapes, aware of him moving behind her. The bathroom door closed and she sighed with relief.

Her swirling thoughts would drive her insane if she didn't get a handle on what to tell Lola. Sophie had had no business making any kind of deal with him. Would Mandy ever negotiate with a bail jumper? Not in a million years.

The minute the rodeo started tomorrow, anyone who cared would know exactly where Ethan Styles was, so she had to tell Lola something.

The smartest story to tell was mostly true. Ethan had unknowingly violated the terms of his bail and he was willing to cooperate. Which saved Sophie from having to fight off hordes of fans. Yes, some gray area existed, since she had Ethan in her clutches at this very moment, but no one had to know…

It didn't feel good lying to Lola like that. In fact, Sophie couldn't recall having ever lied to her cousin, not about anything important, anyway. And here she was doing it now because of Ethan?

God, he was like a drug. And she felt like a junkie. A cocky junkie telling herself she'd clocked in enough sobriety. She could resist him. Easy. Might as well have had *denial* tattooed across her forehead. She'd tempted fate, and fate had kicked her right in the butt.

Her phone buzzed. It was Lola's ringtone. Sophie hesitated, briefly before deciding it was better to talk now, while she had privacy.

Just as she accepted the call, Ethan opened the door.

With his damp hair slicked back, it looked darker, more like the dusting of hair visible above the waistband of his jeans. Which she could swear now rode even lower on his hips than before.

"Sophie? You there?"

"Yeah. What's up?" She started to turn, then decided she'd rather keep an eye on him. He really needed to put his shirt on.

"I thought I'd hear from you by now," Lola said. "Where are you?"

"Blackfoot Falls. I texted you when I arrived."

"Yeah, two hours ago. Have you seen him yet?"

"Yes." She watched him open the closet and pull out a duffel bag. He appeared to be ignoring her, but she wasn't stupid. He was listening, hoping to hear something he could use to his advantage. Fine. As long as he stayed quiet.

"And?" Lola's impatience came through.

"I'll have to call you later."

"Got it. Just tell me this," Lola said. "Will you be able to pick him up tonight?"

She swallowed. "No."

Ethan turned in time to see her wince. Or maybe her voice had given away her guilt over the lie. He studied her a moment before swinging his bag onto the bed and sorting through his clothes.

Lola was still there—Sophie could hear the police scanner her cousin liked to keep on low volume in the background—but she hadn't said boo.

"Okay." Sophie swallowed. "Give me an hour."

"Hey, kiddo." Lola's voice had softened. "This turning out harder than you thought it would?"

Sophie sighed. Her head hurt, as did every lying bone in her body. "Yes," she admitted. "But I can do this." She realized what she'd said and spun to face the window. It was too late. Ethan had heard. "Gotta go."

She disconnected, then stared out at Main Street until she was satisfied no telltale blush stained her cheeks.

Ethan was watching her when she turned to him. He gave her a small crooked smile that didn't help at all.

"I have to move my car and get my bag," she said with deliberate gruffness. "You going to be here when I get back?"

"I gave you my word."

"Okay." She glanced around, pretending to search for the keys she knew were sitting under her jacket. "Guess I'll just have to hope that means something to you."

"I expect so," he said, his tone making it clear he didn't like his integrity questioned. "Mind picking up a six-pack? There's a market at the other end of Main." He dug deep in his pocket, pushing the jeans down another inch before producing a twenty.

It occurred to her that he was trying to buy time by sending her to the store. Not likely. She believed his word did matter to him. And even if she was wrong, he knew he'd be a sitting duck tomorrow, so why bother disappearing now?

She grabbed her jacket and keys. "What kind?"

"Your choice."

Sophie laughed. "You're not getting me drunk."

"Sharing a six-pack? I didn't think so."

Funny, she didn't remember him having such an intense stare. It made her jumpy. She spotted the room key and scooped it up as she passed him.

He caught her arm. "You forgot this," he said, trying to give her the money.

"My treat." She pulled away. His touch had given her goose bumps she didn't want him to see. "A condemned man always gets a last meal."

Ethan's slow smile wasn't altogether pleasant. "I was going to be a gentleman and sleep on the floor. Not anymore. We're sharing the bed."

"I wouldn't have it any other way," she said with a toss of her hair, and then fled the room before she hyperventilated.

6

FUZZY WITH SLEEP, Ethan opened his eyes to slits, just enough to see if the room was dark or if morning was trying to sneak in. He wasn't a big believer in alarm clocks and only used them if he had to.

Still black as night. Good.

Yawning, he changed positions and tried to get comfortable. The mattress wasn't bad, but not great, either. He lifted his lids again, trying to remember where he was…

Not Sioux City. That was last month.

Ah, Blackfoot Falls.

That's right...the Safe Haven Rodeo.

The shock of seeing the steel handcuffs dangling from the bedpost jerked him awake. Memories of a dark-haired beauty teased him. Not just any beauty, but the girl he remembered from Wattsville High.

He looked over his shoulder at Sophie. Her long brown hair was everywhere, and so was the rest of her. One arm was thrown out clear to his pillow while she slept partially on her side, her body slightly curled away from him. Her left leg was straight, but her right leg bent at the knee, bringing her foot up near his ass.

How could someone her size take up most of the bed?

No wonder he felt cramped and achy. He needed more room to stretch out.

He rolled over to give her a gentle nudge but stopped. His eyes had adjusted to the darkness, but he couldn't see much with her other arm plopped over her face. Her chin was visible, and so were those damn pouty lips that had distracted him as a teenager and were doing a number on him now.

Ethan had a feeling she underestimated how sexy she was. More so now that she was in her twenties and had filled out. He smiled at the oversize U of Wyoming T-shirt and men's plaid pajama pants that couldn't hide her curvy body. Sophie had insisted on sleeping on top of the covers while he stayed cozy under the sheet and blanket. As if that would've stopped them from doing anything if the mood had struck.

Hell, the mood had struck plenty. At least for him. He just refused to do anything about it.

Sophie was the sort of trouble he needed to avoid. Not because she wanted to drag him back to Wyoming, although the phony accusation bullshit was something he had to straighten out. Sophie herself was the problem. That nice toned body and gorgeous face would turn any man's head, so, yeah, the packaging didn't hurt, but half the women following the tour fit that description.

But he couldn't think of a single one who had Sophie's keen curious brown eyes. The kind a man could stare into and know he was in for a real interesting ride. Hell, he knew he'd get thrown before it was all over, maybe even stomped on. But for as long as he managed to stay in the saddle, he sure wouldn't be bored.

He liked that she wore her hair longer now, past her shoulders and kind of messy. What he liked most was that she didn't seem to give a shit how it looked. Which had been pretty bad when she pulled the wig off. Any other woman he knew, including his grandmother, would've fixed it until it was just so. But not

Sophie, and when she tossed back all that long hair, it was with impatience. She sure wasn't flirting.

Another thing that struck him as sexy was the way she walked. Slow and easy. And with that almost-smile teasing her lips. That was why he'd noticed her in the bar. He hadn't recognized her then. But it was the same understated sexiness that had gotten her bullied in school.

Unfortunately Ethan might've had something to do with the bullying, too.

She shifted in her sleep, making a soft throaty sound that got his cock's attention.

God, he wanted to touch her.

The thought had barely flickered when she pulled her arm from his pillow, effectively removing his best excuse. And then she turned completely over on her side, her body curling away from him so that he couldn't see her face.

Well, shit.

No, he was better off staying away. This close to the finals he needed her cooperation more than he needed anything else she could offer. Because he still wasn't convinced that he shouldn't head straight to Vegas while his agent figured things out.

Statistically the odds were against him winning another championship title. At twenty-nine he was getting too old. He had to compete against younger riders. The guys who made it to the top ten were mostly in their mid-twenties. Very few guys close to his age had claimed the title in the past fifteen years. And lately, each time he strained his left shoulder, it took longer to heal.

Damn, he wanted that second title. He wished he could say winning was strictly about funding the rodeo camp he was eager to build. But his pride was equally invested in getting that buckle for the family trophy case. His sister had a good chance of claiming another title this year. The little shit wouldn't let him forget that she'd shown him up. He knew Cara didn't really mean anything with all the jabs. In their family, competitiveness was a sport unto itself.

He stared at the back of Sophie's head, then followed the line of her body, the dip at her waist, the narrow strip of exposed skin where her shirt had ridden up, the curve of her hip.

Her hair had spread to his pillow and he picked up a lock. Rubbed the silkiness between his thumb and forefinger. He hadn't expected it to be this soft. Or to smell faintly of roses. He figured she'd be into something more edgy, spicier. But the floral scent was nice, too.

This wasn't doing him any favors. His heart started pumping faster. He should be trying to go back to sleep, not letting himself get worked up. Had to be close to sunrise. Turning his head, he searched for the time. The small bedside clock reflected the old boardinghouse feel. It was useless in the dark.

He could flip on the lamp. Instead he rolled back to face Sophie. She hadn't moved. He didn't think she was faking sleep, either. She would've tugged down her shirt and covered herself.

Hell. She was just too tempting.

Ethan inched closer. He listened to her steady even breathing before sliding in to spoon her. She didn't move, not one tiny muscle. He'd half expected a startled jerk, or an elbow to his ribs. Was she used to sleeping with someone? Maybe she had a boyfriend. Yeah, probably. Why wouldn't she?

Now, why did that idea rub him the wrong way? He hadn't seen her in over ten years. And he'd barely known her then. What did he care if she was involved with someone?

He waited a moment and then carefully put an arm around her waist. She'd stubbornly refused to take the blanket, and now her skin was cool. A lit candle would do a better job than the overtaxed heater.

Sophie moved suddenly. Just when he thought he was about to get busted, she wiggled back until they were touching from knees to chest. Her body was instinctively seeking warmth, and he was fine with that. But if she were to wake up right now, she'd blame him for where she'd stuck her sweet round bottom. And slap him into next year.

It would be worth it.

Tightening his arm, he buried his face in her hair and closed his eyes. She was soft and sweet. They fit together real well. It felt so nice having her in his arms that maybe he could get a couple more hours of sleep. He settled in and she pressed her backside closer. His damn boner would be the thing that woke her.

"What time is it?" she murmured, her voice husky.

Ethan braced himself. "Go back to sleep," he whispered, waiting for her to go all out ninja on him.

Slipping her small hand in his, she let out a soft contented sigh.

The moment passed. Her breathing returned to steady and even. Ethan closed his eyes again, hoping for sleep. So he'd quit wondering whom Sophie thought was snuggled against her.

SOPHIE SQUINTED INTO the sunlight that managed to creep in between the drapes and hit her in the face. Morning was always her favorite time of the day. She took pride in being one of those annoyingly energetic people who jumped out of bed ready to conquer the world.

Today she felt sluggish. No, that wasn't right. The feeling was more pleasant. Warm. Comfy. Safe. Was she coming out of a dream? Smiling, she closed her eyes again and snuggled down under the weight of a—

Her eyes popped open.

She pushed the arm off and shot up from the bed.

"What the—" Ethan lifted a hand to block the sun now shining in his face. He rolled onto his back, rubbing his shoulder and frowning at her. "Christ, you damn near took my arm off."

"Don't put it where it doesn't belong." Sophie tugged down her T-shirt, then remembered she wasn't wearing a bra.

"Huh?" His expression dazed, he seemed to be having trouble focusing on her. He was still under the blanket, his lower half, anyway. Okay, so he must've been sleeping and hadn't pressed against her on purpose.

She could see how that might happen. He was probably used to having a different woman in his bed every night. Arms folded across her chest, she headed for the bathroom.

It was too cool in the room. She vaguely remembered trying to adjust the thermostat last night, for all the good it had done. Since the inn had been recently renovated, she would've expected a better heater. Tonight she was using the blanket. Ethan could just—

No. Tonight they'd be long gone. Headed back to Wyoming. No more negotiating. Someday Ethan would realize she was doing him a favor. His best shot at making the finals was to show up in court Monday.

After taking care of more urgent business, she turned on the shower. The water didn't have to be hot, just warm. That was all she asked. And since she'd stupidly forgotten her bag, if it were to suddenly appear, that would be great, too. Fresh out of magic wishes, she sighed and opened the bathroom door, then made a dash for the leather carry-on she'd left by the closet.

Ethan didn't say a word and she risked a look at him. He was lying on his stomach, arms around his bunched pillow, his face buried. No shirt. She paused just inside the bathroom to admire his well-defined shoulders and back. He had to keep himself in good shape to ride bulls. But she was glad he didn't go overboard like so many guys she knew at the gym.

His elbow moved and she hurriedly closed the door. First, she tested the water. A bit warmer would've been more to her liking, but she wasn't complaining. She stripped off her clothes and got under the spray.

Damn, she shouldn't have been so hasty to leap out of bed. Of course she'd had no way of knowing he was asleep. But if she'd lain still a few seconds to find out, it would've been nice to feel his arm around her. To bask in his heat, maybe touch him and pretend…

Oh, brother. Did she want him to carry her books and save her a seat at lunch, too? She was almost twenty-seven, had pretty much taken care of her mom and herself after her father left on Sophie's fourteenth birthday, and she had a master's degree in computer science. So how was it that she could stay stuck at fifteen when it came to Ethan?

She finished showering, dried off and got dressed without once letting her mind stray from the day ahead. The rodeo started at two. Whether he liked it or not, she was waking his ass up right now. She wanted him packed, their bags stowed in her Jeep and both of them ready to go the minute his event was finished.

Breathing in deeply, she reminded herself she was a warrior, not a silly schoolgirl. She grabbed her bag and flung the door open. Ready for whatever he—

The bed was empty.

Sophie blinked. Panic rushed through her. "Son of a bitch."

"Looking for me?"

She turned toward the sound of his voice. He stood to her left pulling a shirt out of the closet with a look of amusement. "The bathroom's all yours," she muttered, and set her bag on the bed so she could rummage through it.

Somewhere in the mishmash of clothes and toiletries was a Ziploc bag with a tube of mascara, an eyeliner pencil and lip gloss. She found it and saw a couple of blush samples the saleswoman at the makeup counter had given her some months back, maybe a year. Sophie wondered if they were still good.

She felt him watching her and looked up. "Need something?"

He shook his head, his gaze narrowed. "You didn't have to rush. If you still need time in there," he said with a nod at the bathroom. "No problem."

"Nope. Go for it."

"Okay." He drawled out the word, but it was his faint smile that made her think she should be worried. He pulled out jeans and socks from his duffel. "I'll be quick so we'll have time to grab some breakfast."

"Fine. I'll run to the Food Mart now while you—"

"We're going to the diner," he said, walking over to her and forcing her chin up. "So you'll probably want to fix your face."

Sophie gasped. She reared back and shoved his hand away. "Forgive me for not meeting your standards."

He looked confused. "That's not what I meant," he said, and had the nerve to sound frustrated.

"Go. Take your shower." She turned back to her bag, trying to hide her disappointment and hurt.

The second he closed the bathroom door, she sank onto the edge of the bed. Screw him. The stupid insensitive jerk. She pushed her fingers through her damp hair, working past the tangles and wincing at each tug on her scalp.

She eyed the bag beside her. She doubted she had a mirror, and even if she did she'd hate herself for caring enough to look. He thought she should fix her face? Asshole.

Gee, she wondered if she looked sufficiently presentable to pick up breakfast at the Food Mart. He could forget about the diner.

All of a sudden she felt totally drained. The kind of bone-deep exhaustion that followed an adrenaline high. Great. So much for getting a good start for Wyoming tonight.

How could Ethan have said something so hurtful?

She fell back on the mattress and rubbed her eyes. After a pot of coffee and some protein, she'd feel better. She wouldn't let the remark bother her.

She had to stay sharp, remember her objective. Pulling herself into a sitting position, she glanced at the clock.

No way. It couldn't be almost noon.

She yanked her phone from the charger and stared at the numbers. This wasn't possible. She'd never slept so late in her life. Never. Last night she drank one beer. Read for an hour while

Ethan watched TV. The moment he'd fallen asleep, she got into bed and conked out herself around midnight.

Huh.

She noticed something black on her fingertips. She checked the phone, but it was fine, so she set it down. Her other hand was also smudged. Glancing down at her red shirt, she saw that it was clean. And her jeans, well, who could tell…they were brand-new and still dark blue.

The dye maybe?

A thought struck her.

She grabbed her bag and turned it upside down on the bed, not sure whether or not she wanted to be right about the cause of the mysterious smudges. After checking every inside pocket, she dumped the meager contents of the purse she hated carrying but kept on hand.

God bless Lola and her makeup addiction. And for giving Sophie some of her castoffs. The blush compact was small, the mirror tiny. But it did the job.

Sophie stared at her raccoon eyes and laughed. She wasn't used to wearing the epic amount of makeup she'd put on with the wig and obviously had done a poor job of removing all of it.

She found some tissue and went to work fixing her face, relieved she'd misunderstood Ethan. Though she had the feeling she would've been better off thinking he was a jerk.

7

"ARE YOU SURE this is a private ranch?" Sophie asked as they pulled into the Lone Wolf in Ethan's truck. They'd argued over who would drive and ended up flipping a coin.

"Yeah, I'm sure. It's been in the Gunderson family for several generations. Matt owns it now. Keep an eye out for a place to park."

Sophie recognized his friend from the bar last night. "Look, isn't that Matt motioning for you?"

"Yep. He must've saved us a spot."

Sophie glanced around at the rows of parked cars close to the gravel drive, the trailers and motor homes lined up to the right of the beautiful two-story ranch house with green shutters. The two barns were easy to identify, and so was the large stable, but she had no idea about all the other smaller buildings.

"That must be the new arena he built," Ethan said as he pulled up to Matt and lowered his window.

Sophie saw the large structure standing north of the corrals. Behind it were acres of sloping pastureland.

"Were you expecting this kind of turnout?" Ethan asked his friend.

Matt's sigh ended with a mild curse. "We've got some kinks

to work out, that's for sure." He looked at Sophie, nodded and then did a double take.

"Long story," Ethan muttered. "I'll explain later."

"Should be good. See that kid with the yellow flag?" Matt pointed. "He's holding a place for you. I'll catch up with you in a few minutes." He smacked the side of the truck and stepped back.

They were shown to a parking spot next to the arena. The huge building was definitely new with a green roof and rust-colored wooden siding. She couldn't imagine what it was used for besides hosting a rodeo, and she wouldn't find out anytime soon judging by the mob about to converge on them.

Or rather on Ethan.

The crowd barely let the poor guy climb out of the truck before they swarmed him. Two reporters pushed their way to the front. The thirtysomething man wore credentials around his neck, and the woman had a cameraman with her. A cowboy Sophie had seen at the bar last night stood to the side, grinning and watching fans shove pens and pictures in Ethan's face.

He accepted the attention better than she would have. He smiled politely, greeted a few people by name and pretty much ignored the pair of blondes wearing skintight jeans and showing off their boob jobs.

Sophie took a discreet glance at herself. Okay, so she had no room to talk. Her jeans could've been sprayed on. The boobs were all hers, though. She pulled her shoulders back. It helped some.

A heavyset man wearing a diamond pinkie ring the size of her Jeep, and who'd been talking with Ethan, turned and gave her a friendly smile. "Now, who do we have here?"

Sophie had purposely stayed back and hadn't expected any interaction. She cleared her throat. "Sophie," she said, and stuck out her hand.

He seemed surprised but broadened his grin and shook hands with her. "You're here with Ethan?"

They should've discussed this in case someone asked. For God's sake, why hadn't they? She smiled, nodded, managed a quiet "Yes." And hoped the man would leave it at that.

"Sorry, Hal," Ethan said, appearing at her side. "I should've introduced you two right off." He slid an arm around her shoulders and smiled at her, his eyes asking her to go with it. "Sophie's my girlfriend."

"You don't say." The man seemed delighted. "Good for you, Styles. Though you best watch yourself. Your young lady has quite a grip," he said, chuckling and flexing his hand.

"Um, sorry." She'd been told that many times.

"No need to apologize," he said, winking at her. "This boy needs a firm hand." Hal was mostly bald, had no facial hair, but for some reason he reminded her of an overly friendly Santa Claus. "I'll leave you to finish signing autographs, son. I'm sure we'll meet again, Sophie." He gave her a nod and then wandered toward the arena entrance.

"Hal's a good guy," Ethan said, intently watching the older man stop and shake hands with a young cowboy. "I didn't expect to see him here."

She wondered if Ethan realized his arm was still around her shoulders. "Who is he?"

"Hal and his brother own Southern Saddles." He glanced at the sponsor patch he was wearing on his sleeve, then returned his watchful gaze to Hal and the young man. "Probably checking out the new talent. Danny just joined the pro tour this year, but he's kicking ass."

"What does he do?"

"Bull rider." Ethan finally lowered his arm from her shoulders but then resettled it around her waist.

"You're not worried about being replaced, are you? Companies sponsor more than one athlete all the time."

He shrugged. "If I miss the finals again, yeah, I'd expect they might replace me. That's what I'd do if I were in their shoes."

"That's not fair," she said, and noted his small tolerant smile.

"I understand it's just business, of course I do. But if you miss the finals, for whatever reason, yeah, it'll totally suck, but the fact remains that out of hundreds you qualified to ride in the first place. That has to count for something."

He just kept staring at her and smiling. "How about a kiss?"

With a laugh, Sophie leaned away from him. "People are waiting for autographs."

"How long does a kiss take?"

She moved back in close, brushed her lips across his ear and whispered, "Depends how slow and deep you go."

Ethan promptly released her and started laughing. "Yeah, thanks, I need to ride a nineteen-hundred-pound bull while I'm distracted by a hard-on."

"Go sign autographs. That should cool you off."

He kissed her right on the mouth before she could stop him. "Remember, anybody asks, you're my girlfriend."

"I could've just as easily been your cousin," she grumbled, which she knew he'd heard as he walked back toward his waiting fans.

Ethan Styles's girlfriend for the day, she thought, and actually caught herself stupidly twirling her hair around her finger.

How pathetic.

ANOTHER THIRTY MINUTES and the rodeo would officially start. Sophie sure hoped Ethan wouldn't give her a hard time about getting on the road right after his event.

Damn, the man knew everyone. Rabid fans, casual fans, the volunteers from Safe Haven who'd helped organize the fundraiser…

Sophie couldn't keep track of all the people she'd met. But she'd taken an instant liking to Matt and his wife, Rachel. She was friendly and outgoing and treated Ethan and Sophie as though she'd known them forever.

The four of them stood near the stable, the only open area where cars weren't parked bumper to bumper.

"If we do this again next year," Matt said, eyeing the swelling crowd with unease, "we're setting up a table for autographs. Off to the side, maybe near the east barn."

"Oh, trust me, we'll be doing this again." Rachel scanned the list on her clipboard. "Here you go, Ethan," she said, and passed him a number to wear.

Ethan removed the protective sheet to expose the sticky back and slapped it on the front of his shirt.

"This should've been a one-day event," Matt muttered, too preoccupied with what was going on around them to keep up with the conversation. Poor guy. He did seem tense.

"I wondered about that," Ethan said.

Matt strained to look beyond them and nodded to someone.

"My fault." Rachel sighed. "You warned me, and I was stubborn and wanted to help, but..."

"It's okay." Matt caught her hand and pulled her close. Looking into her eyes, he smiled before kissing her. Someone yelled for him, but he was completely focused on his wife. "Ethan and I have to go. Call me if you need anything." Matt gave her another quick kiss before pulling back and winking. "Everything will be just fine."

Rachel nodded. "Thank you," she whispered.

Busy being a voyeur, Sophie hadn't noticed Ethan moving closer. She felt his hand at her waist and with a start turned to him. "What?"

So much for a tender moment à la Matt and Rachel. Sophie had barked like an old harridan.

Ethan grinned. "I'm waiting for my kiss."

She knew Rachel was watching, so Sophie leaned in to plant a peck at the corner of his mouth.

He slid his hand behind her neck, preventing a retreat. "I know you can do better," he murmured near her ear. "Kiss me like you did last night."

She was about to warn him not to push it, but he slipped his tongue inside her mouth and didn't pull back until her heart almost thumped out of her chest.

"Come on, Styles," Matt yelled. "She's not going anywhere."

"He's right about that," Sophie whispered with a gentle shove to his chest.

Ethan stared at her a moment, his smile so faint it barely qualified. "You had to ruin it."

Her breath caught. She had no idea what he meant. Or how to respond. Somehow he seemed disappointed and it bothered her.

And dammit, that bothered her, too. Why should she care?

He glanced at Rachel, touched the brim of his hat, then turned and jogged toward Matt.

"Did you mess up his ritual?"

Sophie dragged her gaze from him and looked at Rachel. "Excuse me?"

"I know a lot of rodeo cowboys are superstitious, especially right before they ride. At least that's what Matt told me. I wasn't around when he was part of the tour."

"Did you meet him after he quit?"

"No. I've known Matt most of my life. We both grew up here in Blackfoot Falls. Although we had a ten-year interruption." Rachel waved an acknowledgment to someone motioning for her. "Mind walking with me?"

"Not at all. If you have something for me to do, put me to work."

"I probably will," Rachel said, grinning at first, and then she glanced back toward the guys and sighed. "Poor Matt. I don't know how he puts up with me. I had no idea this thing would be such a headache. He's right. One day would've been enough, but everyone in town got so excited about the business the rodeo was bringing and I just figured, why not add a day?"

"You want to help your community. That's nice." Sophie smiled, starting to feel better. She liked Rachel and really hoped there was a way to help. "I have a feeling Matt isn't too upset with you."

"Oh, I'm sure he'll think of some way for me to make it up to him," she said, her green eyes sparkling even as she blushed.

"How long have you guys been married?"

"Almost eight months."

"Wow. Not that long. You mentioned a ten-year interruption?"

"Matt's four years older and he left town at nineteen. I had a stupid crush on him and was completely convinced my life was over. Oh, but please don't tell anyone. God forbid the other half of the town should find out." Rachel rolled her eyes, making Sophie laugh. "A few years later I went off to college. After graduate school I came home—it was only supposed to be for the summer." She shrugged. "I stayed to help with my family's ranch and never left again."

They reached the frazzled woman who'd waved for Rachel. How to handle the collected entry tickets was briefly discussed and then Rachel and Sophie headed for the concessions.

"What do you do here at the Lone Wolf?"

"Not much. Most of the hired men have been here forever, so they take care of the cattle. Matt's more interested in raising rodeo stock. The horses and bulls they're using today are his. In fact, that's why he built that monstrosity," she said, glancing at the building that housed the arena. "He wanted a year-round place for demonstrations and such."

"Is he riding today?"

"Oh, God no. I'd be a nervous wreck." Rachel pressed her lips together. "Sorry, I shouldn't have—"

"No, it's fine." Sophie shrugged. "Frankly I'm not a fan. But I try not to say much."

"Yes." They exchanged looks of mutual understanding, and then Rachel said, "Okay, I want to hear all about you and Ethan."

"It's not what you think." Sophie saw they were approaching the hot dog booth and hoped a mini crisis would distract Rachel. Nothing big or awful. Just a little something—

"Oh? How long have you two been together?"

"We're not, really. When he calls me his girlfriend, it's not like— We knew each other in high school." Sophie was a horrible liar. "And honestly we hadn't been in touch for years until… well, recently."

"Huh. How weird. Kind of like Matt and me."

Sophie sniffed the chilly air. "I think the hot dogs might be burning."

"Oh, great." Rachel glanced over her shoulder. "We'll talk later. At the barbecue." She was already backing toward the booth. "There won't be too many people staying."

"Barbecue?"

"Yes, at the house. Ethan said you two could make it. Didn't he tell you?"

A woman passing out programs intercepted Rachel. Sophie thought about reiterating her offer to help, but she figured she'd mostly be in the way. She also was anxious to go inside and find a seat, though not thrilled about having to sit through so many other events before it was Ethan's turn.

Dammit, she was nervous for him.

Bull riding was dangerous enough without Ethan's eerie penchant for having one thing or another go wrong just before the finals. So how could he not be distracted? Which only upped the chances of something bad happening.

Sophie felt her stomach knot. A stiff breeze coming off the mountains made her shiver. The Lone Wolf was a beautiful spread carved into the foothills. Thousands of pines made up for the barren trees. Up this far north and at this altitude, the leaves had fallen weeks ago.

She looked up at the overcast sky and wondered if snow was expected.

Her Jeep was okay in snow. Though she had yet to put it to a real test, since the county where she lived kept the roads plowed. Out here, driving could get tricky. They could take Ethan's truck and get to Wyoming in time, but not if he insisted on being pigheaded.

A barbecue?

Right.

Under different circumstances it might've been fun, Sophie thought as she finally entered the new arena. The place was huge and, according to some people in line, had only been completed last week. There were rows of bleachers on two sides, wooden picnic benches and folding chairs directly across. Metal pens and chutes for the animals finished the makeshift rectangular arena. The floor was a combination of concrete and dirt, and whiffs of sweat and manure had already taken Sophie by surprise. She tried not to inhale too deeply. No wonder the food concessions had been set up outside.

She studied the ticket Rachel had given her earlier. Her seat was supposed to be close to the action. She sure hoped it wasn't in the row of folding chairs. Yes, there was a steel barrier separating spectators from the bucking animals. And yes, she was confident Matt knew what he was doing. But no way in hell was Sophie going to sit that close.

Volunteers from Safe Haven, identified by orange vests, were running around, answering questions, directing people to seats and, in general, looking harried.

Wow, there were a lot of people. Families with kids dressed as little cowboys were just too adorable. Herds of teenage boys crowded the barricaded pens, dividing their attention between the horses and the lists of names printed on the white poster boards hanging on the wall. An older gentleman climbed a metal ladder and, with a fat felt-tipped marker, added another name. *Mayhem.*

Horse or bull? Sophie wondered. Then decided she didn't want to know.

Of course the buckle bunnies had turned out in considerable numbers. The women stood close to the chutes, mostly in pairs, and some of them were really gorgeous. Sophie wished she'd put a bit more effort into her makeup.

When her phone rang, she saw it was Lola and quickly picked up. "Sorry. I meant to call you earlier."

"Everything okay?"

"Yes." Sophie pressed a finger to her free ear to buffer the noise and walked as far away from the crowd as possible.

"Sounds like you're at the rodeo," Lola said.

"I am, but it hasn't started yet. And unfortunately Ethan rides last."

"A lot of people show up?"

"I'm guessing over four hundred."

"Whoa. He'll get mobbed when it's over."

"I know. He's already been overrun with kids wanting autographs." She saw Rachel walk in, and the first thing that popped into Sophie's mind was the barbecue. "Oh, did I mention it might snow?"

Lola responded with silence. And then, "Is that pertinent?"

"No. Not at all." Sophie gritted her teeth.

"So what's the plan?"

Luckily an announcement that the rodeo would begin in three minutes bounced off the walls at an ear-shattering volume. The crowd responded proportionately.

"Lola? It's crazy in here. I can't hear you very well. I'll have to call you later."

The noise level was settling down and Sophie could've finished their conversation. Instead she disconnected and turned off her phone.

8

AFTER SITTING THROUGH three hours of calf roping, team calf roping, steer wrestling, saddle bronc riding and having to listen to the pair next to her, Sophie figured her penance for blowing off Lola was paid in full.

The two middle-aged men had opinions about every damn thing in the whole universe. They certainly were entitled to express themselves. Sophie didn't have to listen. Now, the tobacco chewing? That was getting to her.

She was mentally rehearsing what she could politely say to get them to keep their tobacco juice to themselves when the announcer mentioned Ethan's name. She straightened and concentrated on what the commentator was saying. His slight twang wasn't always easy to understand.

"Think he'll wear a helmet?"

"Shh." Sophie scowled at the bearded man next to her. Then she processed what he'd said. "Who?"

The man gave her a long look, then nodded toward the area behind the chutes. "Ethan Styles."

Sophie panned the faces of three cowboys. "I don't see him."

"He's not riding yet. Danny Young is up next. Then Cody Clark. Weren't you listening?"

Sophie sucked it up and just smiled. Okay, now she remembered. There were supposed to be three bull riders today.

Danny Young was announced and she leaned forward, watching him secure a protective blue helmet, then lower himself onto the back of a bull already bucking to get out of the chute.

So far all the other cowboys had worn Stetsons or another brand of cowboy hat. But then their events weren't as dangerous as bull riding. She couldn't recall seeing a helmet in Ethan's truck. She knew not all bull riders liked wearing a helmet…

After wrapping a short bull rope around his left hand, the rider gave the nod. The chute gate swung open and the black bull charged out bucking and whirling and twisting. Dirt flew from the animal's hooves. With his free hand held up high, the rider clung to the rope with his other gloved hand. The crowd shouted and cheered.

A buzzer sounded and more cheering as the crowd leaped to their feet. The rider pulled the rope free and bailed to the right, landing on his feet while two cowboys distracted the bull. As the announcer sang his praises, Danny Young jogged to safety and then pulled off the helmet and grinned at the crowd.

"I bet the kid makes it to the finals next year," the bearded man said. "He finished the season ranked forty-ninth. Damn good for this being only his second tour."

"I'd sure like to see how he does on a fiercer bucker," said his friend with the weathered face.

Sophie turned and stared at him. "Are you saying that bull wasn't scary as hell?"

The other guy laughed and leaned back. "Hey, Lenny, she's talking to you."

"What?"

Sophie sighed. "That bull looked pretty intimidating to me."

"Is this your first rodeo, honey?" Lenny asked, his craggy features softened by a kind smile.

"No, but…" She breathed in deeply and glanced toward the

chute. She wished she could see Ethan. Wearing a helmet. "Bull riding is nerve-racking."

"Then you might want to sit out the last ride."

"The last— You mean Ethan Styles," she said, a sickening wave of dread swelling inside her. "Why?"

"Matt Gunderson's new to the stock contracting business. But he's raising some good rodeo bulls. I heard Twister is one mean son of a—" Lenny gave her a sheepish grin, then shifted his gaze to the arena.

She realized the next rider—Cody something or other—was being announced, so she kept quiet and let the two men enjoy the event. Although how they could voluntarily watch a bloodthirsty bull try to pulverize someone, she'd never comprehend.

Yes, she understood some rodeo basics. For instance, the bulls were scored on their performance, just as the riders were. The scores were then combined for a potential of one hundred points. So clearly the more difficult the bull was to ride, the more points the rider received overall. But points didn't matter here. Ethan had told her so last night. Matt was supposed to be his friend. So why give Ethan a son of a bitch to ride?

No, it hadn't been Matt who'd made that call. It had been Ethan. She'd bet anything he'd insisted on riding the toughest bull. Stupid, reckless idiot.

She stared down at her aching hands. And only stopped wringing them to drag her damp palms down her jeans. The crowd's collective gasp made her look up.

The rider had been thrown over the bull's massive head. He landed face-first in the dirt and then crawled until he could finally stand. When he staggered, it was Matt who jumped into the arena and helped the cowboy to the side. The bull continued to furiously buck, trampling the man's tan Stetson. Why wasn't he wearing a helmet?

He lifted a hand to let everyone know he was all right.

The crowd responded with deafening applause. Sophie squeezed her eyes shut. Ethan was next.

Please, please, please be wearing a helmet.

"All right, folks, you all know who's up next… Having finished the season at number two, Ethan Styles is arguably the hottest rider on tour," the announcer said, which inspired a few catcalls. "Whose agility and athleticism has won him the respect of his fans. And once again a trip to the finals in Las Vegas—"

Applause and cheering nearly drowned the man out. Handmade signs had popped up in the crowd. Some clever, some incredibly corny. One sign read Marry me, Ethan.

"Settle down, folks. It might be another minute or two. Looks like he might be having some trouble with Twister, who I've been told is a savage bucker. Like the other two bulls we've seen today, Twister belongs to Matt Gunderson. No stranger to you all, but new to the world of raising bulls. He assured me we won't be disappointed with Twister, says he's a real killer. I guess we'll all find out soon enough…"

The announcer continued talking, but Sophie had stopped listening. She rose from her seat, trying to catch a glimpse of Ethan. She could see his sun-streaked hair as the bull rocked him against the metal railing. No helmet. Damn him.

"Miss? You mind sitting down? We can't see from back here."

Sophie heard the voice behind her, but not until someone touched her arm did it register the man was speaking to her. With an apology she sank back onto her seat. Maybe it was a blessing that she couldn't see. Her nerves were already frayed. Why wouldn't he wear a helmet? It was just plain foolish.

"Styles is nuts," Lenny said. "I can't figure out why he's riding this weekend. With his track record you'd think he'd be holed up somewhere with the door double-locked."

The bearded man spat into a cup. "That's what I would do. He gets injured today, he won't never forgive himself. Sure would be a shame if he missed the finals again."

"You get a chance to see him ride Bad Company at the season opener?" Lenny asked his friend. "Reminds me of this bull. Thrashing and lunging against the gate like that, he ain't about to let Styles get comfortable. What was it that happened last year before the finals? Was it his elbow—"

"Please stop saying those things." Sophie turned to the two men. "Riders are superstitious enough. Ethan doesn't need to be reminded of what's happened in the past. So, please..."

Lenny frowned at her. "It ain't like we're saying it so he can hear."

"But you're still putting it out there in the universe."

The men glanced at each other and laughed. "Ma'am, you might wanna find another sport that's easier on your blood pressure," Lenny said.

Sophie hadn't been looking for a clear shot of Ethan. But that was what she got between a pair of Stetson-wearing cowboys sitting two rows in front of her. He was still tying his rope.

"What's he doing?" Lenny mumbled. "He can't be using a suicide wrap."

"He'd be a dang fool, since he's not looking to qualify."

"A what?" Sophie asked, but the men ignored her. A suicide wrap? Okay, maybe it was better she didn't know.

Gripping the edge of her seat, she leaned forward, her heart racing. "Damn you, Ethan," she muttered under her breath, her attention glued to him. "Put on the goddamn helmet."

"You know Styles personally?" Lenny asked, frowning at her.

"Yes," she said, swallowing when she saw him give the nod. "I'm his girlfriend."

AFTER WHAT FELT like an hour inside a blender, Ethan heard the buzzer. Another two seconds and he ripped free of the bull rope and jumped off Twister. He managed to land on his feet while a bullfighter lured the bull in the other direction. Pulling off his Stetson, Ethan waved it at the cheering crowd.

Good for Gunderson. He had a winner with Twister. That son of a bitch could buck and change direction with the best of them. When he'd burst out of the chute and cut to the left, Ethan almost let go.

Sophie wasn't in her seat.

What the hell?

He'd known exactly where she was sitting. He'd spotted her after watching Kenny get an ass-whooping by one of Matt's broncs.

People were on their feet, still applauding, so Ethan waved again before he exited the arena. Once he made it to the reserved area behind the pens, he stopped to dust off his hat and the front of his shirt. Matt was waiting for him with a mile-wide grin.

Ethan laughed. "You trying to kill me, Gunderson?"

"What did I tell you?"

"I didn't think the bastard was gonna let me outta the chute." Ethan wiped his face with the back of his sleeve. "You ride him yet?"

"Nope." Matt handed him a clean rag. "If Twister didn't kill me, Rachel would."

"Smart woman."

Ethan recognized the irritated voice even before he turned around.

Sophie had slipped behind the fence, ignoring the man who tried to stop her.

"It's okay," Matt told the cowboy, and the man backed off.

It didn't appear Sophie was aware of anything going on around her. She was focused solely on Ethan, and she looked pissed.

She stopped a foot away and glared up at him. "Styles, there is something very wrong with you."

"Okay." He grinned and put on his hat. Her cheeks were pink, her dark eyes flashing. He couldn't imagine what this was about, but he didn't like that her lower lip had quivered. "Are you gonna tell me why?"

"We'll talk later," Matt said, nodding at Sophie as he passed her.

She gave him an apologetic smile. When she met Ethan's eyes again, she didn't look angry but afraid. "Why didn't you wear a helmet?" Her voice was so soft he barely heard her. "I know you don't owe me an answer," she said. "I do. But God, Ethan, you're a smart man. Bull riding is dangerous. And I'm just trying to understand—"

He touched her hand, and she threw her arms around his neck. She'd looked so sad and small standing there he wasn't sure what to do or say. Except to hold her close until she stopped trembling. He just rubbed her back and waited for her pounding heart to slow.

"I'm sorry if I'm embarrassing you," she murmured, her face buried against his chest. "Just give me a minute, okay?"

"Hell, you're not embarrassing me." He almost made a joke, but the words seemed to stick in his throat. "A beautiful woman cares about whether I wear a helmet or not, and I should be embarrassed?"

Keeping her face down, she bumped him with her knee.

"Ethan?" The soft voice belonged to a Safe Haven volunteer. "Sorry to interrupt, but folks are waiting for autographs."

Sophie tried to pull away, but he held her tight.

"Tell them it'll be a few more minutes," he told the older woman standing at the fence. "Please."

"Will do." With a smile she turned and left.

"No, Ethan." Sophie pushed at his chest. "Go. I'm fine."

"Twister couldn't buck me off. You think I can't hold on to a little thing like you?"

"Oh, brother." She sniffed. "Watch it. I kickbox," she said, and slowly lifted her chin. Her eyes were bright, but no tears. "Don't make those people wait."

"Why not? They get bored and hit the concessions, that's more money for Safe Haven."

Sophie laughed. "And here I thought you were just a pretty face."

"See how wrong you can be?" He smiled at her mock glare and wondered what had set her off. He doubted it was just about him not wearing a helmet. But he couldn't get into it now. "How about you come with me?"

"Oh, for heaven's sake, I'm fine. Embarrassed as hell," she said. "Though not fatally. I'm sure I'll live to embarrass myself another day. So go." She tugged at his arm. "Good grief, I think your muscles have muscles."

Ethan caught her chin and tipped her face up so he could look into her eyes. "I usually do wear a helmet. But I left Wyoming in a rush to get here and forgot it." He brushed a kiss across her mouth. "That's no excuse. It was dumb to forget something so important."

Her bottom lip quivered again. Not from fear this time. How was he supposed to go shake hands and sign autographs when all he could think about was tasting every inch of her? He trailed a finger down her throat, then traced the ridge of her collarbone. The satiny texture of her skin drove him nuts. So smooth and soft everywhere he touched. What must the skin of her inner thighs feel like?

"We can pick one up tomorrow," she whispered, pressing into him and making it damn near impossible for him to think straight.

"Pick what up?"

"A helmet." Her eyes started to drift closed, but then she widened them. "Oh no. We leave tonight."

"I'm not going to do that, Sophie."

"Ethan…"

He kissed her lips, silencing her. And tormenting himself. All he wanted was for them to be someplace far away, alone, without distractions. Someplace where he could explore her body with his hands and mouth. Listen to her soft breathless moans when their kissing got hot and heavy. He wondered what sound she would make when he sank deep inside her.

Her stubborn lips finally yielded, letting him slip his tongue between them.

He jerked a little when her fingers dug into his bum shoulder.

"Can people see us?" she asked, slightly breathless.

"Probably."

"An awful lot of kids are out there."

"Yeah." Ethan straightened and released her. "Let's get this over with," he said, taking her hand.

She pulled it back. "I'll wait in the truck."

"Come on…" Wasn't this just great? They were gonna end up arguing. So be it, but they weren't leaving tonight. "Matt and Rachel are barbecuing."

"I heard," she said, staying a step ahead of him.

"There won't be a lot of people, mostly the riders who are staying here in their trailers." He watched her squeeze between the fence post and the wall. No way he'd fit so he just moved the whole damn temporary fence. "Did you hear me?"

"Yes, I heard you, and you already know what I have to say to that."

"My agent called," he said, and that stopped her. "He's in the middle of something with a football client. We're talking later."

"Did you not tell him how important this is?"

"I will."

She shook her head. Then without so much as a glance, she walked in the direction of the truck, leaving him to face a dozen squealing kids and a pack of buckle bunnies.

9

SOPHIE WAS IN TROUBLE. She slumped down in the truck's passenger seat, grateful for the tinted windows, and checked her texts. Two from Lola, one from Mandy and a voice mail from her mom. Since she could set a clock by her mom's Saturday phone calls, she'd listen to the message later.

But Lola was getting impatient, and Sophie could hardly blame her.

She thumped her head back on the leather headrest. It was far too comfortable to knock any real sense into her thick skull.

God, she was being stupid. Not just stupid. She'd risen to the level of too-stupid-to-live. When had she become the kind of ridiculous airhead she and Mandy liked to make fun of in bars?

Well, payback was a bitch. She was allowing Ethan to make a complete fool out of her. He probably knew she'd gotten all giddy inside when he'd announced she was his girlfriend. He was only using her to buy time and to keep the buckle bunnies at bay.

And yet, a part of her refused to believe that he'd be so heartless. Something other than ego was driving him to go after that second championship. Maybe that something was more important than her ending up as collateral damage.

She really hadn't expected to like Ethan. He was nothing like the self-centered man she'd imagined. But he was being naive. Clearly he hadn't explained the gravity of his situation to his agent. If he had, Brian wouldn't be shelving the problem for later.

Sitting up straighter, she adjusted the rearview mirror, hoping she could see how the fan schmoozing was going. She recognized a young saddle bronc rider dividing his attention between a blonde and signing a kid's T-shirt. The crowd had thinned, but her view was still limited. She couldn't see Ethan and assumed he was around the corner of the building.

A volunteer picked up trash while two more were closing down the hot dog concession. Hopefully the fans would clear out soon. The sun had gone down, and so had the temperature. She should probably offer to help. But there was a call she should make first.

Ethan needed a lawyer. And Craig Langley was an excellent defense attorney. Every deputy and assistant DA she knew couldn't stand the man, which spoke to his success at getting his clients off. The reason she didn't care for him was more personal. For months he'd been asking her out with the same dogged persistence he used to wear down prosecutors. But he was too smooth in his thousand-dollar suits and not at all her type.

She stared at her phone, well aware that if she asked Craig for help, she'd owe him. Just the thought of having dinner with him gave her the creeps. And if any of the deputies found out, she'd be the laughingstock of the whole county.

"Damn you, Ethan." She sucked in a breath and checked old incoming calls. Yep, there was his number.

Craig answered on the second ring. "Sophie?"

"Hey." She forced a smile, hoping it helped make her sound less as though she'd rather be eating worms. "Got a minute?"

"Well, now, honey, for you I've got all night."

"I need a favor," she said on an exhale, and then summed up the problem, leaving out names for now.

"Hmm, you know I always have a full caseload..." he drawled.

She held back a sigh. Fine. She'd figured he would milk the

situation. "I know you're busy, Craig," she said shamelessly using that husky tone men liked. "That's why I hated to even ask, but it's a time-sensitive matter. And frankly there's no one I could trust more with this little problem."

"You were absolutely right to call me. How about we meet for dinner to discuss the details?"

"I'd love that. I really would, except I'm out of town at the moment. In Montana, actually."

"Montana? When will you be back?"

"Monday, I hope."

"All right, that's the day after tomorrow. How about I make dinner reservations at La Maison? Would you like that?"

Cringing, Sophie shoved a hand through her hair. "See, this little problem my friend has, it really can't wait that long," she said, then tensed at his silence. "But dinner at La Maison sounds—"

She hadn't realized Ethan had opened the driver's door until she saw him standing there.

"That sounds great," she said in a rush, and saw Ethan frown. "But I need to go right now."

"We don't have to eat at La Maison," Craig said, sounding confused. "I know this little bistro—"

"I'll call you later, okay?"

"Sophie?"

She hung up on him. "All done?" she asked Ethan.

He frowned. "Am I interrupting?"

"Nope. Let's go."

He slid behind the wheel and closed the door. "Did you have to cancel a date?"

"No." She noticed he didn't have his keys out.

"The food's good at La Maison."

"You've been there?"

"A few times."

"Don't they require a jacket and tie?"

Ethan cocked an eyebrow. "I happen to have both."

"Huh. I can't picture you in a tie," she said, and failed to see why he seemed to find that objectionable. "Come on, why aren't we moving?"

"Because I'm not ready to move." He turned most of his body toward her. "Do you have a boyfriend?"

"No." He had some nerve. So why did she want so badly to help him stay out of jail? Might as well change her forehead tattoo from *denial* to *stupid*.

"Well, somebody sure wants to impress you."

She glared at him. "And if he does?"

"Nothing." Ethan took his hat off and tossed it into the backseat. "I'm sorry I screwed up your date. If you want to go to La Maison, I'll take you there myself."

Sophie snorted a laugh. Good to know it wasn't just her who was acting like a ridiculous child.

"What?"

"You like the food at La Maison? How about I bring you a takeout while you're sitting in jail?"

It was Ethan's turn to glare. "You're picking a fight so we don't go to the barbecue."

"You're unbelievable," she said. "You really are." She laid her head back and rubbed her eyes, careful not to streak her mascara. Out of her peripheral vision she saw him take out his phone.

"Arnie? Tell me something good." Ethan stared out the windshield while he listened. His mouth tightened. "Arnie." He drawled the name into a warning, then waited, listening, the muscle in his jaw working double time. "You dumb fuck, you slept with her, didn't you?"

Sophie lifted her head and stared outright.

He dropped the phone into his lap and hit the steering wheel with the heel of his hand.

Cursed.

Hit the wheel again.

"Tell me," she said, the tension in her chest beginning to hurt.

"Wendy isn't going to admit she lied. She can't change her story now."

"But her husband..."

"Fullerton already knows. His ranch foreman doesn't like Wendy, so he told the old man he saw me leaving around midnight. That's why she made up a story about turning me down at the bar and me following her home."

"But as far as Fullerton knows, you could've just been giving her a ride home or dropping something off..."

Ethan smiled.

"It's possible," Sophie said, annoyed that he thought she was the one being naive. "So, why did Arnie sleep with her? And anyway, doesn't that just prove she's a serial cheater?"

"She played him. Wendy found the perfect way to keep the dumb ass from telling her husband the truth. Claiming I'd ripped her off was overkill. She must've regretted it as soon as she realized she'd have to get rid of the jewelry and deal with an insurance investigation. So when Arnie showed up in front of a bunch of witnesses she jumped at the chance to tell everyone he'd brought the jewelry back to get her to drop the charges. He made it real easy for her to keep her jewelry and stick to the lie."

"That's crazy."

"Crazy or not, I don't need that kind of publicity dogging me at the finals."

"Yeah, but who'd believe you would do something like that?"

"Probably no one but her husband, if only to keep the marriage intact and save face."

"Men and their damn egos." She saw his eyebrows go up. "Yes, I'm talking about you, too." She huffed out a breath. Something had been bothering her... "What's a suicide wrap?"

His eyes narrowed. "Where did you hear that?"

"Some guys sitting next to me on the bleachers."

Shaking his head, he sighed. "We wrap the hand we use to hold on to the leather strap. Weaving the rope between the ring finger and pinkie makes it harder for the bull to pull it out of your hand," he said. "It also makes it harder for a rider to let go."

"And he can get hung up on a thrashing bull."

"Yes, sometimes that happens."

She tried to control a shudder. "Did you use one of those wraps today?"

"No."

"Do you ever?"

"Yes," he said, his gaze steady. "But I'm not reckless, Sophie."

"Uh, do you even know what the word *suicide* means?"

"Sorry we can't all be as smart as you," he said, his expression stony. "That doesn't mean I'm stupid."

Sophie briefly closed her eyes. "I'm sorry. I know I'm snide sometimes—of course I wasn't saying you're stupid." This was another reason kids had picked on her. She just didn't know when to keep her mouth shut. "If anyone's stupid, it's me. I'm supposed to be taking you back, not trying to find a way to— You don't even care what happens. Why should I?"

He caught her waving hands and held them both in one of his. "I care," he said, and looked directly into her eyes. "I thought Arnie would come through. Brian will, but probably not in time to avoid court, so we'll head to Wyoming tomorrow."

"In the morning?" she asked hopefully.

"No. After my ride."

"That's cutting it close."

He shrugged. "I got here in twelve hours with one stop. What about you?"

"The same."

"I'll talk to Matt about switching the schedule. We should be able to leave by midafternoon. Stop at a motel halfway and get a few hours' sleep." Ethan leaned over the console to brush a kiss across her lips. "How's that?"

She nodded, happy she could call Lola and not have to lie. Happy she was sitting here in Ethan's truck, feeling his warm breath on her face. "You might still need an attorney."

"I guess it'll depend on how far Wendy pushes her story."

"I bet she wants this to go away as much as you do."

"Sure hope so." He cupped the side of her face and studied her lips, his mouth curving in a slow smile.

"Wait. Let me say this before we get crazy and I forget."

A low chuckle rumbled in his throat. "Make it quick."

"Uh-huh." She touched his jaw, intrigued by the stubble that hadn't been there this morning. The rasp against her fingertips was oddly arousing. Imagining how amazing it would feel pressed to her breasts had her holding her breath.

"Last chance," he said, sliding his fingers into her hair.

Whatever she'd been about to say was already in the wind. She hoped it wasn't important. It didn't matter. She was more interested in what Ethan was doing to her scalp. His touch was sheer heaven. The soothing massage turned into a slight tug. She realized she'd closed her eyes.

Apparently he wanted them open. Watching her face, he held her still as he lowered his mouth. Their lips barely touched and lightning shot through her. His tongue didn't politely wait for an invitation. He demanded entrance, coaxing and teasing his way inside, stoking the fire that had ignited low in her belly.

She clutched his arm, digging her fingers into hard muscle, and met each stroke of his tongue. The console was in their way. She wished they could push it to the floor. Or what if they climbed into the backseat?

A light came on somewhere behind him, closer to the house. She didn't care. Her existence had narrowed to the urgency of Ethan's touch, his greedy mouth, the feel of his warm hard body and the longing about to burst out of her chest. Her young girlish fantasies hadn't prepared her for this, not for Ethan in the flesh.

He moved his shoulder to block the light from hitting her face. But he kept kissing her, touching her jaw, the side of her chin, testing how their mouths fit together from different angles. He traced her ear with his thumb, then followed the curve of her neck, and dipped his fingers under the neckline of her top. He thrust his tongue deeper into her mouth and still she couldn't get enough of him. Finally, gasping for air, they pulled apart.

Trying to catch her breath, she looked around. When had it gotten so dark? Where was everyone? Low-voltage security lights from the stable and barns provided a soft glow. A couple of ranch hands stood outside the well-lit bunkhouse. Lots of activity happening where the fifth-wheelers and motor coaches were parked. But it was the porch light from the house that had shone in her face. No one was close enough to see them, though.

The fog had lifted from her brain and she looked at Ethan, who was staring at her.

She smiled at him.

He smiled back.

A wave of distant laughter came from the direction of the house.

"The barbecue," they said at the same time.

"Bet they won't miss us," Ethan said, reaching for her again.

Who cared if they did? she thought, and bumped his nose in her haste to get to his mouth. He murmured an "Ouch" and she started giggling.

"I barely touched you, Mr. Big-Tough-Bull-Rider."

"I never said I was tough. I get a paper cut and I cry like a baby." He ran a palm down her arm, then worked his thumb underneath the sleeve, stretching the fabric as far as it would go so he could probe her muscles. "You're the one who feels pretty tough. Work out much?"

She knew the question was rhetorical. "Every chance I get," she said anyway, and punctuated it with a quick teasing kiss.

"Remind me not to mess with you."

"I tried to warn—" She gasped at the feel of his hand sliding under her shirt.

"Nice abs." He smiled against her mouth, then brushed his tongue over hers. His hand skimmed her right breast, proving the bra an ineffective barrier.

Her nipples tightened immediately. He dipped his fingers

inside the satin cup and grazed the puckered flesh. His touch sparked a surge of liquid heat that spread throughout her body, seeking release. Seeking more…

“We’re making out in your truck,” she whispered.

“I noticed,” he murmured, his breath coming quick and short.

“People are inside…” She tried to swallow, but her mouth was parched. “The barbecue. We have to—”

“No, we don’t.”

“We can’t stay here—”

“Right.” He caught her earlobe between his teeth and tugged lightly. His fingers pushed deeper, plucking at her nipple, while his lips trailed the side of her neck. “I don’t know where my keys are.”

“They aren’t in my bra.” She felt his smile against her flushed skin.

“You sure? I should check.”

“In high school you might’ve found tissue, no keys, though.”

Pulling back to look at her, he laughed.

Sophie sighed. Not something she would’ve shared had she not been so fuzzy-headed. “That was a joke.”

“I figured,” he said, still laughing.

She cupped the bulge straining his jeans, and that shut him up. Holy cow, he was hard. Yeah, they definitely had to go someplace private. And the second she got her thoughts and mouth in working order, she’d tell him just that.

And after he stopped hissing.

And she supposed she’d also have to move her hand. Eventually. She shifted in her seat, causing the light to shine in her eyes again.

She lifted her hand to blot the brightness.

Ethan leaned way back against the seat, and it took her a moment to realize he was having trouble sliding his hand into his pocket.

“We have to go inside,” she said.

“No, we don’t. Matt doesn’t care.”

"You have to talk to him about changing the schedule. So we can leave early tomorrow."

With a grunt, Ethan finally withdrew the keys. "I'll call him in the morning."

"It's better to give him a lot of notice. So you won't put him in a tight spot. Otherwise you'll give in and we'll be delayed." She watched his jaw clench and understood why he was resisting. She wanted to get back to the inn, herself. "Please. I really don't want to have to go out with Craig," she murmured.

"Who's Craig?"

"What?" Oh, crap. That thought wasn't supposed to have left her brain. "Craig who?"

"That was my question."

Dammit. If they were both naked already, they wouldn't be talking. "He's an attorney. From Casper. A very good attorney, and if you need him, then..." She waved a hand, wishing he'd just go inside already. "I can probably make that happen..." She trailed off as she turned her head to stare at the darkness outside her window.

Finally he opened the door, which triggered the interior light. Something she could've done without. "We won't need your friend Craig," Ethan said, and got out of the truck.

"He's not my friend. I don't even like him." She opened her door and slid off the seat. By the time she met him on the driver's side something had occurred to her. "There's really no reason for me to—"

Ethan cut her off by backing her against the truck. He had a good eight inches on her, and with his shoulders broad as they were she couldn't see the porch or even the house. But she heard a door open and close. Heard voices and laughter.

And then Ethan's big, rough hand touched her face. The fingers from his other hand were tangled in her hair. Aware that he had pinned her with a thigh partially nudged between hers, she stood in shock for a moment, feeling the truck's cold metal against her back.

"Ethan?"

"They can't see you," he whispered, and kissed her. "You don't know them."

"But—"

His openmouthed kiss silenced her. She heard the catcalls, so of course he did, too. And when a man with a heckling tone called Ethan's name, one hand briefly disappeared followed by rowdy laughter, so she was pretty sure Ethan had flipped him off. But even then Ethan didn't miss a beat. He slanted his mouth across hers, hungry and demanding, deepening the kiss until he'd left her breathless.

She gulped in air. "What are you doing?"

"Come on," he murmured, not breathing so easily, either. "Let's go."

She eyed the hand circling her arm and realized he meant they should leave the Lone Wolf. "But you were going to talk to Matt."

"I can't go in there. I'll call him."

A funny feeling slithered down her spine. Since she couldn't bodily force him inside the house, she rounded the hood and climbed back into the truck. He already had the keys in the ignition. "You've changed your mind about going back tomorrow, haven't you?"

He frowned at her, then reversed the truck. "No, I have not." Once he'd steered them toward the driveway, he said, "This has nothing to do with tomorrow. And everything to do with a certain physical condition that is completely your fault."

Sophie smiled when he stopped to kiss her hand. She just wished she believed him.

10

BAD VIBES WERE coming off Sophie in waves. They were halfway to town and Ethan still couldn't figure out what had caused the shift in her. It had started right after he told her he wouldn't be going inside to talk to Matt. Whether Ethan called him to change tomorrow's schedule or asked in person made no difference. And she was well aware of the damn hard-on that wouldn't quit. He couldn't have walked into the house like that.

"Did I embarrass you?" he asked after a long silence.

"When?"

"Just before we left. When I kissed you in front of Travis and those other folks."

"No. You said I didn't know them." She finally turned and looked at him. "But why *did* you kiss me like that in front of those people?"

"Travis Mills. I heard his voice and I did the first thing I could think of to avoid him." Saying it out loud made him sound like an ass. "That was rude. I'm sorry." He tugged at his snug jeans. "I got paid back, though. This hard-on is never gonna ease up."

"You could do a commercial for one of those pharmaceutical companies. I bet they'd give you a nice endorsement contract."

Ethan choked out a laugh. Nice to hear the smile back in her voice. "Yeah, I think I'll pass on that." He saw a turnout and pulled off the highway. He had a feeling he knew what could be bothering her. Might as well put her uncertainty to rest.

"What are you doing?" She twisted around to peer at the dark road behind them.

"Don't worry, I won't jump you. Not yet, anyway." He got out his phone. "I'm calling Matt."

"We'll be in town in ten minutes."

"Like you said, better to give him as much notice as possible." He listened to the rings, aware that the tension in the cab was easing. So she hadn't believed that he was serious about returning to Wyoming. It irritated him, since he'd given his word, but then he hung around with a dumb ass like Arnie, so what was she supposed to think?

Arnie didn't know it yet, but this time Ethan had had it with him. Back in school the jocks had picked on Arnie; so had the geeks, which was really pathetic. Ethan used to think he was one of those kids who just couldn't catch a break and he'd gone out of his way to befriend him. Once Ethan had turned pro he hired Arnie to do odd jobs and help him manage his schedule and social media. But the bastard hadn't only screwed Wendy; he'd screwed Ethan. And it hurt.

No surprise he was sent to voice mail, what with Matt having a houseful and all, but he hated leaving a message. For Sophie's sake, he left one anyway. It was short, to the point, and judging by her smile, it did the trick. He was glad she seemed relieved.

"I'm going to call Lola—she's my partner—oh, and my cousin. She was a year behind you in school."

He watched her pull out her phone. She was about to hit speed dial when her words sank in. "Your partner?"

She looked up, her expression wary. "We own Lola's Bail Bonds together. I'm good with computers. And Lola…" Sophie shrugged. "She's better with just about everything else."

"Why isn't your name in there?"

"I nixed it. The business is more Lola's gig. I wanted to help her get started. She knows I don't want to do this forever."

"Yeah, I'm thinking you're a little better than good with computers." He sat back and left the truck idling. "When I first thought I recognized you, I figured I had to be wrong. I mean, why would someone like you be working as a bounty hunter?"

"Fugitive retrieval agent," she muttered. "Scratch that. I like bounty hunter. Sounds pretty cool."

Was she acting flighty on purpose? Sophie was crazy smart. It wouldn't surprise him if she'd skipped her senior year and had gone on to college early. "Is this something you don't like to talk about?"

"I don't understand why you would think I'm such a computer whiz or why the bail bond business wouldn't be for me."

"Because you're too smart, that's why. Jesus. You were a freshman taking junior and senior classes and you were still bored."

She stared at him, her mouth open. "How would you know that?"

Shrugging, he put the truck in gear and eased them back on the highway. "You don't think I noticed you, but I did." He smiled at a memory of her hiding under the bleachers, nearly choking to death on her first and only cigarette. "You used to wear that ugly, oversize blue coat. Remember that? It could be a hundred degrees outside, the sun hotter than hell, and you'd be wearing that damn thing."

She was still staring at him. "After that day you saved me outside the locker room, you never said a word or even looked at me..."

Oh, he'd looked plenty, before and after. Only, he'd learned to be more sly about it after the friggin' incident over the dress. "I *saved* you? When did you get so dramatic?"

She turned away and fixed her gaze on the road ahead, arms crossed in front of her. "You did save me," she said softly. "You were my hero."

Grinding his teeth, he stepped on the accelerator. Kept his attention on the road, wishing like hell he hadn't brought up the coat or the past. He'd been such an asshole.

"You were popular. Everyone liked you. You don't understand what it's like to be different from everyone else and be thrown into a new environment with no friends or…or anybody who's willing to give you a chance." Sophie sighed. "Or pull you aside and explain why everyone thinks you're nothing but a dork."

The sadness in her voice made his gut clench. "I promise you those girls didn't think you were a dork," he said, reliving the anger and shame.

He should've broken up with Ashley that very day. She and her spiteful followers had been mean to Sophie, and who knew how many other girls. All because he'd looked one second too long and Ashley had felt threatened. But he'd put up with her random cruelty because she gave great head. Yeah, some hero.

Sophie surprised him with a laugh. "You don't have to say that, Ethan. It was a long time ago. I'm over it. If anyone calls me a dork now, I'd just put them in a body cast."

He looked over and saw her flexing her left biceps. He relaxed enough to smile. "I'll keep that in mind."

"Excellent idea." She slumped back and blew out a breath. "Okay, I have to say it… You can't claim to have noticed me now, not when you basically treated me as if I were invisible back then. Why didn't you ever talk to me after that day?"

"Well, for one thing, I had a girlfriend."

"Um, yeah. Ashley. I know. Anyway, I said *talk* to me, not ask me out on a date."

"That's the other thing. You were a lot younger than me."

"Guess what? The math hasn't changed."

Ethan shook his head. "Okay, I'll say this…being sarcastic doesn't do you any favors."

"Yes, I've heard that before," she murmured sheepishly. "I'll try to remember."

How was it that he could feel this comfortable with her? She said what she wanted without holding back. And he said whatever he said, and they just moved on, no sweat. Go figure. "You were fifteen. I was eighteen. At those ages it mattered."

"I see your point."

He opened and closed his mouth. Hell, he needed to think about what he was willing to admit. Or whether telling her anything would make her feel worse.

"Just so you know..." She pulled her legs up and hugged her knees. "I thought you deserved better than Ashley. She was a total bitch. But I respect your loyalty and that you didn't mess around with other girls."

"Look, Ashley was..." How should he put this?

"Hot. I get it. You were probably thinking with your dick," she said, and Ethan had to laugh. "How long after graduation were you guys together?"

"We broke up that night."

"No way." Sophie lowered her feet to the floorboard. "There was that big party at what's his name's house."

"Justin."

She'd turned in her seat so she was facing him. "What happened with Ashley?"

"She had one of her tantrums because I complimented her friend Shannon."

"Huh. I always thought they were BFFs."

"So did everyone else, including Shannon."

"Ashley didn't break it off, though. She was too crazy about you." It wasn't a question, but Sophie was obviously waiting for an answer.

He stretched his neck to the side to loosen a kink. "I couldn't take it anymore. She was a little drunk at the party and tried to use it as an excuse, but I knew that was bullshit. Like you said, I was thinking with the wrong body part."

"Wow. See? I was so far out of the loop I hadn't even heard about it. Had to be pretty big news."

"I don't know. I was so glad to be done with school I stayed out of the loop myself."

"Why? You must've had decent grades, since you weren't on the need-a-tutor list like most of the jocks."

"I never really considered myself a jock."

"Yeah, you kind of were. You and the quarterback were the two hottest guys in school."

"Says you."

"Said a whole locker room full of girls every friggin' day. It got pretty annoying."

"Glad I didn't know." He was straight-up serious. It would've been embarrassing. "Some of the guys I hung with thought you were hot."

She stayed quiet a long time, and then she turned back to face the windshield.

He swung his attention between her and the road. "What?"

"I don't understand why you feel the need to lie. I mean, yeah, if I think about those days too much, I can get cranky. But I'm good with my life."

"Do you know why Ashley and her posse destroyed your dress?"

"Because she'd worn the same one a week before I started at Wattsville. So?"

"That was enough to piss her off," he said. "But there was more to it. She overheard me telling the guys that you looked better in the dress. And two of them agreed."

"Why would you say something like that?"

"It was true." He saw lights up ahead and hoped it was Blackfoot Falls.

"You actually said that I looked better?"

"Swear to God."

Her laugh was nervous. "That's crazy. Ashley had the biggest boobs in school."

"Not all guys like big breasts, Sophie."

"You sure?"

Ethan smiled. “Yep, pretty sure I know what I’m talking about.”

She stared at him in silence for almost a minute. Who knew what was going on in that head of hers? But it gave him time to recall last night, her standing there braless in a T-shirt while he’d been handcuffed to the bedpost. Sophie fell into the perfect category. He’d had a sample feel less than an hour ago and he was itching for more. His foot automatically pressed down on the gas.

They were getting closer to the lights.

Lord, please let this be Blackfoot Falls.

“I think I like you even more now,” she said finally.

Considering that he hadn’t gotten to know her in school, and it had been years since he’d laid eyes on her, it was odd how she already wasn’t surprising him much. It was that comfort level and familiarity he’d been feeling with her. She wasn’t flirty, and she didn’t try to dress sexy, which was kind of sexy in itself.

“I had fantasies about you,” she said. “When I was a kid.”

“Uh, do I want to hear this?”

She adjusted the seat and leaned back. “After you rescued me, I felt really special. I mean, you even loaned me your jacket and told those girls to back off. And they did. Ashley and Shannon gave me the stink-eye, but that was it. Then I heard that you’d stepped in before. For other kids who’d been bullied. Like Arnie. So I knew I wasn’t so special after all.”

“I’d never gotten in between girls before.”

“Really?”

“Nope. The rest of the guys thought I was nuts.”

“You were brave. And noble.”

More than the words themselves, the conviction in her voice made him feel like crap. “I hate bullies just about more than anything, but what I did had nothing to do with being noble.” Guilt had played a big part. “Can we leave it alone?” he slipped in quickly when he saw by her body language she was ready to beat the issue to death.

"Okay." Sophie smiled. "Remember this moment. So you know I can be reasonable."

Ethan held in a laugh. "We're about two minutes from the inn. Have you eaten since breakfast?"

"No. You?"

He shook his head. "I guess we should get something in our bellies." Now that he thought about it, he was hungry. He just hadn't wanted to waste time eating. After they turned onto Main Street, he reached for her hand. "We can hit the diner, or pick up something to eat in the room."

"I vote for the second option," she said, lacing their fingers together.

"Sounds good. I want to shower first, though."

"I can pick up the food. And we should make it an early night, since we might have a lot of driving to do—"

He brought her hand up and kissed the back. "I think we can forget the early night."

"You're probably right," she said, her voice a husky whisper.

"I know I am." He resented having to release her because he needed both hands on the wheel. After he pulled up to the curb, he slid an arm behind her shoulders. He leaned in just as she turned her head.

"This is the diner," she said, and then turned back to him. "I thought—" She blinked, her confused expression fading as she realized he'd been about to kiss her.

He brushed his lips across hers. "What did you think?"

"That you would shower while I got takeout."

"Or..." He zeroed in on that sweet spot at the pulse in her neck. "We could shower together," he whispered.

Her throaty moan hit him low in the belly. "Who needs food?" she murmured, turning to meet his lips.

Ethan felt her tongue slip into his mouth. She practically climbed over the console, which he was seriously tempted to rip out. People strolled down the sidewalk past the truck. Half of them probably rodeo fans, trying to peer through the darkened windows. What the hell was wrong with him? He should've driven them straight to the inn.

He promised himself he'd do just that, in a minute, probably two. Sophie tasted like heaven with a scoop of sin. Her heat filled the cab and fogged the windows. He wanted her so damn bad it was messing with his head. From her pouty lips to her untamed hair and curvy body, they all did it for him. Those soft brown eyes, though, they got to him the most.

It had taken him months to blot out the image of her the day he'd slipped his jacket over her shoulders. She'd looked so small, her dress in tatters, but she hadn't cried or uttered a single mean word. She'd just looked up at him with so much trust and gratitude that he hadn't deserved. Afterward he'd nearly busted a hand punching his metal locker. Fixing the big dent he'd left had come out of his own pocket.

After that he'd avoided her as much as possible. Arnie had retrieved the jacket from her the next day. Once Ethan left for college the memory had started to fade and eventually disappeared.

When he realized his hand had slipped down to her breast, he tried to cool down the X-rated kiss. Sophie wasn't interested in complying, so he forced himself to pull back.

"What's wrong?" she asked, then jerked a look at the center console under her left knee. She sank back into her seat, ducked her head and swept a gaze down the sidewalk.

"Yep. Too many people around."

"Oh, jeez. Well, they don't know me, but most of them probably recognize you. Sorry."

"I'm not." He drew the pad of his thumb across her lips. They were puffier than usual. From the kissing. He wanted more of that. Leaning forward got him a firm hand to the front of his shoulder.

"We should go," she said, laughing. "As in right now. Before we get carried away again."

"Honey, we haven't even gotten warmed up yet." He turned the key. The engine made a god-awful grinding noise.

Heads turned. They both cringed.

Fine way to learn the truck had been idling all along.

He shook his head, and Sophie laughed.

The drive to the inn would take three minutes tops. He doubted he could make it.

11

SOPHIE GRABBED THE room key from him and unlocked the door. She laughed when she felt his hand mold to her backside, then quickly sobered and huffed. "What did I tell you? No touching until we're…"

He gave her ass a light squeeze and smiled.

Oh Lord. He wasn't listening, so why had she bothered? She practically shoved him inside the room before their neighbors from down the hall caught up with them.

"Wait. Okay? Just wait."

"Why?"

She turned away from him because she couldn't think straight while staring into his darkened blue eyes. But Ethan put his arms around her and pulled her back against his chest. There was no missing his very insistent erection. So avoiding his gaze wasn't working at all. She was beginning to think nothing would.

He kissed the side of her neck and then trailed his lips to the slope of her shoulder. She closed her eyes, wondering if he knew what he could do to her with only a look, a smile, a brush of his lips.

It was humbling to accept that she was defenseless when it came to Ethan. In the past five years she'd made progress. She could honestly say she hadn't thought about him much. She'd stopped monitoring his standing with the tour. If a rodeo was televised, she'd sometimes watched him. But she hadn't gone out of her way.

But after only twenty-four hours in his company, she could no longer deny the cold, hard truth. Once an addict, always an addict. And when this was all over, and she and Ethan again went their separate ways… Well, God help her. The road to recovery was going to be infinitely harder this time.

With a sigh, she pushed aside the silly notion that she could save herself some pain by walking away now. No chance of that happening.

She turned around in his arms and pulled on the front of his Western-cut shirt. The snaps came apart easily. He yanked her top up and over her head. Her peach-colored bra distracted him while she pushed his shirt open, exposing well-developed pecs.

He slipped the bra strap off her shoulder, then bent his head to kiss the narrow strip of skin he'd uncovered. The light touch of his lips on flesh that had never been sensitive before almost sent her through the roof.

She went for his belt buckle and he reached behind to unclasp her bra, which he seemed determined to get rid of. Except she was equally interested in unzipping his jeans. Their arms momentarily tangled. Then it became a free-for-all with shirts, boots and socks flying everywhere.

Sophie couldn't contain her laughter, intensified by Ethan's impatient battle with her snug jeans. He was still wearing his Wranglers and wouldn't let her near the zipper while he struggled to get her jeans down, making it only as far as her hips.

"Peel, don't pull," she said, then yelped when he picked her up and dumped her on the bed.

His piercing gaze took her in, starting with her hair and eyes, before locking on her breasts. "You're perfect," he whispered, the gravel in his voice a turn-on all by itself.

"Take off your jeans," she said, her eyes feasting on his strong chest and muscled shoulders, on the flexing and release of his pecs. His skin was still tanned, no sleeve lines, nothing along his low-riding waistband, which made her wonder about a whole bunch of things. Like what she was going to find under those jeans. "Please."

He leaned over and touched his tongue to her left nipple. The light contact sent warm pleasure flowing through her body. His mouth was hot, and so was the hand he used to cup her other breast. So she didn't understand why she was shivering. Or why she couldn't seem to stop.

Ethan took the hard tip into his mouth and gently sucked while he eased the jeans down to her thighs. She put a hand on his shoulder, and with the other she strained to reach his zipper. He intercepted her, using less effort than it took to swat a fly.

But he got the message to hurry it up. In seconds he'd pulled off her jeans, leaving her in skimpy peach panties that seemed to fascinate him. She sat up, but he gently forced her back down and put his mouth on the tiny triangle of silk. His warm breath breached the material and sparked a fire inside her.

"Dammit, you're killing me," she murmured, afraid she was going to have the quickest orgasm in history.

He lifted his head. "I didn't want to rush you," he said, and slipped a finger under the material. With a sharp intake of breath, he pushed his finger intimately between her lips. "Jesus, you're wet."

His patience evaporated, replaced by a fevered haste. He stripped off her panties, dropped them right there on the floor and scooped her into his arms.

Startled, she hung on to his neck. "Where are—"

They reached the bathroom. The very small bathroom with its tiny shower. He set her on her feet and turned on the water.

"I don't know about this," she said. "It's going to be a tight squeeze."

"Luckily I'm very good at that."

Sophie looked at him and laughed. He held a hand under the

spray, the other one rested on the curve of her butt and in his eyes, amusement and pure want warred for dominance.

He slipped his arm around her waist, pulled her against him and kissed her. "The water's warm," he murmured against her lips.

"Are you planning to shower with your jeans on?"

"Nope." His kiss was slow and thorough, and with her breasts pushing against his bare chest, she was never going to stop shivering. He broke the kiss. "You're going to get under this warm spray while I take off my jeans."

"Hurry, or I'll use up all the hot water." She stepped inside the narrow stall. It was almost too small for two people. They'd have to be careful—

Sophie found the soap and turned to see if Ethan was getting out of his jeans. He'd unzipped them but was just standing there watching her. It was startling. She'd never been watched like this before, and her first instinct was to yank the shower curtain closed all the way. But it was made of clear plastic, and this was Ethan. It was kind of hot knowing those hooded eyes were focused completely on her.

She rubbed the soap between her breasts and tipped her head back as she slid the bar up to her throat, taking her time and working up a lather. With her free hand she followed the suds sliding down her body, then cupped the white foam and brought it to her breast. She lingered on her nipples, plucking at the stiff peaks with her thumb and forefinger, before soaping around them.

It was easy to sneak a look at him. He sure wasn't staring at her eyes. Never in her life had she been happier that she took working out seriously. Her body was by no means perfect, but she was in good shape, especially considering her weakness for dark chocolate.

Ethan had pushed down the Wranglers, but he'd made it only to his hips. She knew the brand was one of his sponsors, and oh Lord, if they advertised with a picture of him right now, the company would sell out of jeans into the next millennium.

Their problem, not hers. She needed to give him a reason to speed things along. Slowly she turned around and used both hands to soap her butt and the back of her thighs before "dropping" the bar of soap.

Oops.

She bent all the way over until she could flatten her palms on the shower floor, knowing exactly what she was putting on display for him. Before she had a chance to straighten she heard the curtain being yanked across the rod.

Dammit. She'd wanted to get a good look at him before he—

His large hands settled on the curve of her hips. His erection slid up against her butt as he bent forward to kiss the middle of her back.

"You're driving me crazy," he practically growled the words, and removed his hand only to aim the intrusive shower spray toward the wall.

As she rose he banded an arm around her lower ribs, pulling her against him and kneading her left breast, tugging gently at her nipple. She felt his hot breath at the side of her neck, and then the slightly rough texture of his tongue, the scrape of his teeth on her skin.

She reached behind, trying in vain to touch him. But he held her body so tight to his she doubted a breeze could sneak in between them. Turned out the stall had room to spare.

"Do you even know how much I want you, Sophie?" he whispered hoarsely. "I've thought about this all day."

She hoped he'd pinch her soon. Just so she'd know this was real. That she wasn't having one of her adolescent fantasies.

No, she couldn't have come up with this scenario as a teenager.

When she tried to turn around, he wouldn't cooperate. His mouth went from her neck to her shoulder and his hand switched to kneading her other breast. But when she forced the issue, he loosened his hold. She whirled around to face him. And made herself dizzy. She laughed and swayed against him.

Holy crap, he was hard.

She had to look.

He seemed to know what she wanted and even took a step back for her. But he didn't release her arms. Good thing. If he hadn't been holding her up, she would've gone straight down to her knees.

God, he was beautiful. His tan ended about three inches below his belly button. She put her hand out to touch him.

Ethan dropped to a crouch. Apparently he had something else in mind. She gasped at the first intimate brush of his tongue. He parted her sensitive flesh and she slapped a palm against the tile for support. His tongue was sure and pointed, using just the right amount of pressure, circling the spot where she wanted it most. He dipped in for a quick second, just long enough to convince her that dying of bliss wouldn't be so terrible.

His leisurely and confusing retreat turned her thoughts to *his* possible demise instead.

And then he was kissing and licking the soft skin of her inner thigh and he was somewhat forgiven.

He slipped two fingers deep inside her, and she clenched her inner muscles for all she was worth. Her stranglehold on his fingers had him moaning and cursing under his breath.

As soon as she released him he pushed to his feet. "Jesus, Sophie," he murmured, the rasp in his voice making her skin tingle.

He took her face in his hands and claimed her mouth. Thrusting his tongue between her lips, he probed deep inside, stroking her tongue, circling it and keeping her off balance with the heady dance.

He lowered his palms to her breasts. They'd been aching, waiting for his touch, though she hadn't known it until he closed his hands over them. Her head and body swam with so many shimmering sensations that she almost missed her chance.

Finally the path was clear. She curled trembling fingers

around his hard, pulsing erection. The smooth taut skin was hot to the touch.

His breath caught in her mouth. His whole body tensed. She fully expected him to shove her hand aside, and damned if she would let that happen. She stroked upward, adjusting her grip in harmony with the urgency of his moans.

He didn't try to stop her. His hips moved in a slight thrust against her palm before he went still. She slid her hand to the base of his cock, hoping to break through the tight control he was struggling to maintain. Not very nice of her, considering that she was fighting the same battle herself. They were both dangerously close to the edge.

And she wanted to push him over first.

"We should switch to cold water," he said, partly laughing, mostly groaning.

"Don't you dare." She shivered just thinking about it.

"I'll keep you warm, honey," Ethan whispered close to her ear, and released her breasts. His hands slipped around and over her bottom and firmly pulled her against him.

She lost her grip, the damn sneak. "Hey, no fair cutting short my playtime."

"Tough," he murmured, his lips and teeth doing amazing things to the curve of her neck.

Somehow he'd managed to take the soap from her. Or maybe she'd dropped it. Things were starting to blur. With a wicked smile, he slid the soap between her breasts, then over her ribs, down to her belly. She snatched the small bar from him. His hand just kept heading south until it slipped between her thighs.

"You're a devil."

His gaze locked on her face, Ethan wiggled his fingers.

Sophie bit her lip, moved a little to the left and gasped. "If I have heart failure, it's your fault."

"I'll take full responsibility." He leaned back to look down at her breasts, the tips flushed to a deep rose. Lowering his chin, he tried to catch a nipple with his mouth, but there wasn't enough room to maneuver. He sighed. "I hate this shower."

"I know." She smiled at his grouchy expression, then got up on her toes and kissed him. It wasn't a long kiss or especially sexy, but his attitude quickly shifted to enthusiastic. She dragged her mouth from his and reached behind him to give his rock-hard backside a light smack. "Turn around so I can get your back."

Wrapping her in his arms, he lifted her off the shower floor.

"Hey," she said with a muffled giggle. "What are you doing?"

"Hang on." He redistributed her weight and lifted her higher. A little nudge from him and she locked her legs around his waist. Her arms circled his neck. "You should be able to reach my back from there," he murmured, his stubbled chin lightly scraping the tender skin above her breasts.

Even if she stretched she'd only be able to reach his shoulder blades. "Um, pretty sure there's an easier way." As good as his trailing lips felt, she was kind of anxious to trade the cramped shower for the queen-size bed…

She gasped at the unexpected brush against her clit.

Oh hell, the bed would still be there.

Another fleeting touch and her body jerked, then quickly settled, hoping…no, begging for more. Begging for Ethan. She tightened her thighs around him and the pressure increased.

It was his thumb. Right? Had to be his thumb, she thought, her speeding pulse in obvious disagreement.

With each tiny movement she felt more pressure build. Heat swept off his body in great waves. Calloused fingertips dug into her butt while his palms supported her, shifting her higher when she started to sag…

Oh God, it wasn't his thumb.

She dropped the soap and clutched his shoulders.

"Don't worry," he whispered. "I won't enter you without a condom."

She just nodded, barely managing to do that. The weak shower spray glanced off the tile and hit her hair and the side of her face. She'd put herself there by moving her hips, seeking his touch. And now her hair was completely wet, yet her mouth was so dry she had to moisten her lips.

He watched the swipe of her tongue, his eyes black with desire and torment, but he kept moving, rubbing the swollen head of his penis over her clit. He was doing this for her. And she loved the hot feel of him. But God, how she wished she could sink down, let him fill her to the brink. This was torture. Mostly for him, she imagined.

"Put me down, Ethan," she said, her hand sliding off his shoulder and pausing at his bulging biceps.

"Am I not hitting you right?" he asked, repositioning both of them and rocking her against his erection. The friction made her breath catch. "Is this better?"

"The only thing better would be you inside me." She kissed him. Hard and fast. Before they got distracted again.

His lids lowered to half-mast as he lifted a hand to her face. The arm still anchored around her waist kept her suspended while he exacted a more satisfying kiss.

She wasn't that light, either. She pulled back. "Jesus, you're going to hurt yourself."

He smiled. "I bet you aren't even a hundred pounds."

"That would be a horrible bet."

Somehow he'd found another way to rub her clit, the pressure lasting until her feet hit the floor. She raised her eyebrows at him. "One for the road," she said, and then blushed like crazy. She didn't even know why.

She tried to laugh it off and would've escaped him if she hadn't tangled with the stupid shower curtain. One thing she both loved and hated about Ethan was that penetrating gaze of his. He seemed to be constantly watching her, mostly in a good way. Like when they were making out, it was nice to know he was fully engaged. But if she was being sneaky or wanted to slide something by him, forget it.

Turned out she needn't have worried. Ethan finished washing up while she dried herself and blotted some of the moisture from her hair. She thought about turning down the covers but she wanted that perfect view of him that she'd been cheated out of earlier.

With her damp towel wrapped around her, she waited for him to turn off the water and push back the shower curtain. He shook back his wet hair and smiled at the dry towel she held up for him. The light hit him just right. Drops of water glistened on his bronzed skin. His erection had gone down some. Such a pity. Although there was still enough heft there to make her happy.

"Where did you get the tan, cowboy?"

"Mending fences."

"You lie."

"What? You think all I do is ride bulls and pimp products? I have a ranch to take care of."

"Really?" Why didn't she know about that?

"Yes, ma'am, I do. You gonna bring me that towel?"

"Nope. Come and get it."

"All right," he said, stepping out of the stall. "But you can bet that sweet little bottom of yours I'm coming for more than that."

"Bring it."

A second later it was *her* towel wrapped around *his* hips, a smug grin curving his mouth. He used the other towel to dry his hair and chest while he gave her a leisurely once-over.

Well, duh. He had lightning reflexes. Terribly stupid thing for her to forget.

She felt like an idiot standing there naked and trying to hide the goods with her hands over her breasts, her bent leg angled over the other thigh barely covering the short landing strip from her last waxing. Ridiculous, considering that she'd given him a show through the shower curtain. She probably looked like a damn cartoon character.

Ethan wasn't laughing, though. The feral intensity of his eyes had her on the move.

"Watch it," she said, backing out of the bathroom. "The handcuffs are ready and waiting..."

Sophie froze.

Oh, shit.

She looked at him, her eyes wide.

He stopped in the doorway, staring back at her, realizing the same thing.

They both turned and looked at the gleaming metal cuffs dangling from the bedpost. The bed had been made. The whole room had been picked up.

"Oh God," Sophie groaned.

Ethan choked out a laugh.

"I'm glad my name isn't on the register," she muttered.

"Yeah, thanks." He caught her hand. "How about you make it up to me?" The towel fell from his hips before he pulled her close, chest to chest, thighs to thighs, skin to breathtaking skin.

12

ETHAN SKIMMED A HAND down Sophie's back and she pressed her body closer to his, as if they hadn't already melded together. She liked touching him. Not in just a sexual way. It was the smooth, firm texture of his skin that felt so good under her fingertips, the ridges of lean muscle absent of bulk that allowed him to move with grace. He truly was a gorgeous man.

"What's that smile for?" Without waiting for an answer he kissed her.

He didn't rush, even as his arousal grew harder and thicker. His lips moved over hers at a leisurely pace. How many times had they kissed already? And yet he was nibbling and tasting as though he were learning her mouth for the first time. Her breasts were tight and beginning to ache. He might've sensed her waning patience, or lost some of his own. Sliding his hands to her hips, he moved her back toward the bed.

She crawled in between the sheets first, and Ethan, his hand on her ass, slid in right behind her.

"We used the same soap," he said, cupping her breasts and squeezing gently. "Why do you smell so good?"

"You do, too."

"Not the same." He rolled his tongue over her nipple, pulled back to study it, then plucked at it with his lips. At the same time he rubbed his thumb across the other one, over and over, until she was ready to scream.

"What are you doing?"

He lifted his head and did a quick check. "Watching them darken," he said with a self-satisfied smile.

Before she could even blink he'd spread her legs and wedged himself between them. Propping himself on both elbows, he got into a position that put his mouth over her chest. He kissed each nipple, then cupped the sides of her breasts, pushing them together and sucking both nipples at the same time.

She wasn't quite busty enough to make the task easy. But he managed to send her back into an arch as she clawed at his arm.

"Your nipples are hypersensitive," he murmured, looking at her face and kissing one tip very gently. "Am I sucking too hard?"

"No. They usually aren't this sensitive. But what you were doing— It's perfect. All of it."

He used his tongue to swirl and soothe, and then reached over her, putting his chest just above her nose. She surged up and licked his flat brown nipple. He jerked, managed to grab the pillow he was after and tucked it next to her hip.

"For that," he said, dropping back down to his elbows and shifting so that his mouth was closer to her belly, "I will show no mercy."

With her legs still spread, she couldn't be in a more vulnerable position. Or be more excited about what was sure to come. Well, besides her.

Ethan moved down a few more inches and kissed inside each thigh before lifting his head. "What? No 'bring it'?"

Sophie frowned. She had no idea what he was talking— Oh, right. "Yes," she murmured, already out of breath, her brain misfiring. "Do that."

He smiled, but courteously didn't laugh. He tapped her hip so she'd lift her butt, and he slid the pillow underneath her. Reaching behind her head, she centered and plumped the pillow supporting her neck. She wanted to watch.

Their gazes met.

Ethan dipped his chin. She felt the long, flat swipe of his moist tongue against the seam of her lips. Her insides clenched, and her lids drooped.

"Open your eyes, Sophie," he said softly, and took another long, slow lick.

She tried not to whimper. Even when he parted her and slid his tongue along her sex. But then he used his fingers, too, and the steamy blend of sensations elicited a moan from her that could've been made by an animal in the wild.

She clutched at his shoulder, at the sheets, and finally caught a handful of his hair. His answer was to slip his hands beneath her butt and pull her more firmly against his mouth. His fingers went right back to work, plunging in so deep she couldn't breathe. And he refused to stop.

"Ethan?" She tugged on his hair. "Condom. Now."

He lightly sucked her clit.

Sophie exploded.

Her orgasm rocked the bed, shook the entire room. Maybe the whole building. Closing her eyes, opening them, it didn't matter. She couldn't see. Cold one second, and hot the next. Trying to drag air into her lungs, she wiggled and squirmed and whimpered. She pulled Ethan's hair and shoved at his shoulder until he finally eased up.

"Shh," he whispered close to her ear. He was lying beside her, propped on one elbow and petting her hair.

"What?" she mumbled. When had he moved up? "Was I loud?"

He smiled and kissed her mouth.

Able to taste herself on his lips, she shuddered.

Coming from the hall outside the room she heard receding laughter.

Reality heralded its rude reentry. "Oh God." She was never

loud. Or this breathless. Or still this warm and tingly. "On a scale of one to ten?" she asked, cringing. "Ten meaning I didn't need a mic."

Ethan didn't answer, but the grin he was trying to hold back told her a lot.

"Okay," she said, wrapping her hand around his erection. "Let's see you top that."

Two strokes and his head fell back.

She took the smooth, velvety head in her mouth, and his groan filled the room. She licked and sucked the crown and stroked the rest of him with her hand until his breathing grew ragged. His long fingers circled her wrist and he gently tugged her hand away. He already had a condom out. Wow, she really had missed a lot.

Ethan tore open the foil packet and sheathed himself. Slowly. Very slowly, his tortured expression hot as hell. He'd been ready for her a long time and close to climaxing himself. Yet he'd been patient and generous, making sure he'd taken care of her first. She hoped she didn't disappoint him. She wouldn't orgasm just with him inside her. Long ago she'd given up on the elusive G-spot. The damn thing was a myth, and no one could convince her otherwise.

She pressed her lips to his shoulder. He seemed surprised when she swung a leg over his hips to straddle him. Surprised, but not displeased. He stacked a second pillow behind his head and then held on to her hips as she sank onto him.

Every millimeter sent new waves of bliss shooting straight to her pleasure centers. She slowed down, just until she could inhale once more before she died.

Before she knew it, he pulled her up, then flipped her over, sliding his knee between hers and settling in with a kiss that was so hot it left her breathless.

"What was that?" she asked. "Are you okay?"

He smiled as he nodded. "I didn't want to come too fast."

"Oh. Well, I was kind of hoping this part of the evening would include you. Inside me."

"Ah, so you didn't want to just chat, hmm?"

"I—" She closed her mouth, tilted her head and said, "No. In fact, if you don't do something right now, I'll—"

"You'll what?"

"Ethan. I swear to God…"

He raised his right eyebrow as he lifted both of her knees to his shoulders.

She waited, watched as he pressed a kiss on each nipple. Then, with the control of a man who rode bulls for a living, he entered her. In one swift, sure move.

"Holy mother of—" Sophie put her arms over her head and braced herself on the headboard.

"Okay?"

"Quit talking. And don't hold back."

With a feral growl he thrust again. Only this time he changed the angle just a bit. She moaned, and when he started to pull back, Sophie squeezed his cock.

"Sorry," she said, when it sounded as though she'd hurt him. "Are you all right?"

"On a tightrope here. Real tight."

"Wouldn't hurt you to fall," she said, touching his hair with one hand.

"Not yet." He shifted his angle once more. Higher than she was used to, and when he pushed in again, she cried out.

This was different. She had to rethink the whole G-spot issue. Damn, Ethan had found it.

He thrust again. And she let out a scream.

Again.

Another scream.

God, they were so going to get kicked out. But she didn't want him to stop. It was the sweetest torture she'd ever endured. She'd given up trying to keep her eyes open.

One more thrust and then…

Her whole back arched and she came so hard things turned a little gray, shifted upside down, started spinning. They both hit their final shudders within seconds of each other. She'd always known Ethan was a drug, and he'd just proven it.

It took a while to catch her breath, and Ethan, too, but he still managed to lower her legs. When her heart rate slowed to about a hundred beats per minute, she shifted and he tossed himself to the left side of the bed. Good thing he had a lot of practice on his dismounts.

Thinking how loud she'd been, she pressed a hand to her warm cheek. "I can never come back to this town, can I?"

"Nope," he said, and they both laughed.

ETHAN ROLLED ONTO his back and tucked her against his hard, languid body. They sure hadn't needed the heater tonight. His skin was warm from exertion and downright hot in some places. Places that happened to be some of Sophie's favorites. In fact, she was pretty toasty herself.

She barely had the energy to glance at the clock. It was two-thirty and they'd just finished making love for the second time. They'd managed to sleep for a couple of hours before that, but then Ethan had gotten frisky again and she'd been more than happy to oblige him.

And the thing with Ethan—a very admirable, wonderful thing—there was no rushing him when it came to sex. He liked taking his time, trying different angles, milking every last drop of pleasure out of her. Now that she knew she could orgasm without manual stimulation, she wanted to do it every time. She really had to give him props for being the most patient lover ever. Although she'd been with only three other guys and they'd been just okay.

Drowsy and sated, her cheek pressed to his chest, she traced a circle around his belly button, wondering if he'd been like this as a teenager. Probably not. But if he had, good thing she hadn't slept with him. A bar set that high first time around… she would've been destined for disappointment.

"Sleepy?" he asked, idly rubbing her back.

"Why?"

Ethan laughed. "Don't worry. I'm not going to ravish you again so soon."

"Ravish? Is that what you said?"

"Too many syllables for you?"

"Ha." She stifled a yawn. "Probably." Not just sleepy, but exhausted. Yet she was unwilling to give up a single minute with him. Tomorrow they'd have twelve hours together on the drive back to Wyoming, if one or the other wasn't snoozing. "Tell me about your ranch."

"Ah yes. The ranch," he said with a quiet chuckle. "I wondered when you'd bring it up."

"Meaning?"

"I'm busted."

"What?" She brought her head up. "You lied?"

"Technically, no. I own five hundred acres over in Carver County. Including a dilapidated barn and a two-room cabin that were on the property when I bought it."

"You live there?"

"Hell no. I'm a cowboy through and through, but I like my modern comforts. And describing the place as rustic is putting it way too nicely." He shrugged. "Someday I'll build a house. I don't know—maybe next year."

She hated that he'd tensed, though she didn't know why. He'd been living on the road most of his adult life. Maybe the idea of putting down roots made him nervous. "So, would you raise cattle? Breed horses?"

"Don't ever cut your hair." He pushed his fingers through the thick wavy mass, stopping at a tangle and working some magic that quickly loosened it.

"I hate my hair. I always have." She'd made peace and given up on it. "At least with it long I can pull it back."

"How can you hate this?" he asked, fisting a handful and holding it up before slowly letting the locks fall over her shoulder and onto his chest.

"It's frizzy and wavy and yuck."

He shook his head. "Soft and sweet—" he tugged on a curl and smiling at it "—and very sexy."

"Too many concussions," she murmured, not knowing what else to say. Joking was her go-to when she was embarrassed. Or she'd escape through sarcasm, but she was working on that particular shortcoming.

"You know Matt's arena?"

Sophie nodded, curious and confused. He was still preoccupied with her hair, but his tone had changed.

"After I build the house, I'm going to put up something similar. Probably not quite as big, but I'll leave room to expand. And I'll have to do something about the barn. Hell, it may have to be torn down and built from scratch. Then there's the stable, and after that the corrals, more fencing. I've got a lot of work ahead of me."

"Are you going to do most of it yourself?"

"If I wanted to live in a lean-to, sure." He laughed. "I can handle the corrals and fences, but that's about it."

"Okay." She was still processing the information. "Building an arena means you're going to have rodeos?"

"Not the kind you're thinking of." He stretched his back and neck, but his jaw was clamped tight as he stared up at the ceiling. "I want to open a kids' rodeo camp."

"Oh, like your parents have."

"That's not what they do. For one thing, they cater to adults and it's strictly for profit." He glanced at her. "Nothing wrong with that. It's a business. And mine will be, too. I'll charge a fee. But I won't turn away a deserving kid just because his parents don't have the money or he's not athletic. The goal is to help the kids with self-esteem. Let them come into themselves at their own pace."

"Wow, Ethan." She pushed up to look at him full on. "That's terrific."

"Yeah?" Some of the tension seemed to melt from his jaw and shoulders. "You think so?"

"Are you kidding? That is so awesome." She meant it with all her heart. For a guy like Ethan, who had money, good looks and skills that most men could only dream about, it was amazing that he understood not everyone was handed a life wrapped with a pretty bow. "I'm so excited for you."

"I can tell." He was grinning when he leaned over to kiss her. "Somehow I knew you'd understand."

"Well, of course I do. I was the one who got picked on, remember?" She placed a palm on his chest, right over his big wonderful heart.

"You weren't bullied a lot, were you? You seemed like a pretty confident kid."

"If I kept to myself, then no, I wasn't bothered much. But basically, a smart kid thrown into a new school isn't generally well liked."

"I'm sorry, Sophie." He covered the hand she'd put on his chest and squeezed before he kissed her fingertips.

"Okay, what you just did?" She snuggled against him. "Made it all worth it."

"I'm serious," he said quietly.

"Me, too." She shrugged. "I spent a lot of time in my own head. Only-child syndrome, I guess. Plus, before my dad left my mom and me, he hadn't been around all that much."

"What do you mean by *left*? He just walked out on you?"

"He worked in construction and jumped around for different jobs while my mom and I stayed in Idaho. And then he met a woman—a waitress working at a diner, I think. Anyway, he came home to pick up his things and that was that."

"Jesus, what an ass."

"Oh, I had a much stronger word for him," she said with a

wry grin. "Once Mom and I moved to Wattsville to be near my aunt and her family, things were better." Sophie sat up to look into his eyes. "If there's ever a single-parent kid who wants to go to your camp but doesn't have the money, you have to take him or her in, okay? Promise me."

He tucked a lock of her hair behind her ear and smiled. "I promise."

She nodded, satisfied that he'd keep his word. "Are you thinking of a day camp, or more like a summer thing where you board the kids?"

"I haven't decided for sure, but I imagine it'll end up being both. I'd prefer to have the kids for six weeks at a time, but that means we'd open only for the summer."

"That's kind of too bad." Sophie thought for a moment. "You know, lots of schools are open year-round now. I'd have to check, but I think that means they have three weeks off between sessions."

"I hadn't thought of that. Three weeks at a time isn't bad." His brow furrowed in thought, he stared off and absently rubbed her arm. "So maybe I could offer different programs for three weeks or six weeks and put something together in the afternoons for the local kids."

Her hand still rested on his chest and she liked feeling his heartbeat accelerate with his excitement. "Anyway, you have a lot of time to mull over all your options."

He looked at her, his mouth curving in a peculiar smile. "Between you and me, I've already hired a contractor. He's drawing up plans for me to look at after the finals."

"Ethan! That's so terrific."

"You can't say anything. No one else knows."

"Not even your parents?"

"Especially not them." He sighed, looking as if he regretted the remark. "It's nothing. Just another story in itself."

"Want to hear something I've never told anyone?" She lowered her hand to his belly. Not on purpose, but now it seemed he might be interested in something other than what she wanted to share.

"What's that?" he asked, moving her hand up a few inches.

"It's kind of weird, but I've thought about doing something with kids, too. Not on such a grand scale as what you have in mind. I don't have that kind of money, but just a small no-frills martial arts studio. I didn't take up kickboxing and tae kwon do until my first year of college but getting physical and learning discipline made a big difference in my life. I know a couple of qualified people who would volunteer to help teach the kids."

Ethan was silent for a few moments. "I can see how that changed things for you," he said, his slight frown confusing her. "And don't get me wrong, I think it's great you want to give back. But I still don't get why you're not doing something more challenging. I mean, now that I know you're not even from the area, I can't figure out why you'd stick around."

"You sound like my cousin." Sophie sighed. "I told you about my dad, who I don't see and don't care to see ever again. And my mom is a perfectly nice woman who also happens to be clueless. If I were to tell her I was leaving for the moon tomorrow, she would say what she always does, 'That's nice, dear.'" Sophie saw his left eyebrow shoot up. "Seriously. I like being around family. My aunt and uncle, my cousins…we all do stuff on holidays, and if somebody's car is in the shop, we help out.

"I know, it sounds corny. Whatever." She leaned into him while her hand reclaimed those few inches of warm belly. "Who knows? Now that I've gotten you out of my system, maybe I can move on to bigger things."

She felt him tense. Not just his chest and stomach but his whole body seemed to tighten. He should be relieved that she had no expectations beyond this weekend, but instead he looked annoyed.

"We have a long drive tomorrow. You should get some more sleep," she said, and pulled her hand away.

He caught it and peeled open her fingers. "Later," he said, and put her hand back on his lower belly.

13

SOPHIE CRANED HER NECK to see inside the arena. Now that she finally had some time alone, she'd phoned Lola. This was supposed to have been a quick call, but her cousin kept placing her on hold. "Is something wrong?"

"What do you mean?" Lola was rarely this curt. With others, yes, but usually not with Sophie. And here she'd called with good news. Lola sighed. "Sorry. It's that fight I had with Hawk. I think I told you about it—well, now he's being a goddamn baby and not taking my calls."

"Let him stew," Sophie suggested when she really wanted to say good riddance. "Stop calling him and he'll get worried and call you."

"Yeah, you're probably right. So, tell me again. You're at the rodeo now, but you think you'll be leaving in an hour?"

"Basically, yes. Ethan had hoped to be moved up on the schedule sooner, but there was a mix-up. We're still leaving earlier than we originally thought." Sophie waited. "You're quiet."

"Are you a hundred percent sure he isn't playing you?"

"Two hundred percent." A nasty remark about not mistaking Ethan for Hawk sat on the tip of Sophie's tongue. It was mean, so she pressed her lips together. "Do you want me to call you once we're on the road?"

"Are you driving straight through?"

"I don't know. It depends. We're both really tired." The last word had barely tripped off her tongue and she wanted to shoot herself. Eventually she'd tell Lola about Ethan, but not yet.

"Damn," Lola muttered, half to herself. "Hold on, would you?"

"I'll call you later," Sophie slipped in. Then she disconnected without knowing if Lola had heard. She wasn't about to wait around on hold for the umpteenth time and miss Ethan's ride.

She reentered the building, but instead of returning to her seat, she stood by the privacy fence close to the arena. A few buckle bunnies had made camp near the gate used by the riders and volunteers. In the looks department the women ranged from gorgeous to holy shit. And Sophie had overheard enough earlier to know that half the buckle bunnies here had come because of Ethan.

It made her smile to imagine their reaction over him choosing plain Jane her over any of them. There had been a time when she would've been beside herself with jealousy, crippled by self-doubt and mired in suspicion over his motives.

The suspicion part, that wasn't something to be ignored in her line of work. So yeah, she'd been wary at first, wondering if he was playing her. But the 200 percent she'd quoted Lola, that was real. Ethan was one of the good guys. Who just happened to be hot.

On the other hand, maybe she'd idealized him for so long she was being selective about what she wanted to see. He certainly was no monk, not that she expected him to be, but she wondered how difficult it was going to be for him to give up being a rodeo star. Being the guy all the women wanted. Having a slew of companies eager to give him money to endorse their products. Some of that would carry over into his post rodeo career.

And it seemed as if his head was on straight enough he could separate his ego from all the nonsense.

But, again, was that what she wanted to see? And heaven help her, she couldn't discount last night. The most incredible, stupendous, holy-crap-I've-died-and-gone-to-heaven night of her entire life. Past and future. And screw anyone who said otherwise.

Ethan wanted to open a camp for kids to help with their self-esteem. Oh, for God's sake, he was just a little too perfect. Maybe she was being punked. Maybe a tiny camera had been hidden in the room. She'd see herself on some stupid reality show in two weeks. Lying next to him in bed, staring at him with big goo-goo eyes. And then she'd have to move to outer Mongolia. Sadly, last night would still have been worth it.

Sophie sighed so loudly the woman next to her turned to eye her. She hoped she wasn't going to be this same idiotic person for the rest of her twenties. So this was what happened after only three hours' sleep.

And in a few minutes Ethan, who'd had the same amount of sleep, would climb on top a two-thousand-pound bull that wanted to annihilate him.

Okay, now she was feeling nauseated.

She pressed a hand to her tummy and watched a young woman with long blond hair, tight jeans and killer boots walk up to the fence. The other buckle bunnies who'd staked their claim an hour ago turned to give her a sizing-up. She ignored them and called out to some of the bronc riders, who acknowledged her with waves. Popular girl.

The team roping event finally ended, and bull riding was up next. Murmurs rose from the crowd. Fans were used to the bull riders being last. Sophie just wanted the whole thing to be over, period.

Her phone signaled an incoming text. It was from Peggy, Sophie's contact at the sheriff's office. Nothing had changed as far as the charges against Ethan went. And Sophie owed Peggy lunch at her favorite barbecue joint.

Sophie liked the older woman, so hanging out with her was always fun. Now, dinner with Craig, that she dreaded as much as a pap smear. She stared at her phone, trying to decide if it was time to suck it up and call him back.

Ethan's name being announced stole her attention. The signs held by fans shot up in the bleachers. She recognized a few from yesterday. The blonde newcomer let out an ear-piercing whistle, stomped one of her pricy boots and yelled, "Go get 'em, Styles."

His other female fans cast her looks of disdain. She either hadn't noticed or didn't care. Sophie ignored everyone and moved to a spot where she could see Ethan getting ready to be let out of the chute. Again without a helmet, since there hadn't been time to drive to Kalispell and back to buy one.

Today he was riding another bull and not Twister, so she was thankful for that. Although she'd missed the name of the brown bull that was giving him a fit. If Matt had found reason to call him something like the Devil's Spawn, she didn't want to know.

She saw Ethan give the nod for the gate, and then everything happened quickly. The instant the bull lunged from the chute and the clock started, Sophie began counting the seconds.

One thousand one, one thousand two...

The furious animal reared and bucked and did everything in its power to throw Ethan off its back.

One thousand five, one thousand six...

The bull whirled, then changed directions.

She closed her eyes. The crowd's roar had them popping back open.

Ethan was on the ground scrambling away from the monstrous animal. He made it clear of the dangerous hooves coming down like spiked sledgehammers and waved to the fans. The buzzer had gone off at seven and a half seconds. The announcer said something about the heartbreak score and lucky this wasn't the finals.

Sophie wasn't a violent person, but she really wanted to smack the man. He was safe from her. She couldn't move. Not until she was certain Ethan wasn't limping or holding his arm funny. He seemed fine as he left the arena, dusting off his hat and himself. Finally able to breathe again, she headed off to meet him in the back.

She recognized the husky Lone Wolf ranch hand who was acting as security guard and smiled at him when he opened the gate for her. She'd made it a few steps in when the blonde with the cute boots came barreling past her. The poor ranch hand tried to stop her, but the determined woman was too fast.

At the burst of commotion Ethan turned. With a shriek, the blonde jumped at him. He caught her, but unprepared, he staggered back.

"What the hell are you doing here?" Ethan set her down and gestured to the cowboy that it was okay.

Sophie wasn't quite sure what to do. Ethan's gaze had swept over her, so she knew he'd seen her. But his attention was directed at the other woman.

"I bet you're pissed. Damn. Half a second." The blonde shrugged. "At least it didn't count." She jerked a look toward the pen where another bull waited, cupped her hands around her mouth and yelled, "Hey, Matt, the place looks awesome."

Matt flashed her a smile, then went back to doing whatever he and another guy were doing to ready a scary-looking bull for the next rider.

Ethan scrubbed at his face and motioned for Sophie to join them. Nope, he wasn't a happy camper.

"So I was on my way to Vegas, and I thought what the hell…?" The woman paused when she noticed Sophie standing there. Her gaze swept from Sophie's hair to her boots. With a dismissive frown, the blonde turned back to Ethan. "I figured I'd zip up here and see how you were doing. Make sure you weren't laid up in the local hospital in traction or anything."

"Yeah, thanks." Ethan sighed.

Sophie wasn't feeling quite as charitable. The woman was

much younger than Sophie initially thought, but that didn't excuse her stupidity.

Blondie grinned, then turned abruptly back to Sophie, staring at her as if she were an intruder. "Who are you?"

"If you'd shut up long enough," Ethan said, "I'd introduce you."

Something in his expression or tone spurred a sudden realization. "You must be Ethan's sister," Sophie said, noting a faint resemblance around the mouth and eyes. "Cara?"

She nodded and shook Sophie's outstretched hand.

"I'm Sophie," she said, and because Cara had the decency to look embarrassed, Sophie liked her better. "A friend of Ethan's."

"Sure, go ahead, introduce yourselves. You don't need me," he said, and Sophie gave him a private look that said otherwise.

She wanted more than anything to put her arms around him, make sure nothing hurt and kiss him into tomorrow. But not with his sister watching.

Cara barely spared him a glance. "Sorry about before," she said, staring at Sophie with open curiosity. "Some of the buckle bunnies get too pushy and I try to run interference. The ladies seem to just looove my brother. I don't get it." She gave him a cheeky grin. "They don't know you like I do."

He was still grumpy. Probably overtired. And here they were supposed to hit the road right away.

Damn. It occurred to her that Cara showing up out of the blue could complicate things.

Sophie studied his face, the weariness around his eyes, the smudge at his left temple, the streak of grime on his chin. Everything else fell away. Nothing mattered as long as he was okay. She promised herself she would never let him stay up so late the night before a rodeo again.

That is, assuming she'd be in a position to carry out the promise.

He was staring back at her with those intense blue eyes, the corners of his mouth quirking up a bit.

"How are you?" she asked softly. "Everything in working order?"

His smile took over. "Come check for yourself."

Sophie hesitated. Silence doubled the awkwardness that fueled her uncertainty.

Cara must've felt it, too. She glanced around, then looked from Sophie to Ethan. "How do you guys know each other?"

"From high school," he said as he wiped the remaining dust from his face and moved to stand next to Sophie. "I want to have a few words with Matt..." He trailed off, leaving words unsaid, his gaze steady with hers. "Okay with you?"

"Of course." She knew he meant before they left, but he was reluctant to talk in front of Cara. That proved they had a problem.

When he moved in to kiss her, Sophie gave him her cheek. Clearly he didn't care for that one bit. He caught her chin and forced her to face him before he pressed his lips to hers.

"Okay, then," Cara muttered, glancing around again. "I'm gonna grab a hot dog. You guys want anything?"

Ethan might've responded in some way. Sophie hadn't said a word, but she saw that Cara was already headed for the gate.

Sophie raised her eyebrows at him.

"Look, before you rip me a new one, I kissed you because you looked as though you didn't know what to do in front of my sister." He shrugged and touched her arm. "And I figured it might get rid of Cara for a few minutes." He sighed. "Goddammit, I kissed you because I wanted to. Is that a problem?"

"No," she said. "Are you done?"

Ethan frowned. "Kissing you?"

A short laugh escaped her. "You know what? No more late nights." Sophie rolled her eyes at his instant grin. "I mean it. You could've gotten hurt today."

"Oh hell, I'm pumped so full of adrenaline before a ride I could go all night." His eyes lit and he ducked in to steal another kiss. "We should test that out."

Sophie laughed and pushed him away. "We kind of did last night."

"Let's go for two out of three."

"Come on, we have to get serious," she said, glancing over her shoulder and ignoring his murmured assurance that he was extremely serious. "I'm assuming Cara doesn't know about your little legal problem."

"No." That sobered him. "Definitely not and it's gonna stay that way."

"Okay, so—any idea why she's really here?"

"She has a friend who lives in Great Falls, maybe that's part of the reason." Ethan looked out toward the crowd, frowning. "It won't be easy getting out of here without kids wanting autographs."

Sophie groaned. "You couldn't have thought of that yesterday?"

"Did you?"

"Sorry. Guess I'm tired, too." She sniffed. "One of us didn't have that extra adrenaline boost."

He barked out a laugh. "You did okay without it."

Sophie tried to think of something clever, but settled for "Oh." And then of course she had to blush.

Ethan's gaze darkened. "Come on, baby," he murmured near her ear. "Don't make me hard. Not here."

Indignant, she drew back and stared. At his face. Nothing lower. "I didn't do anything."

His quiet groan sounded so damn sexy it vibrated all the way down her spine and pooled in the most inconvenient place. And then he had the nerve to look deep into her eyes and smile as if he knew exactly what he'd just done.

Wow, she'd have to figure out what had set him off. She'd definitely do it again. Later, though. She checked her watch. Right now they had to get out of Blackfoot Falls as soon as possible.

"Go sign a few autographs," she said. "You know you'll feel

bad if you don't. And if you need to talk to Matt, just please be quick?"

Ethan shook his head. "I realized the timing is wrong. He's got too much on his plate until the rodeo is over. I'll call him tomorrow."

She saw him discreetly adjust the front of his jeans and she tried not to smile. "What about Cara?"

"I don't know. But she's headed back this way."

To make room for the other riders leaving the arena, Ethan and Sophie met Cara closer to the gate. Going beyond that would put them at the mercy of insistent fans. Sophie had really had no idea how much fan and media activity surrounded the riders. A minute ago she'd seen Cara get stopped for her autograph by two excited kids dressed like cowgirls.

"I just talked to Dad," Cara said after chewing a bite of hot dog. "I told him you're still in one piece. Nothing broken that I could see. He's still pissed at you, by the way."

Ethan shrugged. It seemed he couldn't care less about his father's disposition. Except Sophie saw his jaw clench long enough to tell a different tale.

"Mom and I just think you're crazy." She grinned, her eyes sparkling with mischief. "If I were you, bro, I'd be sitting in an isolation chamber until five minutes before the finals started."

"If you were me," Ethan said, "you'd have the good sense to keep your mouth shut." He turned to watch a rider lower himself onto a restless bull thrashing against the metal chute. "Matt has himself a good contender there with Tornado Alley. That sucker's gonna be a high scorer."

"I like Matt," Cara said, ignoring her brother's dismissal. "I always have, you know that. But I think it was shitty of him to ask you to ride this close to the finals."

"The benefit was planned for September. Something got screwed up. When he told me it got pushed back, I could've dropped out. So don't blame Matt."

"Well, that just makes you even more stupid." Cara tossed

back her hair. "You get hurt between now and next weekend, and you'll regret it. I'm taking home my second buckle from Vegas this year. You know I will," she said with a nasty gleam in her eye. "And won't your little corner of the family trophy case look lonely?"

Sophie fumed. She pressed her lips together to keep from saying something sarcastic to the little twit. How could she treat her brother like that?

"Too bad you drove all this way to tell me something I already know, runt." Ethan ruffled her hair, which she obviously didn't like. "Why are you here?"

Cara smoothed back her hair. "I told you, to make sure you're in one piece and haven't done anything stupid. Well, stupider than this," she said, gesturing to nothing in particular. "Miss the finals again and you'll feel like a big loser."

"Wow." Sophie couldn't keep quiet a second longer. "I used to wonder what it would be like to have a brother or sister. If this is any example—" she shook her head "—I'm glad I don't have any siblings."

Cara glared at her, a deep red creeping up from her chest to her face.

Sophie tried not to glare back. She figured she'd said enough when Ethan put an arm around her and sighed.

"Cara didn't mean anything," he said. "Our family is competitive. And sometimes we egg each other on."

"Would you ever call Cara stupid and a loser? You can't tell me that doesn't hurt, Ethan." Sophie's voice cracked at the end. Ethan visibly swallowed, and she knew she'd struck a nerve. She lowered her lashes, thoroughly ashamed of her outburst. "I'm sorry. I shouldn't have said anything." She forced herself to look at Cara. "I really am sorry."

The woman's stricken expression made Sophie feel worse. "I wouldn't hurt my brother," Cara said, reverting to her bratty temperament with a contemptuous glare. The next second she deflated into a look of dismay. "Did I, Ethan? Did I hurt you?"

He left Sophie's side to ruffle Cara's hair again. "Hell, runt, you have to do a lot better than that to get under my skin."

He was lying, of course. And Sophie for one was glad he'd done so. For now, it was better that the tension eased.

"Quit messing up my hair," Cara said through gritted teeth. She made a show of smoothing back the long blond locks. Mostly, Sophie guessed, to hide the sheen of tears in her blue eyes. Sophie was right behind her in that department.

She glanced helplessly at Ethan.

He smiled and to Cara he said, "You still haven't told me why you're really here."

Cara dumped the rest of her hot dog in the trash can behind her. "I thought we could drive to Vegas together. But you already have company, so no problem."

"I'm going back to Wyoming first. I have some business to take care of in Casper tomorrow morning."

"Are you serious?" Her eyes widened. "You have to be in Vegas in four days."

"I know."

"Ethan…" She darted a look at Sophie, who wasn't about to say a word. "Can't your business wait? I mean, you don't want to cut it too close."

"No." Ethan inhaled deeply. "No, I don't. But I'll get to Vegas in time. No matter what it takes."

"I hope so," Cara said with a concerned frown.

Jitters flared in Sophie's tummy. She hoped so, too.

14

SOPHIE WASN'T THRILLED about leaving her Jeep behind, but it would be safe in Blackfoot Falls. The main thing worrying her as they drove toward Wyoming was Ethan's uncertain future. It was possible he'd have to fly to Vegas to get there in time. And it was also possible that he wouldn't make it to the finals at all. The thought made Sophie's stomach turn.

If that crazy Wendy Fullerton refused to drop the charges and Ethan ended up spending time in jail, not having a car would be the least of Sophie's worries.

Sophie adjusted the truck's air vents for the hundredth time. They were only five miles outside town. Maybe they should turn around and get the Jeep. The sensible thing was to follow Ethan to Wyoming. No, they were both too tired to drive separately.

"What's wrong?" Ethan took her hand. "You've been quiet and edgy. Are you still upset about Cara?"

"I'm mad at myself for butting in," Sophie admitted. "And I hope your sister doesn't hate me forever, but I'm okay. Just tired." She liked that he had twined their fingers together. "So are you. Don't forget I can take over driving anytime."

"Cara doesn't hate you. And she's really not a bad kid."

"I doubt she'd like being referred to as a kid," Sophie said. "She's only four years younger than me."

Ethan frowned. "Really? Only four years?"

"Technically, four and a half. But we women of a certain age have let that half thing go."

He smiled. "Cara can be a spoiled brat at times. That's for damn sure. And sometimes her teasing can get out of hand, but you have to understand, we were raised in a competitive environment."

"You mean, like riding in junior rodeos and stuff?"

"No. Well, yeah, we did some of that later on. But I'm talking about our parents and how they viewed childrearing. Always pushing us to succeed, to be the best. They can be fairly intense at times. I don't know that I agree with their method. I think using more praise would've been better, but I wanted to explain where Cara's coming from."

Sophie didn't dare say a word. She wouldn't dream of badmouthing his parents. But they sounded like bullies and they might've turned Cara into one. Lucky for Ethan, he'd taken the opposite path. No wonder as a teenager he'd championed the underdogs and misfits who'd been picked on. He'd understood what it was like to be bullied, though she doubted he saw it that way.

Her chest hurt suddenly. So much made sense now. His need to win that second title. Even the kids' camp he wanted to build. More than taking the opposite path, Ethan had turned out to be a really good man. Did his family value him for *that*? He did the right thing, and not the easy thing. Like riding for the Safe Haven Benefit even if it ended up costing him a trip to the finals.

"Did you fall asleep on me?" he asked, lightly squeezing her hand.

"No." She managed a small laugh. "I'm just thinking."

"Uh-oh. That doesn't always turn out so well."

"You got that right," she muttered, her brain beginning to speed ahead. "I have an idea." She forced herself to slow down. "First, may I totally butt into your life again?"

"So, now you're asking?"

"I'm being serious here," she said, looking at him.

He gave her a sober nod before turning back to the road and putting both hands on the wheel.

"I know you said your agent would find you an attorney, but it won't be quick enough." Sophie had done a brief search on the man. He was good, had an A-1 client list. Big sports names who made a lot of money. Like the football star he was currently tied up with. If push came to shove, Ethan wouldn't be the agent's priority. Not that she'd tell Ethan any of that. "I should call Craig."

"The La Maison guy?"

"Yes, but I promise that's not important. He's local and good. If there's a way to nip this thing, he'll figure it out. Next, Wendy Fullerton needs a wake-up call. She has to know, or at least believe, that you're willing to let the media have a field day with her accusation and the arrest, everything. Her husband may pull a lot of weight in Beatrice County, but you have fans across the country and a lot of other parts of the world."

"Jesus. I'm trying to keep it out of the media."

"She doesn't have to know that. And anyway, if the charge messes up your chance to go to the finals, you won't have any choice about what's reported." She saw his lips thin and she touched his arm. "I'm sorry, but that's the truth. And honestly I'm thinking it won't go that far. Even if it's a matter of getting a continuance."

Ethan gave a grudging nod.

Sophie took a deep breath. "Hell, if Wendy still refuses to tell the truth, I can always tell the judge you were with me that night. I'll say you came over after you left the bar."

He slowly turned to her. "Forget it. I won't have you perjuring yourself for me."

"I know it's wrong, but so is what's happening to you. I'd just be canceling out Wendy's lie. Hey, what are you doing?"

He pulled the truck off the road, only there was no exit or

turnout. And not all that much of a shoulder for anything other than an emergency.

Ethan left the engine idling and turned to her.

She twisted around to see if any cars were coming.

"We're fine," he said with a quick glance in the rearview mirror. "I want you to know I understand how much it took for you to make that offer. And how much I appreciate your belief in me. But I would sit in jail for a year before I'd let you do that."

Sophie sighed.

He kissed her. "Thank you." He stroked her cheek and looked into her eyes for as long as he dared considering where they were parked. "I mean it, you're a special woman, Sophie."

She dropped her chin, embarrassed and a little sad. Feeling helpless wasn't one of her strengths. "Yeah, let's go before I end up a special pancake in the middle of the highway."

"I've been watching. You think I'd let anything happen to you?" he said as he got them back on the highway.

Oddly she truly believed that if it was within his power, he would do anything to keep her safe. Just as he'd done eleven years ago.

Somebody really needed to call Wendy and ask the lying cheat if she was prepared for a media circus. Not only would Wendy and Broderick Fullerton's names be dragged through the mud, but who knew how many guys might come out of the woodwork willing to tell the world Wendy had picked them up in bars, as well? Sounded like a good job for Ethan's agent.

Sophie was suddenly exhausted. All she wanted to do was stop thinking. About the past. About his sister's taunts. About how his parents had failed to appreciate what a terrific son they'd raised in spite of themselves. She needed to turn off her brain. Maybe take a nap. At least they were on their way back to Wyoming.

She'd laid her head back as soon as they were on the highway again, but the shutting-down-her-brain thing? It wasn't going to happen. She kept thinking over and over how this whole situation was so unfair on every level.

What if she was leading him back to the slaughter? He needed a top-notch lawyer, someone local who understood Fullerton's reach. With enough pull in the DA's office, Fullerton could be petty and have Ethan locked up long enough to miss the finals. Craig might be his best hope. "Ethan?" she said, and smiled at the hand he'd placed on hers. "We should get off at the next exit."

"Sure." He didn't ask why.

"We need to talk," she said, and stifled a yawn. Screw Wendy, screw his family, screw the unfairness of it all. "About turning around and going to Las Vegas. It's your call. Whatever you decide, I'm with you a hundred percent."

ETHAN LET HER SLEEP. It was already dark. They'd been driving for three hours and he knew she was exhausted. So was he, but not so much that he'd come up with the crazy idea to drive to Vegas.

Maybe he should've argued with her more. Or simply turned the truck around and headed back toward Wyoming after she'd fallen asleep. Hell, she'd made it clear that it was his career, his life, his decision.

It was weird because all along she'd been adamant about him showing up in court tomorrow, but now she seemed to think they could handle things— No, not they—he had to stop thinking of her as a partner in this nightmare. Not only was this his problem, but Sophie could get burned if things went sideways.

She had a lot of faith in this Craig guy, not him personally, but his legal skills. And she seemed confident that through him Ethan could take care of everything long-distance. Damn, he wished he knew what the favor would cost her. Beyond dinner at La Maison.

Ethan snorted. Like hell. He'd pay the hotshot attorney twice his fee before he'd let Sophie go on a date with Mr. Slick. What kind of man coerced a woman into going out with him by doing her a favor? For that reason alone, Ethan didn't like the guy. But Sophie had convinced him to get over himself, that his situation was too serious for him to be a dumb ass. Her exact words. They made him smile.

Sophie made him smile. A lot.

He saw their exit coming up. He hoped the motel he'd found on his iPhone was decent. In rural places like this part of Montana, you couldn't be too choosy. But if they continued on to Vegas as planned, they didn't have to rush. So no sense driving more than they had to tonight.

Once they arrived in Vegas, Sophie was going to be real happy with the suite he already had booked. He could almost hear her squeals when she saw the huge jetted tub. On second thought maybe he should find something off the strip. Damn, she could get loud when she came.

Almost on cue, she brought her head up and yawned just as he parked near the motel's ugly stucco office. He surveyed the row of mud-brown rooms. Damn place looked nothing like the website pictures.

"Where are we?" she asked after a second yawn.

"Some motel I found online. They exaggerated by a lot. We don't have to stay here."

She blinked at him. "Have you slept?"

Ethan laughed. "Not that I'm aware."

"Oh, right. You were driving." She gave him a sweet drowsy smile. "Neither of us should be driving, so this is fine. We're just going to sleep here."

"I hope not," he said, and opened his door.

She made a face at the overhead light.

"Stay here while I register." He quickly got out and closed the door so the light turned off.

The owner seemed keen on making small talk, but Ethan took care of business quickly and drove them to the room at the end. He found out their closest neighbor was two doors down. Just in case.

"It's not so bad," Sophie said, glancing around at the queen bed with a green-and-tan floral comforter that matched the curtains.

Ethan put their two bags in the closet. "Brace yourself, they even have a luggage rack."

"Oh my. Very fancy." She seemed to be waking up. "I want to see the bathroom. The size of the shower is the true test."

"Why?" He followed her inside and put his arms around her from behind. "What do you have in mind?"

"I don't even know what to call that color," she said, leaning back against him as they studied the ugly tile walls.

"Well," he said, deeply inhaling her sweet scent until he felt as if he'd had one beer too many. "The bathroom is bigger than the one at The Boarding House, and so is the shower."

"And everything is very clean."

"No bugs."

"Oh." Her gaze darted across the floor and she shifted her feet. "Why did you have to say that?"

He laughed. "Don't worry. I'll protect you."

"Yes, you will. I don't do bugs or mice."

He kept the straightest face he could. "Now, if the bed isn't lumpy or too soft—"

"And doesn't squeak."

He turned her to face him. "And since I have the most beautiful woman in all of Montana in my arms..."

"Right," she drawled with a mocking sigh, and glanced at the ceiling.

"Hey, you're talking about someone I happen to like very much. So knock it off."

Sophie blinked and blushed.

Ethan smiled and kissed her nose. Man, he liked it when she blushed. He didn't know why, but it got to him every time. "I'm thinking shower. Sex. Nap. More sex."

She was smiling up at him, her hands flat on his chest, her brown eyes sparkling. "Individual showers." He started to object and she pressed a silencing finger to his lips. "Only to save time."

He sucked her finger into his mouth.

She pressed closer. "This isn't working."

He released her finger. "Pardon me, ma'am. Please continue."

"Then sex."

"Now we're talking."

"Then sleep for as long as we can. If there's time when we wake up, then maybe..."

This wasn't what he'd expected at all. "You're serious?" He leaned back and searched her face. "This is, what...our third date and you're already cutting me off."

Sophie laughed. "Oh, sweetie, you think we've been dating?"

"Ah, that's right. You're just getting me out of your system." The remark had pissed him off and apparently he was still getting over it. Now wasn't the time to talk about it, though. He released her. "I'll take a shower first if you don't mind."

Staring at him, she nodded. She stepped around him to leave the bathroom, then looked back. "I was just teasing about the dating thing. I mean, I did handcuff you."

"I know." He smiled. "If you change your mind, you can shower with me."

"Actually I have to make a couple of calls."

He nodded, closed the door and turned the water on in the shower, but he didn't get in yet.

Looking in the mirror at the dark stubble shadowing his jaw, he thought about the past three days since he'd met up with Sophie again. Two days, three nights if he counted tonight. Jesus. Not long, but it felt like it. She was easy to be around, even when they disagreed. Or when things got prickly. His sister showing up, for instance.

He knew Sophie had gotten the wrong impression of his family. His parents weren't self-centered ogres. They did what they thought was best. But since when did he give a shit whether a woman he was involved with liked his family? That right there was the problem. He was feeling things that he probably shouldn't.

He pulled off his boots and unsnapped his shirt. Normally he'd wait and shave in the morning, but he wouldn't do that to Sophie. He opened the door and saw her sitting on the bed, talking on her cell.

She looked up in surprise but then smiled at him, her gaze slowly lowering to his open shirt. The way she moistened her lips was so damn sexy he had to force himself to keep moving to the closet. His shaving kit sat on top of his bag.

"I heard you," she said into the phone. "Call me tomorrow as soon as you find out, okay? The earlier the better. Yes, I do."

Just as he was about to close the bathroom door, he heard her say, "Thanks, Craig. I owe you."

15

"I HAVE A QUESTION," Sophie said after she'd had her shower and was crawling into bed with Ethan.

"Why do you have clothes on?"

"It's just a T-shirt."

Ethan was sitting up, pillow behind his back, the sheets at his waist, showing off a chest of the gods while looking at her with the frown of a ten-year-old. "It hides everything."

"Well, duh." She laughed until he pointed the remote at the TV and turned it off. "Okay," she said, and pulled the shirt over her head.

His hands were covering her breasts before she could even ditch the tee.

"Impatient, aren't we?" Already she was shivering from his touch. So much for them having a talk first.

"Damn right." He dragged his gaze away from the nipple he was circling with his thumb and looked at her mouth. "Kiss me now," he said in a dramatically low voice.

"Oh no, were you watching cartoons again?"

Before she knew it, he'd pulled her against his chest and claimed her mouth. She readily opened for him. He tasted minty and achingly familiar. Which was such a crazy thought she could hardly stand it. No, this wasn't a young girl's fantasy, but it wasn't her real life, either. They were two people attracted to each other and using sex to deal with a stressful situation.

His hand moved to her face and he stroked her cheek with the back of his fingers. She liked the smooth feel of his jaw against her chin and cheeks. But she also liked it when he had a day or two's worth of stubble. His tongue stroked hers, gently, seductively, taking nothing for granted. She might be a sure thing, but Ethan wanted her to be present, eager to take this journey with him because she was helpless to do anything but.

If she slid the hand she had pressed to his chest lower, she'd find him hard and ready. It would be easy to get lost in the many ways he could make her feel so good, so content, put her in a state of temporary euphoria. She was an addict, after all.

Oh yes, she had no doubt he could make her forget the things she had to tell him. The difficult question she had to ask, if only to ease her own mind. And hopefully his.

His mouth moved to her throat, leaving a trail of kisses and light nips down to her collarbone. She quickly drew in air and then leaned back, breaking contact with his mouth.

He looked up with a lazy smile. "Where do you think you're going?" he murmured, and wrapped an arm around her.

Constantly amazed at the gentleness of his large hands and strong arms, she tried to remain firm and not give in to his seeking mouth. "I'm not going anywhere," she said. "Actually I wanted to talk." She saw his expression fall, and with a laugh she cupped his jaw. "It's nothing horrible." She lowered her hand. "At least I hope not."

He sat back against the pillow and leveled his intense gaze with her eyes. She took a moment to arrange her own pillow, quickly compose herself and pull the sheet up to her breasts. He very obviously didn't care for that.

"When I said—" She cleared her throat. "The other night, when I made a crack about getting you out of my system… I swear I didn't mean anything by it."

Ethan snorted, shrugged a shoulder. "I know that."

She shook her head. "I hurt you. And I'm so sorry."

"You think you hurt me?" He lifted his eyebrows and gave her a look that bordered on patronizing.

Sophie didn't just think, she knew. She'd seen the same wounded expression in his eyes with Cara. Fleeting but unmistakable.

"All right, I mentioned it earlier, so I get why you think it upset me, but you're wrong. So don't worry about it."

"It was a thoughtless line directed more at myself than at you." She sighed at his stony reaction. "I had a huge crush on you after that day in school. It was so bad I couldn't even concentrate on studying."

His features softened. "Huh. For what it's worth, I couldn't tell. And I'd checked you out plenty."

"Liar."

"I did," he said with an odd laugh that told her he might be telling the truth. "But I was a lot more careful so Ashley wouldn't go nuts again."

"Wow, high school really sucked."

"Yes, in many ways it did." He reached for her hand. "Is that it? That's what you wanted to tell me?"

She held his gaze. "You haven't asked me about what the lawyer I hired on your behalf had to say."

"Craig?"

"Yes, Craig Langley."

"Okay." He released her hand. "I'm listening."

Oh, brother. It wasn't as if she'd done something behind his back. Ethan knew she was going to contact Craig. And yet the same brooding expression was on his face from a minute ago. "He's contacting the sheriff's office for a copy of the arrest report and Wendy's statement. Then he'll get back to us tomorrow first thing. He understands this is time-sensitive." She absolutely had no idea what Ethan was thinking. He'd closed her off. "I know you don't like talking about this, but—"

"I don't like that you feel you owe the guy. Certainly not on my behalf. Hell, it's not as if we're asking him to represent me for free."

Sophie relaxed a bit. "He's super busy, so yeah, I do owe him. And I don't care even a tiny bit. I've said it before, and I'll say it again. Craig is your best shot at making this all go away."

Ethan stared back a moment too long. "Why are you here, Sophie? Helping me like this. Do you feel you owe me?"

It was a fair question, she supposed. The answer, though, wasn't an easy one. Not if she wanted to be truthful. She swallowed around the lump forming in her throat. "No," she said. "I don't feel like I do, which is kind of odd, actually." She forced herself to keep her eyes even with his. "That stupid crush I told you about… I might still have a tiny itty-bitty piece of it left."

Ethan's mouth curved in a heart-stopping smile. "Good," he said, gathering her in his arms. "I might have a crush on you, too."

Before she could respond, he began kissing and biting her neck. She let out a shriek of laughter, then promptly covered her loud mouth.

"It's okay," he murmured, taking another nip. "The next two rooms are vacant."

She shoved him away to look at him. "And you know this because…?"

"Yes, honey," he said without apology, "I asked."

Sophie gasped, embarrassed, flustered… And then she just laughed.

Mostly because he was tickling behind her ear with his tongue. His hands were busy rubbing a nipple and cupping her butt. She loved having the freedom to skim her palm over his pecs while watching his shoulder muscles ripple. He was so damn beautiful it almost wasn't fair.

"Have you ever modeled for your sponsors?" she asked, and when he didn't answer, she rephrased it. "Like for a magazine ad?"

He kissed her collarbone, paused. "Once. When I was younger," he said, and continued blazing a path to her breast.

"Shirtless?"

When he didn't answer, she grinned. How had she not found the ad in one of her many searches back in her obsessive years?

He flicked his tongue over a very hard, sensitive nipple. Just as she thought she couldn't stand another second, he sucked it into his mouth and she arched slightly. The moment she relaxed he slid a hand between her thighs, then surprised her by going in the direction she hadn't expected.

He cradled the back of her calf in his palm, lightly caressing the muscle as he moved toward her ankle. His mouth moved to her other nipple, lightly biting the tight bud, then licking and sucking it until fire had spread through her veins.

Sophie reached under the sheets and found her prize. He hissed at her touch. Groaned when she wrapped her hand tighter and stroked him to the base of his erection. She took her time learning his shape, the smooth texture of his fever-hot flesh. She wanted to feel everything before she got lost in all the sexy things he did to her.

Ethan murmured some indistinct words—it might've been a mild curse—and then he pulled the sheet back and stared down at her hand wrapped around him, stroking upward. She paused at the rim of the crown and kissed him there.

"Sophie," he whispered, his breathless rasp so hot she felt it all the way to her swollen center.

He'd abandoned her leg, and she was sorry she interrupted him before seeing where he was going with that. But then he urged her thighs apart and slid a finger along the seam of her lips, and her mind went blank. Unconsciously she squeezed him tighter, and he dipped two fingertips inside her. Not far, just enough to tease her. To make her whimper.

He leaned forward at a slight angle so he could kiss her mouth. He kept his fingertips inside her and she hadn't given up her hold on his erection.

"I want to try something," he murmured against her mouth before leaning back to look at her.

"Okay," she said, and released him. It briefly occurred to her she should probably be wary. Or at least ask what he had in mind, but gazing into his blue eyes, she knew he wouldn't harm her.

He brought their faces close together and rested his forehead against hers. "It's nothing kinky or weird," he said. "I promise."

"I didn't think it would be."

Ethan smiled as he drew back. His fingers were still inside her. He pushed in a little deeper, his nostrils flaring, his expression strained, as if he might be rethinking his plan. Finally he pulled out.

He threw the covers to the foot of the bed. Grabbed a condom off the nightstand. Pushed the pillows out of the way so there was a clear spot in the middle of the mattress. He shifted until he was sitting close to the center, his legs crossed loosely at the ankles.

She tried not to stare at his erection, but that was asking too much of herself. She figured out what he wanted to do, and her heart was already racing toward the finish line.

"I want you to sit on me," he said as he rolled on the condom. "As if you were going to wrap your legs around my waist. You'll be sort of sitting on my thighs at first. We'll find a fit to accommodate our height difference."

She nodded, and Ethan put his hands on her waist to help guide her as she climbed on board.

"Making the adjustments should be fun," she said.

Ethan's laugh turned into a groan as she sank down on him.

Maybe that was why he didn't notice that it was still an awkward arrangement. If her legs were a tad longer, it would be easier. She wiggled into a better position and ignored his tormented groans.

He reached behind and cupped her butt with both hands. He lifted her a tiny bit to the right and an inch closer against him. The angle of his erection covered a lot of territory…

Her breath caught at the base of her throat. No air was going in or out. He lifted his hips in the slightest thrust and he filled her utterly and completely to the max. A small cry escaped her lips when she felt her body stretch for him. How could he keep filling her?

She hoped this was good for him.

For her it was like hitting the jackpot.

One hand stayed on her butt, and the other slipped between them and found her clit. His thumb circled and rubbed with varying pressure.

Sensations bombarded her from both sides. They came down from the top and up from the bottom. Everywhere. They shimmered around her, ruled over her. Awareness of her surroundings slipped in and out. She knew she was with Ethan, though. He was doing all of these miraculous things to her.

His body was warm and solid. Her hands rested on his shoulders, her fingers curling into his flesh and muscle.

"Open your eyes, Sophie," he whispered softly. "Come on, look at me."

She forced them open.

He was right there, his face inches from her face. His darkened eyes looking deeply into hers. And his smile… God, his smile melted anything that might've been left of her.

Holding his gaze, she rocked gently against him. He was still rubbing her, but she moved his hand away. It felt amazing, but she wanted to wait. She wanted to stay in this moment with him for as long as they could bear it.

Each of their movements was so tiny, so overwhelming. Neither of them had blinked. She was too afraid of missing something in his gorgeous blue eyes. He was trembling, his whole body straining to hold back. Sophie couldn't decide if that was what she really wanted.

Freezing this particular snapshot in time was amazing, but watching this incredible man shatter…for her… She had a feeling that would keep her heart warm forever.

She moved her face closer to his, wanting to kiss him without losing eye contact.

It didn't work.

Ethan's smile widened a little. He knew what she was doing. "Guess you have to make a choice," he said, his voice sounding weak from the strain of his tight control.

"Why?" She barely got the word out.

"Can't have both." He ran his fingers through her hair and it felt so great she almost closed her eyes.

"I think I might die," she said. "Right here. In whatever town this is. Cause of death…sensation overload."

"Then I'd better hurry up and come."

She laughed and the forward motion had him hissing through his teeth. It affected her, too. She could've sworn he'd rubbed her, but he didn't have a hand down there.

"I made a decision," she said.

"Good." His eyes were completely black. "I don't think I'm gonna last."

Sophie smiled. "Ready to rock and roll?"

In answer Ethan lifted his hips and her.

"Dammit. You made me blink."

Still watching her face, he smiled. And thrust again, only deeper.

She had to hang on to him.

He used both hands to anchor her hips, holding her steady to receive his thrusts. Semi-controlled at first, consistent, precise, but then that disappeared along with the eye contact.

She wound her arms tightly around his neck, her breasts cradled by his chest, the friction caused by his thrusts driving her crazy. Their whimpers and moans permeated the room.

Again, the pressure began building inside her, expanding and stretching, accelerating beyond her limit. And the heat. God, the heat rolled over them in shimmering waves of otherworldly pleasure, seducing them into the fire, fooling them into thinking they were warm and safe. Suspended here in the eye of the storm.

Ethan's strangled groan penetrated the sensual fog. His arms shook. Sweat beaded on his skin. His hands slipped from her hips. One landed on her thigh. She hadn't let go of his neck. Her own body hadn't stopped quaking. The spasms quivering inside her left her breathless and as weak as a newborn kitten.

She knew she should climb off. She couldn't move.

Ethan kissed the corner of her mouth. He lifted her up and laid her back on the mattress carefully, so her head landed on the pillow. Letting out a big whoosh of breath, he collapsed at her side.

"I think I know what it feels like to ride a bull," she murmured between gulps of air.

His laugh barely made it out. "You stayed on for more than eight seconds."

"I expect a buckle," she said, and then just breathed for a while. "That position really was ridiculously amazing. We have to do it again."

"Not right now."

"Wuss."

Chuckling, he rolled toward her. "We will. Do it again. And again."

"Many times."

He kissed the side of her neck. "Many times," he agreed, the warmth in his voice bringing a tightness to her chest.

She snuggled up against him.

He drew away for a moment, but just to pull the covers over them. And then he wrapped an arm around her, bringing her close.

Many times.

Repeating the words in her head made her smile. Though it was easy to say glib things now when she was here with Ethan, quite literally the man of her dreams.

But there was only one thing she knew for certain.

Ethan Styles was impossible. Impossible to understand. And impossible to resist…

16

SOPHIE WAS SITTING on a picnic bench near a snack bar about two hours from the motel where they'd stayed last night. No one else was sitting outside. The air was warm for November, but that wasn't saying much. The sun felt good, though, and she wanted to get the dreaded conversation with Lola over with—if she'd ever call back.

If Craig called soon, that would make her exceedingly happy, but she wasn't expecting to hear from him for another hour. He would've only received the paperwork this morning.

Lola was beginning to worry her. She hadn't been answering her texts or calls. Which wasn't like her at all. She couldn't be *that* busy just because Sophie was gone. Anyway, Lola had been anxious to keep in close touch, and since she was expecting Sophie and Ethan to be arriving in Wattsville this morning, it seemed very odd she wouldn't answer her phone.

Sophie sure hoped this weird behavior didn't have anything to do with Hawk. When Sophie checked him out early on, she hadn't found anything significant or violent in his past. She would've definitely alerted Lola.

Just to make herself feel better, she texted Mandy to see if she knew what was happening at the office. Talking to her would be better, but Sophie wanted to be the one to tell Lola about the last-minute decision to go to Las Vegas. Yes, she could've left a heads-up on a voice mail, but she hadn't felt right doing that. She wanted to explain everything, even let Lola yell and scream at her if she wanted.

Best-case scenario, everything with Lola was fine—just the regular Monday madness keeping her busy. And Sophie would hear from Craig telling her the charges had been dropped, and Lola and Sophie wouldn't be on the hook for the full hundred-thousand-dollar bond.

If only she lived in a perfect world…

She looked up from her phone to take the cup of coffee Ethan had brought her. He bent to kiss her and even before their lips touched, she got that giddy feeling in her tummy that had been hanging around since they left Blackfoot Falls yesterday.

"They didn't have lattes or anything fancy. You should've seen the look I got when I asked for your part-skim, caramel-drizzled whatever."

"Well, if you didn't know what to ask for, how do you know if they have it or not?"

"Trust me, the second I mentioned the word *latte*, the old guy stopped listening. He was too busy mumbling something about yuppies ruining the world."

She eyed the Danish he'd brought for himself. "We just had breakfast."

"So?" He took a big bite, chewed, then sipped his coffee. "Do you know how many meals I've missed since I hooked up with you?"

"Is it my fault you think sex is a meal replacement?"

Ethan touched the brim of his hat and smiled at some phantom person behind her. "Mornin', ma'am."

"Yeah, like I'm going to fall for that," Sophie said, and heard a tsking sound. She refused to turn all the way around, but managed to catch sight of the little white-haired woman walking toward the snack counter.

She looked at Ethan and they both laughed.

"You're the one who wanted to sit out here in the sun for a while," he said.

"Yes, and now I want a bite of that Danish."

"Then you'd better ask nicer." His next bite demolished half the pastry.

Her phone buzzed and she completely forgot about everything but the fact that she had a confession to make to Lola. And she sure didn't want to do it in front of Ethan.

As if he'd read her mind, he got to his feet. "I'll go pick up more Danish," he said.

"Hey, Lola, you were starting to worry me," Sophie said, watching Ethan stroll toward the snack bar.

"Where are you?" Lola asked. She sounded as if she'd been crying.

"Are you okay?"

"No. Not really."

"Are you at the office?"

"I was, but I'm at home now."

Sophie's chest hurt. Lola practically lived at the office. "Does this have anything to do with Hawk?"

Lola burst out crying. She tried to talk but couldn't seem to catch her breath.

"Can you tell me if Hawk is there with you now? Just say yes or no."

"No," Lola managed to choke out.

Sophie swallowed, feeling helpless and close to tears herself. "Did he hurt you?"

"No. Yes." Her voice broke, but the sobs were easing. "Not like you think."

"Okay, don't rush. I'll be right here when you can talk." Sophie caught herself rocking back and forth, an arm wrapped across her stomach. She quickly glanced around. No sign of Ethan. She didn't want him to see her like this. He'd want an explanation she might not be comfortable giving. "Lola? I just wanted you to know I'm still here."

"I'm okay," she said. "Or getting there. Where are you? Are you close by?"

"No, I'm not." Sophie bit her lip. "I'm sorry. Is Mandy there?"

Lola sniffed. "No. I have to call her, though. She needs to help me find that goddamn, lying son of a bitch. I could kill that bastard."

Sighing with relief, Sophie listened to her cousin throw in a few more curses. Lola was sounding more like herself. Anger would serve her better than hurt right now.

Sophie's cell signaled an incoming call. She saw that it was Craig and winced. He'd have to leave a message. "Lola? Can you tell me what happened?"

A sob broke. "I'm sorry, Soph. Please don't hate me. I was such a fool. My God, I can't believe I'm that woman."

"I'm not going to hate you, Lola. Just tell me what happened."

Silence turned to quiet sobbing before Lola finally spoke. "He ripped us off," she said. "Hawk stole everything."

Sophie tried to quickly process the information. They really didn't have much for him to steal. "What exactly did Hawk take?"

"I really do mean everything, Soph," Lola said softly, then paused, trying to control her breathing. "He got into the safe."

Sophie felt the blood drain from her face. A violent shiver surged through her body. "How did—" She wouldn't ask. It didn't matter. Staying calm, keeping Lola calm, those were her priorities. Not dropping her phone would be good, too. Her hands were beginning to shake. "Since you guys had a fight maybe he's just trying to get your attention."

"No, I think he might've been planning this for a while. I'm gonna kill him. I am. God, I'm so stupid. This is all my fault."

"Don't go there, Lola. We need to stay focused. Okay?" Hell, Sophie was one to talk. She'd made her own mess. "How long ago could he have done this?"

"Last night, I think. Late. After we talked around midnight."

It was eleven-forty now. That gave the prick a head start. Sophie had to get to the research she'd done on him a few months ago. With any luck, there would be a clue as to where he'd gone. First, she'd get a hold of Mandy. And she had to talk to Craig. Jesus. Ethan was supposed to be in court in two hours. Hopefully Craig had worked his magic and it was a moot point by now. But she couldn't count on it.

"You're awfully calm," Lola said. "Do you understand what I'm telling you? He took *everything*." Her voice had risen and she sounded close to losing it again.

"I know. I'm just trying to think about our next step."

They'd always disagreed about how much cash to keep in the office. But after business had picked up, Lola had stubbornly insisted on having a minimum of twenty thousand dollars they could get their hands on quickly. "Okay…so, I'm going to call Mandy first, but she'll still want you to fill in the details, and then I'm going to see if I can track him electronically. We both know Hawk is too stupid to hide his trail."

"Yeah," Lola said with a small laugh. "There is that."

"So…" Sophie had to ask. "Just so I know what we're dealing with, can you narrow down what you mean by *everything*?"

Lola let out a sob. "Thirty-five thousand cash," she said, and Sophie wanted to faint. "And two pieces of jewelry we were holding as collateral."

Sophie held her breath. How could she have forgotten about the collateral items? "Do you mean the antique brooch Mrs. Sellars gave us for her son's bond?"

"Yes," Lola choked out. "And the signed Mohammad Ali glove from Mr. Polinski."

Sophie held in a whimper. Mrs. Sellar's ruby-and-diamond brooch alone was worth about sixty thousand. So Lola's Bail Bonds was pretty much ruined financially. "Anything else?"

"I don't know how you can be this calm. I really don't."

Guilt, probably, because Sophie had created her own mess.

She turned and saw Ethan approaching. He looked worried, so she tried to clean up her body language. "I don't know. Maybe I'm still in shock," Sophie said. "But let's use it to our advantage. Let's hang up and I'll contact Mandy, then get online."

"You have to call me soon, or you know I'll go nuts," Lola said. "I think I'll go to the bar and ask around. Hawk might've shot off his mouth."

"Mandy should probably do that."

"Everyone there knows me." Lola sighed. "They probably all think I'm a dumb ass, too, so what the hell?"

"For the record, I didn't say you were a dumb ass, nor do I think you are a dumb ass. We all have our blind spots," Sophie said, watching Ethan advance on her. "I'll call you soon."

"Wait. You have Styles, right? He'll make it to court?"

"Let's worry about Hawk for now."

"We really don't need to fork out money for Styles."

"I know that," she snapped, adding another layer of guilt to the growing pile. "Sorry."

"Nope. You have every right. Call me." Lola disconnected.

Sophie wanted to lay her head down and sob her heart out. She found a smile for Ethan when he set the paper bag on the table in front of her.

"Problem?" he asked, his eyes narrowed.

"Nothing I can't handle. Duty calls, though, and I have to get my tablet out of my bag." She glanced around, mostly because she was having trouble with that intense gaze of his. She couldn't explain anything now. She'd lose it and be tempted to hide in the comfort of his arms. He'd feel guilty they hadn't returned to Wyoming and she didn't want that. He had the finals to worry about.

THERE WAS ANOTHER ISSUE. She needed privacy and good Wi-Fi. "How about we find someplace where you can get some rest while I do a little work? Would that be okay?" she asked lightly. "I don't care if we go back to the same motel for a while."

Ethan's eyebrows went up. He looked as though he had a hundred questions. "Whatever you want."

"I have to make a quick call first, okay? To Mandy. She works in our office," Sophie said, trying like hell to sound normal. "Oh, and Craig called while I was talking to Lola. I had to let him go to voice mail, but I'll get back to him. Fingers crossed that he has good news."

Ethan stood there stone-faced, just watching her. She wasn't fooling him at all. He stepped back so she could get up, then offered her a hand. His skin was warm, his grip solid and sure. She felt safe with him. Alive. Happy. Whole. Which made her feel all the more a fool. This bubble in which they'd existed for the past three days was only a blip in time. A page torn from their normal lives and soon to be discarded. Yet she'd been willing to give up so much of herself, jeopardize the reputation of the business she'd built with Lola.

But Sophie couldn't afford self-pity or to let her shame interfere with finding Hawk. There would be plenty of time for all that later.

They were halfway to the truck when a sudden flash of memory stopped her cold. That day in the office when she'd announced she was going after Ethan… Hawk had sided with her. Lola had already been annoyed with him, yet he'd spoken out against her, taking Sophie's side. It made sense now. Lola was right. The bastard had been planning the theft for a while. Hawk knew Sophie didn't like him and he'd wanted her out of the way. But even worse, he'd used Lola.

Sophie was going to find that asshole. She would, because she was smarter than him and she knew so much more about him than he could imagine. And when she finally got her hands on him…

"Sophie? Please." Ethan put his arms around her. She'd never seen him look this worried, not even about his own problem. "Is it me? Am I causing you this grief?"

This wasn't fair to him. And anyway, she couldn't avoid his

gaze forever. "We have a problem at the office. It's—" She cleared her throat. "My cousin Lola's boyfriend... We were robbed. The office safe was cleaned out."

"Jesus." Ethan touched her cheek. "I'm sorry. Did he get away with a lot?"

Despite trying to be stoic, she let out a whimper. "It's bad. He stole a lot of cash, some expensive jewelry we were holding as collateral, a piece of valuable sports memorabilia that might be irreplaceable."

When Ethan touched her cheek again, she realized he'd been wiping tears. She jerked away, embarrassed and twice as furious with Hawk.

"Obviously we have to do something," Ethan said, easily staying abreast of her on the brisk walk to his truck. "I'm sure you have an idea."

"*You* will do nothing. Except whatever it is you do to get ready for the finals." She checked her cheeks for moisture. "I'm calling Mandy, a bounty hunter who works with us. She's the real deal. Totally badass. She'll help me find the stupid prick. Hawk really is stupid, probably left electronic footprints all over the country. I'll work on that while Mandy does her thing. Oh, we will find him, and when we do..."

They got to the truck and Ethan opened the passenger door for her.

"Look," she said, keeping her gaze lowered, "I feel horrible for Lola because she's blaming herself, and she shouldn't. This has nothing to do with you." As soon as Sophie was seated, she glanced at Ethan. He'd been so quiet.

His expression grim, he closed the door. She watched him round the hood. He looked angry.

She understood. She'd been incensed with Wendy Fullerton on his behalf, so she got it. Of course Ethan would be upset for her. And then she thought of something else. Damn. She couldn't afford to lose it now. Craig. She had to return his call. God, she really, really hoped the news was good. She wasn't about to leave Ethan twisting in the wind. Maybe he was angry because he thought she'd dropped the ball on him.

After he slid behind the wheel, she laid a hand on his arm. "I haven't forgotten you. I'm calling Craig now."

"You think I'm pissed about that?" His eyes were blazing mad when he turned to her. "You're a smart, capable woman, Sophie, I'll give you that. But obviously you're in trouble. Do you honestly think I could stand by and not help? Is that the kind of man you think I am?"

"No, of course not, but—"

"Frankly I don't give a shit what you have to say about it. I'm going to help you any way I'm able."

She'd never seen him this angry. Maybe that day back in high school. "Okay."

Looking straight ahead, he turned the key and started the truck. His lips were a thin line, his jaw clenched. Leaving the engine idling, he reached over the console, grabbed her upper arms and pulled her toward him.

"Damn independent little cuss," he muttered, and then kissed her hard on the mouth. He released her, took a deep breath and asked, "Now where the hell are we going?"

17

AFTER CONTACTING MANDY and receiving the bad news from Craig, Sophie worked from her tablet at the small table in the dinky motel they'd found three miles down from the snack bar. The room sucked, but the Wi-Fi was good.

Ethan had stepped outside so he wouldn't disturb her while he called his agent. Brian would probably come in person to strangle Sophie. If they'd gone straight to Wyoming last night as they'd planned, Ethan wouldn't be missing his court date in—she looked at the time and felt a little sick—five minutes.

There was still a possibility that everything would work out for him. Mandy was on the case, and Sophie had a great deal more faith in the bounty hunter than she had in herself at the moment. Sophie was pretty damn close to blowing everything.

Craig was furious that she hadn't warned him about Wendy being Broderick Fullerton's wife. Apparently Craig was on retainer with two of Fullerton's subsidiaries. They'd exchanged a few choice words, and Sophie might've called Craig a yellow-bellied chickenshit. It was actually one of the nicer names that had come to mind after discovering he'd called Lola and told her everything. So now her poor cousin was a complete basket case, worrying that Fullerton would have his bank call in their loan and kill their line of credit.

Sophie had only herself to blame.

Sighing, she rubbed her eyes. The screen blurred. She was tired from stress and lack of sleep, and staring at Hawk's—no, Floyd's—background file was frustrating. She was missing something, but she couldn't seem to pinpoint it. For the third time, she searched through his late teenage years, the job-hopping, being nailed for shoplifting cigarettes, petty stuff. Mostly his past was uneventful.

Her cell buzzed. She picked it up and read the text from Lola. A warrant had just been issued for Ethan's arrest. Sophie briefly closed her eyes. She wanted to call Mandy, but there was no point. If she had news, she would've called.

Sophie stared at the text, wanting so very much to curl up into a ball. Oh God, what had she done? He could've made it to court. They had been on their way to Wyoming. Did she have to pick then to rail against life's injustices? Did she need any more proof that she was hopeless when it came to Ethan? She had no judgment, no ability to reason, and now two people she deeply cared about had been caught in her well-intentioned but destructive wake.

She wondered if she should call Lola. And say what? Sorry I wasn't there for you? Sorry I was too busy chasing a childish dream? Sorry I didn't warn you about Hawk? Sophie could go on forever about the ways in which she'd failed. And she hadn't even gotten to Ethan yet.

Speaking of which… She heard the door being unlocked. She looked up as Ethan walked into the room. He looked grim but gave her a smile. She tried to return it. Had he been keeping track of the time? Was he expecting to hear about the warrant? She had to say something.

She moistened her lips. "A warrant has—"

"I know."

"I'm sorry, Ethan."

"Why? You tried to warn me." He slipped behind her chair and massaged her cramped shoulders.

His strong, gentle hands felt so good, but she didn't deserve his kindness. Or his forgiveness. She didn't deserve him. "I'm also the person who encouraged you to drive to Vegas instead. I was so sure Craig would come through, or that Wendy would finally—"

"Shh, it doesn't matter."

"Of course it does." She stopped when her voice shook.

"Aren't you going to check that?" he asked.

"What?" She realized she'd gotten an alert and looked at the corner of the screen. Floyd had used his credit card to buy gas—he was in Reno, Nevada.

Ethan took the other chair. "This is good. You've located him, right?"

"For now." Something clicked in the back of her mind that made sense about him being in Reno. "I have to check something before I call Mandy," she said, knowing Mandy would head for the airport as soon as she heard the news. So if she hadn't made progress solving Ethan's problem… Well, that was that.

"You should be happy," he said, frowning.

"I am." She paused. "Ethan? Why do you think this might be your last chance to go to the finals?"

His face darkened. "I never told you that."

"I overheard you mention something to Arnie."

He shrugged. "It's nothing." He glanced at her tablet. "Shouldn't you be moving on this information?"

"Please tell me." She begged with her eyes even though she wouldn't blame him for never trusting her with anything again.

He stared back, then sighed. "You ride long enough your body's bound to suffer some wear and tear. I've had some trouble with my shoulder. Nothing serious, but I'm going to quit before I blow my future. That's all."

"Really?"

"Really. I'm being sensible. Imagine that."

Sophie smiled. She wanted to kiss him. It would be a stupid move. She'd already proven she couldn't think straight when she was around him. She glanced at the file on her screen just when her phone rang. It was Mandy. Sophie told herself not to get excited yet. "Tell me something good."

"Something good," Mandy said in her usual calm voice.

Sophie's heart lurched. "How good?"

"Mrs. Fullerton turned out to be extremely cooperative once I explained all the possible ramifications of making a false charge against a popular rodeo celebrity. She agreed it would be best to explain she'd misplaced her jewelry and drop the charges. Done deal. I just left the sheriff's office."

Sophie looked at Ethan. "What about the husband?"

"He's out of town again," Mandy said. "But hell, that's her problem. Have you got anything yet?"

"I think I might. Call you in ten?"

"Yep."

The moment they disconnected, Sophie hugged Ethan.

"She found him?" He held her tight, his smile matching hers.

"No, not yet. Wendy dropped the charges. You're in the clear."

He frowned. "I thought you guys were looking for Hawk."

"I am. Ethan. Aren't you excited? No more charges against you. They'll cancel the warrant."

"Well, yeah, of course I am. How?"

"Mandy had a talk with Wendy. She pointed out how easily a trial could get out of control with other men stepping up to swear Wendy had sex with them and turning everything into a media circus." Sophie didn't mention that she'd thought up the tactic during their drive. She'd told Mandy, who thought it was a brilliant maneuver and volunteered to do the deed. "Of course Wendy didn't know that you've been trying to keep it out of the media. I told you. Mandy totally rocks."

Ethan smiled. The relief on his face lifted her spirits. "Well, now that I've given Brian heart failure," he said, "I'll call back and tell him to relax. What about Hawk?"

"The prick's real name is Floyd," she said, focusing on the information on the screen. Sophie had finally realized what she'd overlooked in his file. Annoyed with herself, she shook her head. "We got you, you dumb ass."

She grabbed her phone again and while waiting for the connection, glanced at Ethan.

He was watching her and frowning. "What?" she said. But then Mandy answered. "He's twenty miles outside Reno," Sophie told her. "The idiot was too lazy to walk inside and pay for his gas with *our* money. He used his credit card."

"Reno's a big place," Mandy said. "Any thoughts on whether he's passing through or sticking around?"

"I think he'll be hanging around," she said. He'd had some petty scrapes over gambling with a fake ID when he was a kid. She should've figured he'd want to go play big shot in a high-stakes poker game at a casino where they'd kiss his ass.

"Have you told Lola yet?"

"No, but I bet he's bragged about something or other that could point us in the right direction. Lola can help us there."

"Or he's cried over being mistreated," Mandy said. "Either way, I say we meet in Reno."

"I agree." She looked over at Ethan, who of course was still watching her. Why hadn't he gone to call his agent? "Let me know after you book your flight. I'm kind of in the middle of nowhere. Driving might be quicker for me. I'll call Lola."

As soon as she hung up Ethan said, "We can check flights out of Billings and see if it's worth backtracking, but I think you're right. We'd be better off driving."

Hell no, she would not let him tag along. She felt guilty enough for the messes she'd created. Yes, they'd avoided one disaster, but they still needed to nail Floyd before he blew all their money. That was where her focus needed to be. Not on Ethan, who had to get himself mentally psyched for the finals.

Couldn't he see they were reaching the end of the road anyway? The thought hurt. She could barely think about it, so why prolong the agony?

"No. *I'll* be better off driving." She gathered her things. On the way out she'd call Lola. "I'd appreciate a ride to pick up a rental car, though. I'll be fine, Ethan." She wanted to kiss him, but better she stay detached. It was for his own good. And for hers. "You, on the other hand, are driving to Las Vegas."

ETHAN GLANCED AT Sophie's boots scuffing up his once-clean dashboard. "Are you going to sulk all the way to Reno?"

"Probably," she huffed. "Yes, I am. You deserve it. What part of *please drop me at the car rental office* did you not understand?"

Sighing, he nodded to himself. Yep, he knew she was a handful. Stubborn. Irritating. A real pain in the ass when she wanted to be. Sophie was also fiercely loyal. Smart as hell. And she was softhearted, which he could never say to her and expect to live.

She looked so damn tired it made his gut knot. He'd bet anything she was beating herself up over failing Lola. Which really wasn't the case. Not that Sophie would listen.

"It wouldn't hurt for you to get some shut-eye," he said. "Nothing's going to change because you're asleep."

"Why don't I drive for a while?"

"No, thanks."

"You are so damn stubborn."

He snorted. "You would know," he said, turning on the radio. He kept it low and found an easy-listening station.

She surprised him by not complaining. Ten minutes later, just as he'd hoped, she was asleep.

He drove for another hour and then stopped at a motel. Even if they slept for six hours, they had time to get to Reno and meet Mandy. The best flight she could get had two stopovers.

After checking them in and paying for the night, he drove them closer to the room. She slept through it all, even when he carried her inside and laid her on the bed. He thought about undressing her but decided that would be a bad idea. Yeah, they'd both better keep their clothes on or they wouldn't get any rest.

He lightly kissed her parted lips, hid the truck keys, just in case, then set the alarms and crawled in beside her.

THE PALACE CASINO AND HOTEL wasn't the snazziest of the large casinos in downtown Reno, but it looked to be the busiest.

A steady stream of mainly older folks led the way into the hotel, where dings and trills of electronic music mostly covered up the piped-in oldies. The purple carpeting and gold chandeliers had probably been daring in their day.

As they headed toward the front desk, Ethan took her hand, and a shiver ran up her spine. Such a simple touch brought so much pleasure. She'd add this moment to her mental scrapbook.

They had to wait in a short line to reach the front desk. But that was okay, because Mandy was still ten minutes away and Sophie wouldn't proceed without her. So she waited with Ethan, who stood right behind her, draping his arms over her shoulders. Her hands were on top of his where they met on her chest.

She'd meant it when she told him to head to Vegas, but she was still glad he was here. The feel of his body warm and comforting. She was a horrible, selfish person. By tomorrow he would have no more grace period. He'd have to leave first thing to check in for the finals.

"I could eat a whole buffet," he said. "Not including the desserts."

"That's the best part." Dammit, now she wanted chocolate.

It was their turn at the desk, and by the time Sophie explained the importance of speaking to the casino manager himself, Mandy had joined them.

When Sophie made the introductions Ethan thanked Mandy for her help in getting the charges dropped. She looked pleased with the recognition, and not surprised by their clasped hands.

It took a few minutes for the manager to arrive, and he was surprisingly young considering his title. Maybe late thirties?

However, the way he sized them up before inviting them into his office said he was going to be a challenge.

His office was small, nothing ornate. Behind him, though, was a door opened just enough for them to see a wall of monitors showing every cash transaction, second by second.

"How can I help you?" Dan Pfizer asked, waving them to the seats in front of his desk.

Mandy took the lead. She showed him her ID, a picture of Floyd, and offered a video of the idiot emptying the company safe.

He stopped her when she brought out the flash drive. "It won't do you any good. Even if I watched him steal from you personally, without a valid warrant there's nothing I can do."

"We're going to call the police," Sophie said. "We already know you have private poker rooms, and that he's in one of them. Probably throwing all our money on the table."

"We saw his Harley close to the valet booth," Mandy added. "So we know he's here."

Pfizer shrugged. "Show me a warrant, and I'll be happy to call the police myself. You have no idea how many times I get asked to do this. Wives wanting their husbands to come home. Vice versa. My hands are tied."

"Actually you might want to reconsider, assuming you want to keep all this quiet. Do you know who this is?" Sophie asked, nodding at Ethan, who didn't even blink at her tactic.

"I'm afraid I don't," Pfizer said. "But I really do have to be—"

"He's the number-two-rated professional bull rider in the world. In fact, I saw a poster out there inviting people to watch the National Finals Rodeo on your HD TVs starting this weekend."

That got his attention. But it wasn't enough.

"Hey, if you can't help us, I understand," Ethan said, shrugging. "Just like you understand why we have to call the police. And since we don't have access to your poker room, I'm pretty sure they'll have no problem meeting us in front of the sports book. That is where people place bets, right?"

Picking up a pen and toying with it, Pfizer frowned.

Sophie could almost hear the wheels turning in his head. "We'll try not to make too big a fuss," she said with a smile.

"By the way," Ethan added, "I saw the odds you have posted out there. I'm the five-to-two favorite. Just out of curiosity, what happens if I get hung up and miss the finals?" His jaw tightened for a split second, and Sophie's heart slid right down to her toes. After that he didn't so much as blink. "Do you guys have to return the money people have already bet?"

And there it was. The look of a man defeated.

"If we could all step outside my office, I'll be with you in a few moments."

They did, and Mr. Pfizer in his neat suit and tie walked hastily toward the poker rooms in the back.

Mandy pulled out her phone and moved a few feet away to give them privacy while she called Lola.

Sophie turned to him. "Why did you say that?"

"Hey, it worked." He looked tired, but he smiled. "Don't tell me you're superstitious."

She didn't buy his act of indifference. He'd been worried about the finals all along. His concern hadn't suddenly disappeared. "No, just a bad-luck charm."

"Come on." He put an arm around her. "Knock it off. What were the chances you'd find Floyd as quickly as you did? That he was still here by the time we showed up? This was a best-case scenario."

No, it wasn't. She and Mandy here taking care of business while Ethan was already in Vegas was a best-case scenario. But she wouldn't argue. He looked so exhausted. Tonight he had to sleep. Tomorrow, if he was still tired, she'd talk him into catching a flight while she took care of his truck.

She dug up a smile from somewhere. "Thank you. Without

you here, I don't know— You've been—" She inhaled deeply, hoping it would help keep her eyes dry.

"I would never have deserted you," he said, and squeezed her hand. "I told you I'd help any way I could."

Even if it had cost him the finals? Oh God. She would've just died. But in truth, he wasn't there yet. If she wanted to be a good person, a friend, she'd let him check in to the hotel alone. Sleep as much as he could without her distracting him.

She nodded. "I think it's okay for you to go right after they bring that moron out. If you don't want to stay here, I'm sure you'll find a room in another hotel."

Ethan frowned. "Don't you mean it's okay for *us* to go?"

Mandy, who'd approached and was now on the phone with the Reno cops, turned around again.

"You need sleep," Sophie said. "What you don't need is any more distractions."

"I'm a grown man. I'm pretty sure I know what I do and don't need."

"I didn't mean it like that. It's just— You know I can't go with you now. I have to go back to Wyoming. Once Floyd's arrested, we won't automatically get back what he's stolen. I can't leave everything to Lola." Most of that was true, but she had trouble meeting his eyes.

"Yo," Mandy said.

Walking toward them, right behind the casino manager, Floyd was staring daggers at her. But the two beefy security guards weren't about to let him make a move.

Pfizer stopped in front of Ethan. Behind him, on the monitor on the wall, Sophie saw a man in a cowboy hat being interviewed. The closed caption said the broadcast was coming from Las Vegas. Her stomach turned over. She literally felt sick. Ethan had claimed he didn't need to be there yet.

"If you'll join us at the security office when you're ready," Pfizer said.

Mandy waited until the guards and Floyd had passed. "The

cops will be here in about five minutes. I'll give them what we've got, and then we can head back."

Sophie nodded. "I'll be right there. Ethan has to get his butt to Vegas."

Mandy held out her hand, and Ethan took it. "Good luck. I bet a hundred bucks on you. So get some damn sleep, would you?"

"I'll try," he said, unsmiling.

Mandy shrugged, met Sophie's eyes, then started walking.

"You promised you'd come with me," he said.

"I did, but that was before all this crap happened." She swallowed hard. "I didn't know Floyd was going to rip us off, or that we'd actually find him. But Jesus, Ethan. You told me you didn't have to be in Vegas yet." She motioned to the monitor. "You should be up there being interviewed. Not here mixed up in my mess." She forced a smile. "Look, we had fun, right? But we knew it would end. Like you said, you know what you need to do, and I need to go home. It's as simple as that."

He stared at her as if she'd just ripped his heart out of his chest. "If it's that simple to you, then yeah, I sure did misunderstand."

Despite the pain that squeezed the life out of her, she nodded. He wasn't thinking clearly. She had to be strong for both of them. "I hope you win the title." She stepped back.

"That's it?" He looked stricken.

"I'll call," she said, wondering if she dared. Wanting so much to tell him all the things she couldn't say on the purple carpet of this damn casino. Like how he'd rocked her world. How she used to think she had it bad for him, but now? She'd never recover.

But he didn't need her as baggage or a distraction. He'd never forgive her if he missed the finals, and she'd never forgive herself, either.

Ethan stared, looking confused and angry. But then he turned and walked past the security office, past the police who were headed in to arrest Floyd.

And he just kept walking.

18

SOPHIE SAT IN front of her small TV and shoved another piece of chocolate into her mouth. She wasn't crazy about television. She didn't even have cable or satellite, but she'd watched most of the National Finals Rodeo. Well, she'd kept track of the bull riders, anyway. And now she was watching reruns of Ethan.

Sometimes it had been nearly impossible to watch. Two riders had suffered serious injuries. If Ethan had gotten hurt, she had no idea what she would've done. Except blame herself for having distracted him at the most important time of his entire career.

But she didn't have to worry about that. Ethan had won his second championship title. Last night had been the buckle ceremony.

She'd thought seriously about calling, just to congratulate him. But she couldn't bring herself to pick up her cell. She'd handled the goodbye at the casino so badly. It still stung.

She should've at least offered to drive his truck back to Wyoming. Drop him at the airport first. Sophie had replayed her words and the expression on his face a thousand times in the past two weeks. She'd sounded so cold. How he must hate her.

Seeing the cowboy being interviewed on the monitor had done something to her. Panic had taken over. And she knew if she'd given herself an inch, she would've done the thing she wanted to do instead of doing what was honorable. Intellectually she realized it wasn't completely her fault that he'd driven her to Reno when he should've gone to Las Vegas. She'd begged him to take her to a car rental office. But he'd insisted. And she hadn't fought him hard enough because she'd been thrilled he'd stayed with her.

Someone knocked at the apartment door. She grabbed something to throw at it. Then stared at the bag in her hand. What the hell was she thinking? Not the chocolate. That would make everything worse.

Another knock. It was either Lola or Mandy, most likely Lola. Mandy knew how to buy a clue.

"Go away," Sophie yelled loud enough to be heard by half the residents in the apartment complex.

"Not gonna happen."

"Goddammit, Lola," Sophie muttered, and got off the couch. She opened the door and growled at her cousin.

Lola walked right in, uninvited, as usual. She surveyed Sophie's mess after three days of hibernation. Every glass she owned was sitting out somewhere.

Finally Lola eyed Sophie's baggy gray sweats and the sock with a hole over the big toe. "You look like shit."

"Should've saved yourself the trip. I could've told you that on the phone." Sophie plopped back down on the couch. Wincing, she lifted her butt and moved the bag of chocolate out of the way. "What do you want?"

"Get up and take a shower, then put on something nice. We're going out."

Sophie snorted a laugh. "Are you high?"

"Come on, Soph." Lola's gaze shifted briefly to the TV. "You can't keep moping."

"Yes, I can. Except I'm not moping."

Lola sighed. "Please get up and get ready. Mandy is meeting us at the—"

"Nice try. Mandy knows better. Yet she's only known me for a fraction of the time you have. Explain that." Sophie stretched her neck back. She'd stayed away from the gym too long. Tomorrow she'd get herself moving.

"The Reno police called. They found the brooch at a pawnshop."

Sophie shook her head. Anyone could tell the piece was an antique and too valuable to sell to a pawnbroker. Anyone but Floyd. "How much did he get for it? Did they tell you?"

"No. I didn't ask. I want this whole thing over with and I never want to hear his name again."

Sophie gave her a sympathetic nod. "I'm glad they recovered the brooch."

"You know what pisses me off, Sophie?"

"I'm coming in to work tomorrow. I'll be my old cheery self. Promise."

"That's not what I'm upset about." She sat at the edge of the couch. "Ethan is a really good man, and you're tossing him away. Do you have any idea what I'd do to find someone like him? What most single women would do? You've never been a quitter. I've always admired that about you."

Sophie had to look away. She wasn't good at hiding her emotions lately. "Not now. Okay, Lola?"

Her cousin sighed. "Please get dressed and come out. Would you do that for me?"

"I can't. I'm sorry."

Shrugging, Lola stood. "You can't say I didn't try."

Sophie watched sideways until Lola opened the door. She would've felt worse if she thought her cousin really wanted a drinking buddy tonight. Lola was only trying to cheer her up.

Sophie turned her head. Lola had left. Why hadn't she closed the damn door?

Muttering a curse, she pushed to her feet.

Ethan appeared in the doorway. He looked at Sophie, glanced around the apartment and then looked at her again and laughed.

Her mouth wouldn't work. When it finally did, she said, "I'm going to kill her."

"Ah, right. She asked me to remind you that she tried."

"I'm still going to kill her. Stay right there." She skirted the coffee table, thought about taking some glasses and empty bags with her, but what was the point? "Right there," she repeated before disappearing into her bathroom.

She washed her face, brushed her hair and teeth in record time, then splurged with some mascara and scented body cream. She exchanged the sweatpants for jeans. Thank God she'd taken a shower earlier.

When she returned to the living room, plastic trash bag in hand, the door was closed and Ethan was sitting on the couch, staring at the TV. He hadn't pushed her crap to the side. He'd just made himself comfortable.

He looked up at her and smiled.

She pointed at the door. "I told you to stay there."

"You really have to quit being so damn bossy."

"I doubt that's going to stop," she said, sighing, and picked up empty cookie packages, dropping them into the trash bag. She hated feeling this awkward with him.

"I know," he said, his quiet tone making her look up. He nodded at the TV. "You've been watching the finals."

"Oh." She cleared her throat. "Congratulations, by the way." Should she give him a quick kiss or maybe a hug? A kiss wouldn't be out of line. She leaned over and he pulled her onto his lap.

Sophie let out a startled gasp.

"Is this okay?" he asked, uncertainty in his blue eyes.

"Uh-huh."

"I want to explain why I didn't call."

"You don't have to. I never expected you to—"

"Can you please just be quiet for a few minutes?"

She pressed her lips together and jerked a nod.

Ethan gave a short laugh. "At first I was really mad. And

then I started thinking about the moment everything had gone sideways with us at the casino. I figured out you weren't trying to get rid of me but get me to Vegas. That was just before the first round.

"I was going to call then. Hash things out. But I knew the moment I heard your voice I'd lose my focus. And I couldn't afford to do that. I owed it to both of us to be on my game."

Sophie blinked. *Us?* A quiver started in her tummy. Like the feeling she'd gotten when she saw him wearing a helmet that first round. He'd worn it until the very end. She'd told herself he was doing it for her and then realized that was the fifteen-year-old inside her who still believed in fairy tales.

"Sophie..." He was watching her, waiting for her to look into his eyes. "Honey, I know you were trying to help get me to finals because you knew how important it was to me. But something had happened that shifted my priorities."

"Okay," she said. "What?"

"You."

"Me? How?"

"By believing in me. When you said my fans would believe me over Wendy, you were probably right. They'd rally around me. But they don't really know me. They just wouldn't want to believe their rodeo idol could be a thief. But you believed in *me*."

"Well, of course..."

"Look, you're a beautiful, capable woman who's built a business and a nice life. And I suspect you got here mainly by yourself. But you don't have to go a hundred miles an hour all the time. You don't have anything to prove. Now, how about believing in yourself, Sophie?"

Her mouth was so dry. Eleven years ago she'd been cowed and humiliated, and she'd been running so fast, so hard ever since to never be in a situation like that again. To be in control at all times. But she hadn't always succeeded. "May I speak now?"

"Go ahead."

"First of all, I'm obviously not all that capable, because I wasn't the one who helped you. It was Mandy. I couldn't even—"

"All right. Stop." He shook his head.

"What? Shouldn't I be able to have my say?"

"You can't expect me to sit here and listen to this crap. Remember, you're talking about someone I love."

The air left her lungs. "You can't love me."

Ethan's eyes blazed. He clearly did not like that response.

"I'm not saying I'm not lovable. I just meant, you don't really know me. You can't. Not after only four days."

He said nothing, just looked at her with a hint of sadness. "Sophie, I know all the things that matter about you. I promise you that. Even if it takes a year, two years, whatever it takes to prove it to you, I'm going to do that. I can be stubborn myself."

She held back a sob and dashed a tear away with impatience. "You're right."

"I am?" He smiled, looking so boyishly delighted, she laughed.

"I think you do know me. Maybe better than I do." She wasn't ready to explain that she had been trying to prove something she hadn't realized until now. She'd needed to feel she deserved the small kindness he'd shown her. Her teenage years had been so damn lonely.

He put his arms around her and pulled her back against him.

That alone made her want to cry as she curled up in his lap. She'd missed his arms so much.

"I owe you a congratulatory kiss." She turned her face, and their lips touched. He kissed her softly, eyes open. She kissed him back and heard the bag of candy scrunch. Now, how could she not love a man who'd seen her mess of an apartment, the mess of her life, and hadn't run in the other direction?

"Dammit, Ethan," she murmured against his lips.

"What?"

"I love you, too."

His smile could've lit the room. "With the finals money, I'm going ahead with the construction of the rodeo camp. And there's plenty of space for you to set up your martial arts studio. If you want to."

She kissed him again, so hard they both nearly fell off the couch. And when she finally caught her breath, she said, "I know the important parts about you, too, Ethan Styles. But it'll be fun to explore the rest."

"I'd like to do a little exploring myself." He stood with her still in his arms. "I'm guessing you have a bedroom somewhere in here."

Sophie grinned. She might not be the best bounty hunter in the world, but she'd set out to get her man and ended up with the man of her dreams. "You can have me anywhere, cowboy."

* * * * *

A Cowboy Returns

Kelli Ireland

Kelli Ireland spent a decade as a name on a door in corporate America. Unexpectedly liberated by Fate's sense of humor, she chose to carpe the diem and pursue her passion for writing. A fan of happily-ever-afters, she found she loved being the puppet master for the most unlikely couples. Seeing them through the best and worst of each other while helping them survive the joys and disasters of falling in love? Best. Thing. Ever. Visit Kelli's website at kelliireland.com.

Books by Kelli Ireland

Pleasure Before Business

Stripped Down
Wound Up
Pulled Under

All backlist available in ebook format.

Visit the Author Profile page at millsandboon.com.au for more titles.

Dear Reader,

It's with absolute pleasure I am able to introduce you to Harding County, New Mexico. It's a land of grassy plains that give themselves up to the beauty of the Sangre de Christo Mountains, a range that is in some places sparse and in others the most beautiful country you've ever seen.

When his father passes away, Elijah, the oldest of the three Covington boys, comes home after fourteen years away. He's reunited with the beautiful Reagan Matthews, the woman he loved and left behind—the only woman he's *ever* loved. And it's an emotional, passionate, thoroughly satisfying ride!

Having lived on a ranch myself in New Mexico after marrying my very own cowboy, I have to tell you that there are a few things in each of the Covington books that I've experienced firsthand, but I'm not telling which ones. Rest assured that every character and every situation is entirely a product of my imagination, though.

The one thing I *can* tell you with certainty? New Mexico's cowboys are every single bit as sexy as *anything* Texas has turned out.

Happy reading,

Kelli

This book is for Vivian Arend,
one of the absolute best mentors a writer could
ever hope to find.

1

ELIJAH COVINGTON NEVER thought he'd find religion on a commuter flight, but when the tiny plane plummeted the last fifty feet to the runway, he prayed. Little more than a closed-cockpit crop duster, the little plane skipped down the cracked asphalt runway hard enough to compress his spine. He would have given anything for the firm's corporate jet and his chiropractor right about then.

Of course, he should probably just be grateful they weren't landing on a dirt strip. They'd had to circle several times while the neighboring rancher retrieved his cows from the runway. That had been bad enough.

The flight attendant made an inane joke at the pilot's expense, but Eli only half listened. Thumbing his smartphone on, he waited for a signal. His service indicator showed a single bar. *A single bar.*

"I'm in hell," he muttered, but that wasn't true. Hell undoubtedly had better cell service.

Scrolling through emails, he ignored the flight attendant's glare. He might have been obligated to come home to manage the distribution of his father's estate, but that didn't require he cut himself off from civilization entirely. With any luck, he could get to the ranch, go through the estate paperwork, file the will and be gone within the week. Had his old man been remotely organized, this could have been done by mail. And had the estate been reasonably solvent, they could have hired someone to manage the distributions altogether. No doubt, there wouldn't be any money.

That had to be why his youngest brother, Tyson, had emailed and asked him to come home and handle estate "issues." Otherwise? They never would have called him home. He'd have just received whatever his old man left him via certified mail.

Eli glanced out the window at the desert landscape. New Mexico always looked caught between centuries and droughts. The landscape was as foreign to him as Austin would be to his brothers. Here in Tucumcari, the wide plateau created a backdrop decorated with cedar shrubs, barbed wire fences and black grama grass. Cows outnumbered people twenty to one, and if you didn't drive a pickup, you'd better be riding a horse.

The only beef Eli cared about was braised, his vehicle was an Audi R8 and the only horses that mattered were under the hood.

He'd always been the piece that didn't fit this particular puzzle.

Elijah snorted and shook his head, pulling his small travel bag out from under his seat. *Might as well get this over with.*

Fifteen minutes later he was standing beside a tiny Ford Fiesta with a dented fender, an AM/FM radio and questionable air-conditioning. It was the better of the two cars available at the only car rental service in town.

"I'm in hell," he repeated, struggling against a temper he'd all but mastered over the past fourteen years.

Fourteen years.

He'd been gone almost as long as he'd lived here.

Peeling off his Canali suit jacket, he tossed it across the passenger seat before folding himself behind the wheel. A generous layer of grit on the rubber floor mat ground under his heel. The little car shimmied as the four-cylinder engine sputtered and choked before it caught and, obviously under duress, whined to life.

The rental attendant tipped the brim of his hat in salute and wandered inside the tiny office as Eli drove away. He hadn't remembered Elijah, or had pretended not to as a matter of convenience to avoid unnecessary chitchat. Small towns worked that way. You were either on the inside or exiled for life.

The next few days would be a lot of the same. Tight-knit communities were very unforgiving when one of their own escaped, and his leaving *had* been an escape. As well loved as his father had been, everyone saw his departure as a first-rate betrayal—oldest son to old man.

Elijah refused to feel guilty for wanting a different life, a *better* life. He had it now and hadn't asked for handouts along the way. He'd earned his place, and he wasn't sorry that place wasn't here. With one exception…

Caught up in his own thoughts, he ran one of the two traffic lights in town.

An extended-cab four-wheel-drive pickup swerved, brakes chattering and tires squealing. It hit the curb, skipping up and over with a hard bounce before coming to rest in the hedges in front of the Blue Swallow motel.

Heart lodged in his throat, Eli shut the little car down and left it in the middle of the road, racing toward the truck. He couldn't see anyone moving inside. Then a black-and-white head popped up and looked out the rear window.

A dog.

If anything, the dog seemed exhilarated at the wild ride, his feathery tail wagging with obvious enthusiasm.

Eli reached the driver's side and found a cowboy-hatted individual slumped forward, forehead against the steering wheel, arms lax, hands resting next to trim thighs. *A woman.* He reached for the truck door. The dog objected, going from excited to back-the-hell-off between breaths. The animal crossed his owner and bared his teeth in a feral growl, blatantly daring Eli to open the door.

Not interested in losing any body parts, Eli knocked on the window hard enough to rouse the woman.

She rolled her head to the side, green eyes narrowed in an impressive glare. The moment those eyes focused on Eli, they flared with almost-comedic alarm. Almost.

Because his did the same thing.

Reagan Armstrong.

The one person he'd intended to avoid altogether stared at him in utter disbelief. Her mouth hung open in shock. She didn't move.

History rose up between them, an invisible, insurmountable wall of differences that stole every word that might have allayed old hurts or bridged the gap of time to allow them to communicate. At least while he was here.

Leaning one arm against the truck's door frame, Eli gave a small jerk of his chin. "Reagan? Lower your window."

She mouthed something that, if it matched the look in her eyes, was seriously foul.

He was prepared for that. What he wasn't prepared for was for her to shove the door open. The mirror folded as it nailed his shoulder. Then the hot metal of the door's edge slammed into his sternum hard enough he wasn't sure if he'd been burned or if the bone had cracked or both.

She spoke before her boots hit the dirt, her voice as smooth as the truck's diesel engine. "Well, well. If it isn't Elijah Covington. Or would that be Mr. Covington, Esquire, since you're an Austin attorney now? Just what you always wanted—bigger, better and worlds away from here—so I suppose congratulations would be appropriate. I mean, you made it out, made your way and managed to break your word, all in one impressive feat."

His brows drew together. "What are you talking about, 'break my word'?"

"You said you'd come home. Promised, in fact. But I'd be

willing to bet you hit the county line at a dead run and never thought about us again. Good on you, Esquire." The last was offered with near indifference or would have been if she hadn't begun to clap slowly for emphasis.

It was that last action that betrayed her, because, despite their fourteen years apart, Eli knew her.

The aged and seasoned hurt that lurked beneath the surface of her words sliced through his conscience with cold efficiency. He'd wanted her to come with him, but she'd made it clear her life was here. And his life could never be here.

"You knew we wanted different things. I was never going to fit in here. Not like you did. My dad. My brothers. Leaving was my only option. And I didn't just skip out on you." Running his hands through his hair, he huffed out a heavy breath. "Look, Reagan," he started, and then the wind shifted, carrying her smell to him, all fresh-cut hay and sunshine on warm skin.

Overwhelmed with sensory memories, his gaze homed in on lips that parted in almost curious shock. And just like that, she was the girl he'd loved. And yet, with time and distance, she had somehow evolved into more.

She'd always been his sun, chasing away the shadows he hadn't been able to banish himself. Unwelcome memories of yesteryear hovered at the fringes of his consciousness. He needed to touch her, needed the tenderness he'd always found waiting in her.

He closed the distance between them. His lips closed over hers and he pulled her into his embrace. The shock of cinnamon on his tongue told him she still loved Big Red gum, and the flavor transferred between them. Her lips were soft, pliable and so familiar his heart ached with the memories of a thousand and more shared moments. Being here, in New Mexico, didn't hurt so much with her in his arms.

He wasn't only "Covington's oldest boy." He wasn't burdened with the unshakable disappointment his father had found in him.

He wasn't a failure of an older brother. He was Eli. Just Eli. And he could survive that.

His troubles became manageable as their tongues touched, tentative for the briefest moment. Then he took over the kiss. Dominating the moment, he took comfort in her nearness and yelped like a scolded pup when she bit his lip. Hard.

Parking both hands on his chest, she shoved and shouted, "What in the Sam Hill are you doing?" Eyes wild, she dragged a hand over her mouth. "You don't waltz into town after fourteen years, run me off the road and then… You don't… You can't kiss me like…like…you *ass*!"

"'Ass'? I kiss you and you call me an *ass*?" Eli's lips thinned as his once-infamous temper, second only to hers and all but squashed under years of educational and professional training, raced forward like a laser-guided missile, target locked, impact imminent. "I'm going to point out the obvious here, Reagan. You kissed me, too."

"I didn't… That is… No. There was no mutual… No, I didn't!" Chest heaving, she drove a finger into his chest. "Why are you even here? The funeral was two freaking weeks ago. You should've been here *then.* But you show up now, expecting everyone to bend to your expectations. That's so typical, Eli. It's always been the way you operate," she snapped, backing up until she bumped into her truck. She hopped in, never taking her eyes off him. "You haven't changed at all. You're still smart as shit when it comes to business and dumb as dirt when it comes to people."

"Hey," he objected, but she powered on without pause.

"You're too late to do any good, Eli, but, then, you taught me what to expect a long time ago. I'd truly thought you'd show for the funeral, though. For your blood." She looked him up and down with a critical eye as she delivered the blow he should've anticipated but never saw coming. "I might have been your girlfriend once, but Cade and Tyson are your brothers, Eli. They *needed* you." Her gaze met his, anger turning the normally moss green color of her eyes deep and vibrant. "They needed you here to help them manage the mess your old man left behind, but you clearly couldn't put your high-society life aside for a few days to come home and help them out of the bind they're in. You never could be bothered. Not for them. Not for anyone."

She moved to slam the door, but he grabbed it, stepping close. "That's why I'm here now—to probate my father's estate. But that's irrelevant. You don't get to sit there in your shiny truck, that captain's chair your personal throne, and pass judgment on me, Armstrong."

Jerking away as if struck, she stared at him with wide eyes. "It hasn't been 'Armstrong' for eight years. It's Matthews. And to you? *Dr.* Matthews. Nothing less, and never, ever anything more. Now let go of the door, Eli."

His hand fell away from the truck.

She'd married Luke Matthews. He'd had no idea.

The reality he'd likely see her and Luke together while in town made Eli's stomach lurch up his throat until he seriously wondered if he might puke. Wouldn't that be awesome.

Then there was the fact she was a doctor. From the size of her truck and the type of work boxes, he didn't have to ask what kind. A vet. She'd always wanted to be a large-animal vet.

He cleared his throat once, then twice, before he managed to croak, "Great. Happy for you."

Slamming the truck door shut, she made it a point to click the locks down. Couldn't get much clearer than that.

Her dog whined loud enough for Eli to hear the cry over the soft rumble of the truck's engine. Reagan absently soothed the animal, her hand shaking.

Eli could totally relate. Years in court had trained him to present a totally calm and controlled exterior under extreme pressure. That didn't mean his insides weren't rattling, though. The emotions buffering him now were both uncomfortable and unrecognizable. But there was no point examining them too closely. This visit didn't center around assuaging years of curiosity and doubt; nor did it have anything to do with healing old hurts. It was about finally closing this part of his life. Permanently.

Swallowing his anger and determined to keep things civil, he motioned for her to roll her window down.

Green eyes that had always before met his with open trust and absolute passion narrowed and glared. She punctuated the stare with a one-fingered salute. Without waiting for him to move, she slammed the truck into Reverse and punched the accelerator.

He leaped aside with a shouted curse.

The truck surged off the curb, suspension squeaking in protest. She shifted the truck into gear and, leaning on the accelerator, she rapidly put distance between them.

The dog, its tail still wagging, watched him with open curiosity thought the rear window.

Closing his eyes, Eli parked his fists on his hips and let his chin fall to his chest.

What the hell am I doing here?

"Settling an old debt," he answered quietly. He was here to make sure his brothers were okay. Yet according to Reagan, he was already too late for that.

Trying to wipe the unforgettable taste of her off his lips, he crossed the still-vacant street and crammed himself into the compact car before making a left and heading up Highway 54.

He was going to get this done and get gone. That would spare everyone involved any further awkwardness. Then he'd return to Austin, to the career he excelled at and the life he'd carved out for himself.

And Reagan was right. He wouldn't look back.

REAGAN MATTHEWS MUSCLED her heavy-duty truck around the corner and shot down the highway as hard and fast as the GMC would go. She had to put distance between herself and that... that...*man.*

But it wasn't just the man—it was the memories. She'd tried

to put up a good front with Eli, to come across as both indifferent and controlled. Even *she* knew she'd botched it up and let emotion get the best of her. The apathy she'd dug for had been, at best, a shaky mirage. A strong gust of wind would have swept the bulk of it away, a million seeds of discontent that simply wanted answers.

But then he'd kissed her.

If her apathy hadn't stood a chance against a simple breeze, it couldn't hold out hope for survival when faced with the force of nature that *was* Elijah Covington.

He'd been the sole shareholder of her heart, the one thing she was sure she couldn't live without. All those days spent at the river, just the two of them listening to music, talking, watching the sunset against the Sangre de Cristo Mountains. Then there were the nights. Hours spent stargazing and more hours spent discovering each other, learning the touches that elicited the most pleasure, the sensitive spots to kiss softly, the right time to love gently and the time to let it all go and be as wild and free as the world around them.

Then he'd left.

So many years she'd held out hope he'd come back. She'd been the talk of the town for so long, first with shared hope, then pity and then the fool who simply couldn't let go of a man long gone. She'd never stopped loving him. She'd just stopped looking for him.

Reagan traced her numb lips with trembling fingers. Her chest had constricted to the point she couldn't draw even half a breath. But her heart… She rubbed her sternum. Her heart hadn't hurt this bad in years, and wasn't that a testament to the way she'd lived her life.

She allowed reality to sink in, accepting that Eli'd had his arms around her again, and it had felt as familiar as it did foreign. A broken sob ripped out of her chest. She'd spent the past fourteen years trying not to drown in heartache and regrets. Then he showed up and, with a single kiss, pulled her under those dark emotional waters again. He acted as if it had meant as little to him as if he were ordering a cup of coffee to go.

When she'd broken away, she'd begun to sink.

Taking the first dirt road she came to, she slid to a stop, dust billowing around her. She rested her head on the steering wheel and rolled her forehead back and forth, trying to force her roiling thoughts to fall into place.

She'd have to repair the Blue Swallow's landscaping. But the damage *really* hadn't been her fault. Most people reacted poorly when a ghost ran them off the road.

Elijah Covington.

"Not a ghost," she said, voice hoarse. "Just a memory. A… mistake."

But that wasn't true, either. Loving him had never been a mistake. Holding on to the faith he'd figure out he belonged here, too? That she was the one for him? Those were her major screwups, the two things that had given him the power to thoroughly and effectively decimate her heart.

Swiping her cowboy hat off, she cursed as she rewound her hair and tucked it under the hat. "It's been fourteen years now, Matthews. You've moved on. You have a career and a life story, neither of which include him."

She didn't have much of a life at the moment, though. What she had were long, backbreaking days and endless, lonely nights.

In the passenger seat, her dog, Brisket, whined.

"It's fine. I'm fine." Untucking her shirt, she wiped the sweat—*not* tears—off her face.

The iPad alarm sounded. She glanced at the screen with a physical wince. Almost nine. She was due at the Jensen place in a little less than an hour to draw up health papers on their steers before they shipped the yearlings to the livestock auction in nearby Dalhart, Texas.

Scrubbing her hands over her face, she forced a deep breath. All right. Eli had come home. So what? He was fast-flowing water under the charred remnants of a bridge burned long ago.

She could avoid him for however long he was here. And knowing him, it would only be temporary. He had run before; he would run again. That was what he was good at, after all.

Shifting the truck into Reverse, she backed out onto the highway as a faded red car started up the two-lane highway from the boulevard. Slow but sure, the car closed in on her. The driver was hunched over the wheel as if he were nothing but an origami miniature of a large man. Dark hair blew in the breeze from the open window. Large hands wrung the steering wheel. If the poor thing had been alive, he'd have killed it a thousand times over.

Eli.

Reagan punched the accelerator. Her tires chirped on the hot asphalt before gaining hold. The truck belched and then roared to life. She watched in the rearview mirror as the little red car disappeared in a dense cloud of diesel exhaust.

The truck's tires slipped off the highway shoulder and into soft sand, forcing her attention to the road. Overcorrecting, she crossed into the opposite lane before muscling the truck onto her side of the road again.

Heat burned up her neck and settled on her cheeks. *Freaking wonderful, Matthews. Exactly the kind of impression you wanted to leave him with.* Then she grinned. She'd just filled the guy's car with a solid layer of diesel exhaust. Sure, she'd almost wrecked her truck.

It was totally worth it.

2

THREE HOURS LATER, Reagan wiped the sweat from her brow with a grungy bandana. “Is it me or is it about a hundred and ten out here today?”

“Only supposed to be about ninety.” Tyson Covington, youngest of the three Covington brothers, tipped the brim of his hat up and leaned on the saddle horn to grin down at her. “I’m no expert in female anatomy, but I’d say you’re far too young for hot flashes, Doc.”

She barked out a laugh. “Not an expert in female anatomy, huh? The only person in Harding County who’s seen more action than you, Ty, is the gynecologist, and that’s only because he’s been in practice longer than you’ve been alive.”

Ty’s grin widened. “I suppose I’ll just have to work harder to catch up then, won’t I?”

Her snort was answer enough. Turning back to the chute, she called out, “Push ’em through, gentlemen.”

“You heard Doc Matthews,” Ty shouted to the other cowboys. “Let’s get the first truck backed up and help the Jensens make a little money.” He let out a sharp whistle as he wheeled his horse around and pushed his way into the thick of things.

She grabbed her pad and jotted down a couple of notes as

the semi parked, trailer gate open to the chute. The herd looked pretty good. A few were underweight, but calves sometimes lost a little mass to stress when they were gathered and penned. They'd also lose a bit of water weight when they shipped, but it would be easy to replace that. Picking up her vaccine gun, she climbed up the pipe panel and started inoculating the animals as they moved by.

Once the first group of animals were loaded, they began sorting the second pen. Bawling protests decorated the dusty air. Cowboys called to each other as they moved the calves and pushed the current bunch down the chute, peeling off those Reagan indicated she wanted to assess a little closer. One truck driver after another climbed around shipping trailers like monkeys, opening and closing interior gates to make sure the weight distribution of the oncoming cattle was beneficial for the haul to the sale ring.

A larger yearling turned back. Nose high, the whites of his eyes showed as he tried to work his way against the flow.

Reagan scanned the corral. "Brisket!"

A blue merle body darted between the men and their horses, arrowing toward her. The Border collie stopped twenty feet away, crouched and ready, focused on her as he waited for instruction. With a short whistle and pointed finger toward the offender, she set him loose.

The dog wove through the masses. Reaching the bottleneck, he started nipping with a strike-retreat-strike approach, turning the steer around and driving the herd forward with unparalleled efficiency.

It took a couple more hours to sort the remaining calves, and Reagan was officially exhausted by the time they finished. Carol Jensen approached her with a tall glass of tea, a barbecue sandwich wrapped in waxed paper, and a genuine smile. Such a nice person, and her husband was much the same.

Accepting the drink first, Reagan sighed. "Thanks, Carol." "What was the total count?"

"We vaccinated and loaded 812 today. I held back a handful that weren't ready or seemed a little sickly to ship to market. The other cows are ready to be driven to the bull pasture for breeding. Overall, with price-per-pound holding steady at $212 a hundredweight? Should be a very profitable day."

"Glad to hear it." Reaching into her pocket, Carol pulled out a second sandwich. "Brisket around?"

Reagan smiled and shook her head as the dog trotted up and sat at the other woman's feet. "No wonder he likes to visit you."

"He works hard enough he should probably be paid day wages."

"We talked about it, but he decided long ago that self-employment taxes suck. Besides, I'm pretty sure he prefers to be paid with barbecue."

In apparent agreement, Brisket took his sandwich and sprinted across the arena. He dropped down in the shade of the barn and began ripping off the waxed paper to get to the treat, his tail thumping a happy beat.

Ty sauntered over, his horse's reins draped loosely over his shoulder. The giant quarter horse followed along, appearing to be more docile pet than high-dollar cutting horse. Ty smiled and winked, the picture of innocence. "You have another sandwich for a starving man, Mrs. Jensen?"

"You're a menace to the female population," Carol said primly. Still, she started to head for the house. "I'll bring you a couple sandwiches. You want tea or lemonade?"

"Whatever you have is fine. I'd get it myself, but I'm too dirty to do much more than strip down and wash in the stock tank."

Reagan hid her grin when Carol blushed.

Flustered, the woman fled.

"You're a nuisance, Ty." Reagan finished her sandwich and leaned against the corral fence, one boot heel hung on a rail.

"I'm harmless," he countered, pulling his hat off and shaking out light brown hair darkened with sweat.

"You're as harmless as a bad case of ringworm. Treatable, but still a pain in the ass."

Denim-blue eyes sparkled with mischief. "Treatable, am I? Come over tonight and I'll play patient to your doctor."

Reagan pulled her vaccine gun out, the massive needle glinting in the bright sunlight. "Why wait? Drop your drawers, and I'll take care of you right this minute."

Ty blanched. "Not exactly the kind of action I had in mind if my pants came off."

One corner of her mouth curled up. "Chicken shit."

"Hey, if you weren't so hot, I wouldn't feel compelled to flirt."

This time she laughed. "Ty, you'd flirt with an octogenarian if she was the only woman around. You can't help yourself."

His horse nosed him, shoving him toward her a step. "You know it's all in fun."

She waggled the vaccine gun at him and fought the urge to smile. "Only because my gun's bigger."

"That's an unfair comparison. You've never seen my gun."

"No offense, but I'm not interested in your caliber." Her stomach tightened at the memory of just what caliber she had once been *very* interested in—the same caliber that forced her off the road only hours earlier. Keeping busy had helped her forget him, but now her mind raced.

Chewing her bottom lip, she glanced at Ty. "Today, in town, I…well, I was run off the road by…"

He scrutinized her, and Reagan wondered what he saw. When he sobered, she knew. The barbecue sandwich that had cut through hunger pangs only moments ago now sat like a lead cannonball in her stomach. She swallowed convulsively. It took a minute to work the question around the emotion lodged in her throat. "What's he doing here, Ty?"

Dark brows winged down and he shoved sunglasses on to cover his eyes. "I asked Eli to come home for this thing involving Dad."

Her chin snapped around. "Doesn't the fact you had to *ask* him to come home tell you where he stands in all of this?"

"He should be here, Reagan. It's his mess and his legacy as much as it is ours." Full lips thinned. "Cade and I are going to need his help to sort out the mess Dad left us in. Our best chance at saving the ranch involves Eli...and you."

The blood drained from her face at being paired, even loosely, in a sentence with Eli. "You can't be sure your herd's got Shipping Fever until the lab results come back and I get out there and look at the steer we drew from."

"I grew up around this stuff. I know what it is." He snorted and shook his head, hooking one arm through the pipe panel. "It's going to ruin Dad's perfect reputation."

"He wasn't perfect," she said softly, remembering how Mr. Covington had always been so cold and rigid in his expectations of Eli. Those expectations had succeeded in driving Eli away for good, and she'd never forgive the old man for it.

Carol's return with two sandwiches and a giant glass of lemonade interrupted the conversation. She'd also brought Ty cookies. "I thought you might want something sweet."

Reagan fought the urge to steal a cookie.

As if the conversation hadn't been deadly serious only moments before, Ty looked at the older woman and grinned wide enough to reveal a single dimple. "You're an angel, Mrs. Jensen. You ever get tired of Mr. Jensen, you pack up and we'll run away together."

She flushed prettily. "You're incorrigible, Ty."

"Can't blame a man for being attracted to a pretty woman... Carol."

Reagan only half listened as Ty bantered with Carol and then a few of the day workers as he ate his sandwiches. She offered absent, one-word answers when someone said something directly to her, but she couldn't manage to tease and joke in return.

"Hey."

She glanced up to find her and Ty alone again. Coughing, she nodded. "Yeah."

Ty ran a hand around the nape of his neck. "I probably should have warned you Eli was coming home."

She winced at his name.

"I just wasn't sure how to bring it up."

She waved a hand in dismissal, but the words that matched the gesture wouldn't come. Her chest was too tight. Shrouded in panic, she pushed off the fence. It had been years since this had happened, since she'd given in to the devastating loss that had changed the course of her life and affected every aspect of it, from what she'd taken in school to five years of marriage.

A hard gasp escaped her at the same time large hands spun her around. She said the only thing she could say to him. "Keep him away from me, Ty."

"You want the Bar C to use Doc Hollinsworth? I don't want to, but if you ask, I'll do it."

She swallowed convulsively. He was offering her a shameless out. All she had to do was seize it.

"You know we're in trouble," he continued. "None of us are sure just how bad it's going to get, but I'll wager my assless chaps it's going to get ugly. We've got to have a vet on call. You know that, too. I can't imagine Eli's going to keep his share of the cows, even if they survive. Probably ship them off as soon as we can prove they aren't infected. If that's the case, I can try to put off getting the shipping papers until after Eli's gone, maybe handle that part myself—me or Cade, anyway—and just send Eli the check."

She straightened. "Call me when you're ready. Hollinsworth isn't half the man I am."

Ty grinned, but it didn't lessen the tight lines at the corners of his eyes or the crease between his brows. "Hell, Reagan, not many of us are." Curling a finger under her chin, he nudged her face up. "You've managed really well."

Her laugh was bitter. "Survival isn't admirable, Ty. It's the only option they ever left me with, him and Luke."

"Luke didn't die on you on purpose."

She nodded, swiping viciously at the tears that fell for the loss of each man. "He might not have done it on purpose, but gone is gone. The only difference between Luke and Eli?" Backing away from Ty, she didn't bother to try to hide her misery. "Luke didn't have a choice. Eli did. But in the end? They both left me."

Spinning on her heel, she called hoarsely for Brisket. The dog leaped into the truck bed, and she didn't try to coax him into the cab.

Vaulting herself into the seat behind the wheel, she cranked the engine and took off, pretending not to hear Ty calling her name.

There was nothing left to say.

3

ELI MADE THE 120-mile drive to the Clayton County courthouse in average time considering his rental car was powered by little more than a two-stroke lawn-mower engine.

His first order of business was to determine whether or not anything had been filed on his old man's behalf or—worse—against the estate. Nothing showed up, so he went through the rest of the probate process.

Privately, he was grateful for the mundane tasks. They kept his mind busy, kept him from thinking too much. He made the appropriate inquiries at the courthouse and filed the required documents as the estate's representative. Then he'd gone to the newspaper to arrange for the mandatory ads to run in the classifieds. That done, he started for the ranch.

Less than ten miles from the courthouse, he was the only car on the highway. No surprise. The locals would consider traffic heavy if they passed a dozen cars. He was as far from Austin's bumper-to-bumper lifestyle as he could get. Considering the clown car and his surreal surroundings, it was as if he'd been fired from civilization's cannon into the wilds of wide-open space. Every instinct he had screamed the landing was going to suck. Bad.

The memory of Reagan—her summertime smell, her cinnamon taste, her feminine strength, her lean body—had haunted him all morning.

She'd always been at the heart of the community. It made sense, then, that she'd married the community's son.

Everyone loved Luke. He was the kind who stopped to help a stranded motorist and not only fixed their car but topped off their gas and gave them food and a fresh set of directions before sending them on their way. Always neighborly, he'd be the first to volunteer for day work during shipping season. He'd be the last to leave. As a kid, every son had been compared to Luke—his dad had told him several times he would have preferred Luke as a son over him any day. Even Reagan's mother had expressed her opinion, pushing her daughter toward Saint Luke—and away from Eli. She must have been overjoyed when Reagan married the right man.

Eli would put money on it the guy had evolved to the ultimate cowboy, the type of man every boy wanted to grow up to be. He and Eli had always been casual friends, but at the moment? Eli hated every damn cell in the man's body.

Rolling the car window down, he breathed in the dry air. New Mexico's unpopulated roads and wide-open spaces never failed to press their beauty on him without apology—right before they reminded him how insignificant he was.

He'd never been able to accomplish enough to stand out as his own man, always living in his father's shadow. Never Elijah Covington, but always Max Covington's boy. And even in that, the only thing that set him apart was that he was the eldest of the three. His greatest distinction was that he'd been his dad's biggest disappointment. Never quite country enough, never quite smart enough, never quite proud enough of his name, just… never quite enough.

The only one who'd ever made him feel he was more, could *be* more, had been Reagan.

Seeing her today had shaken him. Hard. She'd been more

beautiful than he remembered, those moss green eyes set in a deceptively feminine face. Most people just saw a pretty girl who'd make a good rancher's wife. He'd always known there was far more to her than that. It had terrified him they'd both end up doing exactly what the community expected of them—him taking over his father's ranching operation, and her staying on in the little town because she loved her man.

She *had* stayed, but not for reasons he'd ever understood.

Emotions whipped through him as unchecked as spring winds, tearing up certain pieces of his life and battering others until he was a mess of overlapping memories. When he finally reached the right road, Eli pointed the little car across the first of eleven cattle guard and started through the sand hills. It was a different world out here, yet nothing had changed. He could find his way through this alien landscape with his eyes closed.

Rounding a corner, he rolled to a stop. Cows blocked the road, completely unconcerned with either him or his cartoon car. Waving his arm out the window and shouting, pair after pair of huge brown eyes lifted to blink at him. He honked and snorted at the almost comical beep that made him think of circus cars that dumped out twenty clowns in the ring.

"I am *not* getting out of this car," he shouted at them. Laying on the horn, he whistled and eased into the mass of bodies. Slowly, the herd began to move off.

Eli tunneled his fingers through his hair and fought the urge to turn the car around. He could get to Amarillo and catch a flight back to Austin tonight, be in his own bed by midnight and back in the office first thing tomorrow morning. And if it weren't for the fact Tyson had asked for help, he would have done just that.

Damn it.

His youngest brother had never asked him for anything. Ever. The realization yoked him with heavy guilt. He'd do this for Ty and leave.

And what about Cade? his conscience whispered.

Oh, Cade had asked him for something once, had asked for the one thing he couldn't give. He'd never forgiven Eli for saying no, either.

Eli whispered dire threats to the little car as it struggled up the final hill. It peaked and the world opened up. From the Sangre de Cristo mountain range to the west, the uninterrupted northern horizon and the plains to the east, open range spread before him with regal silence. His breath caught and his chest ached.

This would always be his place, his heritage and his home. But it seemed as foreign to him as another country, as if a passport should be required to visit his past. He was nothing more than a visitor and an unwelcome one, at that. Trying to ignore the undeniable beauty of the land and the way it called to him, soft and familiar, he put the car in gear, starting forward again. The car rattled over the washboard road. A bolt fell out from under the dash and clunked against the passenger floorboard as Eli's teeth clattered together.

A dust trail caught his eye. Somebody was tearing through the sand hills. If Eli'd had a four-wheel drive, he would've ducked down a side road to avoid being seen. In this thing? He'd be dooming himself to walking, and it was way too far to the ranch to run the risk. Instead, he eased forward at the same time he rolled his window up. It would be easy enough to stay focused on the road and ignore whoever passed him. Might be the smartest thing to do, too.

He gained momentum heading down the hill, the little car bucking over the rutted road. A pickup truck roared by. Eli didn't look up. Instead, he leaned on the accelerator, jaw tight, wheel strangled in a death grip. Habit had him flipping a hand up in absent greeting. Brake lights lit up the rearview mirror as the truck fishtailed to a stop.

Curiosity got the better of Eli. He slowed as he watched the driver's side door swing open. The driver jumped down, boots stirring up small puffs of dust as he stormed toward the slowing car. Tall and clearly furious, the man yanked his hat off and tossed it aside without a care. Long legs ate up the distance between them. Lips thinned and eyes hardened the closer the guy came.

Eli let the car drift to a stop even as his stomach went into free fall. His mouth was so dry he couldn't have share-cropped the space without subsidized water rights. Slipping the car into Park, he couldn't make himself stop staring until the man was so close Eli could only see his torso in the little mirror.

Eli reached for the door handle.

The man beat him to it, yanking the door open. "Get out."

Eli's jaw set. "Out of the car or out of town?"

"Car first, town second." The low voice was so raw it sounded like it had been dragged over sharp gravel.

His hands ached with the urge to clench into tight fists. "That's not your call."

Work-roughened hands reached into the car.

Shoving the man away, Eli lunged to stand. "What's your—" A meaty fist connected with his jaw, whipping his head to the side. Stars exploded in his vision. Shaking his head, he rounded on the man, considering him through narrowed eyes. "What the he—" A short jab split his lip. "That's. It."

Eli threw himself into the fight. Grunting as the other man's fist connected with his ribs, he spun and kicked out. He connected with a hip, forcing the bastard off him.

The man regained his balance and, chest heaving, charged Eli.

They went down in a heap, arms swinging and legs kicking as they pummeled each other for all they were worth. A hard shot to Eli's temple made him see double. The guy grabbed him by the front of his oxford and twisted so he knelt over Eli, fist raised.

Eli set his jaw. He wouldn't fight anymore. Not like this.

"You sorry son of a bitch," the man gasped. "All these years. You been gone all these years. Why now?"

Eli swallowed hard. "It's good to see you, too, brother."

Cade Covington shoved off Eli, panting. "Can't say the same."

Seemed karma was determined to put the screws to him by dumping every ounce of history in his lap all at once.

Excellent.

Eli dabbed his split lip with his shirttail. "You still hit like a freaking truck."

"You used to be faster." Cade shook out his fist. "What're you doing here, Eli?"

Cade's tone was cold and Eli glanced at his brother. "Ty didn't tell you?"

"Tell me what?" Cade asked, the words flat.

"He asked me to come home and probate the estate."

His brother cursed, low and harsh.

"I'll take that as a no." Eli leaned against the little clown car and, one at a time, emptied his shoes of sand.

Cade turned away, his voice carrying on the wind. "I've got this covered. We don't need your brand of help."

The words hit Eli harder than any of Cade's blows. He watched his younger brother, the middle of the three of them, retrieve his hat and head for his truck, his gait as long and sure as ever.

"I'll see this through," Eli called after him.

Cade shook his head, slapping his hat against his thigh as he paused beside his idling truck. "Why bother? You don't want to be here, and we don't want you. So just…go on. Get back to Austin and do whatever it is you do down there."

Eli clenched his jaw so tight his molars ached. His nostrils flared on each exhale. "I have a client roster that proves I finish what I start."

Cade settled his hat on his head and glanced over his shoulder. "A client roster, huh?" He shook his head and grinned sardonically. "And how many of those clients have you stuck by through the years, Eli? How many have you seen through the hard times because it was the right thing to do?" When Eli didn't answer, Cade shook his head, grin fading. "They *pay you* to stick. You don't do it because it's the right thing, and that makes all the difference."

"I've never walked out on my professional responsibilities," Eli snapped.

"Then I can honestly say I wish we'd been professional associates instead of brothers." Slamming the driver's door behind him, Cade shifted the truck into Drive and took off.

Hurt and anger warred for dominance, an internal battle that bloodied Eli with every volley. *Who the hell does Cade think he is?*

The idea that he could leave this whole mess to someone else crossed his mind again. He could send a check to cover the attorney's fees, let it be someone else's headache. Epic temptation that it was, it would only reinforce Cade's opinion that he didn't care about his family.

Eli glared down the empty dirt road. He might be a lot of things, but a quitter? No. His leaving had been about survival and what was best for everyone. If Cade didn't get that?

"Screw him." Folding himself gingerly into the car, he winced as it gained speed and resumed rattling over the dirt road. Each jarring bump hammered every new bruise. By the time Eli reached Highway 102, he was pretty sure at least two fillings were loose.

He had no idea how he would manage staying at the ranch with Cade and Ty, but there wasn't a decent hotel within a hundred miles. What there was would be historic—thereby archaic—and that translated to dial-up internet if he was lucky, rotary phones and curious proprietors. The ranch would at least have a rudimentary office. His brothers might not appreciate his presence, but one-third of the house was his, and he intended to put it to use before deeding it to them jointly. Breaking all ties with this place was long past due.

Eli buzzed by the ranch's main gate. The black iron arch over the gate had the ranch's name centered at the top arch, the family name below. Their individual brands were showcased on either side of the ranch name. His, the E-bar C, was to the right.

The battered mailbox stood weather-beaten and worn as ever. The red flag hung broken and listless, the ever-present breeze swinging it back and forth sporadically. Behind the mailbox stood the metal road sign—Road to Perdition.

He'd helped weld and post it with his old man's help. He'd been…what? Eleven? Twelve? The irony had been lost on him at the time. Now? Now it just seemed prophetic. His mother had died two years later and cemented his understanding of perdition. Spiritual ruin. Utter destruction. Hell.

He passed under the sign and onto Covington land.

Tension built in knots across his shoulders, spreading down each side of his spine the farther down the road he went. Long-suppressed memories were close enough to the surface to shove into his consciousness. They dragged him through an entire lifetime of highs and lows that he'd lived in the measly nineteen years he'd been here. So much to remember. So much he wanted to forget. Too much to survive all over again. Shutting his thoughts out, he took in the landscape.

The range looked good. The pastures had benefited from heavier-than-usual summer rains, the black grama grass already heading out. To the west, the mountains rose in a wild spray of desert colors. Fences were tight. Windmills spun in lazy circles, pumping water in a slow but predictable push-pause, push-pause cadence. Yet for all that, something was wrong. It took him a minute to figure it out, but when he did, he felt like an idiot.

As pretty as everything appeared, the pastures were empty.

The ground around the stock tanks should have been soupy from cows stomping through the overflow. Not so.

Grass shouldn't be thickening along livestock trails. It was.

The roads shouldn't have been clear of cow pies and other evidence of a herd. They were.

This wasn't the picture of a working ranch but rather an idyllic snapshot of grasslands. Postcard perfect.

His brows drew together. It was the end of the stocker/grower season. His brothers should be getting ready to ship the contracted stocker steers to the feed yards, yet there was no evidence of activity. Anywhere. Following the road toward the main house, his confusion increased when he found the fields closest to the place empty. That should've been where his brothers were holding the cattle and where the work was happening.

Trying to sort out what might have gone wrong, he suddenly recalled Ty's email. His little brother had asked him to handle the estate's "issues." Eli had assumed his brother meant the difficulty of probating such a physically large estate without a will or, at the very least, without a sufficient will.

Then there was Reagan. She'd accused him of not being here to help his brothers.

Looking around as he pulled up to the main house, the inactivity made his skin tighten. The "issues" his youngest brother had mentioned were clearly going to be larger, *much* larger, than Eli had assumed.

He parked in the main house's half-circle drive. His childhood home hadn't changed at all, from the silver tin roof to the stone walls to the aged, wavy glass of the picture windows. The sense of familiarity sans family left him empty. Steeling himself, he stepped out of the car.

The first thing to strike him was the smell. Someone had cut hay, and recently. The rich, clean smell tickled his nose. Below that hovered the subtle, distinct aroma of ammonia that was inherent to large animals. The barn door squeaked as the breeze curled around the corner of the building to shove the door to and fro. And the sky—man, the sky was so much bigger and bluer than he remembered.

All of that he could break down and compartmentalize by sense. It was the massive quiet that demanded recognition, though, calling forward all those memories he'd been fighting to suppress. They echoed endlessly through the aching hollow of his chest.

Pocketing his keys, he dropped his bag and headed for the barn. Somewhere nearby, a mule brayed.

Eli grinned. Before he'd left, Ty had been bottle-feeding a little jack. The thing had followed the kid around like a damn dog.

Not a kid anymore. Ty would have grown up while Eli was away. He wondered if Ty was half as big as his feet and awkwardness had forecast he'd be. A dull burn settled in his belly when he realized he might not recognize his little brother after so long.

Rubbing his abs, Eli slipped into the dim barn.

The smells of leather and horse sweat joined the mix, dragging his past forward. He'd lived out here as a kid. It had been the one place he'd been entirely comfortable, with the cowhands and the horses. Leaning into the tack room, he was surprised to see a few extra saddles. The ranch must've taken on more hands, but for what? With the empty fields, he couldn't imagine there would be enough work to justify the number of saddles on pegs or money to pay them.

Several horses stuck their heads over their stall doors and peered at him, curious.

He ran a hand around the base of his skull and pulled. A cloak of unease settled around him. It had to be coming here, to the ranch. *Back home.*

A diesel engine rumbled into the yard and saved him from that particular train of thought. Avoiding that sentimental bullshit was beyond necessary. As it was, his life was far too close to turning into a country song full of loss and longing. Eli didn't have room for those emotions.

And with Reagan married, he'd never chance that road again.

4

Reagan pulled up in front of the southern corrals at the Covington place. Several trucks were parked at the bunkhouses, but she didn't see Ty's or Cade's anywhere. She had expected she'd beat Ty to the Bar C, but she'd thought Cade would be around. As serious as things were likely to get, she couldn't imagine the brothers would be too far out of pocket.

Grabbing the backpack she carried her paperwork and iPad in, she slid out of the truck. Brisket leaped down and trotted along beside her, eyes glued to her hands, as she strode toward the main bunkhouse. Chances were someone there would know where Cade had run off to.

"Can I help you?"

She stumbled to a stop. Numb, her hands hung at her sides. Her feet wouldn't move no matter what she silently shouted at them.

"I asked if I could help you."

She might have shaken her head. Could have been she was just shaking. She had no idea.

"Hey. I'm talking to you."

That dark chocolate voice wound around her chest and tightened, and her heart suddenly didn't have enough room to hammer so wildly. She wondered if it would break free of her ribs or just break. *Are there even enough pieces left?*

Brisket pressed up against her legs as he looked over his shoulder.

"That dog… Reagan?"

Steeling herself, hands fisting, she turned with incrementally small steps. "Yeah?"

"Why didn't you answer me?" he asked, exasperation woven through the question.

She shrugged as she mentally reached for her pride. "I figured I'd weigh the odds of you assaulting me again if I turned around. But with Brisket out of the truck this time, I'm feeling lucky."

He smiled slowly. "Feeling lucky, huh? I didn't think married women were supposed to cop to that with another man."

Ice lodged in her chest and her vision wavered through unexpected tears even as a fierce blush stole up her neck and across her cheeks. "Go to hell, Esquire. It's right back the way you came, so you shouldn't have trouble finding your way."

The smile faded. "Look, I'm sorry. I shouldn't have kissed you earlier."

His apology caught her off guard. Picking up her pack, she called Brisket to her as she started toward the bunkhouse again. "Stick with the insults. They go with the suit better than apologies."

"I didn't know you were married." His irritation escalated with every word. "And stop calling me Esquire."

She didn't really want to be petty, fought not to smile. And lost. Pausing, she glanced over her shoulder. The smile morphed from snarky to humorless when their eyes met. "But it fits you so well. There's the attorney thing, but there's also the fact you're out here—" she looked him over just as she had earlier, head to toe "—apparently rolling around in cow shit while wearing designer duds I bet were featured in your namesake's magazine. Esquire, it is."

"I don't remember you being so bitter," he said, absently brushing at his clothes.

"And I don't remember you being so worried about how you looked or what people thought," she volleyed.

Something wounded passed through his gaze. "Then you weren't paying attention."

The breeze shifted. Eli's cologne carried across the air, teasing her with its rich, crisp scent. She drew a breath, intent on offering him a creative suggestion on what to do with his cuff links, but the words hung in her throat. Beneath the cologne was the familiar scent that was all him—midnight and dark promises and sensual heat.

She remembered the taste of his skin on her tongue, the half promise of heaven, half threat of heartache. The feel of his body wrapped around her. But the sound of his voice? That was all too real. It hadn't changed, not with age and time or education. Not any more than the brutal, irrational desire she still harbored for him, desire she'd warred against so long...and lost every battle.

Uncomfortable with the way the conversation was devolving and scared he'd want to talk about the kiss, she faced him and put up her hands. "Enough, okay? Enough."

He crossed his arms over his chest. "Fine. What are you doing out here?"

"I'm the Bar C's vet."

"And?" he asked, rolling his hand in a get-on-with-it gesture.

She hesitated. "If neither Cade nor Ty said anything about this, I'm not sure I should be discussing it with you."

"I own one-third of this ranch, Reagan."

"On paper, yes." Shifting from foot to foot, she let her gaze wander, let it rest anywhere but on him. "But by operational standards, I believe you'd be considered an owner in absentia."

"And how would you know the appropriate legal term?" His voice was lethally soft.

She finally met his gaze. "That's between you and your brothers, Esquire."

"So they called me home to officially shut me out?"

"If that's what you think, what I said earlier about your intelligence in business is wrong. You're dumb as dirt in that arena, as well," she snapped. "How many ways do you have to hear that they need you, Eli, because I'm running out of ways to say it." She sighed in the face of his silence. "Ty either called you home or he didn't. He either asked for your help or he didn't. But consider this, Eli. How often does a proud man go to his knees and plead for help from the one man least likely to give it?"

His visible flinch was followed by a wince as he touched his split lip. "Yeah, well, I don't think Ty and Cade are seeing eye to eye on what they 'need' from me at the moment."

Reagan stared at him long and hard, noting the split lip, the bruise beginning to blossom on one cheekbone, and the ripped buttons on his shirt. "Cade do that to you?"

Obviously watching her for a reaction, he blinked slowly. "What would you say if I told you I ran into Luke and he called me out on kissing you?"

Every ounce of blood left her face. Spots danced in her vision. She moved in slow motion, closing the distance between them and watching detachedly as her fist connected with his unbruised cheek. Observed his chin whip to the side with absolute indifference.

"What the hell!" Eli bit out, spitting fresh blood.

"You don't talk about Luke. Never again."

"I mention his name and you hit me?" The demand hung between them.

She met his angry stare, her own eyes flat. "Luke was killed three years ago."

Eli's mouth worked silently before he managed a gruff response. "Oh, shit. Reagan, I—" He reached for her, but she waved him off.

"Don't." She spun away and moved stiffly toward the nearest bunkhouse. Her voice hollow in her ears, she called back to him. "Tell Ty I'm taking a few men and heading out to pasture twenty-one."

She battled against the urge to turn back to Eli, to lose herself in the comfort of his arms and the heat of his touch like she had all those years ago. The moment she'd recognized him in Tucumcari, she'd known with perverse certainty that nothing had changed. Eli had left her, broken her heart and left it an empty muscle, but his brand was still there, clear as day. She craved the sound of his voice, wanted his body against hers again and had the strongest...*need* to lose herself in him one more time.

But with Luke's death hanging between them, it seemed as if it would be the ultimate betrayal of the man's legacy. Luke had deserved better than she'd afforded him in life, and she hadn't been able to give it. She'd damn sure try to do a better job after his death, no matter what her heart wanted.

EVERYTHING IN ELI had rebelled at Reagan's admission. He crossed his arms tighter over his chest to hide its shaking and leaned against her truck.

She'd stared at him with that achingly familiar face, those stunning green eyes, her lean body backlit by the late-summer sunshine, and he'd realized she was as familiar as the landscape—and just as foreign.

Everything he believed about her had shifted when he'd discovered she was married. She'd stood up in front of God and everyone and committed her life. *To someone else.* But he'd said it himself—it had been fourteen years. Expecting her to wait when he'd given her no hope had been a kid's dream. No more.

Yet, here he stood with every belief he had regarding Reagan changing all over again. He wanted to ask how Luke had died, but the words stalled deep in his chest. Death wasn't so uncommon out here, but communities were small enough that losing one of their own was like losing a family member. And Luke had definitely been one of the community, their charmed favorite who'd never done anything wrong. Hell, he'd even got the girl.

Guilt swamped Eli at his disrespectful thoughts and he shoved off the truck.

"I've got to get my stuff inside," he said to her retreating form. The urge to run, fast, hard, far, to push every physical limit he had, to go and go until he collapsed made his skin twitch and his muscles tighten even as his breath came shorter. He needed to get away from here. From her. He waited until he was sure his legs wouldn't give out and then started for the house.

"Fair enough. I need to get the herds sorted as soon as possible. Tell Ty I'll have the walkie-talkies."

Eli stopped but couldn't bring himself to face her. Instead, he focused on keeping his voice steady. "What's going on, Dr. Matthews?"

Her breath might have hitched, but it could've been wishful thinking on his part.

She cleared her throat. "Ty really didn't mention anything to you?"

"Apparently there are a lot of things Ty didn't mention to me."

He tipped his chin to his chest, ignoring the emotional hole rapidly unraveling in his chest. All of this—hurt, anger, regret… sweet heaven, the regret—was brought on by the simple sound of her voice, husky and made for whispers in the dark. "If it can wait, I'll just get the news from him." Cowardly, maybe, but too much had happened since he landed in Tucumcari, and he was pretty damn sure he'd reached his breaking point.

She hesitated. "I'm pretty sure it can't wait."

"That bad?"

"Yeah. I'm afraid it is."

Closing his eyes, he gave her profile, just enough that she'd know she had his attention.

"Look, Eli, there's not an easy way to say this. The Bar C is facing quarantine."

Muscles across his shoulders tightened. "Pardon me?"

"You guys may have contracted Shipping Fever on a broad scale."

"Shipping Fever?"

"Bovine Respiratory Disease—temp over 104, nasal discharge, dull eyes, diarrhea, stumbling about, muscle wasting. You've been gone more than a decade, Eli, but I'm sure you remember how the disease appears and what it can do to a ranch, or even a region, if it's not contained."

He blew out a hard breath, ignoring the barb. "How'd the Bar C herds come down with it? It's the wrong time of year for Shipping Fever. All the stocker cattle should have arrived months ago."

She lifted one shoulder in a shrug. "The ranch recently bought some new replacement heifers of its own. Then there are the late stockers taken on. With the drought and prices high as they are, the ranchers who *do* have grass can feed through the winter and demand premiums. It's messed up the delivery schedules as stockers and feed yards vie for the best growing environment for their steers." She chewed on her bottom lip for a second and then continued. "Everything that came onto the Bar C had health papers—I checked them all—but logic says the disease somehow originated in the new heifers. If it originated with Bar C's stocker cattle, that's one thing. If it's because of the ranch's new stock..."

She didn't finish, but Eli didn't need her to. If the Bar C's own cattle had infected those they'd been contracted to put weight on through the year, the liability would destroy the ranch. The ranch would be quarantined. The cows that didn't die wouldn't do well this year. That meant low revenue. Worst-case scenario would be a huge die-off that would force the ranch to compensate the brokers and owners for the casualties. That would permanently shutter the Covington operation.

He gave a single nod. "I'll tell Ty where you'll be. Four-wheelers or horseback?"

"Horseback. I want to keep from spooking the herd any more

than necessary. I'll take one of Cade's horses. We'll trailer them as far as we can to save time, and we'll ride on from there."

Eli nodded and she walked away without another word.

He grabbed his travel bag and then took the porch steps two at a time. Pausing at the door, hand resting on the iron doorknob, he hesitated. Then he depressed the lever, the door swung in and nostalgia claimed him, reeling him across the threshold like the catch of the day.

The inside of the house still smelled like lumber, wood smoke and leather. Wide-planked floors were scuffed and marked by age and heavy use. His old man's recliner still sat in the corner as if waiting on Max himself to pull up a seat at the end of the day. Curtains his mother had made still framed the window, threadbare with time. A pellet stove had replaced the archaic potbellied beast in the stone fireplace. Leather sofas and club chairs were scattered around the room in a haphazard way that announced "bachelor pad" as efficiently as did the abandoned boots near the door and the boxers on the coffee table.

Eli wove through the room and down the hallway to the stairs. Taking a deep breath, he opened the basement door. These he took one at a time. The air was cooler with a bite of dampness to it. He used to love it, especially in July's heat. Breathing faster, he crossed the family room and stopped outside a familiar wooden door. Twice he reached for the handle only to stop. It was stupid, really. Nothing on the other side of the door changed anything about who he was now.

He traced his fingers over the rough-hewn pine door. How many nights had he spent in this basement? How many nights had he sworn that he'd find his way out of a life that had never fit him no matter how he twisted or stretched it as he tried to fill his old man's expectations? How many times had he imagined how fulfilling it would be to make it on his own and *force* his dad to be proud of him? The answer was the same for every question: too many.

On a sigh, he shoved off the casing and stood. One silent twist of the doorknob and the door swung open without a sound. His past crashed into him. Shallow shelves held trophies from FFA and 4-H and high school sports. Laminated newspaper clippings were tacked to a small corkboard exactly as he'd left them. His bed was made. That was different. Looking closer, he realized the room was clean. No dust, no cobwebs, nothing out of place. He was suddenly nineteen all over again and awkward with it. All of the familiar, unwelcome insecurities were still there, waiting, still unresolved after all these years.

Crossing the threshold, his heart stopped. There, on his nightstand, was his favorite picture of his mother. She smiled out at him. Even though her dark hair had been burnished by sunlight in the picture, time had faded the effect. Still, he could remember the way she appeared. The love on her face still radiated from the photo, though. In spades. The years had passed, indifferent to his family's grief at the loss of her, but not even time could change how much Eli'd loved her. Nothing could.

He traced the face in the photo and imagined he could still hear her puttering around upstairs. "I miss her, too."

Eli dropped the picture and the glass frame shattered. "I—" He glanced at the picture and back to the door, where a large man filled the doorway. "Tyson?"

"I don't remember her as well as you and Cade, but it was still hard to lose her."

His youngest brother was now definitely not the littlest. He was a couple of inches taller than Eli's own six feet two inches and clearly comfortable in his skin as he moved into the room. "Grown a bit since you last saw me."

Backing up, Eli stepped on the broken glass and winced at the sound.

Tyson paused, his brows winging down. "What the hell happened to your face? You look like someone dragged your ass down the runway. You do know you're supposed to stay *inside* the plane until it comes to a complete stop at the gate, right?" He snorted. "And here I figured you were the debonair, well-traveled brother." Stepping across the small room, he wrapped Eli in a rib-cracking hug. "It's so good to see you, man."

Eli wasn't sure what he'd expected from his little brother, but given the brutal reception he'd gotten from everyone else, it definitely wasn't this.

He wanted to hug Ty back. He wanted to put distance between them. He wanted someone to shock his heart back into a normal rhythm.

Instead, for just a second, he reveled in a brother's love.

REAGAN AND THREE of the ranch hands trailered their rides as far northeast as they could go on the Bar C. Unloading at the gate to the last pasture on the place, she tossed walkie-talkies to each man and left one in the truck in case Ty or Cade showed up and needed to contact them. Mounting one of Ty's geldings, she adjusted her stirrups and checked her saddlebags. Everything was there, from medical supplies and antibiotics to a pistol for animals that were suffering and beyond help.

Coiling her rope and securing it to her saddle, she whistled for Brisket and headed for the gate. The dog slipped in close, trotting along to keep up.

The men followed in a tight group. Jake Peterson, the most seasoned of the men and another childhood friend of hers, moved up beside her. "How far out do you think the cows'll be?"

She glanced at the midafternoon sun. "I'm hoping we find them in the front half of this pasture. If not, it'll mean getting a chopper out here to push them toward us, and that's not cost effective. It'll also stress them out more than they already are. We'll save it as a last resort." Leaning forward, she tightened her saddle's cinch without stopping her horse. "Regardless, we've got to do whatever it takes to get this contained, Jake."

He settled his hat more firmly on his head and frowned. "This is going to be bad, Reagan, isn't it?"

"Let's not borrow trouble," she said softly, eyes on the horizon. "No need to borrow when the coffers are full."

She snorted. "Aren't you a bundle of joy today?"

"Just worried. Forgot my canteen. Be right back." He wheeled his horse around and galloped off.

The soft voices of the other men around her and the methodical clop of horse hooves were almost carried away by the sound of the wind whispering through the grass. Being out here on horseback with nothing but the sky above her and the power and potential of one of Ty's cutting horses beneath her proved spiritually cathartic. She hadn't realized how much she'd truly needed the privacy to process the day's events.

Never in a million years would she have suspected today would be the day she ended up facing off with Eli Covington. So much history. So much hurt. She had no idea how she was going to survive the next week or two as she did what she had to do, and he did the same. He'd want the estate probated as quickly as possible. That made sense. But if this was truly Shipping Fever, it was the worst case she'd ever heard about. She'd have to get the state vet involved.

Wanting more distance, she urged her horse into a swift lope. No doubt the men would catch up, but she'd have a few minutes to herself to just breathe. She never expected the tears that first caught up and then overran her.

Leaning over the saddle, she spurred the horse into a dead run. Ghosts of the past chased her across the plains, nipping at her heels. Their teeth had been finely honed on the sharp clarity of memories she'd once cherished and now resented. Every touch, every kiss, every promise they'd made—every promise they'd broken—it all rushed over her in a ruthless barrage of brilliant recollections. But the taste of him today… It had broken the fragile levee she'd finally managed to build to keep her feelings contained.

The wind whipped her hat off her head. She didn't slow down. If anything, she urged her horse faster, then faster still. Giving him his head, she buried her face in his mane and just held on.

A harsh sob escaped as years of blinding heartache flooded through her.

Hoofbeats thundered up behind her. Sitting up, she scrubbed one hand over her face and fought to catch her breath. No one would say anything, but there would be curiosity. And out here, curiosity led to speculation, which led to probabilities, which led to the birth of the most insane gossip. She didn't want to suffer through it. Particularly not with Eli in town.

It had been bad enough when Luke had died. For months, all she'd heard were condolences. The sentiments had been heartfelt, yes. But they'd all been as empty to her as her bed had been at night. No casserole, phone call or sympathy card could take the place of the man who had loved her for five years. She'd learned to hear the words without listening, without assigning them value.

A broad hand reached for her reins.

Sitting deep in the saddle, she parked her feet in the stirrups and shut the horse down. Like the brilliant athlete he was, the horse sat on his hindquarters and slid to a hard stop. Barely winded, he righted himself and stood waiting, ready.

Ty spun his horse and trotted up to her, her hat in hand. He offered the Stetson without comment.

She accepted it, absently reshaping the brim.

"You were running as if the hounds of hell were hot on your heels." Reaching out, he grabbed her wrist. "I checked. No hounds. What's going on?"

Her smile was wobbly as she drew a deep breath and blew out hard enough to puff her cheeks. "I'm good." When he arched a single brow, she nodded quickly. "Honest."

"Don't ever bullshit a bullshitter, Reagan. What happened?"

The noise that escaped was half laugh, half sob. "I thought, just once, I'd indulge myself and try to outrun a past I can't seem to escape. That's what happened." Slapping her hat on her head, she realized the group was quickly catching up. She glared at Ty. "Not a word, Ty. Not to anyone."

"You should probably know that I, uh..." He tugged at his collar and whipped his head to the side, popping his neck.

"Know *what*?" she asked with a snarl.

"That he brought me along." Eli had stopped several feet away, his eyes hidden by reflective sunglasses. He'd changed into jeans and a pair of beat-up boots she recognized from years past. His shirt was clean but wrinkled.

"Great." *How much had he heard?* Whatever it was, she couldn't take it back. Instead, she stared at the very man she'd so wanted to avoid. "Been a while since you've sat a horse, Eli. Do your best not to fall off, would you? Earlier, it seemed you'd already taken the opportunity to roll around in shit. Once a day is our limit out here."

Tyson barked out a laugh. "You rolled around in shit? Where was I?"

Eli never took his eyes off Reagan when he answered. "You missed Cade taking it upon himself to reintroduce me to his fists."

Ty sobered instantly. "So you didn't jump from the plane?"

"No." He shook his head, his eyes still on her. "While I'm flattered you're worried about my well-being, don't bother. I can take what you dish out, Dr. Matthews."

Ty sobered instantly. "That's right. She said you knew about her marrying Luke and—"

"The marriage. Nothing more, Ty, and I insist it stay that way." Reagan reined the horse to the side with a heavier hand than necessary. The animal protested by tossing his head and crow hopping. She settled him down and pointed him toward the northeast again. "Chances are, the herd has holed up out here where they can be sick and miserable without human intervention. I want to get to them as quickly as possible. Either keep up or go home, Esquire."

"You've gotten bossy as hell," Eli muttered.

"And you've got a great manicure. Your point?"

Ty bit his lip and nearly choked on his laughter.

"You always were a smart-ass." Eli coiled his rope with a practiced ease that made her fight the familiarity of him. "Some things never change."

Settling her hat tight, she forced herself to calm down or she'd transmit her tension to her mount. "True, but some things, and people, do. Don't pretend to know who I am anymore, Eli."

Clucking at the gelding, she slipped into an easy lope.

The sooner she got this job over with, the sooner she could get home and start piecing her life together again. But after Eli's reappearance, it was going to take more than all of her life experience and surgical skill.

It was going to take a miracle.

5

ELI'S LEGS WERE sore by the end of the first hour. By the end of the second, he wasn't sure he still had an ass. He shifted in his saddle as Ty reined in next to him, a wicked smile decorating the kid's face.

"You ever do those *Buns of Steel* videos?"

The casual inquiry caught Eli off guard. "What? No. Why?"

"I was thinking I might market a cowboy version, *Buns of Leather*. You know—ride 'em rough, ride 'em tough, fifteen minutes is never enough."

Eli laughed out loud. The ranch hands glanced their way before casually returning to their own conversation. They'd extended due courtesy to Eli. Their words and behaviors stopped long short of respect, though. To Ty, on the other hand, they were deferential. It chafed.

Ty caught him shaking his head. The youngest Covington reached over and punched the elder in the shoulder. "Give them time, Eli."

"Time to what? Drown me in the stock tank? Drop a branding iron in my lap? Dump my ass in the bull pasture before they take off with my horse? No, thanks."

"I'd forgotten Cade and I did that your last summer at home.

Dad was pissed." His mouth twitched. "If it makes you feel any better, the bulls are on the south side of the place now."

Eli shook his head. "You guys almost got me killed."

"Never saw a guy climb a windmill so damn fast."

"I was up there overnight!" Reaching out, he flipped his little brother's hat off his head.

Ty caught it before it hit the ground, grinning. "And you're still whining about it."

"Shut up." Eli smiled through the grumbled command. In a weird way, it hurt to remember the good times. He'd spent so many years hating who he'd been and where he'd come from that looking back with affection felt wrong, like a betrayal of who he'd fought so hard to become. Being reminded that it hadn't all sucked…it stung.

Then there was the little bit he'd overheard of Reagan's admission to Ty. That more than stung. Way more.

Clearing his throat, he twisted in his saddle and found her. She rode among the men with the surety of one who belonged. He envied her the ease with which she fit in. She'd always been that way, though, so confident and aware of where she belonged. He'd had to scramble to keep up, always feeling one step behind.

Her eyes met his.

A shock of awareness burned through him. He twisted around so quickly he nearly unseated himself.

"She's an amazing woman," Ty said softly.

"Always was." The admission scraped at emotions that were already raw. He adjusted his sunglasses. "When did she marry?"

Ty slouched in his saddle. "Eight years ago."

So long. "Any kids?"

"No. They never—"

A sharp whistle interrupted the conversation. Brisket streaked across the field toward a small cluster of weanlings that had just topped the rise. A second whistle stopped him short. The dog focused on the herd and waited for Reagan to direct his next action.

Eli jerked his chin toward the Border collie, watching as Reagan sent him wide. "She's good with him."

Reagan spread the cowboys out. "Bring these in slow. We'll get them pointed toward the working pens and walk them in. Don't rouse them."

"C'mon," Ty said, heading in the opposite direction of the other three hands.

Eli followed along, his gaze constantly roving as he watched for more steers. Pushing closer to Ty, he considered the black calves with their white faces. "What are you guys running now?"

"Bar C's running all Angus cows. The Charolais bulls provide hybrid vigor and give us the black baldies. Market's still paying a premium for them." Ty jerked his chin toward the little cluster of black steers with white faces. "Those are some of ours. When it comes to stocking, we'll contract anything brokers have and we'll grow 'em out and put weight on 'em for the fall sale ring, provided the price is right."

"Who's running the ranch now that Dad's gone?"

Eli watched the weight of responsibility age Ty a good ten years.

His little brother glanced over and shrugged. "We're managing."

Before he could ask who constituted "we" in Ty's books, one of the steers broke free and headed for the hills. Eli simply reacted. Laying his heels to his horse, he loosed his rope. Someone shouted something after him. He didn't slow down.

Wind whistled past his ears. His eyes watered. The hammering of his heart competed with his horse's hooves pounding the turf. Shaking out a coil of rope, the horse put him right on top of the runaway. Eli's movements were effortless, remembered—as if his muscles had never forgotten. He swung the rope with fluid wrist rolls and watched for the right moment to snag the calf. One swing, two, three—and the horse shut down.

Eli's reaction was a matter of total self-preservation. Dropping the rope, he pushed up on the pommel and vaulted the saddle horn before his junk was relocated into his spine. Over the horse's neck, he ended up straddling the beast's head. His legs clamped around its jaw. The animal backed up rapidly. Eli stumbled forward and rolled, landing flat on his back staring at a stunning blue sky just beginning to turn pink toward the west.

Ty reined his horse in and hit the ground running. "Eli!"

All he could do was weakly hold up a hand.

"Bro, are you okay?" Ty slid to his side on his knees, his hands roaming over Eli as he searched for injuries.

"Me? I'm fine. But my nuts are so damn traumatized they've entered the Witness Protection Program and are passing as acorns."

Ty winced. "I'm not checking your nuts."

Eli rolled his face toward his brother. "That would be bad touch, Ty. Bad touch."

His brother's mouth curled up at one corner. "Your sunglasses didn't fare so well, either."

"No?"

The younger man held up half of the frame, sans lens. "Nope."

"What the hell made the horse balk?" Eli groaned as he sat up, running a hand across his chest and stretching muscles that were grumbling now but would be flat out protesting by sunset.

Ty shrugged. "He's a roping horse."

"So?"

"He put you where you needed to be. Gave you your three swings before he shut it down."

"That's insane. Horses don't count." Eli glanced around and was less than thrilled to discover said horse headed in the direction of the truck and trailer.

"Yeah. Well, around here, we train 'em with pixie dust so they do. Count, that is." Ty rubbed his upper lip. "You, uh, crashed—" a rich laugh broke free "—rather spectacularly."

"Points for style?"

"Definitely. Some free advice, though?" Ty offered Eli a hand up. "Next time try to stick the landing."

"No 'next time,' thanks." Hands on his hips, he stared at the ground. "Cade'll be sorry he missed my humiliation. Listen, I've got to catch a ride to the truck. I'll mend any broken gear and get back out here to help."

"No need." Ty vaulted into his saddle.

It was only then that Eli realized how sore he really was.

"Grab a ride with Doc Matthews while I get the boys to try and regather the calves."

"Ty, I'm not going to—"

But Ty had already taken off, calling the men along with him.

Eli caught the furious look on Reagan's face. Yanking her horse around, she galloped up to him and slid to a stop, no doubt purposely positioning the gelding inches from Eli. "You lost them all."

"If you want to beat on me, you're going to have to take a number, Reagan. It's been a really crappy day."

Her gaze flitted between him and the retreating men.

"Go on," he muttered. "I'll walk."

"You'll spook the herd." She tilted her chin toward the cattle that had crested the nearest hill to check out the commotion. With a heavy sigh, she kicked her foot out of the stirrup and hooked her leg over the pommel as she offered him her hand. "Get on. I'll take you to the truck. You can wait for us there."

Eli crossed his arms over his chest. "I'll walk."

"Unless you're the Pied Piper, get your ass in the saddle, Covington. With you on foot, the calves will *never* come in. I won't debate means and methods with you. If we can get these steers into the pen tonight, it means I can test them sooner."

He opened his mouth to argue.

She whipped her hat off, her long brown hair tumbling past her shoulders. "Get on before I give in to the urge to hog-tie your ass and drag you to the truck."

Scowling, pride bruised and ego down for the count, Eli

climbed up behind Reagan. His thighs molded to hers and he fought to ignore the fire that burned through him at every point of contact. The horse sidestepped. Eli settled his hands on her hips for balance.

She jerked and twisted away as if pained. "Don't touch me." Her voice was low and harsh.

"How do you suggest we make it to the truck without touching?" Her whole body tensed, and he wondered if she'd jump ship and catch a ride with one of the other men.

The idea of her pressed intimately against anyone else made him grind his teeth. He tried reminding himself she'd been married, but that only conjured images of her and Luke locked in each other's arms. His fingers dug into her hips.

"I said 'don't touch me.'"

Settling his hands on his thighs, he leaned away from her and closed his eyes. "Just get me to the truck, Reagan."

The pain was intensifying, and he suspected the worst of it had nothing to do with hitting the ground.

REAGAN WAS MISERABLY aware of Eli's body, from the way his thighs molded to hers to the way his chest kept brushing against her back, his movements in sync with the horse. How many times had they ridden this way? It might have been a hundred years ago, but the heart didn't forget. She wanted to relax into him, have his arms settle around her waist. Let her head fall into that spot between his neck and shoulder where she fit so well.

"Hold on," she muttered, shifting her weight forward. The horse slipped into an effortless lope.

Eli's fingers brushed her ass as they gripped the cantle.

She moved farther forward, nearly standing in the stirrups. This had been an epically miserable mistake. And Ty? She was going to kill that man. Her mind wandered to the contents of the saddlebags Eli straddled. Maybe she wouldn't kill Ty, but she might shock him with a cattle prod. Maybe grab the tattoo pliers and leave him a more permanent token of her appreciation. Her grin was feral, but she'd never follow through with it. They kept up that pace for more than half an hour, her mind working the entire time.

Eli leaned into her, his chest rubbing against her back. "Slow him down."

She touched the reins and the horse slowed to a walk, blowing softly. The trucks were just over the next hill. "What's wrong?"

"Nothing. He's getting tired." His voice moved around her, a promise of things long past, his breath skating across the bared skin of her neck. Warmth radiated from him and seeped into her.

Being with Luke was never this good.

And she hated both men for that fact.

Fisting the reins, she stopped the horse. "Get off."

"What? We're almost there."

"Get. Off."

He slung a leg over and slid down, grunting as his feet hit the ground. "What's your problem?"

She shrugged. Guiding the horse with her knees, she pointed him deeper into the pasture only to find the herd cresting the hill. *Damn it.* If she rode toward them now, she'd scatter them all to hell. Instead, she retrieved her saddlebags, slipped off the horse and handed Eli the reins. "Man the gate." Digging through one pouch, she retrieved two cattle prods. Flipping the wands open, she switched them both on before tossing him one as he settled into the saddle.

He fumbled it and managed to shock himself before gripping the handle. "Damn it!" Glaring down at her, his face clouded with thunderous fury. "How long are you going to punish me for doing what you knew I had to do, Reagan?"

Staring at him, her heart stopped. For years she'd dreamed of this opportunity, this chance to tell him what he'd done to her. That moment had arrived, but the words wouldn't come. There were too many variables. She didn't want to hear that she'd been part of what he'd needed to escape. He might respond by explaining to her he'd had to experience life without her. Or he could say that he'd never loved her.

She had only survived this far because she didn't know how responsible she was for his never coming home. Would that change if she did? It wasn't worth finding out.

Stepping away and cursing herself for being a coward, she said the only thing she could. "I don't imagine you'll be around long enough for either of us to find out." Spinning on her heel, she strode toward the working pen. Her tight grip on the cattle prod's handle pressed its checkered pattern into her palm. A sharp whistle brought Brisket to her. Before he stopped, she redirected him with a sharp "Away." Swinging wide and crouching low, he moved counterclockwise as he trotted around the approaching cattle.

Reagan swung the gate open and moved out of their path. Listless and wheezing, the yearling steers moved into the portable corrals with stumbling steps and zero protest. Not good. One calf stood apart from the others, head hanging low. He was gaunt, his sides drawn up. Pointing at him, she whistled for Brisket. "Push 'em. Easy."

The dog slipped into the pen and began weaving back and forth as he herded the steer toward the chute.

"To me," she called as she shut the gate behind the young animal, and Brisket came to heel.

Scrutinizing the black-bodied, white-faced steer, she knew what she faced. From the cowboys' silence, they all did. Didn't matter. She had a job to do. Digging a thermometer out of one saddlebag, she donned a pair of nitrile gloves. Slipping the thermometer into the calf's rectum, the digital readout stopped and beeped at 105 degrees.

The calf coughed—a deep, rattling sound—and stumbled forward a step before going to his knees.

Her arm was caught between the panel and the calf's hip. She yelped involuntarily.

Movement in the corner of one eye said someone was moving in to help.

"Don't," she snapped. "Brisket, bite."

The dog raced around to nip at the calf's heels, forcing him up.

Reagan pulled her arm back, massaging the spot that would be black-and-blue by dawn tomorrow. "Get him into the trailer. There's no point waiting on the results of his blood work. He's not going to make it until tomorrow. I'll put him down when we get to the house. Ty, you'll need to get his information—originating ranch, transport papers, other cattle he's been exposed to here—while I do the necropsy. I'm going to go ahead and say y'all should treat the entire ranch with a broad-spectrum antibiotic that'll address all three major bacteria that could be involved."

Ty shoved his hat back and cursed as he leaped from his horse. "Damn it, Doc, we can't afford to treat every last animal."

She glanced over her shoulder, working to keep her face neutral. "You don't have a choice if you want them to survive. The alternative is letting this run its course, but it's going to cost you a hell of a lot more in death loss and potential lawsuits than if you do the right thing now."

"What's it going to cost, Dr. Matthews?" Eli slipped from the borrowed horse and moved to stand beside Ty.

"You've got, what? Fifteen hundred head contracted and another five hundred of your own? I'm going to guess your yearlings are averaging 900-plus pounds each at this point. On Draxxin, that'll run about $21 per animal. Then we'll be required to monitor them for at least five consecutive days, which means additional feed and, for each group, draining and cleaning out water tanks and hauling off the waste. That's your best… no, that's your *only* hope of getting this cleared up."

Eli stormed forward, his jaw set and eyes hard. "Damn it, Reagan. You're talking about eating up every last penny of profit the ranch might see from its own animals this year, not to mention destroying our relationship with clients when we disclose to them they're facing negative net gains for the early sale ring. They'll have to leave the animals with us longer to make up for their losses, and that costs everyone money. Our pastures will be overgrazed and we'll have to take a full season off next year to allow the pastures to recover. That means everything, and *everyone*, goes hungry this winter *and* next."

She nodded once. "It's not about cost, Eli. It's about stopping this before it becomes an epidemic." Taking a deep breath, she steeled herself for the impending storm her next words were going to bring. "Until then, I have to notify the state vet we've got a BRD outbreak. The Bar C is quarantined."

6

ELI STORMED AND STEWED, his temper tangling with common sense as he worked to fix the tack he'd broken in his "equine dismount." He refused to use the word "fall" because he'd been freaking *ejected* from the back of that horse like his ass was a gymnast and the saddle was a springboard. Despite his irritation, he snorted. Ty would get a kick out of that comparison, and a small part of him breathed easier to realize he knew one of his brothers at least a little.

The cowboys were quiet as they penned the herd and loaded the sick steers into the trailer. They'd push the healthy cows toward the main corrals at the house so Reagan could treat them and begin watching them for the next few days. Once these were treated, the cowboys would begin working through the rest of the herds as they waited on the state vet's arrival. This was about to get very, very expensive.

The horses weren't at risk from the steers' BRD, but the steers could easily have additional complications or infections that *would* affect the horses, so someone would trailer the steers to the main house and corrals while everyone else rode home.

Home.

It had been so long since he'd considered this place that way.

His gaze rested on Reagan as she took notes and pictures of the sickest of the steers. Her fingertips flew over her iPad screen. She mumbled to herself as she worked, ignoring everything and everyone around her. Including him. Irritated she could dismiss him so easily, he gripped his horse's repaired reins and started toward Ty. "I'll drive the truck."

"I already asked Everett to drive," Ty responded. He twisted to hook his far leg over his saddle horn. His horse dipped its head low and began grazing as if it hadn't a care in the world. "Gizmo and I'll ride the rest of the herd in with the ranch hands."

Eli arched a single brow. "Gizmo? Last I heard you were raising prized cutting horses, not… Gizmos."

Ty shrugged. "I am. His official name is Doc Bar's Dippy Zippy Gizmo, but all the ladies know him as Gizmo."

"He's a stud?" The surprise in Eli's question was undisguised. The horse should've been as high-strung as a runway model during New York Fashion Week. Instead, he was working "sedated Labradoodle chic."

"Yeah." Ty patted his neck. "I want you and Doc Matthews to ride in ahead and tell Cade we're coming in with some sicklings so he…you and he…" He scratched his jaw and force his gaze elsewhere. "Y'all will need to create a quarantine situation."

Translation: kill the sickest of the animals.

Eli narrowed his eyes, gazing hard at his brother. "I'd prefer to drive."

"And you'd also prefer to do anything that allows you to avoid Reagan and Cade." Ty met him stare for stare. "Neither can happen if we're going to fix this, brother. Best learn whether or not we can work together now, or we might as well put the for-sale sign out by the road."

Guilt twisted Eli's belly into knots a seasoned sailor would have been proud of. He hated that his little brother was right, that Ty had clarity while Eli was blinded by every new revelation.

Ty glanced over his shoulder before jerking his chin slightly in the same direction. "Go easy with her."

Eli looked at Reagan, the hole in his chest beginning to unravel again, slower this time. The destruction was just as devastating. "'Easy' and 'Reagan' don't play well together," he said softly.

"She married Luke eight years ago—"

"I'm well aware of that," Eli bit out.

His little brother shifted in his saddle, and Eli watched some foreign cocktail of emotions—hurt, anger, grief, rage, regret—slip through Ty's eyes. "She married Luke eight years ago," he said again but with a hardness that had been lacking before, "and was widowed three years ago."

Eli moved closer to his brother and kept his voice very low so no one would overhear them. "She told me he died. How'd it happen?"

"Gored by a Hereford. The owner brought the cow to Luke and Reagan with a severe prolapsed uterus. Luke went out to help, got pinned by the chute gate when it failed and the cow broke loose just enough to reach him." Ty swallowed several times before finishing. "Reagan witnessed the whole thing. She tried to save him. Couldn't. The cow had severed some major artery and Luke bled out before the EMTs even got there."

Eli nodded, the movement entirely reflexive, totally numb. "How'd she do? After."

"She's been working her backside off trying to hold on to the place they'd just bought together." Ty dipped his chin. "Rumor is she's going to have to sell, though."

"Why?"

"She can't manage a place that size by herself. The Russell ranch neighbors her, and they've offered to pick up her place at fair market value."

The skin along Eli's shoulders tightened. "She ought to sell."

"And do what?" Ty demanded, that low, hard edge decorating his words again. "It's the last piece of him she has left."

"She loved him." Eli choked the words out so softly the wind all but carried them away.

Still, Ty heard him. "She married him."

"Same thing." His chest felt as if it had been filled with something highly flammable that began to burn so hot it reduced his insides to ash. *She'd loved Luke.* That meant, at some point, she'd stopped loving *him*.

The trailer rattled as the steers lumbered inside. Everett shut the gate behind him and said something to Reagan. She answered, the other man shook his head and she handed over her pistol. Rancher-speak for *If he's worse when you get home, put him out of his misery.* Compassionate, yes, but killing had always been something Eli struggled with. One more way he'd disappointed his dad.

"A Covington doesn't flinch when he pulls the trigger, boy," the man had snapped the last time Eli had been given the rifle with instructions to use it on a deformed calf.

The memory drew a line of cold sweat along his hairline.

His attention shifted as Ty straddled his horse again.

The youngest Covington picked up the reins and, nudging his horse forward, called out, "Let's get 'em home. Doc and Eli will ride ahead and call Cade soon as the walkie-talkie is within range of the base."

Reagan mounted her borrowed gelding without comment and took up the reins to Everett's riderless horse, turning toward the main house that was a good fifteen miles away. She didn't wait on Eli, though, just urged her horse into a swift gait.

Eli caught up without any trouble and trotted beside her until they were far enough ahead of the herd to spare the horses and slow to a walk.

The setting sun burned up the horizon in a blaze of fiery colors. As the colors faded and darkness began to seep in, it seemed to offer nature's equivalent of amnesty to the perpetual breeze. The night went still. Crickets and frogs collected around the streams and creeks they crossed, the chirping and croaking lost to the splash of the horses through the water and the huff of breath as the horses climbed the opposite banks.

Eli had just opened his mouth to say something when a doe and her fawn, spots nearly gone, shot out of a nearby mesquite stand and bounded away, the whites of their tails raised in alarm.

His breath caught. There was an innate beauty to this place he'd absolutely forgotten. He gazed up at the stars. *Man, the stars.* Night hadn't even fully descended, but the sky was bigger than he'd witnessed in years.

"You ever take astronomy in college?"

Reagan's voice startled him enough he twitched in the saddle. His horse sidestepped in response, and he settled the animal down as he hunted for his voice. Clearing his throat, he nodded. "Yeah. It was one of my favorite electives. Took as many classes as I could. You?"

"Same." She sounded indifferent to the tentative link between them. "I missed the size of the sky out here while I was at school."

"Where'd you go?" he asked.

She rolled her head back and forth. "Undergrad at New Mexico State University. Vet school at Colorado State. Did my degrees consecutively, never taking summers off." Glancing at him from under the brim of her hat, her face was as neutral as the color of a hospital wall. "I didn't want to be too far from home."

"Reagan, I—"

"I heard you went to UT-Austin," she quickly interrupted. "Did you get your law degree there, too?"

"Yeah." He settled deeper into his saddle. "I was accepted to Stanford, but there was no way I could afford the tuition."

"I have no idea how people afford colleges like that. I'm still paying off my student loans."

"That makes two of us."

She opened her mouth and then closed it, chewing her bottom lip for a second before speaking so quickly the words ran together. "Are you happy in Austin? Being a lawyer?"

The answer didn't come easily, surprising him. He rolled his shoulders. She didn't press, giving him time to answer or not. It had always been that way between them, with her giving him as much space and time as he required. And he'd abused that. Sorely.

In the distance, a coyote's yip was answered by another's long howl. Then a third voice joined the chorus. The sound—more soulful cry than call—was so bereft that Eli's thoughts slipped back to the loss Reagan had lived through.

Finally he shrugged and answered her question. "It's given me the sense of accomplishment I always seemed to lack here. I get recognition for my efforts with the firm. In fact, I made partner two years ago—youngest ever."

"Congratulations."

"Thanks." That same tight-skinned sensation returned with a vengeance. "It's an entirely different way of life, but it suits me."

"I appreciate the insight, but I asked if you were happy."

"Happiness isn't the only thing that matters, Reagan." His answer came out far terser than he intended, but before he could apologize, even clarify, she cast him a sideways glance.

Running a hand around her neck, she massaged her shoulder muscles. "I don't want to fight with you, Eli. I don't want to waste even another second hurting. And I definitely don't want our history to derail what's most important now—saving the ranch."

If she'd whipped off her shirt and said, *Take me now, you hot badass,* she couldn't have surprised him more. "That's a big change from kicking me off your horse a couple of hours ago and tossing me a live cattle prod."

She grinned. "Yeah. Sorry about that. Still have a temper." Then her eyes met his and she truly looked at him, the layers of her grief mingling until he wasn't sure how much she regretted him, how much she hated him being here, how much she might miss what they had and how much was the shadow left by Luke's loss.

It didn't matter.

Altogether, it combined to age her soul, to make her ancient beyond her years and leave her bearing a burden of hurt he would never have wanted her to carry. He felt responsible and would have given anything for the chance to change it.

Eli's breathing increased. Gripping the saddle horn, he nearly came out of his skin when his cell phone rang.

Reagan glanced over at him. "Impressive service."

"Total fluke if the reception at the airport was any indication of what I should expect out here." He dug the smartphone out of his jeans pocket, annoyed to find the screen cracked, the incoming call's number unreadable. Still, no matter who was on the other end of the call, he'd handle it better than he was handling Reagan. "Covington."

REAGAN HALF LISTENED to Eli talk to someone from his office. His entire demeanor changed. He'd been slouched comfortably in the saddle when the phone rang. Now? He sat so straight it was as if someone had shoved a ramrod up his ass. His crisp enunciation and decisive language made him seem more a stranger than he had since he'd stormed out of her parents' barn all those years ago. She'd watched him seize opportunity that night, and now she knew the results.

"Don't count me impressed," she muttered. Clucking at her horse, she put some space between her and Eli.

He'd asked her about the stars. The *stars*. How many nights had they lain in the bed of his old '74 Ford F-150 and counted falling stars? Too many to count. They'd pointed out the little they'd known about the night sky to each other, always finding the Milky Way, always wishing they could see the Northern Lights. Together. They'd wanted those things *together*. But life had other plans.

It shouldn't surprise her that they'd both pursued astronomy in college, but part of her clung to the small similarity, the hope he'd been thinking of her as they stared at the same night sky. Of course, she may have had nothing to do with him taking the classes. Meanwhile, she'd still been living on the hope he'd find what he needed and come back as he'd promised, then they'd pick up where they'd left off. Together.

A short, raspy breath chased the thoughts out like an emotional exorcism. Those dreams were long gone. She had the sneaking suspicion she'd know where to start looking for them, though. Glancing over her shoulder, she considered Eli.

Guilt hit her mangled heart with a one-two punch and followed up with a kick to the proverbial kidney. Luke had always been steadfast, standing by her when people whispered about Eli leaving. They'd intimated she wasn't enough to bring him home. That's when Luke stepped in and openly began courting her broken heart, had fallen in love with her and convinced the shell of the woman she'd become to marry him. Then he'd set about loving her harder than any man should have to love his wife—hard enough for the both of them.

The truth hadn't been lost on Luke, that she had loved him solid and sound, but she'd never been *in* love with him. God, she'd tried. So hard. But at every turn she crashed into memories of Eli she couldn't escape. She'd finally given up, settling for the fact he and all the memories she had of him were woven into the fabric of her soul. If she was going to have any kind of life, she'd have to settle for what she had instead of holding out hope for the one—the life and the man—she'd believed had been meant for her.

Hooves beat against the grassy turf. Eli reined in next to her, settling his horse into a pace that comfortably matched her own.

She slid a glance sideways at him. "Real life calling?"

He nodded and gave an almost uncomfortable shrug. "Some of my bigger clients are anxious to get me back into the office for upcoming litigation."

"Sounds like… Nope. I was going to say 'fun,' but it sounds like hell, actually."

He laughed. "It's life."

"Seems you'd always be pulled in a million different directions, trying to make everyone a winner."

"As I said, it's life."

"Yeah, well, not everyone wins at life." Try as she might to keep the bitterness from her voice, it still seeped through the tiny pauses between each word.

Urging his horse forward, he cut in front of her and forced her to draw up short. "I'm sorry about Luke and doubly sorry for being a complete asshole about it earlier. I had no idea."

She sucked air into lungs turned to stone. But that's exactly what she'd been doing for years, suffocating. Dying slowly from a kind of emotional asphyxiation that she'd finally stopped fighting. She'd given up living, her choices making her the equivalent of a coward, scared of where every quiet night would take her in sleep and what heartache every new sunrise might bring.

Swinging off her horse, she dropped the reins and started across the field to the small stream that ran through the bottom of the shallow valley.

"Reagan?"

Ignoring Eli's call proved easier than she expected. She just kept putting one foot in front of the other. She ignored the haggard sound of each inhale as she fought for every breath. Thick cedar shrubs crowded the stream banks. She didn't pay any mind to the scratchy twigs and branches snagging her clothes, instead pushing through the brush until she emerged at the water's edge. Two large steps forward and she dropped to her knees, the damp immediately seeping through her jeans as the ranch phone tumbled from her shirt pocket into the creek. Too bad. She dug the tips of her boots through the river rock and buried them in the moist dirt. Plunging her hands into the shallow water, she grabbed fistfuls of sandy mud and squished it through her fingers. Something pricked her palm. She ignored that just as she'd worked to ignore Eli.

Unless she found some kind of anchor, she had the feeling she'd break and simply float away. She sought the reminder that this was her reality, and this—kneeling on the edge of the creek with her hands in mud up to her wrists—was all she could come up with. It was a physical connection with the very land that had kept her safely tethered all these years.

But maybe that was the problem, *her* problem—always playing it safe. The last time she'd gone out on a limb and done something crazy, she'd said "I do" to a man she had known she'd never love. The man behind her *now* had been the ghost that chased her whether she was awake or asleep. She couldn't outrun him. And look how that had ended for Luke, a good man who had deserved better than she'd ever been able to give him. Especially the day he died.

Ever since then, life had been about playing it safe and working hard enough during the day that she fell into bed at night in a heavy and hopefully dreamless sleep. The biggest difference since Luke's death? Now two ghosts haunted her—the ghost of what might have been and the ghost of what should have been.

Whatever had pricked her palm dug in. Reagan blinked rapidly. Her reflection was warped in the lazy eddies of the water, her image colored softly by the last of the sun's glow while somehow also paled by the moon's first light.

It was going to be a long, highly stressful night. The next few days didn't promise to offer any relief from the long hours, strained emotions and death. Always death.

A hand settled tentatively on the back of her neck.

She jumped.

The hand tightened, holding her still as deft fingers began to move along the column of her neck. Thumbs dug into the knotted muscles.

A whimper caught in her throat, and Reagan wasn't sure what she wanted, to plead with him to stop or beg him to dig in harder.

As if nothing had changed and more than a decade hadn't passed since he'd touched her, he seemed to understand just what she needed. He dug both his thumbs into the base of her skull and massaged.

Deft fingers moved down to trace the distinct lines of her collarbones and then up until he cupped her chin. Elijah Covington, home again and touching her as if he wanted her. It was everything she'd wanted save for that specter of a love that hadn't been love, a marriage that had been so unbalanced it was amazing it had remained upright at all.

Eli urged her to her feet.

Unfurling her hand, she gasped at the sharp sting. Looking down, she found a mesquite thorn buried in her palm.

"Reagan."

Nothing but her name, an admonishment of compassion. The tenderness in his tone pulled her toward him like a ship toward safe harbor. But she knew what he represented wasn't safety. That voice promised heat, passion and the kind of empty promises made in the dark that would turn to dust at the first touch of sunrise.

And still, she offered him her palm.

With infinite tenderness, he pulled the thorn free. The wound bled, so he pulled his T-shirt off and wrapped it around her hand. "Hold this tight to stem the bleeding."

Her gaze went from his broad shoulders to his wide chest. He was more muscled than he'd been so many years ago, and it was very evident now as he stood with his shirt off, his hand around hers, his bare upper body less than a foot away. A deep valley ran between well-defined pecs. That valley continued lower, carving an admirable runnel between chiseled abs and his external obliques, that fascinating set of muscles that created the V just inside each hip and ran below the waist of his jeans. "Gutters" they'd been called in college before her biology classes.

A faint smile pulled at her lips as her gaze climbed every inch of bared skin with heated appreciation, pausing when she reached his throat. He was swallowing rapidly, and Reagan had to wonder how in the world they'd ended up here, under the starlight with his shirt off, her hand held in his and her desire for him building at an alarming rate. Leaning down, he kissed the pulse point on her wrist. Once, twice, and then his lips lingered, his tongue flicked over her pulse.

She should have said something. It would have been appropriate. But heaven save her, the sight of him shirtless stole her voice, the intimate touch of his lips, innocently suggestive, had rendered her mute. The man was more physically beautiful than she remembered. Years in the gym had made his body a topographical map of feminine delights. And that gesture, that tender kiss, had softened every reservation she had.

Shaking her head, she dipped her chin and closed her eyes, drawing a steadying breath. "Sorry."

"For looking at me?" he asked so gently she glanced up. With infinite gentleness and moving slow enough to give her the chance to stop him, he grasped her free hand and laid it over his heart. Then he wove his hands through her hair and tipped her face back farther. "You never have to apologize for looking at me like that, Reagan. Ever."

"Things are different now, Eli." Her voice shook even as her fingers curled into the thick pad of muscle on his chest, her fingertips registering the hammering of his heart. "We both know it. If we can just get through—"

His hands tightened the second before his mouth came down on hers, all demand and hunger and wet heat that worked her over until she was nothing but one giant, vibrating mass of nerves. Everything ached with wanting him, ached in a way she'd forgotten she could feel.

She dropped his shirt, intent on pushing him away, only to find her hand snaking up his neck and pulling him closer. Every thrust of his tongue demanded her response, refused to allow her to think, gave her no quarter other than to touch him and move with him, to feel the hard muscle under soft skin and to want everything he offered. Everything.

Reagan had missed this ravenous sexual ache. She'd hungered for this fire that branded her, burned her from the inside out and turned her reservations to ash. She had forgotten what it was like to get lost in a kiss. Forgotten what it was to be oxygen to the flame and flame to the oxygen, becoming so intertwined it was impossible to separate the two as they consumed her.

Eli freed one hand from her hair and, gripping her belt loop, yanked her closer.

And God…and Luke…forgive her, she let herself fall willingly into her first love's embrace.

7

ELI COULDN'T BREATHE. Hell, he didn't want to breathe, didn't need air. He only needed this woman. He'd fought so hard to forget the exhilaration of holding her in his arms as she came alive, as she whipped up his emotions like wind to a wildfire, incinerating his common sense. He'd been with other women, had the reputation of a serial dater among his crowd in Austin, but only because no one he'd ever met did this to him. No one else made him burn so damn hot. The best he'd been able to come up with were mediocre conversationalists who translated to disappointing bed partners. The cold memories only made the woman in his arms that much hotter.

Easing them down to the ground, he propped himself on an elbow, his arm beneath her head, his free hand roaming the dips and curves of her body. She'd always been so firm but feminine. Full breasts strained against her T-shirt. The hem had worked its way loose, and his fingertips dipped below the soft, well-worn cotton to find the bare skin of her belly.

She sucked in a sharp breath and, when he flattened his palm on her skin and let his pinky finger slip underneath the waistband of her jeans, her hips came off the ground to meet his touch.

He'd missed her organic responses, the way he could make her mind cloud over and coax her body into uninhibited acquiescence. For so long he'd thought of her, wondered how she'd been and, only now could admit, had missed her.

She whimpered and shifted her hips toward him, a silent demand he love her body. He unbuttoned the top button of her jeans and eased the zipper down. The skin above her practical cotton bikinis was so soft it drew a groan from his chest. Still, he slowed down, gentling his kiss as he nibbled at her lips before dropping his chin and nipping at the soft spot between her neck and shoulder. She tasted of salt and sunshine. Nothing had ever tasted so good.

Twisting her face away, she choked out, "Don't, Elijah. Don't let me think." She wound her hands through his hair and pulled his face back to hers, her kiss hungry and demanding and so damn heartbreaking he was powerless to do anything but give her whatever she wanted. And what she seemed to want, against all odds, was him.

Shifting over her, he settled his hips between the juncture of her thighs. She lifted to meet the hard ridge of his erection and he ground against her, rocking his body into hers as his balls drew tighter and the slow burn began at the base of his spine.

Somewhere nearby, a cow sneezed.

Reagan froze as the voices of the cowboys they'd ridden with carried across the wind. They weren't terribly close, but if Eli and Reagan could hear them, chances were fair the men would be able to hear them—soon.

Shoving and pushing, Reagan scrambled out from under him, pulling at her shirt and attempting to button her jeans, but her hands shook so badly she couldn't manage.

Eli stood and moved her hands aside gently but firmly. When her hands fell away, he deftly did her pants up, straightened her shirt and retrieved her hat from where it had fallen near the stream's edge.

She took it without a word, refusing to meet his gaze.

Reaching for his shirt, he shook it out and scrubbed the bloodstain in the water until it was nearly gone. When he stood and faced her, she still wouldn't look at him. "You okay?"

"I don't want anyone to know about this," she whispered.

Her declaration stung. "We didn't do anything wrong, Reagan."

Her eyes snapped to his. The depth of despair he saw in her gaze stole his breath and rendered him speechless.

Then she spoke, her every word tearing at his heart. "You'll leave, Eli. It's not a secret, not to you and definitely not to me. Whatever happens between us is something I'll be left to bear, the proverbial scarlet-letter-wearing woman who couldn't be true to the memory of her late husband."

"It's been three years—" he started, but she waved him off.

"Luke is a saint in this county and probably in heaven itself. I'm cheating on him whether he's waiting at home—" she swallowed hard "—or not. What I want, what I've always wanted with you, isn't possible, Eli."

"That's not true," he ground out. "I have no doubt you were a faithful wife. It's not in you to be otherwise, so this damn town and its gossipy residents can go to hell as far as I'm concerned. You're entitled to live your life however you want to."

"And where do you fit in that anymore?" She sighed. "You're going to leave and I'm going to stay and it will be just like it was before, except you know about Luke now and I'm tired of hating you for never coming back."

For me wasn't said, but he heard it loud and clear.

"I wanted you to come with me."

"And that wasn't possible. No more now than it was then." She wound her hair up and settled her hat on her head. "Anyway, it's history now and not worth reliving. We both made our choices. I'm asking you to respect mine. I..."

"But this is our opportunity to make a different choice, to get a kind of—" he threw his hands up in desperation "—a do-over, if you will. We can make the choice to be together now, for as long as it lasts."

"And how long will that be, Eli?" she asked quietly. "How long will it be before you return to Austin, to be the partner in your firm, fighting the good fight in court…and never looking back."

He turned a tight circle and then stepped into her space, pulling her hat off her head and tossing it aside as he gripped her shoulders. "You're asking me to pull out a crystal ball I don't have. I can't predict what will happen with one hundred percent accuracy. The only thing I can tell you with absolute certainty is that this is our chance to see what's left between us, to see if we can salvage what might have been and make it into something that could be." At her startled expression, he rushed on. "I'm not asking you to make any commitments or promises. What I am asking you to do is to willingly explore this…this…*thing* between us while I'm here. We'll take it day by day, you have the option to call stop at any point, and if you do I'll respect that." He moved in closer. "Your body doesn't lie. You still respond to my touch as much as I respond to yours. It's something we, as two consenting adults, want." He brushed his lips over hers. "I want you, Reagan. Tell me you want me, too."

"I can't deny that whatever this thing is between us clearly hasn't burned out." A deep flush spread up her neck and across her cheeks. "If I agree to see you while you're here, anything we do has to be done privately. No dates, no public affection, no behavior that gives anything away." When he started to speak, she glanced up, eyes blazing. "That's nonnegotiable. I'm the one who'll be left to suffer any consequences once you're gone again. I lived through it once. I don't have any desire to do it again."

Shame combined with regret to make his response sharper than he intended. "Are you embarrassed to be caught with me?"

"Not embarrassed, exactly. I just don't want the judgment and speculation about my private life that will inevitably come along with the action."

Not embarrassed...exactly. Well, wasn't that a rousing endorsement. He'd never been the secret lover his partner didn't want exposed. It hurt like hell, and the truth surprised him. "And if someone finds out?"

She took a deep breath and squared her shoulders. "Then I fully expect you to deny it. We're working together to get the Bar C out from under quarantine. You're probating your dad's estate. I don't care what you tell people so long as it isn't the truth. If you can live with that, we can explore our mutual physical attraction while you're in town. No strings attached, no expectations." She paused, looking over his shoulder. Her next words were almost lost to the fast-darkening night. "No regrets."

He took a step closer to her, his voice low and hard when he spoke. "So you'd what, use me to satisfy some latent sexual urges and then cast me aside?"

She didn't retreat even one step but went toe-to-toe with him, lifting her face to meet his. "Define it however you want, but you either take it on these terms or pass on the opportunity. Your choice." Laying a hand on his arm, she gave a fraction of a smile. "No hard feelings if you don't want to take it."

Oh, he wanted it, all right. But not with those rules. He didn't want to skulk around as if he was something she was ashamed of or what they might find in each other now was something to regret. It never had been. It shouldn't be now.

But he'd take Reagan any way he could get her. If it meant compromising his pride to keep her reputation intact, so be it. If the terms she'd outlined were the only ones she'd consider, if she truly meant he could take it or leave it, he had no doubt which side of the fence he'd be coming down on.

Illicit affair, it was.

THE RIDE TO the main house passed in general quiet. Eli asked a few questions but cast her a hundred curious looks. It was enough to make Reagan want to take back every word she'd said. They had been uttered in a moment of madness. It was the only explanation. Why else in the name of all that was holy would she offer Elijah Covington a short-term affair?

Intimate images of Luke floated to the surface, and it occurred to Reagan that Eli might think it would be acceptable to come to her house so he could…oh, hell. She couldn't even say it. "To screw your brains out, Matthews," she forced herself to whisper. "To take you every way you can imagine so you burn him out of your system and lay this particular ghost to rest."

Eli looked over. "I missed that."

"It's not worth repeating."

"I'm curious."

"And that should make me a parrot?" she bit out, then sighed. "Sorry. I'm tired. I don't want to have to euthanize tonight, yet it's unavoidable. I'll have to get medical provisions air shipped and start treating in the field. It's going to be hell."

"I figured." He moved his horse in closer. "What do you think the loss ratio is going to be? Realistically, I mean."

She swallowed hard. "If the entire ranch has been affected, if the cows brought in have intermingled, if they've run the same fence line or shared a stock tank? You're looking at a loss ratio of no less than three to ten. It could be worse if the disease has progressed further in different pastures."

"Shit. We can't afford that kind of loss. If Dad didn't keep up the insurance policies, it'll bankrupt the ranch and we'll be forced to sell it either as a whole or to parcel it off in sections." His face paled. "There could be lawsuits."

"There'd be nothing left to claim."

He shrugged, his shoulders seemingly burdened with possibilities. "Depends on how Dad set up the will. I've got to go over it tonight. If the limited liability corporation is in place, we've got some culpability. If it's an S corp, we're better off." He glanced over at her. "How's your place set up?"

"I don't know." She'd been struggling just to make the mortgage payments and keep up with her own obligations around the place. She'd never checked how the papers had been drawn up. No, that wasn't true. She'd avoided checking it after Luke was killed. It was one more thing to remind her he was gone, one more thing she had to handle on her own. "I suppose I should find out."

"Get the deed and I'll look it over for you while I'm here," he said absently, his mind seemingly a million miles away.

While I'm here, he'd said. Even now, Reagan had to mentally kick her own rear for laying out the terms of their affair the way she had. She knew he'd leave, but found she was already dreading the idea of it. She'd fight to keep this a sensory experience—nonemotional and nonconfrontational. It was the opportunity she had to have in order to get him out of her system. She'd love him and be loved by him one last time. Then she could—probably—move on and—maybe—reclaim her life. She would sell to the neighboring ranch and pick up a—God forbid—small place in town. But she'd make it work. As always.

They crested the hill to find the main house and three bunkhouses ablaze with lights pouring out from multiple windows. Blue lights flickered in several of the windows indicating the men had their TVs going. Laughter rang across the smooth night air, and all Reagan could think was, *That's about to change.*

Cade stepped out on the front porch, some sixth sense drawing his gaze their way. Full night had set in but, backlit as he was in the open doorway, it was easy to see his entire body stiffen at the sight of them riding in together. He skipped down the stairs, his shirt unbuttoned and the top button of his jeans undone. Reagan had a brief moment to thank God for the Covington genes before Cade was striding toward them, as pissed off as a horny bull pulled off a receptive cow.

"What the hell are you still doing here?" he demanded, reaching out to grab the reins of Eli's mount. The horse shied, nearly unseating Eli. Cade kept coming and the horse began backing up rapidly.

"Enough!" Reagan shouted, the command harsh.

Cade spun on her. "No offense, Reagan, but this is Covington business."

"Not anymore it isn't. You've got BRD spreading through your herds."

The middle Covington brother froze and considered her, his voice softer when he finally spoke. "I figured Everett had somehow misunderstood."

"He didn't. Eli and I intended to radio you ahead of our arrival, but I had a small accident—" she held up her bloodied hand "—and I dropped the radio in the water. Regardless, we're here now and we've got to get a handle on the outbreak. A large part of that is going to be you two working out whatever it is between you, so the bullshit stops and the collective priority becomes saving the Bar C. Eli might've just shown up today, but he gets that. He's helped me all evening to sort and gather, and Ty and a handful of cowboys are going to be here soon with the first herd. I'll have to have quarantine corrals set up, chutes to work in, lights for night work and food and drink for the men. The horses will have to be moved, preferably to a pasture nearby or to the barn where the doors are kept closed. I'll treat them with a full-spectrum antibiotic as a precaution for anything else the cows might be carrying, but I still don't want them exposed to any more than they have to be."

Cade's eyes widened. "Did you just dare to insinuate *he* cares more about the Bar C than I do?" There was a dangerous undertone to his words.

But Reagan was beyond the point she was willing to play *Family Feud*—Covington Style—with these two. "Out of everything I just laid at your feet, that's what you focused on? Grow up, Cade. I mean it. If I can work with him, so can you. So stop being so self-righteously pissed off over a history that can't be changed and grow a big-boy pair that'll see you through this." She swung down off her horse. "After this is done? You two can kill each other for all I care."

He stared after her as she stormed toward the barn, but she

still heard him say to Eli, "Some days I wonder why you ever left that woman."

And Eli's response: "So do I, Cade. Trust me. So do I."

8

THEY WORKED ALL NIGHT, and by the time the sun began to color the eastern horizon, Eli wanted to fall facedown on a bed. Or the hayloft. Or, hell, even a quiet piece of ground where he hopefully wouldn't get trampled.

He'd forgotten the working-all-night-then-pushing-on-to-do-chores-come-dawn thing that came with ranch life. You did what you had to do, and that's exactly why he found himself still in the barn well after dawn, shirt tucked into the pocket of his jeans and flinging hay bales off the giant stack. Several split on impact, and he cursed a blazing blue streak. He'd have to clean those up and feed them by tractor. Obviously, he'd lost his touch. Used to be he could chuck bales off the roofline and get them to land solid. That had been so long ago.

Soft footsteps interrupted his rhythm. Pausing, he peered over the edge of the giant pyramid-shaped haystack built into the corner of the barn to find Reagan moving from horse stall to horse stall, vaccination gun in hand. Voice soothing, she'd slip inside, inoculate the animal and move on. Ty went ahead of her to indicate which of the mares were pregnant. Reagan would pull out a different vaccination gun and treat those before going back to the regular dosing.

"Seems like you made up with Eli," Ty remarked casually, opening a stall door for her.

"I guess."

"You guys were pretty in sync all night, pushing cattle, treating the sickies, sorting the rest. It was like old times."

"Not quite, but easier than it could have been."

Ty stroked a mare's nose and looked at Reagan. "What made it easier?"

She shrugged. "I've been angry for fourteen years. That's plenty long for the best of women to carry a grudge."

"A grudge, huh?"

"I chucked the voodoo doll I made in his likeness before we got to work last night. You know, just to keep from backsliding." She glanced at him, the irony in her deadpan stare heavy. "But thanks for trying to help us work it out. At *every* opportunity."

"I didn't—" He coughed, then grinned. "Okay. I did."

Eli remembered enough about Ty to know he'd start badgering Reagan about her ride back to the ranch with him, so, he tossed a bale of hay down the far side of the haystack with such lack of care it split and scattered on impact. Both Ty and Reagan jumped. He leaped from bale edge to bale edge, agilely descending the giant haystack. "Thought I heard voices down here."

"Never took you for one to lurk in haystacks and eavesdrop," Reagan said, her words heavy with censure.

"Not my speed. I heard voices, thought one was yours, so I came down." He forced himself to grin charmingly. "You're not disappointed to see me, are you?" His smile faded as the silence drew out between them. When she only stared at him, his eyes narrowed.

"In the name of self-preservation, I'm out of here," Ty muttered. Snatching up the vaccine gun, he passed it to Reagan handle first. "I don't care what he says, don't inoculate Eli. It'll piss me off."

Both Eli and Reagan glanced at the typically affable youngest brother. The sharp edge to his tone said he was less than amused with her poking at Eli and wouldn't hesitate to give her hell if he had to. When Ty spun on his boot heel and strode to the barn door, Eli saw his opportunity and seized it.

"Do me a favor, bro?"

The younger man stopped but didn't turn around. "What?"

"Bar the barn door for me. Both ends."

Ty's brows winged down. "You remember how to get out?"

Eli glanced at Reagan, who had begun to shake her head. "Yep. If it's anything like riding a horse, I'm pretty damn good at it given all the practice I had growing up here."

One corner of Ty's mouth lifted with humor. "Your reputation could stand a good romp in the hay."

"Yeah?"

This time Ty truly smiled. "It might loosen the stick Austin seems to have wedged up your rear end."

"Get out, asshat," Eli called, flinging a flake of hay toward his brother. "And shut the damn door."

"Getting and shutting." He pulled the barn door closed behind him, the action followed by a heavy *thunk* of the wood baluster that pinned the doors closed from the outside.

Reagan looked up at Eli, eyes wide, dark circles easy to see even in dim light. "What are you up to, Covington?"

"Making the most of the time we've got for that illicit affair. I intend to start now."

SOMEONE MUST HAVE sucked all the air out of the barn. It was the only logical reason Reagan stopped breathing and couldn't get her lungs to reengage. "What are you talking about?"

"Hey, you were the one who set the terms—secret, right? With everyone out there working and assuming you're in here doing the same, they ought to leave you alone for at least a little while."

"They'll see Ty out there in the corrals," she hissed, backing away from him.

"And he'll cover for us."

"Why? What's in it for him?"

A strange shadow passed over his face, half pain and half relief. "He'll do it because I came home when he asked me to." He closed the distance between them, hooking a finger under her chin and lifting until their eyes met.

Hot and cold, want and regret, desire and worry—they all raced through her, driving her to want to take up drinking. "This is crazy," she whispered.

"I prefer to consider it in legal terms," he whispered in return, stepping even closer.

"Which are?"

"Temporary insanity. It forgives a great deal, and I want you to forgive me for this."

He moved so quickly she didn't have a chance to defend herself. Getting his shoulder into her hips and pelvis, he stood, picking her up like a sack of grain.

"Elijah Covington, you put me down right this second," she demanded, struggling. "Put me down or you're going to find yourself inoculated for a variety of diseases."

Tightening his grip, he ripped a horse blanket off a saddle resting on the hitching post and started up the hay bale, strong enough that he moved with confidence and ease. "Stab me with that vaccine gun and I'll tan your ass, Matthews."

The temptation to see if he'd follow through nearly had her pricking him with the needle, but she managed to refrain. Barely.

Once at the top, he tossed the blanket down, spreading it out by foot before going to his knees and laying her down gently.

"Eli—"

"Hush, Reagan. I agreed to your terms of privacy and secrecy. I don't like it, but if it's the only way I can get my hands on you? So be it. I've been here a mere twenty-four hours, and it's been one constant reminder after another that I suck at being a Covington. The only thing that I ever got right in my life before I left for Austin was you. Not even my old man could condemn me for that." His throat worked as he swallowed hard. "You were the only thing that was ever right about this place, the only thing that ever fit and the one thing I couldn't take with me. I don't want to have to wait for sundown and convenient timing to touch you. Not now. Now when I have you within reach again, baby."

"No pet names."

"That wasn't part of the original negotiation."

Her eyes narrowed. "Consider it an amendment."

"Sorry. Original contracts have been accepted as presented. No more negotiations," he said softly as he untucked her T-shirt.

Her breath came faster as his soft fingertips brushed her ribs. Then he ran a hand up under her shirt, through the neck and gripped her throat gently. As he stroked her chin with one thumb, her eyes widened. "This is new."

"I left here an insecure boy who couldn't navigate his way through his family's politics. I'm not that boy anymore. I know who I am, know my own worth. I want to know who *you* are now, the type of woman you've become. From what I've seen so far? You're everything I believed you could be and more. Neither of us are the people we were fourteen years ago. We both need to remember that."

His grip tightened momentarily and her back arched hard enough so that only her shoulders and booted feet were in contact with the hay beneath her.

He dragged a hand down her chest, over her sternum, spreading her breasts even as his thumb and pinkie raked over her swollen nipples. She drew in another shaky breath. "And what does that mean exactly, that we're different people?"

His grin was slow. "It means I've wanted this long enough you should probably prepare yourself to hang on tight."

"You've wanted this?" Nerves she'd believed long dead flared hard and fast, and awareness spread across her skin.

Eli's face grew somber, his broad hand resting across her belly. "More than you can possibly imagine. And I have an active imagination where you're concerned." He closed his eyes and drew a breath so deep his chest and shoulders seemed larger in size. When his gaze finally found her, his eyes were so serious.

Her nerves released little butterflies through her body. “Kiss me, Eli.”

“As my mistress commands,” he murmured, lowering his mouth to hers.

His tongue touched hers tentatively before his confidence surged. The years fell away and everything was familiar in a way that was all new. They devoured each other. Her hunger for him burned through her, a gasoline-fueled blaze.

Every time she thought she’d caught up with him, he’d change the way he touched her, change the angle of his kiss or move his lips to her ear to whisper suggestively as he caressed her body.

Raising her up, he divested her of her shirt and bra before laying her back down with a sort of desperate reverence. His eyes skipped over her, leaping hungrily from point to point before settling on the button of her jeans. Toying with it, he began to say something twice but stopped himself each time.

She pushed to sitting and leaned on her hands. “Something you want to say about my brand of denim?”

“You’re more beautiful than I ever remembered,” Eli said in a hushed voice.

Her heart stumbled and threatened to take a dangerous fall in his direction.

Reagan could manage sex. She knew she could. But manage him? Never. So she did the only thing she could to keep herself from baring her soul. “You’ve obviously not been laid in a while if a farmer’s tan is doing something for you.”

He traced the line where deep tan gave way to pale skin on her arm, that point where shirtsleeve began and ended and left a year-round difference in the color on her flesh. When his gaze finally made its way up to hers, she regretted the quippy remark. So much rested in his stare. From regret to contentment, hunger to anxiety, it was all there.

It made him suddenly, unequivocally real to her. She’d spent the past twenty-four hours knowing he was here, yes. But it had been with the general understanding he was temporary, a passing attraction no more permanent than a traveling circus.

But this ringmaster ran her emotions, putting them through their paces with every proverbial crack of the whip that came in the form of his brand of humor, his charm, his compassion. This combination of him and her was dangerous.

She'd truly believed she could manage this affair. Now she wondered if both of them would walk away from this scarred worse than before.

He unbuttoned her jeans. "What's going on in that mind of yours, Reagan?"

Nothing safe, and definitely nothing welcome. So she lied. "Seems I'm in a bit more of a rush than you are. It's unfair." Hooking a leg around his thighs and an arm around his shoulder, she half flipped, half rolled him over so he ended up on his back with her straddling his hips. His erection pressed against the seam of her sex. She grinned. "Maybe you're more rushed than I thought."

Eli settled his hands on her hips. "I wanted this first time to be more than a roll in the hay."

Her belly flipped over. *This first time.* So this was going to be more than a single occurrence. She had to concur.

Once would never be enough.

9

CLOTHES CAME OFF in a confusing rush, and they both laughed a bit manically when Eli couldn't get one boot off. It took both of them to wiggle his foot free.

Then, suddenly, the laughter dissolved into the kind of anticipatory silence that built before a storm broke. And it would be the kind of storm that leveled outlying buildings and sent both man and animal running for cover. Eli held no false illusions about what coming back together with Reagan would be like…or would mean.

Laying her down on the blanket, he started with her jaw, kissing her tenderly before nipping the soft skin and soothing it again with little kisses, small licks and murmured words of affection and encouragement. He wanted to draw the little noises out of her that drove him wild, evidence he'd done the same, was *doing* the same, to her. She was passionate. She was responsive. She was so alive compared to the handful of lovers he'd been with over the years. Not a one of them could hold a candle to this amazing woman.

He was lost to her all over again, to the smell of her shampoo, the taste of hard-earned sweat on her skin, the musk of her undeniable arousal. She was everything to him in that moment—

his sunrise and sunset, every minute of his day and every hour of his night. She was the one thing that had ever been right about home.

Slipping down her body, he pressed her legs open and ran his tongue along the seam of her sex. It thrilled him when her hips bucked involuntarily, lifting her off the blanket.

She cried out.

"Shh," he said, breathing against her cleft.

"Eli," she begged.

He didn't stop. Settling in, he tasted her deeply, reveled in every shudder of her body as he drew closer and closer to her clit.

She moved in fits and starts, trying to force him to get to that magical place that would send her over the edge.

He resisted. At least initially.

Then it was too much—her reaction, her arousal, her unarguable need for him. Dragging the tip of his tongue over her clit, he circled it rapidly, then suckled it. Gently, he built the pressure and at the same time he flicked his tongue over the hard knot.

Her shoulders rose off the blanket as she came. Eyes wild, Reagan bit her lip fiercely. Every breath came fast. She clutched his hair and rode his mouth as the orgasm took her higher, soft whimpers escaping despite her best efforts.

Gripping her wrists, he pulled her hands free of his hair, dug a condom from his wallet and sheathed himself to the root with shaking hands. "Lie back," he commanded softly. "I want to see your face when I take you."

She slumped down, her breathing heavy, her eyes alight with expectation.

He covered her body with his, planting his forearms next to her shoulders and settling his raging erection against her. Adjusting his approach, he gripped his cock. "Spread yourself for me."

She complied.

His heart lodged in his throat. She was beautiful. Perfect. Raising himself up, he settled one hand against the blanket and the other on his rigid shaft. He fed the head into her slowly, shocked at her channel's narrowness, thrilled with how wet she was. He had to take his time—feed in an inch, retreat. Feed in another half inch and retreat.

Then she took control, lifting her hips and taking him to the hilt with a gasp.

He grunted as he hit the end of her channel. She was so tight it almost hurt.

"Move," she commanded, voice straining. When he hesitated, she began to draw herself off him.

"Don't you dare," he nearly growled. Holding himself on his forearms, he used his knees to spread her legs wider. She followed his silent direction, bending her knees more and lifting her hips to meet his thrusts. He began with a slow in and out movement, rolling his hips to insure he covered her G-spot with every entry.

She moaned. "More. Please, Eli. I… I need…"

"What, beautiful? Tell me, Reagan." Shaking her head, she tried to force herself back down his length, but he gripped her chin. "Say it."

"Raw. I want this raw and real." She gasped, pushing against him. "Please, Eli. Please."

And in giving her what she needed, a little bit of him fell into the mix. He fumbled the rhythm when he realized he'd offered part of himself to her, but she couldn't possibly understand, refusing to let him slow down.

Pushing against him, she moaned low but clear. "Yes. Yes, yes, yes."

The unguarded pleasure in her voice pushed aside his intention to make this a matter of gentle lovemaking. Instead, he rode her with increasing roughness, the sound of slick skin slapping slick skin creating the most erotic sound he'd heard in…fourteen years.

She met his every stroke, refusing to let him have the upper hand. She was so different from the gentle lover she'd once been, and he was crazed by the woman she'd become. Her demands drove him higher, made him ride her harder. His fingers dug into her firm flesh as the burn of release began near the base of his spine. "Not yet," he ground out.

Reaching down, he pinned her hips down and shifted higher so he scraped her clit with every drive forward. One stroke, two, three…and she came apart in his arms with a shout.

Curled over her body, Eli rode her harder, his own release bearing down on him with unapologetic force. He came with a shout, gripping her so tight he feared she'd bruise. But damn if he could stop himself.

Slowly slipping down from that precipice of ultimate release, he stroked her pinked skin and ran a fingertip down her neck.

Eyes closed, breathing fast, she managed a small smile.

"What?" he panted as he withdrew and shifted to lie by her side.

"I'm going to go out on a limb here and say that getting to know the man you've become is going to have some serious perks. Unless that's all you've got going on, Esquire."

He rolled her onto her side, following the motion with his own as he draped an arm around her waist. "Not even close, Doc. Not even close."

THE MOMENT REAGAN pulled herself together, she left the Covington place in a cloud of dust. She'd been so worried that everyone could tell what she and Eli had been up to that she'd nearly left Brisket behind.

That had been the litmus test of her emotional well-being. Her life's stability had crashed and burned within twenty-four hours of Eli's return. She didn't even want to think about what that might mean.

Pulling up to her small log cabin, she put the truck in Park and sat staring blankly through the windshield over wide, barbed-wire-fenced fields. Somewhere nearby, a calf bawled, calling for its mother. Reagan could relate. If her mother weren't still so hung up on Luke's memory, she'd give the woman a call and ask her advice. But her mom believed in Luke Matthews's sainthood, and if she suspected her daughter had defiled his memory, let alone with the reviled Elijah Covington, she'd probably have a heart attack. Or a seizure. Or both.

Neither would stop her from condemning her daughter's actions, though, and Reagan couldn't take that. Not right now. But if Eli would hold to his word and keep the affair a secret, Reagan hoped she would never be put in that position.

That was the only downfall to living in such a small town. Everyone took an interest in everyone else's business, and no one hesitated to volunteer their two cents—to your face or behind your back. She hated being talked about. Hated being the object of speculation, be it curious or malicious. Hated that she had to remain above it all in order to keep her business healthy. Her livelihood was contingent on the very people who gossiped about her, and it sucked.

She pulled her hat off and ran a shaking hand through her hair. Brisket licked her wrist, and she turned her attention to him. The dog had never known Luke, but she had no doubt he would have loved the man.

Still, the Border collie's loyalty would have been to her and her alone. It was her gift, building these wordless relationships with animals. It was what had, in part, led her to pursue veterinary medicine. It was also a decent career that had allowed her to come back home with a solid job in the otherwise unstable communities of northeastern New Mexico. No one could leave her or force her to leave. She would be responsible for herself and only herself, and that was exactly what she'd wanted in the wake of Eli's abandonment.

Eli's abandonment.

And she'd just willingly set herself up to be abandoned again. Soon.

Making love with him in the barn had convinced her that

having a private affair had been as asinine a choice as her decision to marry Luke.

She'd known she wasn't in love with Luke when he'd asked, but he'd presented her with what seemed to be, even in retrospect, a hundred excellent reasons why they should make the ultimate commitment to each other. He'd told her then he was well aware she'd always love Eli, but he had been so convinced he could make her love him, too. It would just take time, and he was willing to give her that. All she'd needed to do was say yes, to step out of the shadow of history and live in the light of the present.

So she'd said yes.

But what she'd found with Luke hadn't been living. Because it hadn't taken her any time at all to realize Luke *had* been the perfect husband…for someone else. She'd done him the greatest disservice by marrying him.

From the first, she'd tried to be a good wife, to be a companion and responsive lover. She'd never quite pulled it off. She'd believed herself more a fraud every day, the layers and layers of guilt building a thicker and thicker wall between her and Luke. Then he'd died. And those layers, those walls, had become unsurpassable.

Because while she had cared for Luke, had truly loved him in the dispassionate way of a steady, nonsexual companion and had mourned his loss, she'd never been brokenhearted over it. Not like she'd been when Eli left her.

She was a horrible person, and if anyone ever realized the truth about how she'd felt at Luke's death, she'd be shunned as the county pariah. She'd have to leave.

She threw the driver's door open and hit the ground at a run. She made it to the edge of the porch before she lost the meager contents of her stomach.

The problem? No matter where she ran to, she couldn't get away from herself or her past. Eli had proved that with amazing efficiency. A hard shiver skipped down her spine. He'd owned her body this morning, taking her to heights she'd forgotten a woman could reach. And he'd done it with a finesse he'd lacked as a teen. The realization he'd learned to be such an accomplished lover by *being* a lover to other women made her hands ball into fists. It wasn't as if they'd had a commitment to each other, but she'd been faithful to his memory, had held out hope he'd return for her even though his parting words had been so decisive.

"One of these days, I'll be back," he promised gruffly, moving out of reach as he snatched his duffel bag up and hoisted it over his shoulder. "This damn two-light town will see exactly what I'm made of."

What she'd heard was that he'd be back.

What he'd meant was things between them were through.

Until now.

Brisket whined from the open door of the truck, waiting her command that would allow him to hop down.

"Out," she said softly.

The dog leaped from the truck and nearly belly crawled to her. Canine intuition told him something was very wrong, but the environment gave no clue as to what it was. Being Brisket, though, and loving her the way he did, he sidled up to her and pressed against her legs.

"It's fine." She stroked his head.

His feathery tail wagged, stirring up the dust.

She climbed the stairs and walked across the porch, pushing into the house and tossing her bag on the seat of the hall tree. Stripping as she went, she crossed the living room and went straight to the shower. The water was hot enough to scald, but it didn't faze her when she stepped under the aggressive spray. She craved the benediction of the cleansing heat. Water sluiced over her head, over her face and down her body.

The one thing she couldn't deny was that being well used by Eli had left her with delicious tiny aches and tenderness. It had been years since she'd had sex. Even more years since she'd experienced desire so raw it left her body demanding more than a creative imagination.

She stepped out of the shower and toweled off, wrapping her hair up and pulling on her T-shirt and boxers. The answering machine by her bedside blinked, advertising eight messages. They were probably clients. Maybe her neighbors. Regardless, those callers were going to have to wait. She'd been up for more than thirty hours.

Pulling her quilt back, she fell into bed. Sleep crowded her consciousness before she got the towel off her head.

And for the first time since Luke had died, she went to sleep unafraid of dreaming.

10

ELI FELL OUT of his twin bed. Twice. "Damn it," he shouted the second time he crashed to the ground. Surely the bed hadn't been this small when he was a kid. It wasn't possible. He'd have ended up with brain damage. And the carpet-on-concrete floor certainly hadn't softened with age. Irritated, he shoved to his feet and wrestled the covers into place.

The pristine sky shone through the lone window. The sun was high; he needed to get his saddle-sore ass in gear. Besides, the aches and pains he'd earned from yesterday's manual labor meant there'd be no more sleep. The gym was fine for building a body, but hard work revealed muscles a person forgot they had and, despite his exceptional physical conditioning, he apparently had a hell of a lot of those very muscles.

His phone rang and he dug it out of the pocket of his briefcase. The broken screen again scrambled the incoming number but chances were solid it was an Austin number. "Covington."

The voice at the other end came through so garbled he couldn't understand a single word.

"Hold on," he said loudly, as if yelling would help. Jogging out of the room, he was up the stairs and outside before the signal cleared. "Covington," he repeated.

"Mr. Covington, it's Lynette."

He fought a sigh. Lynette, his paralegal, was the best there was, but she could get a little codependent in his absence. She always had to have more direction on the larger cases when he was out of the office, a bit more reassurance in her decision making. But her output? It was the sole reason she was at the top of her field. She worked circles around the other paralegals once she was set on task, and what she produced was impeccable. Getting her to take the initiative without his approval proved the only challenge.

"What can I do for you, Lynette?"

"Sir, the president of Macallroy Oil is demanding an in-office meeting with you tomorrow at ten o'clock central time. I advised him you were out of the office, but he's insisting you be here to discuss the prosecution's settlement offer." She drew a deep breath. "He's livid, Mr. Covington."

Eli pinched the bridge of his nose. "Explain to him my father passed away."

"That was the first thing I did, sir. He was rather—" she sniffed "—vulgar in his response."

Brows drawn together, Eli couldn't imagine what the old jackass had said to earn his paralegal's disapproval. She'd witnessed and heard plenty to toughen her skin. "Define vulgar."

"I'd rather not."

"And I'd like to know how hard I'll be taking him to task when I return his call."

She took a moment to answer, her voice low when she finally got around to it. "He said he didn't care if you were stuck in the Australian Outback and your dick had been eaten by a dingo. You'd best slap a Band-Aid over your bare balls and get your ass to the meeting or, for what he's paying you, he'd find another lawyer that would make Macallroy Oil his *only* priority."

While it wasn't exactly vulgar, particularly for the man in question, it had offended his paralegal, and Eli took exception to anyone abusing the people he considered himself responsible for. "If he calls in again, tell him I'll be in touch within the hour."

"Should I expect you in the office, Mr. Covington?"

Eli paused, thinking through the logistics. He could theoretically get to Austin today if he left now, but he'd only be able to make a single meeting. Then he'd have to get back here to carry out his responsibilities to his brothers. It seemed pointless, but Macallroy Oil was one of the firm's most profitable clients, and pissing the old man off wouldn't end well for anyone.

Sighing, he closed his eyes and tipped his head to the sky. He usually had no problem prioritizing. But the current demands were all pulling him in different directions, and he didn't know how to manage what everyone expected of him.

In the distance, someone fired the tractor up. Cattle called out at the promise of food, rattling the chains that held the metal gates as they jostled for the best positions at the round bale feeders. Overhead, the sun beat down on his face and warmed his skin.

"Are those…cows?" Confusion infused Lynette's question.

"Yeah." Eli hadn't shared his background with his coworkers. The most anyone at the firm knew, he'd moved to Austin to go to school and had stayed. Nothing more personal ever passed his lips.

"Where are you, Mr. Covington?"

He hesitated. "Taking care of some business." Even now, he couldn't bring himself to reveal his rural upbringing, to admit ties to this place he'd called home for nineteen years.

He'd worked hard to cultivate his image, one of urbane sophistication, not that of an unpolished, dirt-road-driving, tractor-owning cowhand. He rolled his shoulders and ground his teeth.

Shoving a hand in one pocket of his jeans, he forced himself to admit that for the first time, he was ashamed of himself for leaving the ranch and his family as he had. He'd always blamed his old man for not being able to see past Eli's shortcomings. Not once had Eli recognized in himself the longing to be different—he'd just wanted to be "better" than the people he'd grown up with.

He'd dismissed them en masse after his mother died. The lack of civilization had killed her, he'd believed. But in truth? She'd made her place here. She'd been the epitome of class and grace. She'd displayed loyalty and affection, been a good friend and neighbor and more. He'd been the uncivilized one.

He'd been so full of self-righteousness he'd never even tried to look for the good in this place and the people who made it what it was. *Shit*. He'd really screwed this up.

Or being here was screwing *him* up. He'd never questioned his choice to leave, never felt guilty about the man he'd been or the man he'd become. Not until all this emotional bullshit started sticking to his borrowed boots.

"Are you there, Mr. Covington?"

He forced himself to speak. "Yeah. If Macallroy calls, tell him I'll be in touch within the hour. I'll be there for the meeting, but do *not* advertise my availability to anyone else. There's too much left to do with this estate business, so I'll be returning after that meeting."

"Yes, sir. Do you need me to make travel arrangements?"

"No. I've got it. Have a good afternoon." He disconnected and went back into the house, sank into his dad's favorite recliner and used the house phone to call Macallroy.

The old man answered on the second ring. "Don Macallroy."

"Don, it's Elijah Covington."

"So your little secretary managed to reach you? Figured she would if I made it clear I'm prepared to walk."

"Let's not get off on the wrong foot here, Don. While I appreciate your creativity in having me unmanned by a dingo, my father died. There are obligations to the family I have to fulfill."

"Unless those particular obligations fund your bank account, you've got your priorities out of order, Covington. *I* provide the income that allows you to live the lifestyle you do."

"You're not my only client. And my lifestyle and how I pay

for it is none of your concern, Don," Eli snapped. He'd intended to keep this entirely professional no matter how the old man goaded him, but Eli's front-porch epiphany had brought too much emotion to the surface. Still…

"Don, I'm trying to work with you here. The best I can offer is a nine o'clock Skype call tomorrow morning. I'm not coming into Austin for a personal meeting, because I have to attend the first probate hearing at the local court by one tomorrow afternoon. That's not negotiable. But I'm willing to work with you remotely to settle whatever has disturbed you."

"You'd better come to the virtual table with some answers, Covington."

"Anything in particular?" The cold edge to Eli's words was unmistakable.

The old man matched his tone. "I want to know what the hell would prompt you to encourage us to settle for $35 million. You're supposed to be on our side in this, but I get the distinct impression Macallroy Oil is getting the shaft, and the bitch isn't using lube."

Eli's stomach pitched as his ethics bucked wildly. His client had run an oil carrier ashore. The hull had been breached and the crude had been dumped into the North Atlantic. Every study conducted indicated the disaster would affect the environment for the next twenty years. He'd proposed they accept this settlement because, if anything, Macallroy Oil should be paying three times the amount. But it wasn't Eli's job to point out his client was "lucky." It was his job to get the bastard the best deal he could. It wasn't the first time he'd been faced with having to do something that went against his personal beliefs. For some reason, though, this particular event chafed worse than ever.

"Conference call at nine tomorrow, Don. It's the best I can do." He barely refrained from adding *Take it or leave it*, with the hope the old man would leave it.

"Mind yourself, Covington," Macallroy said softly. There was a distinctive click.

Eli fought the urge to punch something. He needed to go for a run, lift some weights, throw some hay around—something. It wasn't an option, though. Not with so much to do.

He called Lynette to let her know he wouldn't be coming in after all, and instead asked her to email him the Macallroy files and arrange the conference call with his fellow attorney on the case, Amanda English, and then Don. He wasn't dealing with the old man without witnesses.

Eli disconnected at the same time Cade came through the front door.

The other man paused, looking him over. "Odd seeing you in Dad's chair. Hell, it's odd seeing you here at all." Then he surprised Eli by moving to the sofa and flopping down. "Damn, but I'm worn-out." His gaze focused on the rolling fields outside the big picture window. "I've got to admit I'm surprised you're up and moving. Figured after last night you'd have packed your bags and be headed to your life in the city fast as your borrowed boots would take you."

"The boots are actually my old ones." Eli shrugged. "They're a little tight, but they fit about as well as this life ever did."

Cade's gaze locked on him, detached curiosity swimming in his eyes. "You ever miss it?"

Eli slid low in the recliner and crossed his hands loosely over his stomach. He took a second to figure out how to answer honestly. He'd realized in the past thirty-plus hours that there *were* things he missed.

Enough to come home?

Never.

His brother started to get up, shaking his head. "Your silence says more than enough."

"Sit," Eli ordered.

Cade's gaze narrowed.

"Please," he amended, breathing easier when Cade sank back onto the sofa. "It's just something I didn't expect you to ask, and I wanted to think about how best to answer. If you'd asked me yesterday, I would've said there was nothing I missed. Now?" He sat forward, propping his forearms on his knees. "Yeah. There are things I miss. Some more than others."

"Saw you with Reagan."

Eli's chin whipped up and his eyes locked on Cade's. "I would argue there wasn't much to see."

"Depends on how hard someone was looking, I suppose." Crossing his arms over his chest, Cade considered Eli. "You came home for Ty."

The rest of the statement was left off but might as well have been shouted—*but not for me*.

"Ty asked me to come home and help with the estate." Eli swallowed, weighing every word twice before he continued. "You asked me to come home and stay. I couldn't, Cade. I don't belong here."

"Did you ever consider that the two of us, me and Ty, might have had dreams of our own? Your leaving meant we were obligated to stay. Me particularly, because I inherited the title of oldest whether I wanted it or not."

Resentment colored his every word, but the exhaustion behind it all was what hit Eli the hardest. "I thought you wanted to be here."

"What I wanted didn't matter after you took off. Dad took me aside and explained what he expected. You know how he was." Cade's gaze drifted back to the window. "I didn't want to leave him, didn't want to put it all on Ty." He faced Eli. "So I stayed."

"What did you want to do instead?" Eli asked quietly.

"Doesn't matter anymore." Standing, Cade stretched.

"I've got a conference call tomorrow at nine with a difficult client. Dad's office have internet?"

"Dial-up. Doubt it's fast enough for what you need. Reagan's place has satellite internet. We've used it before to place large orders."

"I'll ask her if I can use it, then. Thanks."

"No problem." Cade slapped his cowboy hat on. "State vet

will be here at noon tomorrow. Wouldn't hurt to have you around to speak legalese."

"I'll be here."

"We'll see," Cade muttered, heading outside.

"Cade?" Eli called.

The man paused and glanced over his shoulder, one hand on the screen door, waiting.

"I won't leave you guys to handle this alone." It wasn't the apology Eli had intended to offer, but it was what came out. It was a place to start.

Cade gave a short nod and went on outside.

Eli pushed out of the chair and, without thinking too hard, grabbed the keys to one of the ranch trucks and headed out.

THE KNOCK AT the door dragged Reagan out of a deep sleep. Squinting at the late-afternoon sunlight, she sat up and rubbed her bleary eyes. Brisket had crashed out on his dog bed on the floor beside her, but the knock had brought the dog up on all fours facing the front of the house.

A toss of the quilt exposed her overheated skin to the air-conditioned room and goose bumps broke out all over. That's when she realized her hair was half-wrapped in the towel, the bottom half of its length still damp.

"Great," she muttered to the dog. "I'm going to open the door looking like Medusa. If I turn anyone to stone, you'll dig the hole to bury the evidence. Deal?"

He wagged his tail.

"Excellent." Shoving her feet into slippers, she finger combed her hair as best she could and started for the door.

A second, louder knock sounded.

"Coming!" Yes, she worked for people, but damn if their general impatience didn't make her a little crazy at times. She yanked the door open and nearly knocked herself over. "Eli?"

"Hey." His heated gaze roamed over her body, taking in her

thin cami and tiny sleep shorts, before trailing down her legs and back up to her face. "Can I come in for a second?"

"Stay," she ordered Brisket. Heart pounding in her ears, she stepped out on the porch and pulled the door closed behind her. "I'm not sure it's the best idea right now."

He gave a short nod. "You're beautiful."

Heat burned her cheeks. "What are you doing here?"

"I have to talk to you."

Reagan's stomach plummeted. A hundred possible reasons why he would have come raced through her mind, but only one stuck. He was done with her. It had taken him one literal roll in the hay, and he was finished. "So talk."

Dark brows winged down over blue eyes. "You have a problem with letting me in your house for this conversation?"

"Some conversations don't need coffee and a couch. Just get it over with."

He jerked as if she'd slapped him. "This is quite a bit different than my reception this morning."

Lips thin, she lifted one shoulder in an approximation of a shrug.

Eli rolled his head. "I'm here to ask a favor."

That threw her. "I'm sorry?"

"A favor." Eli propped one hip on the porch rail. "I'd appreciate it if I could borrow your office tomorrow morning a little before nine. I have a conference call with a difficult client and some of my office staff. The ranch office doesn't have enough bandwidth to carry the call. Cade suggested I ask if I could use your place."

"You're here to borrow my office?" Heat crawled up her neck and across her cheeks.

"Yeah. Why? What did you think…?" His brows shot up. "You thought I was here to end this thing between us?"

She crossed her arms under her breasts and forced herself to meet his wide-eyed stare. "It crossed my mind."

Slowly standing, he moved toward her. The wild heat in his gaze said she couldn't have been any more wrong.

Reagan retreated up until she was pressed against the front door, her hand fumbling to find the doorknob. He reached out and gently grasped her wrist, pulling it forward and placing it around his neck. He did the same with her other hand. Then he bent, hooked his arms under her butt and lifted her straight up. "Legs around my waist."

"We're on my front porch," she whispered.

"In the middle of nowhere."

"Clients regularly come by without an appointment."

"Legs, Reagan."

She secretly reveled in his brute strength as she wrapped her legs around his waist. And gasped. The hard ridge of his erection rubbed at her sex through the seriously thin cotton of her sleep shorts. Her nipples beaded. Breaths came shallow and fast as he shifted her so her feminine lips parted. The rough edge of his jeans scraped tender flesh and she tightened her arms and legs around him. "Eli," she whispered roughly.

He supported her ass, fumbling to get his zipper down. The heat of his erection nearly scalded her skin as the broad head of his cock slipped inside her shorts. On contact, he buried his face in her neck and let out a tortured groan. "Damn it, Reagan. You're not wearing underwear."

"I got out of the shower and grabbed a nap."

"And now I'm not only thinking about you naked, but soapy and wet, too." He lifted his face and shared a tight smile with her. "You're trying to reduce me to the green kid I used to be and make me come before I've had my way with you." He dug his wallet out one-handed. "Condom's behind the driver's license."

Shoulders propped against the front door as he held her up by the thighs, she fumbled through his wallet, found the condom and tossed the wallet aside. He ripped the condom wrapper with his teeth and sheathed his erection. Then he was there, pushing inside her, giving no quarter as he pulled her down his length.

Chest to chest, he never took his eyes off hers. "You're so damn tight."

Gripping his hips and using his neck as a fulcrum, she pressed her forehead to his before she lifted herself up his length.

He hissed. "Sweet hell."

His mouth claimed hers with authority, challenging her to meet the thrust of his tongue in time with the thrust of his hips. The width of his cock stretched her to a point where pain and pleasure converged and she reveled in it. Every thrust was a kind of claiming. And the words he whispered in her ear, the things he said he was going to do to her, took her higher.

She rode him harder, leaning back far enough to force him to widen his stance and bend his knees a little more. Her tempo increased, nails digging into the soft skin on his neck. "Eli," she breathed, unable to stop herself from calling out his name.

Hands on her hips, he encouraged her to move faster, rougher. He leaned her forward just enough to ensure the root of his cock scraped her clit with every thrust.

Her eyes widened and, before she could think about how good that really felt, the orgasm crashed over her. Her walls tightened around him and her whole body shook with the ferocity of her release. She was carried away on a surge of pleasure unlike any she'd ever experienced.

His fingers dug into her ass and then, with a shout, he let go. Hips pumping hard, she felt the pulses along the length of his cock as his release moved through him. His movements became sporadic, slowed and then stopped. He pressed her shoulders against the front door, pinning her there with his chest as his hands gripped her thighs. Breathing raggedly, he laid a gentle kiss on her lips. "So, can I use your internet?"

The question was so off-the-wall that she burst out laughing. "For this? You can even use my long-distance service if the connection cuts out. Just don't touch my red Swingline stapler."

He narrowed his eyes as he set her down. "What would I have to do to be able to use the stapler?"

"I'm not sure you're cut out for it," she said, getting her feet under her.

Turning, she opened the door and Brisket jumped out, tail wagging. He went straight to Eli and pressed his body up against the man's leg. Big brown eyes lifted to watch as Eli tucked himself inside his jeans and zipped up.

The ease with which Brisket accepted Eli made her chest tight. It was as if the man just belonged, and that was the farthest thing from the truth that could possibly be said. From his expensive haircut to his smooth hands with their fresh blisters, Eli didn't belong here. Never had. This could only last a few days at most, and then he'd be gone. They'd both be in the places they belonged, both alone again, though he was certain not to stay that way, whereas she seemed tormented by ghosts.

"Hey, buddy." Eli rubbed the dog's ears. "Let's get inside." He gestured awkwardly to his groin. "I would pay good money to have the chance to clean up." Brisket trotted into the house. "Smart dog," Eli commented.

"Brilliant," she answered, watching the dog curiously. Trying to recapture the lighthearted mood of moments before, she looked over her shoulder as she headed inside. "Seems his judge of character might be warped, but he's hell on cattle so I'll keep him."

"Hey!" Eli slapped her ass. "My character's just fine."

"Your character's as warped as an untreated two-by-four left out through a good wet season."

"Wench," he growled, scooping her up and starting for the bathroom.

Panic struck her as unexpectedly as a rattlesnake strike. "No. Don't go into the bathroom. I don't want to use the bathroom."

Eli stopped and glanced down at her, the deep V between his brows seeming unnatural. "I'm seriously hoping you're not suggesting we use the stock tanks. Always makes me nervous to dunk my junk in there. A lot of those tanks have catfish." He shuddered.

"Put me down. Please."

He set her on her feet. "What's wrong?"

She pushed her hair off her forehead. How did she explain that this entire house was tied to Luke? How did she tell Eli that she couldn't do this here, have him in the space that Luke had loved so dearly? The porch had pushed boundaries. This blew past them without slowing down to even appreciate the posted emotional speed limit.

"Reagan?"

Truth, then. "This is Luke's house."

Eli studied her until she couldn't meet his direct stare any longer.

His boot steps advertised his approach. Prepared for his touch, she didn't flinch when he gently grasped her chin and encouraged her to meet his eyes. "I respect the fact this was your late husband's house. Would you prefer I use the guest bath?"

She opened and closed her mouth. Words eluded her.

"Which way?" he asked, scanning the open living room.

"Second door on the left," Reagan croaked, pointing in the opposite direction.

"Catch you out here in fifteen? I'd like to shower really fast."

"You're not mad?" she whispered.

His lips were soft, the kiss tender. "Never."

She watched him stride down the hall in the direction she'd indicated and stood there until the door to the spare bath clicked closed.

Moving like an automaton, she turned toward her bedroom. Five minutes to clean up and dress. She couldn't let herself think about anything else, couldn't let history catch up to her. Because if she stood still too long, it wouldn't just catch up with her, it would level her.

That was the power of ghosts.

11

ELI MADE HIMSELF at home while he waited for Reagan to emerge, grabbing a beer from the fridge and sinking into the deep sofa. Guilt that he hadn't thought this through very well—being in her private space with Luke—rankled. Somehow, he needed to make it up to her. He didn't know how, wasn't sure what to do to show her he respected where she was coming from, but he'd figure it out. She deserved nothing less.

There was a sharp knock on the door and he twisted to look out the front windows. A brown Ford four-by-four hauling a four-horse pipe trailer had pulled up with an enormous Charolais bull throwing enough of a fit that the parked truck was being pushed around like a Tonka toy. A second knock sounded but, this time, the door opened a crack.

"Doc Matthews?" a man called out.

"Coming," she shouted. Hair pulled back in a French braid, she came out of the bedroom with her boots in hand. She paused, glancing between Eli and the fiftyish man standing in the doorway. "Hey, Gary. What's going on?"

The man's identity clicked with Eli. Gary Watson had been a good friend of his father's, regularly stopping by to shoot the breeze. Growing up, Eli had done some day work on the Watson ranch off and on, though he'd never cared for the Watson family much. Gary's wife, Linda, always had her nose in business that had nothing to do with her. And she had a gift for pulling other noses in alongside hers. She might not be well respected, but when you wanted to know something, the Watson number was the first one you called.

Gary looked between Reagan, freshly showered, and Eli, also freshly showered, and the older man's eyes visibly cooled. "Found a wallet on your porch, Doc." He tossed it on the nearest counter.

"That'd be mine," Eli said. "Must've dropped it when I stopped in to ask Doc Matthews if I could borrow her internet service. Thanks for picking it up." Eli stood and moved to place himself between Reagan and Watson's assessing stare. "How've you been?"

"Heard you'd come back to handle the estate," Watson said .

He struggled to keep his free hand loose instead of letting it fist as he wanted to. "I did, yes."

"Rumor has it your old man left a hell of a mess—a mess we might all end up paying for." Gary's voice was thick as he spoke around the dip tucked between his bottom lip and teeth. The words were soft, the allegation clear.

"Rumors are nasty business," Eli answered just as softly, picking up his wallet and tucking it into his back pocket. "They tend to be based on a lot of false assumptions that only end up fostering a lot of nonsense and hurting innocent people. Hate to think of such a tight community as this singling someone out without all their facts straight."

The other man's eyes narrowed. "You got something to say, boy?"

"I was Max Covington's boy. Not yours. And if I have something to say, I'll have the good grace to say it to your face." Eli took a long draw on his beer. "Never doubt it."

Reagan stepped around Eli and tipped her head toward the truck in her drive. "What've you got, Gary?"

"The wrong vet." Spinning on his heel, he yanked the front

door closed behind him, his booted steps heavy on the stair treads as he stormed off the porch.

Eli rammed his beer bottle on the counter and took off after Gary. Hell, if the man hadn't lit his fuse with a damn blowtorch.

"Eli!"

"Stay inside, Reagan," he snapped, shutting the door before hopping off the porch and eating up the distance between him and the retreating man. "Hold it, Watson."

The man got in his truck and tried to slam the door, but Eli caught it and held it open. "You have a problem with me or my family? Fine. I've got no problem working it out with you with either civil words or fists. Your choice. But that's between us. You leave Reagan out of it. She works for our place just as she works for yours."

"She don't work for us no more." Watson spit a glob of tarry mess at Eli's boots. "I'd deal with the devil himself before I'd pay that woman another dime, doing Luke's memory wrong with the likes of you."

"Watch your mouth," Eli snarled, leaning into the truck and grabbing Gary by the front of the shirt. "She's a good woman."

"Oughta clean up after yourselves a little better if you're gonna be screwing around where God and country can see." Gary's smile was vicious. "Condom wrapper's tucked inside your wallet. Safe sex don't make her any less a—"

Eli threw up his arm to level the man, but Reagan grabbed him. He hadn't even heard her come up behind him. She shoved him back a step and put herself between the two men. Skin pale, her eyes were livid pools of green fire. "Don't you *dare* come onto my property and accuse me of disrespecting my late husband's memory. He's been gone for three years, and I've done nothing but honor him day in and day out."

"You deny you screwed a Covington?" Gary demanded.

"I don't owe you any answers."

"And that's answer enough," the man said on a sneer. "Luke's probably rolling in his grave."

All the color left her face so fast Eli thought she might faint. He should have known she was made of tougher stuff than that.

Her fist connected with Watson's mouth in a short, sharp jab that bloodied both his upper and lower lips. "Use my phone if you want to call in the assault, you son of a bitch, but don't you ever, *ever* insult Luke in front of me again. Now get the hell off my land. I don't care if your cows come down with chlamydia and your whole herd aborts. Don't call me for help."

Slamming his door, she spun away from the truck and stalked to the house, calling over her shoulder, "Come in or don't, Eli. Your choice."

He couldn't help it. With a parting smile at Gary Watson and his stunned, bleeding face, Eli turned and sauntered up the steps, across the porch and into the house. He shut the door behind him with authority and locked the door.

Continuing across the room, he came up behind Reagan, spun her around to face him and kissed the hell out of her. When he finally came up for air, he was grinning. "That was the sexiest thing *ever*. I'm talking in the history of man, darlin'."

"I think I broke a knuckle."

Glancing at her swelling hand, he leaned down and placed his lips on the split skin with extreme care. "Let's get some ice on that."

"Eli?"

He glanced up.

"Thanks for taking up for me."

He felt his face go slack. "Did you really think I'd do different? I mean, I understand you wanted me to keep it a secret and I agreed, but Reagan, he'd already figured it out. I wasn't about to let him disrespect you."

"I heard what he said—about finding the condom wrapper. He's going to gossip." She let out a shaky sigh. "Everyone is going to know."

He blinked slowly. "Know what, exactly?"

"About this." She waggled her good hand between them. "About us."

"Then I'm not hiding it." He held up a hand when she opened her mouth, presumably to argue. "Did Luke love you?"

"What?" she gasped.

"Did he love you?"

"Yes."

"Would he want you to be miserable?" She didn't answer immediately, so he pressed. "Well? Would he?"

"No," she whispered so softly he read her lips more than heard her speak.

"Then don't be miserable. If he loved you, he'd want you to be happy, and if what we've got makes you happy—" he cupped her face in his hands "—run with it."

"The problem is that this is a fifty-yard dash," she said, "not a marathon. It'll be over and done, my business will be ruined and you'll be gone. Again."

If what he heard in her voice was true, it sounded as if she might regret his leaving. Eli's heart slammed against his sternum. Taking a deep breath, Eli pressed his forehead to hers and closed his eyes. "Let's take this one day at a time, okay? We'll figure it out as we go. But I want to be very clear on one thing."

She closed her eyes. "What?"

"Look at me." When she hesitated, he leaned away just enough to give her a very gentle shake. "Look at me, Reagan."

Her eyes slowly opened.

"Whatever happens between us? It's between *us*. Understand? We don't owe anyone any explanation, nor do we owe anyone an apology. Your work speaks for itself, and I doubt anyone with sense will take their business elsewhere."

Her nod was all he got out of her in the way of agreement, but it would have to do. Because now that this thing between him and Reagan was about to become public knowledge, the opportunity to turn this into a marathon became very real.

He just had to figure out how fast to set the initial pace.

ELI LEFT NOT long after binding her hand in an ice pack. She hadn't wanted to be alone, but at the same time, after the incident with Gary Watson, she hadn't wanted Eli to stay.

The older man's vitriolic verbal attack had left her more shaken than she cared to admit. No doubt his wife would fire up the gossip train the moment Gary got home, burning up the phone lines with the news about the condom wrapper and wallet on the porch. The woman would back up her circumstantial evidence with the image of Eli relaxing in her house as Reagan came out of the bedroom barefoot and with wet hair. As the gossip was retold, the story would be sensationalized until she was wearing a dominatrix getup and Eli had on little more than a pony saddle cinched tight to his back. The idea alone made her grin.

Then she sobered. Lord, this was going to be such a mess. Three years of fighting to be the proper widow and maintain a reputation as an ethical businessperson and she'd blown it with one spontaneous act carried out with the county's very own black sheep.

Now, lying in bed and wide-awake a little after five in the morning, she had little choice but to get up and get the day started. The state vet would be at the Covington ranch by noon, and the guy was thorough.

She had ordered extra vaccine, and she'd be working all morning to continue treating the infected cattle, isolating the sickest, euthanizing those beyond hope and centrally pasturing those who should make it after they'd been dosed. The entire thing would be a circus where she was the ringmaster and every hoop she had to jump through blazed.

Brisket whined in his sleep, and she automatically dropped a foot to his bed and rubbed his back. He snorted and sat up, stretching.

"Morning, sunshine." In a moment of indulgence, she patted the bed and encouraged him up to cuddle with her. The dog snuggled into her side and sighed, totally content.

Reagan couldn't help but wonder what life would have been like if she'd taken Ty up on his offer not to be their vet. None of this would have happened; she wouldn't be faced with attitudes like Gary Watson's, and she would be...what? Hiding out at home trying to avoid Eli?

Shame nearly choked her. She was a bigger person than that. Never had she expected she'd allow history to dictate both her present and her future.

But that's exactly what you've been doing, her conscience whispered.

The thought stilled her hand on her dog's fur. She'd been a coward. It had begun the moment Eli walked away from her that summer night. Ever since then, she'd clung to what might have been and had missed everything that might be. She had to get out of the house. Get out of the immediate reach of Luke's clothes that she hadn't gotten rid of, their wedding pictures, the furniture he'd picked out to surprise her. The stupid antelope head he'd hung on the living room wall.

This place was so much his, so much *him*, and always had been. She'd never considered what it did to her to come home to this every day, to live surrounded by the memories he'd worked so hard to create.

"No more," she whispered. Change was inevitable. It would have been the same whether he'd lived or died. And if he'd lived and Eli had come home?

She jumped from the bed and pulled on the first clothes she found. Whatever might have been, it was just that: might have been. Luke was gone. She'd been living in the shadow of his death for three years, burdened by her guilt, burdened by the community's expectations, burdened by what she'd always wanted versus her reality. Never had she been so ashamed.

She'd been living life like a spectator with a crappy view from the cheap seats. She'd allowed the blind expectations of others to dictate her behavior. She'd spent a sleepless night worrying about the likes of the Watsons. She was done with that.

She wasn't going to spend the rest of her life living on the fringes. If Eli's return had shown her anything, it was that she had more left in her—more life, desire, determination, pride—than she'd given herself credit for.

And if Eli is wrong? If the community continues to rally around Luke's memory and you lose everything? her conscience pressed.

"I'm stronger than a bunch of wagging tongues," she said aloud. "I'll manage." No, that wasn't true. She wouldn't just manage. She was going to come out on top of this mess and reclaim a life she'd been too scared to live. And if people didn't like it?

She'd heard Hell had a handful of openings, and she'd be happy to provide personal recommendations to the devil himself.

12

ELI KNOCKED A second time on Reagan's front door, but no one answered. A glance at his watch told him he had ten minutes to get into her office and log on or his meeting was going to go ass up. No help for it. He'd have to break in.

A sprint to the barn provided a shovel. Even though it was necessary, he still felt bad smashing a windowpane on her front door. Of course he'd replace it, but it wouldn't have come to this if she'd just stayed to let him in. Or left the key under a flowerpot. Or something. Anything.

A quick circuit of the house revealed her office. It looked entirely different than the rest of the house, more feminine in a wild way, less manly hunter/rancher somehow.

He signed into his computer and growled when the internet turned out to be password protected. Grabbing her phone, he called Cade. His brother answered on the second ring, and Eli didn't give him a chance to get through his hello before he asked, "What's the password to Reagan's Wi-Fi?"

"Hold on. I should remember this."

Eli listened to Cade breathing, his own anxiety mounting with his brother's every breath. "I've got to be online in—" another peek at his watch "—two minutes."

"Try *RedCanoe#2*," he said, spelling it out.

Eli's fingers fumbled over the keyboard. "Come again?"

"RedCanoe#2," Cade repeated. "Why? It mean something?"

"It's nothing. Thanks for this. I'll be there before the state guy." Hanging up, he typed the password in and the Wi-Fi began the process of connecting.

"RedCanoe#2." He shook his head, a small smile playing at his lips. They'd lied to their parents one weekend and snuck away together, going up to the Abiquiu Reservoir and camping out in the back of his pickup. They'd rented a canoe, the red one numbered *two*, and fished and laughed and found a remote area to beach the little boat and make love on a blanket on the sand. The sun had been hot on their skin. She'd ridden him, a dark outline in the bright light, her hair blowing in the breeze. He'd realized then that he'd never love anyone else the way he loved her. He'd told her so.

And she remembered.

Throat tight, he plugged his earpiece in and signed into Skype. His screen immediately flashed an incoming call. Taking a deep breath, he cleared his throat and answered. "Elijah Covington."

"Mr. Covington, Ms. English and I are present. I've not been able to reach Mr. Macallroy yet."

"Give him five minutes. If he's not here, we'll call his secretary," Eli responded absently, scrolling through the settlement offer on-screen and his handwritten notes in the small file he'd brought with him.

"How are things, Eli?" Amanda asked.

"My brothers and I are doing what we can..." He trailed off, realizing his mistake.

"You have brothers?" the other attorney asked. "I had no idea."

"I prefer to keep my personal and professional lives separate." He fought to keep his voice calm and cool. "The two don't intersect for me. Ever."

"Fair enough." Papers rustled in the background. "What's the point of today's call? Macallroy Oil is getting off with a proverbial slap on the wrist with this EPA fine. Does the word *Valdez* not mean anything to him?"

"He believes we're not representing him vigorously enough in seeking a smaller fine." Eli continued to flip through his notes. "Feels the environmental impact isn't equivalent to some of the larger oil spills we've seen previously."

"Another case of size mattering," Amanda muttered.

Lynette coughed to cover her laugh.

"Try him again, Lynette," Eli said, ignoring the byplay.

"Don Macallroy's office," his secretary answered.

It was right then that Eli officially despised Macallroy. They'd rung his personal computer, and he'd set it up so his secretary had answered. Such a bullshit power play. Fighting to keep his cool, Eli pulled his professionalism around him like a chain mail cloak. "Good morning, Susan. Will you please let Mr. Macallroy know that his legal team is present and available for the call?"

"Certainly, Mr. Covington. Please hold."

Seconds later, Don came online. "Covington," he said in greeting. "Mike Tibbs, Jeff Orr and Ron Tucker are sitting in." In the background, computer keys clicked.

Eli did his best to ignore the fact Macallroy had essentially dismissed the women on the call by refusing to acknowledge them. It wasn't a secret that the guy was a dick. Still, it ate at Eli. He opened his mouth to say something, but Amanda stepped in.

"Good morning, Don." Her chilled voice conveyed her displeasure.

"English," Don replied.

"I understand you're unhappy with the EPA's settlement figures," she continued.

"Eli and I have already talked. No need to rehash the fact your firm dropped the ball on this one." The old man's gaze bored into the laptop camera. "So, Eli, what are you going to do about it?"

"Nothing." It was out before Eli could temper his response.

"Excuse me?" Don's voice was lethally quiet. "For a moment there, I thought you said 'nothing.'"

Eli parked his elbows on the desk and steepled his fingers in front of him, forefingers tapping against each other. "The EPA has every right to seek three times this amount in damages. They've agreed to settle based on a hell of a lot of negotiating we've done on Macallroy Oil's behalf. Meanwhile, your company is going to be tied up in a public relations nightmare for years. You'd be better off to spend the money the EPA isn't demanding investing in an aggressive, environmentally friendly PR campaign to win back the public's good opinion. Show you give a damn about the impact the oil spill is going to have over the coming years."

Don stared at him, unblinking. "I think we're done here, gentlemen. You and I will sit down, face-to-face, and work this out, Covington. Your grief has clearly screwed up your perspective. I'm willing to discount that. Once. Get your ass back to Austin by the middle of next week or Macallroy Oil will find alternate representation from this point forward."

The screen went blank.

Eli closed his eyes and did his best to avoid the nausea swamping his gut. "Amanda, Lynette, I've got to be somewhere in the next hour so there's not time to discuss this. Lynette, make arrangements for me to meet Don at Peché next Thursday evening for drinks and dinner. And get me a new iPhone overnighted." He rattled off the ranch's address as he shoved paperwork into his briefcase.

He wasn't delusional. The founding partners would have his ass if Macallroy fired the firm. The account was one of the most lucrative year after year, and being awarded the account had been a major coup when he'd made senior partner.

Don had always rubbed him the wrong way. But this was the first time Eli had allowed it to show. He needed to return to Austin and get his game back. This whole experience, being at the ranch, reconnecting with his brothers, being with Reagan—it was throwing him off. Badly.

But he wasn't ready to leave Reagan. She'd weighed on his mind all night and throughout the morning. They'd rediscovered something in each other, a once-in-a-lifetime passion. If they stood a chance of recapturing that passion, they had to get away from the stresses of the ranch quarantine. So why not invite her to come with him to Austin? What he could offer her now was exponentially more than the pipe dreams he'd laid at her feet as a teen. And it was so much more than she had here. Better yet, he could get her away from the gossip hounds that would be dogging her—*their*—heels before the day was out.

If he could get her to agree to go, even for a long weekend, he could show her around the city, romance her more than a little and open her eyes to the life they could share there. And if she felt even half as much for him now as she had all those years ago, they had a real opportunity of making something of this unexpected second chance.

Only yesterday he'd thought his biggest challenge would be figuring out how to convince her they could run the race together. But sitting in her office, considering what it would take to persuade her to come to Austin, he knew he'd been wrong.

His biggest challenge was going to be getting her to agree to leave everything she knew behind.

"WE'RE DOING ALL we can, Dr. Alvarez."

Reagan listened as Cade spoke with the New Mexico state vet. He'd shown up almost two hours early. To say he hadn't been thrilled with what he'd found would be an understatement. Granted, he'd had nothing but praise for Reagan's diagnosis and treatment plan, but Cade had argued it was excessive and would put the ranch out of business.

Ty stood by, taking it all in. He refused to look at her, and that got under her skin.

She'd done what she had to do, not only ethically but legally, and the brothers were going to have to accept that. Yes, the treatment plan she'd come up with was pricey, but it was the only way she knew to contain the disease and keep it from spreading. Already three of the calves she'd held from the Jensen place had tested positive for the same disease. If it continued to spread, there would be little they could do but quarantine the county. That would cut into profitability for all the ranches, and the Covingtons were sure to bear the blame.

"Armando?" Reagan said, addressing the state vet by first name as she stepped forward to break up what was fast becoming an argument.

He faced her, his irritation undisguised.

She held up her hands, palms out. "Let's take this down a notch. There are some options here, things we haven't touched on yet."

A truck roared up the dirt drive and slid to a stop in front of the nearest bunkhouse. Eli stepped out dressed in complete business attire.

Her heart flipped over. She might always think of—and prefer—him in his jeans and tees, but he was freaking *GQ* gorgeous all decked out like he was. The dark expression on his face didn't bode well, though. He looked like he wanted to kill someone with one hand while the other mixed up a strong drink as a chaser to the violence.

He walked up and held out a hand to the man wearing the state's insignia on his sleeve. "You must be Dr. Alvarez. I'm Elijah Covington. I'm representing the ranch in this investigation."

"Are you an attorney, Mr. Covington?" Armando asked.

"I am."

"Then I don't have much use for you." He held up a hand when Eli protested. "The law is the law in this instance, and you can file all the injunctions you want to stop me, but I'm the state-appointed expert. Dr. Matthews has done all the right things, suggested all the most effective treatments, but she also reported a second case involving three steers earlier this morning."

Eli turned his burning gaze on her. "She did?"

"She's ethically obligated to report these things when there's a threat of outbreak." Armando shifted, but Eli didn't look away from Reagan.

His fury was undisguised, as if she'd betrayed him. Then she remembered he'd needed to use her office this morning. She winced. He only arched a brow and faced Armando.

The vet crossed his arms over his chest. "Do you have an insurance policy for the cattle you've contracted to feed out?"

Reagan's stomach fell. "Armando, I don't think we've got to talk about euthanizing in large numbers. Not yet."

He gazed at her, eyes flat but knowing. "It's spreading, Reagan. Until my team and I identify the source, we've got to keep this ranch quarantined and the sickest of the cattle have to be killed off. If we don't, we're just perpetuating the disease and delaying recovery in those that stand even half a chance of making it."

"So that's what your criteria are?" Eli demanded. "We kill everything with less than a fifty-percent chance of survival?" Cade laid a hand on his shoulder, but Eli shrugged it off. "An answer, please, Dr. Alvarez."

"Frankly? Yes."

"You'll ruin the Covington ranch," Eli all but snarled. "I won't allow you to do that." Shoulders tight and neck corded with fury, he rounded on Reagan. "This ranch is my brothers' livelihood. You can't take that from them."

Ty stepped forward and laid a hand on his oldest brother's arm. "Eli—"

Armando interrupted. "I'll say it again—there's nothing you can do to stop me. I have a duty to the State of New Mexico and the states that border her to keep the cattle population healthy. Bovine Respiratory Disease has one of the highest fatality rates of all the cattle diseases. We'll kill off those Dr. Matthews and I deem to have less than a fifty percent chance and burn the carcasses. I'll make arrangement with the Bureau of Land Management to set up a burn zone. The ranch will be financially responsible for funding the firefighters necessary, as well as the equipment they'll have to bring in."

Reagan's heart skipped several beats and then took up a thundering pace when she realized the role she was going to have to play in assessing the herds. She would probably shutter the Bar C. She gripped her shirt at the waist and wadded the fabric, doing her best to keep from shaking. The Covington brothers would never forgive her for this.

Eli stepped up close to Armando, eyes blazing. "I'll make this clear. Once. I don't care what it costs, but you and Dr. Matthews *will* resolve this issue as expeditiously as possible with the end goal of lifting the quarantine on the ranch so these calves can be fed out and shipped before the end of this year."

Cade's voice was tight when he tried to interrupt. "We can't afford—"

"The hell with the costs, Cade." When Cade opened his mouth, presumably to argue, Eli's mouth thinned and his eyes narrowed as he looked first at Cade and then at Ty. "Not a damn word from either of you. This ranch is your legacy. It will *not* be shut down by some self-righteous prick who thinks that because he's been issued a plastic badge and a cheap flip wallet with a state ID, he can come out here and drop a can of whoop-ass, forcing us to run for cover."

"It's the actual costs, Eli," Ty said quietly.

"I'll cover the costs. You're my brothers, and I'd move heaven and hell to see you done right by."

"Between treatment and the burn zone, you're looking at roughly $70,000, Mr. Covington."

Reagan wanted to tell Armando to shut the hell up, to not press Eli when he was so close to losing his temper. The words would have been wasted, though.

Eli rounded on the state vet. "Your personal concern for my financial solvency is touching, Doctor," Eli said, the sound of his voice as soft as a large blade slicing through the air. "Allow me to alleviate your concern that you might not get paid. I'll have my bank wire the initial estimate plus an additional thirty per cent for unforeseen expenses and any overages we may encounter. The funds will be in the Bar C's primary account within seventy-two hours per regulations established by the Federal Reserve. If that timeline isn't good enough for you, take it up with their local office. The money *will* be there. So, by all means, don't let the financial details get in the way of your intent to slaughter and burn the sick and infirm."

Armando shifted to face Reagan, effectively dismissing Eli. "We'll use established criteria to determine which animals are treated and which are euthanized."

She nodded numbly. "Give me a minute, Armando."

He tipped his chin in acknowledgment and started for his truck.

"What happens now?" Ty asked quietly.

"We'll set up a working pen in the first pasture away from the house. All the animals will be run through and assessed." She swallowed hard. "Those that aren't deemed candidates for survival will be put down. It'll be over in about three days, and in another ten days, we can begin the process of applying to the state to lift the quarantine. We just have to prove recovery and clean stock tanks, burn off any residual hay the sick cattle may have encountered, scrape the corrals clean…" She laid a hand on Eli's arm. "We'll work through this."

Eli jerked away from her. "If we treated humans like this, 'euthanizing' those we weren't sure we could save, we'd be labeled sadistic bastards at best, radical supremacists at worst. And there's little difference between the two." Grabbing his briefcase off the ground, he started for the house.

She made to follow him, but Cade moved into her path. "Give him a little while. Killing was always hard on him."

"He doesn't have to do it," she objected.

"Yeah, he does. Don't forget who he is. He won't ask someone to do his dirty work just to cut himself an easy path. We have Dad to thank for that. He forced Eli to put down his first horse when it developed hoof problems. The animal could have been saved, but Dad said it would be cheaper to invest in a new horse and he didn't need a cripple running around. Made Eli pull the trigger. He always had Eli do the worst work. Claimed he was trying to toughen him up."

She swallowed hard. "How old was he?"

"When he had to shoot his horse?" Cade shook his head. "Probably seven. Maybe eight."

Her stomach protested, forcing her to swallow convulsively.

Cade looked at Eli's retreating back. "Never got used to that part of ranch life. Running like he did was the only way he could get out of that cycle. I didn't really understand that until I watched him work side by side with us the other night, hanging in with the tasks I was sure would be hardest for him. Caught him puking behind the barn after he shot the first steer. It might have taken me years to realize getting out was his best option, but it doesn't make it any less true."

"But—"

"Leave it alone, okay?" Cade followed after Eli, who'd slammed into the house. "Call it whatever lets you sleep at night, Reagan. What we're being asked to do is killing in more ways than one."

Cade meant this could be the death of the ranch itself. She knew it, but she couldn't think about that. Not right now. First she had to stop this from spreading and save the animals she could save.

Then she'd deal with the heartache eating a hole in her chest, the one that said by doing the right thing, she just might lose Eli all over again.

13

THE NEXT FEW days were hell. Between attending the probate hearing, confirming his dad had less than $20,000 in cash assets and working through the stocker herds one animal at a time, Eli managed very little sleep. He spent his waking hours split between wearing loafers and cowboy boots, business suits and shit-stained jeans. Never had he been pulled in such opposite directions.

His new cell arrived, and immediately the firm's founding partners began calling. The first two days they were cajoling, joking with him about getting back to civilization. By Monday, their coaxing turned to demands he return. He had, after all, taken his three days of bereavement leave. They needed him to be in the office to handle Macallroy, who was making serious noises about taking his business elsewhere. And, to add to the soup pot of madness, Lynette had begun to call three or four times a day to ask for guidance.

Before the last call, he'd just pulled the trigger to put a young steer down. His stomach had been rolling viciously, and he seriously thought he might lose his lunch.

"What?" he'd shouted into the phone.

"M-Mr. Covington?"

"Not now, Lynette. Go find Amanda if you have questions." And he'd hung up.

They'd sorted the sickest first and, so far, they'd put down more than forty percent of the herds that had moved through the portable corrals. It seemed the rest stood a fairly good chance of making it, but it would mean more round-the-clock work, and he had just about reached his limit.

He and Reagan hadn't exchanged much more than curt conversation as they worked together. Often when he'd grab a couple hours of sleep, he'd wake to find her still at it. She had to be near breaking, too. He'd been so angry with her for all of this, but it wasn't her fault. Realization had taken a few days to set in, but when it did, it had been one more brick of guilt to weigh him down. She hadn't brought this down on them. Not in any way. All she'd done was her job. She'd held to her ethics and obligations, and that was more than he could say for himself lately.

Still, ethics aside, this whole experience had reinforced his long-held belief that this wasn't the life for him. Facing life and death every day, never knowing if you'd be delivering a calf or putting its mother down after a difficult birth—he couldn't live this way. Ranching life was far too brutal. He wanted to give life every chance to persevere. That's why he'd gone into law, though he'd lost some of that idealism along the way.

He had to wrap this up and get home…to Austin, back to a job he was damned good at with people he didn't have to share a house with or a lover he couldn't touch. But he wouldn't abandon his brothers again. He might not be a cowboy, but there were other ways he could help them and the legacy the three of them shared as brothers. He emptied the chamber of his rifle and bowed his head. The urge to plead with the heavens hit him for the second time since he'd started this journey, surprising him no less now than it had when the plane had dropped to the runway.

That's when it hit him—it was far too quiet. Dragging his gaze up, he looked around stupidly. *Where were all the cows?*

A hand settled on his shoulder and he glanced up.

"It's done," Ty said quietly.

"Finished?"

"In more ways than one." Cade handed him a sheet of paper. "The insurance company's dropping us. We won't be able to register or advertise as an insured stocker operation anymore." He swallowed hard and tipped his chin back, but not before Eli caught the sheen in his eyes. "The Bar C is done."

"No." Eli's denial surprised them all. Ty's gaze slowly rose even as Cade wiped his eyes without shame. "It's not done," Eli said vehemently. "This isn't how this was supposed to go."

Cade opened his mouth and had to close it as the first tear tipped over his lower lashes. He spun away and started across the pasture, away from the house and the day's activities.

They watched him go, and Eli experienced the strongest sense of solidarity with his brothers he'd ever had. He looked at Ty. "There has to be something we can do, something to change the course we're on."

Ty's usual fun-loving gaze was flat. "We ought to be able to make enough off the sale to buy a small place somewhere, but it won't be enough to use as a sole source of income. We'll have to take jobs with some of the local contractors around." He blew out a hard breath. "Or sell, save the money and see if we can get hired on as cowboys on other ranches."

"No," Eli ground out, low but fierce. "I have a substantial savings account. I'll buy into the ranch, fund what I can and get a loan for the rest of it to restock the place. We'll just become an independent operation."

Ty gaped at him, face entirely blank. "We?"

Eli opened and closed his mouth. Then the laughter started, soft at first until it had him doubled over. "I've lost my damn mind," he finally said as he stood, "but yeah—*we*."

"You coming home?" Ty asked so quietly Eli had to ask him to repeat it. "Are you coming home, to the ranch?"

"No. I'll keep my job in Austin to insure this place stays afloat. Besides, if any of us should work in town, it's me. I'm better at it, and I make damn good money." Ty's face lost the joy that had suffused it, and Eli reached out to clasp his brother's shoulder. "It's for the best. I'll funnel everything I can back to you guys, and make some investments so we've got money for the lean years. It'll give you and Cade the security you have to have in order to make the Bar C what it should be without depending on brokers. I..." He rubbed a hand across of the nape of his neck and stared at his boots. "The Bar C has to stay in the family, if for no other reason than for you and the family of your own that you'll have one day. You *and* Cade, provided there's a woman out there tough enough to whip him into shape and keep him there. It won't happen for me, but I can make that happen for you two. I want to do that. Please."

Ty nodded and then started across the pasture in a different direction than Cade had taken, his shoulders shaking and head bowed.

Eli hurt for his brothers. They'd borne so much on their own, carrying his weight, his obligations, his legacy for him while he tried to find out who he was and where he belonged. The least he could do was ensure they both had the opportunity to make something of this place. Cade was a good businessman. Ty was an amazing horseman. Both were outstanding cowboys. Between them and the men they had on staff, they could make this work. He'd be a silent partner, and he wouldn't regret it in any way.

Grabbing his rifle, he headed toward the corrals. Several of the Bar C cowboys spoke to him, their deference clear. He'd held with them, worked alongside them and he'd earned their respect. It wasn't something he'd expected. It also wasn't something he'd ever take for granted. Eli searched for Reagan but couldn't find her anywhere. The state vet, though, was sitting in his truck, driver's door open, and filling out paperwork on a metal clipboard. Eli approached the man with caution. They hadn't gotten off on the right foot, and Eli had some fences to mend. The other man had to be receptive, though.

"Dr. Alvarez?" Eli started.

The vet glanced up, his hooded eyes emotionless. "Mr. Covington. What can I do for you?"

Eli held out his hand.

Dr. Alvarez set his stuff down slowly, stood and shook the proffered hand. "Different kind of discussion than I expected."

"I want to apologize for being so harsh the other day." A good eight inches taller than the diminutive man, Eli tried not to lord his height. "I was upset and struck out at the first target I could find."

Dr. Alvarez dropped Eli's hand and got back in his truck, picking up his paperwork and returning his attention to it as he spoke. "I appreciate the apology, but I want to be clear that this won't change my recommendations for the ranch."

"I'm sorry?" Eli took his hat off and scrubbed a hand through his hair. "I was under the impression that we'd be cleared once the stock tanks were sanitized and the ear tags confirmed we'd accounted for all the calves."

The vet shot him a brief glance before continuing to fill out forms. "This is the worst outbreak I've seen in my career. It's spread to two additional ranches now. The Phillips just reported six head with symptoms. Until this is totally shut down, I'm quarantining the county."

"You—"

Dr. Alvarez held up a hand and gave Eli a somewhat compassionate look. "I realize what this is going to cost you. On the heels of losing your father, I would imagine it's harder than it would normally be. I'm sorry for that. But we can't jeopardize the state's cattle population on sentimentality, Mr. Covington."

"I understand," he said woodenly. Everything he'd just talked to his brothers about, everything he'd promised them he'd do, meant more now than ever. They'd have to begin an extensive recovery program and bring in cows as soon as the quarantine was lifted. To keep his word to his brothers, he'd have to sell his Lake Travis home, probably his car, and pare back his lifestyle by half. He'd do what he'd promised them he'd do, though.

His brothers would be able to live the life they'd fought so hard to hold on to. He wanted that for them, if not for himself.

Still, the achievement left him feeling empty. He'd be returning to Austin with a true relationship with his brothers. But in the end? He'd still be going home just as alone as he had been when he arrived.

Unless he could convince Reagan to come with him…

REAGAN SAT ON the back porch of her house sipping beer and rocking her porch swing with one bare foot. The sunset blazed furiously as if the day protested the coming night. But like so many things in life, night would come no matter how hard the sun fought to hold its place.

Armando had left more than an hour ago with his final report. He'd told her he'd be quarantining the county, which meant more work for her. She couldn't bring herself to charge the ranchers for her services, not when the medications were so expensive, so she'd provide top-notch care at cut-rate prices until everyone was on their feet again. It was the right thing to do. But, like everything these days, it came with a cost.

Holding a hand up to shield her eyes, she watched her horses coming up to the barn for the night. Chores were done save stabling those four and feeding them. She'd get to it soon enough.

Brisket rolled over on his back, his tongue lolling out the side of his mouth. He swished his tail against the pine boards, and she gave in, rubbing his belly with her other foot. She absently reached for the phone and dialed her neighbor's number from memory.

Mark Russell picked up on the third ring. "Hey, Reagan. You okay?"

"I'm good, Mark. Have you heard otherwise?"

He chuckled. "The Watsons are burning up the phone lines about you and Eli."

Her throat tightened. "Yeah?"

"Gossipy old bitch." She heard his booted steps echo across his floor and a screen door squeaked open before slamming closed. "What's new?"

Something in her she hadn't realized she'd been holding on to so tightly relaxed just enough for her to ask the one thing she most wanted to know. "What's the general consensus, Mark?"

"About Eli?" He huffed out a breath. "There are a handful who let old grudges die hard deaths."

"Do they never wonder why he left?" she asked a little more harshly than she intended. "He had to be happy, and no one around here seems to give a damn about that aspect of his life. They're too busy condemning him for leaving."

"Most of them judged him for leaving *you* more than his old man."

Struck dumb, she choked on her beer. When she could finally wheeze without coughing, she asked, "Me? But I left, too."

"And came home." He called out a warning to one of his boys about swinging in the hayloft before returning to the conversation.

"He came home when he was needed. That has to count for something."

"You'd think." Mark sighed and, just as she'd trusted him to do, let the rest of the truth go. "There are a handful of people who believe you're making a huge mistake getting involved with him."

"What you're actually saying is they feel I should continue to live a good widow's life." She blew out a hard breath. "I've reached the point where they can kiss my ass."

"Good girl. Just know the majority of us have your back."

"Thanks, Mark." Winding her ponytail around her hand, she fought the shake in her voice. "That's not why I called, though. Well, not the only reason."

"What can I do for you?"

"You've heard the county's going to be quarantined."

"Yeah," he answered, voice tight.

"It's going to mean lower profits for everyone for a bit. I'm going to cut my service rates to dirt, sell meds at wholesale, do what I can to help. That means I can't keep this place."

"Without the income from the calves, I can't afford to buy it."

"I've got the mortgage paid through the end of the year." Her belly flipped like a pancake tossed by a short-order cook. "If I have an attorney draw up a lease-to-purchase that's favorable for you until you get your calves sold and can make the purchase, are you still interested in buying my place?"

"You sure about this?" he asked gently.

"It's time." Her answer was so quiet the words competed with the crickets emerging for the evening.

"Have your attorney draw it up. You want to stay in the house until we close the deal for good?"

She hadn't thought that far ahead. "It'd be great if you'd be willing to let me. I'll include all my livestock in the sale except the horses. I'll keep those," she said, voice tight.

"You sure you're ready to take this step, sweetheart?" Mark asked, the term of endearment nothing more than one of close friendship.

Even though he couldn't see her, she nodded. "It really is time, Mark."

"Then we've got a deal. And if you need to stay at the house longer, just give me a holler. We'll work something out."

"Thanks, Mark. Good night." Disconnecting, she set the phone down.

Being with Eli had proved to her she'd been holding on to the wrong memories for far too long. When he left this time, she'd mourn him, yes. But she would also be able to celebrate what they'd shared. So from now until he left, she would relish every second they had together. If he could forgive her the quarantine mess.

The rumble of a diesel engine came down her drive and cut off in front of her house. She stood and stretched before starting around the wraparound porch toward the front of the house. The truck came into sight first. It was a Bar C vehicle, and the first thing she thought was that something had gone horribly wrong. Her walk turned into a run as she rounded the corner of the house to see Eli raising a hand to knock. She stopped suddenly, rocking forward. "Eli?"

He looked over at her, face solemn. "I brought a piece of glass to fix the door."

"I already had it done, but thanks."

"Send me the bill, okay? I meant to get to it sooner, but…" He didn't have to explain anything to her. They both knew how hellish the past few days had been.

"Why are you here? What's wrong?"

One corner of his mouth lifted. "Nothing."

"Everything is okay at the ranch?" she demanded.

"As okay as it can be given the fact Dr. Alvarez quarantined the county." He shrugged. "It is what it is."

"I'm so sorry, Eli," she whispered.

He closed the distance between them and wrapped her in a hard hug that nearly stole her breath. "Don't you dare apologize. You did what you had to do. Yeah, we were pissed about it. Might even have cursed you once or twice, if I'm honest." He drew back and met her stare. "But you didn't cause this. We have no idea where it originated, had no idea initially that it was something so serious. Maybe we could have, even *should have*, moved faster, but Shipping Fever is so rare nowadays. It seemed logical to assume it was something less lethal. All we can do now is get through the aftermath." He swallowed hard and gazed out over her land. Set in the Cimarron Valley, it was idyllic. Nothing as wild and scenic as the Bar C, but pretty enough. "I'm going back to Austin. Soon. I'll have to make some serious financial changes to my lifestyle, but I'm going to do my damnedest to provide the operating overhead Cade and Ty have to have to keep the ranch."

This time it was she who wrapped her arms around him. A

slight tremor worked its way through her and down her arms, curling her fingers into his shirt. She didn't want him to leave. They'd barely scratched the surface of what might have been between them. She didn't want to let him go. Not again. Not like this. Not knowing she would, at best, be someone he either visited or simply ran into when he came home to visit his brothers. Breaking away, he grabbed her hand and hauled her toward the truck, but she resisted. "What?"

"I'm barefoot."

Without missing a beat, he scooped her up and carried her to the truck. "Shoes are optional tonight."

"Where are we going?" she asked as he deposited her in the cab.

He crawled in behind the wheel, hooked an arm around her waist and pulled her close to his side. "Somewhere I should have taken you already."

The most she could do was buckle up and go along for the ride.

14

Eli turned on the radio and sang along with some of the current country hits, ignoring the surprise on Reagan's face that he was familiar with the lyrics. They drove for half an hour without talking, her leaning into his side, his arm around her shoulders. The night was a brilliant blue-black, the wind little more than a breeze. An owl swooped across the highway close enough to make Eli tap the brakes, but the bird was long gone by the time he even reacted.

"Where are we going?" she finally asked.

"Just hang tight."

Highway 64 curved southwest and Eli slowed, pulling off the highway and up to a metal gate. He'd made sure Cade had pulled the key for him so he wouldn't have to dig through the multiple keys on the key ring. Some nights, like now, it paid to appear like you had your shit together.

Gate opened, he drove through, locked it behind him and continued down the dirt road. A glance to the side showed Reagan twisting her hands in her lap, a wide grin splitting her face. "The river."

"Yeah." Her excitement was a huge relief—*huge*—and he found himself unintentionally speeding up, the washboard road rattling the truck's rearview mirror so wildly it was nauseating. He didn't slow down.

One mile of dirt roads later and two more turns west and he eased off the gas. The rush of the Cimarron River, relatively shallow here but fast moving over rocky areas and hushed in the deeper curve, spilled before them like a wide band of hammered silver in the moonlight.

She shifted to her knees on the seat, grabbed his face and kissed him senseless, all heat and a tangle of tongues. Fisting his hair, she pulled his head back and grinned. "I can't believe you brought me here."

His immediate erection said he should have brought her here that first night. He felt like a kid again, not a thirty-three-year-old lawyer. Smiling in answer, he dragged her across his lap, cradling her in his left arm while he stroked her face with his free hand. "Pretty as you've ever been, but more beautiful in the moonlight than my dreams do justice."

"Careful, Covington," she said, soft and husky. "Words that sweet'll get a guy in my pants."

"Any guy?" he asked, teasing a finger along her collarbone.

"Just one."

He leaned into her, pulling her up so their lips met in a lazy kiss. He nibbled and suckled, whispering to her how beautiful she was, how long he'd dreamed of being here with her, the way the taste of her skin haunted him on sleepless nights—all the things he'd wanted to say to her from the moment he'd first seen her but hadn't been brave enough.

But he understood now there simply weren't any guarantees. Things could be going absolutely right and then the road could end and you'd find yourself in free fall. There wasn't time to waste with her.

Tongues dueling, the taste of the hoppy beer she'd been drinking rolled through his mouth. Their breaths mingled. He nipped her bottom lip, then sucked on it, and when her head tipped back, he traced a line from the hollow of her neck to her chin with the tip of his tongue. Her every gasp, every plea for more—it all drove him crazy. But that wasn't what this night was about. Not in its entirety.

Pulling away, he put a finger over her lips to stop her objection. "We've got all night."

"Yeah?" One corner of her mouth curled up. "Cade lift your curfew?"

"Cade can kiss my ass. I'm out all night." He kissed the tip of her nose. "If you'll have me."

She laughed. "Oh, I intend to have you, all right."

"At least the seduction part of the evening's plans are a go. Takes a lot of pressure off a guy."

"Glad I could help." She scrambled out of his lap and across the seat, pausing when she opened the door. "Don't suppose you've got a pair of irrigation boots tucked between the cab and the bed?"

"Sit tight." He dropped to the ground and went to the rear of the truck, pulling out blankets and a small cooler. "Dig the pillows out from behind the seat."

"Pillows?" she called, the smile in her voice evident.

"Hey, growing up should count for something. In this case, it's pillows."

They flew at him one at a time, and he made them part of the bedroll. Then he went to the passenger side of the truck, reached around her to turn the music up a little, and, before she could object, tossed her over his shoulder. She screamed with laughter, and his heart beat so fast it hurt. So much had changed between them, but not this. *Never again this.*

He carried her to the lowered truck tailgate and set her down gently. "Stars," he whispered, looking up.

She followed his gaze and sighed. "Do you know how many nights, in college in particular, I wondered if you were gazing at the same stars I was? It made me feel closer to you."

"Yeah. Me, too."

He got them settled, her head on his shoulder, a blanket within easy reach to flip over them when the night cooled off. Laying his lips against her temple after fourteen years, he had the most concrete sense of what truly mattered, and it had nothing to do with old hurts or regrets or bad decisions.

They talked for hours, catching up on fourteen years of missing each other. Luke was noticeably absent from the conversation, and Eli was both grateful and curious. Stars filled the New Mexico night sky, so much bigger than he remembered.

What he'd never forgotten was the shape and warmth of the body beside him. He closed his eyes sometime after midnight and let his fingers, his hands, his mouth *remember.* Moving over her, he parted her thighs. She encouraged him closer and he buried his face in her neck.

He breathed her in, the smells of sunshine and warm skin and something soft that was simply her, had always been her. "You're for me, Reagan. You've always been for me. And you always will."

REAGAN'S HEART TRIPPED all over itself. Her hands paused in stroking Eli's back. Hell, she might have stopped breathing. Terror ripped through her. Had he just…

His breath was hot against her skin as he lifted his head and nipped her earlobe. "Living without you has been like living without the sun. I did it, but I don't want to go back to that, don't want to do it again."

She'd wanted this so badly for so long, but she was broken in too many ways. She didn't know what to do. There were too many things to say and not enough words. She didn't want to screw this up, didn't want to—

"I've lived with my mistakes for fourteen years. No more. I won't go another day pretending this is anything other than what it is. It's never been anyone but you. Only you."

She scrambled out from under him, pushing and shoving.

"Reagan?"

Barefoot or not, it didn't matter. She leaped from the truck and took off running for the river. Rocks and grass scraped at her feet. She didn't slow down. Memories chased her too hard and too fast. She was swift enough to outrun them. Almost. But what she had no hope of outrunning was the guilt she'd carried for more than eight years. The knowledge caught her at the same time Eli did.

"Don't," she pleaded, struggling to pull free of his grasp.

"Don't what? Care about you? I can't help it, Reagan. You're the one. You've always *been* the one."

She laughed almost hysterically, gripping her shirt and pulling. Her vision blurred with tears. Everything—her clothes, her underwear, her skin—it all felt too tight.

"If this is about Luke…" Eli swallowed hard and dropped his hand. "Did you love him that much, Reagan?" The question hurt to hear almost as much as it seemed to hurt him to ask.

The emotional floodwaters began to rise at an alarming rate. Reagan shook her head. "Don't. Don't bring Luke into this, Eli."

"If you loved him that much, if what you had with him was more powerful than what we have, not just now but before…" He swallowed so hard she heard it. He moved away stiffly, his words a quiet offering filled with regret and respect. "I'll take you home."

Watching him walk away triggered something in her, something fierce and raw and terrifying. "Stop!" The single, shouted word halted him in his tracks.

"What do you want from me, Reagan?" He angled his head to the side, offering her the dark side of his profile. "You want to rub it in my face that I messed up so bad I can't undo the damage? That I can't—and never could—measure up to the county hero-turned-martyr? Job well done."

Something in his bitter self-reproach resonated with her shame, and she found herself stalking toward him. He faced her just in time for her to plant her hands on his chest and shove. Satisfaction surged through her when he stumbled. "How dare you! How *dare* you! What we had—" The first sob ripped through her. "You left me, Eli! I wasn't enough for you. Wasn't enough to keep you here, to make you happy."

He stood there stunned for a heartbeat before his voice was as raised as hers. "I asked you to come with me! You stayed. You didn't love me enough to take a chance on me! And not once," he hissed, "not *once* did you beg me to stay."

"Don't you get it? I loved you! Love shouldn't ever have to beg." Her eyes filled with unwanted tears. "You should have stayed because you loved me more than you hungered for the idea of escaping. But you didn't. So I let you go."

"And married everybody's favorite son. Clearly you were brokenhearted."

His vitriolic anger forced her back a step. But only because she had to have the extra room to release her own fury. "I was destroyed," she whispered on a broken hiss. "I married Luke because I hoped it might exorcise your ghost. And I failed. *I. Failed.* Luke loved me." She pounded a fist over her heart. "And you know what? I didn't love him in return, not the way he did me. Not even close. And no one ever suspected. No one but Luke," she screamed, beginning to shake. "I didn't love him the way he loved me and he knew. He *died* with the certainty that the only man I ever gave my heart to was *you*."

Sobs racked her body, the confession torn out of her, the history and truth like scar tissue ripped off a wound that appeared healed but had actually festered below the surface.

Eli closed the distance between them in three strides and wrapped her in his strong arms, ignoring her struggles. "He loved you, baby. I know how that feels, and I'm willing to bet that, if you could ask him, he'd tell you there was nothing in the world he would have changed about his life with you."

"But you haunted me, Eli. Every time I turned around, you were there."

"Did he ever stop loving you?"

She choked on a sob.

"Did he?" Eli demanded.

"No."

Pulling her into him, they faced each other in the moonlight, the river the music to his declaration. "I understand how that feels." He reached for the hem of her T-shirt and lifted. "Let me make up for the past, Reagan."

"Don't leave me again," she pleaded. "Don't walk out on me."

"I don't intend to."

Closing her eyes, she raised her arms over her head and gave herself over to the moment. She needed the physical reassurance of him, needed him to lay claim to a heart he'd long ago abandoned.

It took a moment for her to realize that the turmoil that had kept her emotionally off balance 24/7 was gone. It was just the two of them in that moment.

Luke's ghost was gone.

15

ELI REMINDED HIMSELF to go slow, to truly make love to Reagan, but he was desperate for her, the touch of her bare skin as vital to him as his next breath.

In his desperation, he had trouble unbuttoning her jeans. Through her tears, she laughed, undoing them herself and shimmying out of her pants. The rate he peeled first hers and then his clothes off probably set some kind of world record, but he didn't care. He needed her.

Laying her down on the grass, he slipped into her with slow, measured pressure. She wrapped her legs around his waist and arched off the ground. Grabbing her hips, he went to his knees and lifted, fully seating her on his length and forcing her to support herself on her shoulders. Bending over her, he kissed the valley between her bare breasts. That one taste of her skin wasn't enough, though. He traced each beaded nipple with his tongue, suckling them until she was clawing the grass.

Widening his knees, he began to move. Fighting to keep the tempo slow and sure, he loved her body with everything he had. The night was bright enough to cast their shadows on the grass, and he watched the dark impressions move across the ground.

There was truth in that. They weren't the people they'd been.

Maybe they hadn't been ready for each other then; maybe it wouldn't have worked anyway; maybe…who knew. All he was sure of at this very moment was that, as he moved into her slick heat, as she arched higher and tightened around his hard shaft, she was the only woman he'd ever given his heart to. He was hers. And whether she was ready to admit it yet or not, she was his.

Sweat slicked their skin.

She gasped as he shifted a hand to give his thumb access to her clit.

He worked that tiny bundle of nerves, loving her body with every skill he possessed, driving her higher. Increasing his thrusts at the same rate he pressed his thumb against her, he felt her begin to shake. He loved that about her. Loved her uninhibited way of giving him her whole body.

She flung her arms out from her sides and tore handfuls of grass from the ground. "Harder," she pleaded.

He gave her what she asked for, vowing then and there it would always be so. There was nothing she could ask of him he wouldn't give. Wouldn't do. Wouldn't sacrifice. He'd been a fool far too long, and they'd both paid a high price for his pride.

The tremors overtook her and she cried out, her sheath tightening around him until she forced the orgasm out of him before he was ready. But his wants were second to hers. Now. Always. He gave her what she wanted, following her over the edge into the abyss.

The only thing he said was her name, whispering it over and over.

ELI HELD REAGAN until they felt the chill in the air. Scooping his lover up, he gave her a piggyback ride to the truck and set her on the tailgate. Neither of them spoke. There were a thousand things to say, and neither of them seemed sure where to start. Eli was fine with that. He wanted a lifetime with her to get this right.

He had to convince Reagan that coming with him to Austin was not only the best thing for both of them, but it was also the *right* thing. It would have been better if he'd had a chance to plan, to figure out how to approach her. He didn't have the luxury. This night under the stars had been his best shot.

Steeling himself, he settled his hands on her waist. "I have to go back to Austin."

Her fingers stalled against his skin.

Gripping her wrists so she couldn't break free, he shifted until he had positioned himself between her thighs. "Come with me."

Her gaze fell, her hands fisting. "I can't leave the county in the mess they're in. Not now," she whispered brokenly.

"Just come for a long weekend, then. See if you could be happy there." The pleading in his voice was open and obvious, and he didn't care. If he had to get on his knees, he would. "I've got to keep that job in order to make money for the ranch. But I can't just leave you, Reagan. I did it once and I've never been the same. Don't say no. Don't shut me down before we've had a chance to talk it out. Please."

"And after the weekend?"

"We'll figure it out, but this isn't over, Reagan. Not by a long shot."

She took a shuddering breath. Tipping her head back, she stared at the sky long enough he was sure she'd say no. His heart stuttered, his mind went blank. She reached out to trace the line of his jaw, a sheen of emotion evident in her eyes. "A weekend."

"To start."

She nodded, a tear tipping over her bottom lashes. "When do we leave?"

16

ELI RETURNED THE little rental car first thing the next morning.

"Eli," the owner said, tipping his hat.

"Sir," he responded, surprised and not at all sure who the man was.

The bell on the door jangled and they both turned as Reagan walked through the door. "Hey, Walt."

Walt Anderson. The name registered with Eli as if he was an amnesia patient regaining bits and pieces of his memories. "I appreciate the car, Mr. Anderson."

"You're old enough to call me Walt at this point, Eli." The man's tone was dry as dust.

"Sometimes I wonder if I'll ever be old enough," Eli muttered.

Walt laughed.

Eli jumped, surprised. He couldn't remember the crotchety old man ever smiling let alone laughing.

Reagan laid a hand on the small of Eli's back. "Any extra charges?"

"Nah. Car's a piece of shit." He grinned mischievously at Eli. "Figured it'd do you a little good."

"I may have a black lung, but that would be her fault, not

yours," Eli said, affecting the same dry tone. "She filled the cab with diesel exhaust."

Walt chuckled. "Hear you're gonna be outta town a bit, Doc."

"About four days," she answered, shifting from foot to foot.

This time it was Eli who reached out with a comforting touch. The old man's eyes were shrewd. "Anything you want to share?"

Reagan laughed. "Nope."

"Not even a hint?" Walt wheedled.

"Wait for the Watsons to call. One of them is sure to come up with something worth discussing." The bitterness in Reagan's voice cut at Eli.

"Bunch of pains in the ass, the lot of 'em. Y'all better git or you'll miss your flight."

Eli's brows shot up. "We made those reservations early this morning."

"It's a small town." Walt tipped his head toward the front door. "Have a safe trip."

ELI HUNCHED OVER to get through the plane door and did a quick head count. He and Reagan were two of three passengers on the flight.

Had anyone tried to convince him a mere week ago that he'd be returning to Austin with the only woman he'd ever loved, he would have laughed. Or punched them in the face. Now? Here she sat at his side, nervously gripping his hand and staring out the window as the ground fell away.

He leaned over and kissed her temple. "It's just four days, baby."

"I feel so guilty leaving when the community is in such a mess."

"Dr. Hollinsworth agreed to cover for you. Also, I had Ty call in a favor. He found out Dr. Alvarez will be in town until at least next Friday. It'll be fine."

She peered over her shoulder, brows creased. "But these people count on me."

"So do I."

Grinning a bit flatly, she shifted to press her forehead against the window and watch the plateau pass beneath them.

They made their connecting flight to Austin without any trouble. He'd booked them seats in business class, and she fussed with him for spending the money. Spoiling her secretly thrilled him. He let her mutter for about three minutes, then he kissed her quiet. The way she melted into his embrace made the extra costs for first class worth every single cent.

By the time they touched down in Austin, she'd relaxed. It had taken Eli pointing out she had a smartphone and could, in fact, be contacted 24/7 if something arose. And he'd reassured her that he could have her home in only a few hours if need be.

His car, an Audi R8, had been a matter of social standing and pride when he'd left. Now he wished he owned a pickup, even an SUV—something she'd be more comfortable in, and, in truth, something a little less glaringly excessive. Instead of lingering on the discomfort, he opened the door for her and watched her carefully seat herself and fish for the seat belt.

Settling himself behind the wheel, he offered her a small smile. "It's just a car."

"It's a car that costs more than most of the houses in Tucumcari," she responded quietly.

His brows pinched together. "Is it a problem?"

"No," she said quickly. Then much quieter, "No."

Ignoring the voice that whispered in his ear that something had shifted, he pulled out of the parking garage and into Austin traffic. Chaos reigned during the lunch hour. She was silent as he maneuvered through the snarl of metallic bedlam and hit the interstate at speed.

He'd just opened his mouth to ask her what was going on when his phone rang.

"Covington," he barked, completely ill at ease.

"From the lack of livestock in the background, I'm going

to assume you're in town." It was Stephen Smithy, one of the founding partners.

"Yeah." He pinned the phone between his shoulder and ear as he checked his mirrors, then downshifted and switched lanes quickly, heading for his house.

"Glad you made the right decision." Ice rattled in a glass.

"Scotch with lunch?" Eli asked lightly.

"Drinks and dinner with Macallroy have been moved up to tonight. Man's driving us all mad. It's up to you to salvage this, Eli. We can't afford to lose his business, no matter how much I might like to personally string him up by his… Never mind. Peché. Tonight. Reservations are for seven. Come by the office first."

Eli clenched his jaw. "I've already made plans."

"Do what you have to do," Reagan murmured.

He shot her a hot glance and waggled his eyebrows. "What *we* really should do is take my sauna's virginity. He's been trying to give it up for ages."

Her eyes widened and she mouthed, *You're on the* phone.

"So?"

"Much as I enjoy listening to you talk to your female companion—" Stephen started.

Eli interrupted. "Girlfriend, not companion. She's hot as hell and a doctor, so keep your mind out of my sauna."

"Hold the phone. Eli Covington has a girlfriend?"

"A serious girlfriend," he replied softly. "*Very* serious."

Reagan blushed and tucked a strand of hair behind one ear. The almost shy movement charmed him, and he found himself compelled to take her hand and lace their fingers together.

"Eyes on the road," she murmured.

"It's great you brought a love affair home from the wilds, but it doesn't change the fact you have to be in this office by two this afternoon."

Eli fought to ignore the slight jab about Reagan not being

Austin-polished. “I’ll be in the office by three, but I’ve got to be out by four to beat rush hour. That’s not negotiable.”

“Be in the office by two-thirty. You’ll leave when we’re done. That’s all the compromise you’ll get.” His boss’s tone had shifted just enough to warn Eli that he was pushing the man’s tolerance.

“See you then.” Eli disconnected before Stephen could decide he wanted Eli in the office immediately. He tossed his cell down, fighting to unclench his jaw. “I’m going to have to go into the office for a little while this afternoon. Shouldn’t be more than an hour, hour and a half tops.”

She slid her gaze to him, color riding her cheeks and mischief in her eyes. “Gives me time to talk to your sauna about his expectations and reassure him I’ll be gentle. He can let you know how it was for him when you get home.”

“You…” Eli’s mock incredulity was ruined when he had to adjust his swelling cock. Damn, but the idea of her in his sauna, naked, touching herself…

“Eyes on the road, Covington.” Her admonishment was tinged with laughter.

He blinked rapidly. It didn’t matter what they discussed this afternoon in the office. Eli’s mind would be on Reagan.

REAGAN WATCHED THE immensity of Austin spread out as they headed toward the outskirts of town. The homes grew larger, lots became rolling fields and driveways were gated. Appearances were clearly important here, and the realization left her tugging at her jacket sleeves.

She’d dressed in the closest thing to nice clothes she owned—slacks, a jacket and a pair of heels—but she suddenly felt frumpy. She considered herself a simple woman with an appreciation for nice sheets, spontaneous picnics and nights—particularly passionate ones—spent by the river. Riding in such an expensive car with an obviously highly influential attorney as they passed by expensive neighborhoods left her out of sorts, her emotions frayed. Then Eli pulled up to a gated community called The

Canyons. He entered a personal pass code and the iron gates swung open.

"The community is built along the edge of Lake Travis. It's quiet. And the neighbors are really nice."

He sounded as if he was trying to sell her on his address. She peered out the window at huge houses. A woman at her mailbox waved as they drove by. She was dressed in kitten heels, silk slacks and a lovely sleeveless shell, and her makeup was subtle but perfect.

Reagan slid a little lower in her seat. She'd never fit in with people who lived like this, and she didn't want to. No way could she stay here and play dress up to walk to the curb for the mail. She wouldn't pretend to have anything in common with people who would never understand her.

"What's bugging you, Reagan?"

She chanced a quick glance his way, shocked to find him clearly confused. "Seriously? Look at me, Eli. These are the best clothes I own, and I wasn't as well dressed as the woman picking up her *mail*."

He sped up, pushing the boundaries of acceptable speed through the subdivision until he pulled into a large half-circle drive. Shutting the car down, he unbuckled his seat belt and twisted to face her. "Stop it."

She hardly heard him. The house he'd pulled up in front of was enormous, easily five thousand square feet. A combination of stucco and stone, it was stunning. A high entry advertised a tall two-story entryway with a wrought-iron chandelier showcased behind a large window. What appeared to be hand-carved double doors were decorated with more wrought-iron work that matched the railing on the wide steps that led to the deep porch. The landscaping was immaculate. Through the sidelights, she could see through the depth of the house and, in the background, the shimmer of Lake Travis.

"Reagan?"

"You live here? Alone?"

"Yeah." He seemed to struggle with what to say and finally, on a sigh, said, "It was a good investment."

"It's a *huge* investment."

He gripped the steering wheel with one hand, wringing it so tightly the leather creaked. "I put far less into this house than I'll be putting into the ranch. Why does this bother you so badly? It's just a house."

"Uh-huh." She faced him. "And this is just a car. And the credit card you made the travel arrangements with wasn't black. And your lifestyle is really only representative of what anyone who goes to college should expect, right?" Her heart fluttered in her tightening chest.

The realization he lived like this, that he could truly afford to fund the Bar C's recovery efforts on his own? It made her doctorate seem insignificant and the fact she'd agreed to sell off her place a little harder to swallow. Eli would've been able to sell his house here and probably buy her land in New Mexico. In cash. Then it struck her. "With all this disposable income, why did you balk at the cost of treatment for the Bar C's herd?"

Closing his eyes, he took a deep breath before opening them to meet her gaze. "When I first got there—to the ranch, I mean—I was interested in getting in, doing what needed to be done and getting gone. And to be honest, I didn't even *consider* that my brothers might accept more from me. Things… changed." The tightness around his eyes softened. "My brothers and I realized we respected each other. Beyond the respect? We're brothers, Reagan. Neither time nor my absence changed that. I would have done anything to keep the ranch in their hands. But they're proud. I knew Cade would struggle with his pride before accepting the gesture. I wasn't sure how Ty would react. Ultimately? I managed to handle it so neither had a choice. Still, I would have done it for them even if they'd fought me on it." He lifted one shoulder and glanced away. "Bottom line is that they're my brothers and I love them."

Blinking slowly, she nodded, more to herself than in acknowledgment of his statement. He'd told her he cared about her. He'd said repeatedly he wasn't going to leave her again, wouldn't walk away. But he hadn't said he loved *her.*

"Is there something I can say to make this easier?"

What was he—a mind reader? "No," she answered quickly, forcing herself to smile. "Show me around the house?"

He considered her for a moment, then got out of the car. Walking to her side of the car, he took her hands and hauled her from the low-slung sports coupe. The sun's heat radiated off the pavement, dry and unforgiving.

"Listen to me," he said, voice low and fervent. "This is how I've lived, yes. But it doesn't change who I am. I'm Elijah Covington, the kid from Harding County, New Mexico, who grew up driving beat-up trucks and eating beans from a can after my mom died."

She nodded a little too quickly and gave him the honesty that was burning her up inside. "You can dress it up a hundred different ways, but this lifestyle is as foreign to me as if I'd been dropped into another country." Fine tremors ran down her arms, and he tightened his grip on her hands as if she'd run. And she'd be lying if she said the thought hadn't crossed her mind. "This might have been a mistake."

"Hush," he said, the word thickened with harsh desperation. "Don't reject me because of my address or the kind of car I drive. This is all temporary. I'm selling it all off to fund the ranch. We can make this work, Reagan. We can find a place outside the city with a little land where you could run a large animal practice and I can do some telecommuting. All I'm asking is that you remain open to the possibilities."

The laugh that escaped her was tinged with more than a little mania. "You make it sound so easy."

"It can be." At her skeptical look, he squeezed her hands quickly. "More than. Because we'll be in it together."

Somehow, that didn't afford her the kind of reassurance she

wanted, but she didn't argue with him. Instead, she gave a short nod, followed him to the front door and into a house that she knew would never be her home.

17

ELI COULD TELL SOMETHING was off with Reagan. She sought his permission to use the computer. Instead of grabbing a soda from the fridge, she asked if he'd mind if she had one. She was withdrawn, always scanning her environment, forever tugging at her sleeves or touching her hair.

The change in her depressed him. It also made him take a hard look at how he'd been living for the past few years. He'd been successful, yes, but he was living a life of unnecessary excess. No way did he need a house this large or a car that cost more than the median income of the Austin population. The realization left him uncomfortable in his own skin for the first time since he'd left home, and he didn't relish the experience.

Reagan had taken a call earlier, leaving him in his room as he changed to go into the office. When he'd tracked her down in the living room, she'd been hanging up with the state vet. He'd quarantined two more ranches today and was beginning to develop a suspicion on the source of the infection, but he was keeping all information close to his chest.

Eli knew the families who'd be affected by the BRD quarantines, and he'd offer pro bono legal services to every single one of them until this was cleared. And he might even keep his

New Mexico license active after that, just in case. If he'd learned anything over the past couple of weeks it was that life thrived on unpredictability.

He closed the distance between them, regret at having to leave her here making every step heavier than the last. "I've got to head into the office. I should be back before five, though."

She flashed him an irritated glance.

Stepping into her personal space, he encouraged her to meet his gaze. "What's eating at you, Reagan?"

She closed her eyes and shook her head. "Nothing worth discussing."

"Try me," he pressed.

"I don't belong here, and I hate feeling like a fake. I'm capable of looking the part but, no matter how hard I try, I'll never really fit in here." She waved her hand in the general direction of the neighborhood before settling her hands in her lap. Picking at a cuticle, she only stilled when Eli reached out and laid his hand over hers. She glanced up, haunted understanding in her eyes. "This is how you felt, isn't it? Growing up in New Mexico? Like you didn't belong no matter what you did."

He nodded, the observation so astute his throat tightened, making it difficult to breathe.

Reaching out, she gripped his hand. "I never got it. I'm sorry for that."

"How could you have understood?" He pulled free and stepped away, walking to the patio doors and staring out over the infinity pool and to the lake beyond. "You were always so at home there, so comfortable. You belonged from the beginning. It was impossible for you to imagine it could be any different for me as another rancher's kid."

"And now?" she asked quietly.

He shrugged. "It's different."

"How?"

Explaining would take more time than he had. Still, he owed her at least a rudimentary attempt at defining the differences.

He returned to her, grasping both her hands. "Let's talk about it when I get back."

Her eyes searched his for several seconds before she nodded. "Okay."

"I want to take you out tonight, show you around the city, visit some of my favorite haunts and then maybe take a walk through the heart of the music scene." He rolled his shoulders. "I want to show you the city that's been my home for fourteen years."

"We could stay in and I could cook for you." Her suggestion was offered with almost no inflection.

"Why wouldn't you want to go out to dinner?"

"I just thought a quiet night at home might be nice." She shifted from foot to foot. "And frankly? I'm not sure I'm up to diving into city life."

Totally disregarding his suit, he pulled her lithe body against his. "It doesn't matter what we do, sweetheart. Whatever it is, we'll spend tonight together."

She started to say something, but he bent his head and kissed her. It was meant to be a swift kiss, but it quickly evolved, becoming a drawn-out, slow burn. Desperation weighted every movement and made it raw in a very brutal, real way. There was an unspoken reminder that this opportunity to rediscover each other was fragile and should be treated with the utmost care.

Eli wished like hell he had even a single clue how to manage that. If only do-overs came with manuals that guaranteed a guy could learn from past mistakes and not repeat them.

Unease settled at the base of his spine and slowly burned its way up. He would hurt Reagan again if he botched this up. She'd given him that power over her, the move subtle but undeniable. Conversely, he'd done the same when he'd handed his heart over to her. He couldn't be sure she realized the exchange had been a fifty-fifty trade on the power grid, but when things were just right, he'd tell her how he felt.

It just wasn't something he could blurt out, though. Offer it up too soon and she'd think he wasn't sincere. Wait too long and she wouldn't believe it was genuine. There was a window, a brief moment, when he could convince her that what he felt for her was real. He could only hope he was smart enough to recognize it.

Reagan pulled away and met his somber eyes with bright ones, her lips swollen and parted slightly as she gasped a bit to catch her breath. "Well," she said, putting some distance between them and straightening the collar of his shirt. "That's one way to get me to go to dinner with you."

He chuckled. "There's another way?"

She grinned. "Go to the office and do what you have to do, Esquire. While you're gone, I'll come up with a list of ways you might be able to convince me that Austin's charms are exactly what this country girl can't live without." She spun away from him and started up the winding staircase, the sway of her hips mesmerizing.

Eli was more grateful for that moment than he had been for nearly anything in his life that had come before. The woman he loved was currently in his home, headed to his bathroom to soap up, then get all polished so he could take her out. Her belongings—travel-sized or not—were on his vanity counter. Truth slammed into him with runaway-train velocity, knocking him completely off the tracks. He never wanted to be without those small reminders of her again. Ever.

But for now, he had work to do. Then he had a woman to please. And if the sway of her body was any indication, she was telling him just what she wanted. He intended to deliver. And after that? After they had a little fun this weekend and Reagan saw what their life together could be like?

He'd find a way to make her stay.

REAGAN WOKE FROM her short nap when her cell phone alarm sounded. She stretched, Eli's luxurious bamboo sheets sliding across her bare skin. The bed was so sumptuous she promised herself she'd be getting the same setup when she went home. The mattress, the sheets, the pillows—it all tempted her to stay in bed the entire weekend. The man who would be home soon was an even greater temptation.

Her connection to him was stronger than ever, and she wondered for what had to be the thousandth time if what he experienced with her was anything remotely close to what she found in his arms. He'd said repeatedly he cared for her, had brought her to Austin to share his life with her, but she was still lacking that one fundamental admission that would change everything.

Granted, it had been fast for love. A week? Not so likely. But they'd loved each other before. Yes, they'd been kids, but neither age nor the passage of years could diminish what they'd had together. At least not for her. Was that it? Had he stopped loving her at some point over the past fourteen years and was now only easing his way back into the relationship? Or would they trek down the same path where love wasn't enough to get them through the rough patches?

The thought made her want to throw up. Distracting herself seemed prudent, so she shoved out of bed and went to the sumptuous bathroom, turned the shower on and stepped under the stream of hot water. She didn't really have the best clothes to wear to a nice restaurant, but she'd manage. Maybe mix up her jacket with jeans and boots, put her hair up and pay a little extra attention to her makeup. Whatever she did, she wanted to be beautiful and sexy for Eli.

A couple of hours later, she assessed the completed look in the mirror. She was satisfied that she'd transformed herself into the kind of chic and urbane woman Eli would be accustomed to and, likely, expect.

And she hated it. This wasn't her. She wasn't the girl who sat around and waited for her moneyman to come home. She'd worked long and hard to build a life on her own terms, to be proud of who she was. Eli had helped her to do that. And she wouldn't move backward. Not even for him. When he came home, she'd make it clear that he'd either have to adjust and take her for who she was or she'd return to New Mexico.

Alone.

18

THE DAY HAD been interminable. Eli's boss had ridden his ass about having his priorities skewed over this thing with the family. Alternately, Eli's family had ridden his ass via texts and cell about not getting in touch to discuss operational budgets and options for moving forward under quarantine. They were in limbo, and Cade and Ty did not *do* limbo.

Eli understood that. But what they all failed to realize was that he had more responsibilities than an emotional pack mule, and whipping his ass raw wasn't going to do anything but make him lock down.

After an hour in the office, though, just about everyone had the picture. Lynette had all but disappeared, opting to work in her office instead of his. She'd muttered something about "toxic proximity" as she left earlier.

Macallroy had called three times after somehow finding out Eli had come in a day early, and had insisted dinner be moved to tonight. No negotiation, no compromise, nothing.

Eli immediately thought of Reagan. He'd promised to take her out, and she was already sensitive about how she fit into his life. But when he suggested bringing a date, Macallroy made it clear he had no intention of tolerating interlopers to what he obviously anticipated would be a six-course ass-kissing.

Eli had no intention of going anywhere near that wrinkled bum. No amount of money was worth it, and maybe Reagan could lighten the mood.

Then Stephen laid it out in no uncertain terms. "Macallroy called." The man hadn't said "again," but the implication was loud and clear. "It'll be the two of you at dinner."

Eli slouched low and swiveled his chair around to face Stephen. "My girlfriend's in town. I can't just leave her at home."

"I don't care if you pay Lynette overtime to take the woman to the circus," Stephen spat. "You're going to dinner alone."

"So I can sit down with Macallroy and listen to his threats, take his abuse and simply nod along while he insults the firm, Stephen?" Eli slowly stood and toed the chair aside, propping a hip on the corner of his desk and crossing his arms over his chest. "An impartial witness is a good idea."

The older man arched a silvered brow. "And you truly believe your woman's impartial? Juries are generally malleable, but even I can't imagine them following your skewed logic."

Eli's jaw clenched as he fought the urge to snap at the man. Seconds from the mantel clock in his office ticked by with the unrelenting precision of marching soldiers. Stephen made the move to leave, and Eli shoved off his desk. "You're not being reasonable. This is her first night in Austin—it's important that I spend it with her, keep her with me and make sure she knows she matters. It's not reasonable to expect her to accept the fact I brought her home and then immediately left her, expecting her to fend for herself with no car, no friends and no knowledge of the area. You're standing there insisting I treat Macallroy like a benevolent king while also demanding that I treat my girlfriend like an inconvenience. That's not even remotely equitable treatment, and you know it. There's no reason Macallroy can't wait until tomorrow night for dinner, as was originally planned."

The founding partner paused in the doorway. "Stop thinking with your cock and get your priorities straight. This dinner is about preserving one of the firm's top three revenue-generating clients. If that means Macallroy wants to yank your chain a little and get you to grovel, you'll do it. I don't give a damn what you do with your girlfriend or what excuse you make for having to bow out of whatever you had planned." Stephen shifted to offer his profile, but Eli didn't miss the cold visage on the man's face. Eli had never wanted to be on the receiving end of that look and, until now, had managed to avoid it. No longer. "You do a single thing to screw this up tonight, and your position as partner here is done."

Eli's stomach tightened as if a giant fist had squeezed his innards and turned them into a pulverized mess. "I started in the mailroom here fourteen years ago. I've been loyal to you and this firm, working nights, weekends and holidays, and all in the name of taking care of clients. I have billable hours no one here can match and have managed to secure some of the firm's top clients. You'd let me go because I'm asking a client to hold to his original *dinner plans*?"

"You said it yourself," Stephen said quietly. "This is about loyalty and where yours lies, Eli. Nothing more, nothing less." With measured steps, the man left the spacious corner office.

Eli spun away from the doorway and looked out over Austin's premier business district. The streets teamed with life. Vendors hawked their wares at street corners. Entertainers had seated themselves at intervals along the sidewalks to play and accept coin or the occasional dollar bill someone might flip their way. The pedestrians ranged from college students to suburbanites to high-end business people.

The view from his window had always been one that energized and grounded him. He'd survived in this city, *his* city, for fourteen years. Some of those early years had been miserable as he survived on ten-cent noodle packets in order to have enough money to make the rent. He'd worked until he'd earned the respect of his peers and superiors.

The haunting voice of his old man had faded over the years, the taunts that he'd never be anyone had faded from memory with every pay increase, every promotion, every accomplishment Eli claimed as his own.

But in the course of one very short afternoon and an even shorter conversation, Stephen had managed to fracture Eli's surety that this was where he belonged. The man had suggested Eli set his morals and ethics aside and cater to the highest bidder—in this case, Macallroy—if he wanted to experience continued success.

Gathering his things and shoving the case file and his laptop into his briefcase, Eli started for the door. His temper was brewing. No one called his ethics into question or suggested he set them aside in exchange for the almighty dollar. Screw that. He'd manage dinner tonight, but then he had to truly reassess what it meant to stay with the firm. His brothers had remained proud and strong while everything they'd worked for had been systematically destroyed. He would do no less.

His phone rang. A quick glance at the caller ID showed Stephen's extension. Hesitating, Eli rested his fingers on the receiver and then pulled away…empty handed. Stephen had made his position clear. There was nothing left to say. Spinning on his heel, he stalked out of the office, his suit jacket flapping over one arm.

From the curious looks a handful of colleagues shot his way, they'd either overheard Stephen's threat or his boss had advertised it to a select few who would make sure the gossip spread.

More intimidation tactics. He'd watched the old man work long enough to expect this, to know exactly how he'd be treated. Stephen had drawn a line in the sand, and if Eli crossed it, he'd be fired, his reputation ruined and all hope for funding the ranch's recovery destroyed.

He missed the elevator by seconds, so he hit the Down arrow and waited for the next one.

Heels clicked across the lobby's wood floors. "Mr. Covington?"

He lifted his face and stared at the ceiling. "Yes, Lynette?"

"Mr. Smithy tried to catch you in your office before you left," she said, voice breathy.

"Apologies for neglecting Stephen's call," Eli murmured. Then he turned his gaze toward the woman, whose face was flushed and eyes wide. "What did he want, Lynette?"

She wrung her hands together. "He said that, before you left the building, I was to tell you that only a fool would throw his career away over a piece of ass, and he's never considered you a fool."

"You can inform him that his message was delivered. Thank you, Lynette." The elevator chimed its arrival with a soft note before the doors silently opened. Eli stepped inside and faced the front of the elevator, meeting his paralegal's paranoid stare. He leaned one shoulder against the wall, the corners of his mouth kicking up with undisguised insolence. "Go home early tonight. You put in way too many hours."

She grinned. "Yes, sir."

The doors slid together and Eli closed his eyes, reveling in the silence.

If he saved his job to protect the ranch, he'd hurt Reagan. If he ruined his career to protect Reagan, he'd hurt his brothers.

There was no way to win. To lose, though? It seemed there were infinite choices available to him.

He only had to settle on one.

REAGAN HAD JUST finished refreshing her makeup when she heard the front door slam and Eli call her name. "Up here!" she shouted.

He came into the room and smiled at her over her shoulder,

the action reflected in the mirror, but the smile never reached his eyes.

She rounded on him slowly, makeup brush clutched in one hand. "What happened?"

Closing the distance between them, he leaned in and laid a tender kiss on her lips. "You look absolutely stunning."

She didn't comment, didn't blink. "Seriously. Is everything okay?"

"Yes." He shook his head and raked his fingers through his hair. "No. I've been ordered to attend dinner tonight with the very client who's been raising hell since before I left for New Mexico."

"The one you broke the window in my door for so you wouldn't miss the conference call?"

"That would be the one." He shrugged out of his suit jacket and tossed it across the counter before leaning against the wall, chin tucked into his chest. "I don't want to have to do this, Reagan, but he's demanding I come alone. He wants me one-on-one to ensure I sufficiently kiss his ass and make empty promises that the firm will do all we can to get the EPA fines and settlement figure lowered." Eli looked up. "Don't suppose I could talk you into a rain check on dinner?"

Drawing a deep breath, she set her brush down and propped both hands on the counter. "You went into work this afternoon at their demand, and now you're going to leave me here, alone, in order to go to dinner with a client, again at their demand."

He sighed. "Pretty much."

Rising to her full height, she faced Eli. "That's not what I came to Austin for, Eli. This, being second to your job day *and* night, isn't what I want, and it's certainly not what I'm worth." The truth hung between them, her words heavy, the uncensored guilt in his eyes telling. "I'm not the person whose life revolves around her partner's availability, settling for the scraps of time he can scrounge up on weekend afternoons or the occasional weeknight he makes it home for dinner. I won't be that woman, Eli. Not even for you."

"Come with me." The invitation, undoubtedly sincere, didn't disguise the panic in his voice.

"If that were an option, you would have invited me first instead of asking for a rain check."

"It's an option if I make it one. And I want you to be there with me. I want you to be a permanent part of my life, not a space-filler." He stepped closer to her, running his hands from her shoulders to her fingertips. "Please come."

She gestured to her outfit of slacks and a sleeveless shell paired with low pumps. "Is this sufficient dinner attire?"

Eli visibly paled even as one corner of his mouth lifted. "Unfortunately, no. But we can run by an upscale shop and pick up something more appropriate. My treat," he added, as if that would sway her.

"Now you want me to play dress up in order to impress your client," she said.

"The restaurant is very high-end."

That would be a *yes* to her question.

Exactly what she'd decided today she would never do. Pretend to be someone she wasn't. Give up the identity she was proud of.

Her chest ached hard and fast as if someone had reached in and pierced her heart. A tiny pinprick. Nothing more. But it was enough to let her know it was enough she would bleed out. Maybe not tonight, maybe not tomorrow, but eventually it would become an inevitability.

It was over, this thing between them. She had to tell Eli. No doubt he would do his best to persuade her to stay, and the man could be very, very persuasive. But she wouldn't let him take over her life again. She wouldn't spend years waiting on him to figure out she mattered more than whatever Austin held for him. No, she would make plans to return to New Mexico tomorrow. Loving Eli would always be her first instinct, but living in Austin would gradually evolve and that love would become resentment. That was one thing she could never allow. What they had was unique, had survived the trials life had thrown their way. Maybe, someday, their paths would cross and they would be right for each other. But that time wasn't now. Her breath hitched.

Eli pulled her into his embrace. "Talk to me, baby. It doesn't matter what you wear. All I care about is that you're with me."

Had she been wrong? Maybe she'd been too hasty to assume that she couldn't be herself in Austin, couldn't be Eli's partner. She could give him—them—this one opportunity. She'd be here tonight anyway, so she would take the chance, go to dinner and find out where things stood. How he was with her in front of a client would be very revealing.

"You'll smudge my makeup." She wiggled free of his arms and started for the stairs. "If we're going to have time to pick up something appropriate for me to wear, we need to go now."

He didn't answer her, simply went into his closet and began to change into more formal attire.

She would play this game tonight with one goal in mind: figuring out who truly held the strings to Eli's heart.

19

Eli had picked out a black Chanel suit, clutch and sky-high Jimmy Choos for Reagan before cajoling her into having her hair and makeup redone quickly at a tony salon nearby. She was beautiful. The loose chignon emphasized the long column of her neck. Smoky eye shadow made her green eyes luminescent.

But with every change he'd asked for, he'd put a certain amount of distance between them. He wasn't a fool—he knew she was withdrawing. Still, he wouldn't give up, wouldn't lose her. He'd fight to find a way to salvage their relationship he didn't want to give up and the career that the ranch couldn't afford to survive without.

She was quiet on the way to the restaurant, staring out the window as she fidgeted with her handbag, snapping it open then closed repeatedly. When Eli laid his hand over hers, she'd stilled but refrained from comment.

He pulled into the valet lane and put the car in Park, waving the attendant off for a moment. Shifting in his seat, he took a fortifying breath and let it out slowly. "This is going to be a difficult dinner."

"I gathered as much when you buffed and polished your balls before dressing," she said calmly.

His lips twitched. "I did no such thing."

"You also did the same to your ass. You're prepared to bend over the barrel for this guy." Her eyes narrowed. "I've got to say, Esquire, I'm not the least bit impressed with your willingness to give it up to someone else on our first official date, particularly when you had me dressed up like a pretty doll."

"I'm not giving it—" His lips clamped together, nose flaring as he fought to rein in his temper. "This is a delicate situation. You're right about one thing, though. It's literally my ass on the line if I lose this man's business, so yeah, I might be a little..." He ran a hand around the back of his neck and pulled, searching for words.

She reached for the door handle, but Eli grabbed her wrist.

"I'm sorry, Reagan. Truly. After we get through this evening, we'll make this whole thing work out the way it was supposed to."

The small flare of hope in her green eyes made him want to scrap dinner and go straight to planning their future, but there wouldn't be as much to discuss if he lost Macallroy's business.

Squeezing her wrist tightly, he gave the valet a short come-ahead gesture. "You look amazing tonight. Just watch my back so the old man doesn't shiv a kidney when I'm facing the bar."

Shaking her head on a chuffed laugh, she took the valet's hand and rose from the low-slung car.

The front of the restaurant gave off a hip vibe. An eclectic array of well-dressed people waited outside; the warehouse district was already coming alive as the sun set. Eli bypassed the line, slipped through the coat check station and discreetly slipped a bill into the hand of the maître d'. "Table for three. I believe my personal assistant requested the private tasting room."

"You're Mr. Covington." The statement was delivered with smooth assurance. "I was advised there would only be two in your party this evening. Mr. Macallroy has already arrived."

"Of course he has," Eli responded just as smoothly. "I'm sure you'll accommodate my companion, Dr. Matthews, and see her seated with us immediately."

"Absolutely, Mr. Covington. Dr. Matthews?" The middle-aged man swept an arm wide, encouraging Reagan to step behind the near end of the bar and through black swinging doors. The noise from the club abated, and the maître d' said, "Please watch your step, Doctor. The metal grates of the stairs might catch the heel of your shoe if you're not diligent."

"Thank you." She took the stairs on her tiptoes, and all Eli could think was that if it had been him, he'd have one big-ass charley horse by the time he made it to the top of that spiral staircase. Reagan didn't even whimper.

"This is where the club was run in the 1920s when prohibition was in full force. It's why you'll hear nothing from below any more than someone from below will hear you."

Reagan shot him a look over her shoulder. Eli grinned, shook his head and pointed to his kidney. She hid a laugh as they cleared the top of the stairwell.

Moving in close to her, Eli nodded at the liveried man and, placing his hand on Reagan's back, directed her to the only table in the moderately sized room.

Covered in black linens and white china, and with candles burning strategically around the room, the table seemed almost suspended in a void. Eli pulled Reagan's chair out but held her elbow to keep her from sitting down. "Don, this is Dr. Reagan Matthews."

The old man stared up at her with an indifference he could only have achieved if he'd tried. Hard. "Mr. Macallroy." Reagan inclined her head and slipped into her seat. "I understand if it's too difficult for you to rise and greet your guests. Please, don't be inconvenienced."

Both men stared at her, startled. For Eli that was quickly followed by panic and fury. He'd explained to her on the way over what this evening meant, that it was a delicate dance. Now, before the old man had even spoken, she was already provoking him.

Stephen had warned him, had told Eli not to bring her, that it would only make the situation harder to control. But Eli had let Reagan supersede his common sense. And they were all going to pay for it if he didn't rein her in, and quickly.

Pulling up a chair, he missed Reagan's arched brow until he was seated and she'd slid her own chair in. Frustrated, Eli grabbed his glass of water and took a short swallow. "Have you ordered from the bar already, Don?"

The old man offered him a cold stare. "I'm not here for shallow, congenial conversation any more than I'm here to play nice with your newest piece of ass."

Eli's temper flared higher, his lips thinning. A feminine hand squeezed his knee.

"I find that hard to believe," Reagan said quietly, leaning back as she let the waiter settle her napkin in her lap.

"It was clearly stated you were not to be part of the evening," Macallroy barked out. "This isn't a social dinner. It's about your pretty boy here making it clear to me that his loyalties lie where they should. You're nothing but an annoying distraction from business dealings well above your head."

Eli's spine stiffened and he leaned toward Macallroy, but Reagan spoke before he could.

"First, if you weren't here for shallow, congenial, *ass-kissing* conversation, you would have answered either yes or no to Mr. Covington's question. You didn't, so you must not be entirely averse to his gesture." She met Macallroy's hostile stare, her face giving away nothing. "Second, if these business dealings were so far above my head that I'd be nothing but a liability to any conversation, I wouldn't be able to discuss your company's public filings, for example, or the public relations nightmare you are facing because of the oil spill. And while Eli hasn't said one word about Macallroy Oil, I have to believe that's a large reason you insisted on meeting with him in person. Your case goes to Federal Court in less than ten days.

"And finally, if you weren't interested in checking out Eli's 'latest piece of ass,' you wouldn't be paying so much attention to my—" she tugged her jacket "—personal assets." She looked up through thick lashes and met his unabashed stare with an open dare to refute her verbal comeback.

Time stalled, seconds dragging by with echoing booms in the vacuum of space created by Reagan's response. As impressed as he was, her words had pulled the safety net out from under the tightrope Eli was walking tonight.

Macallroy didn't tolerate dissidence of any kind, and here she was, heaping it on layer after layer. Every word could be construed as an insult, every look a taunt of what Eli had and Don couldn't touch.

If Reagan didn't cool it, Eli would be fired before they made it to the main course.

The waiter set a glass of bourbon next to Macallroy's right hand so he only had to shift his fingers to retrieve it. He took a solid swallow, blowing fumes through his nose. "You usually don't go for the particularly bright ones, Covington. She's a different flavor for you." Macallroy blinked slowly and focused on Eli. "And while she might be entertaining in a variety of ways, she's pissing me off. Get her under control before she ruins a perfectly lovely evening."

Reagan looked at Eli, clearly expecting him to say or do… *something.*

"Dr. Matthews is my guest, Don. I'd appreciate it if you'd treat her with at least a rudimentary showing of respect."

Don snorted into his glass.

Eli's fist came down on the table. "Enough."

The old man gazed up at him, a slow smile spreading across his face. "I didn't think you had it in you."

"You'll push me only so far before I'll defend—"

"What's yours," Macallroy finished for him. "It's that very

fire that led me to retain you six years ago. I'd begun to believe it had been squashed out by soft living and easy women." He barely spared Reagan any acknowledgment when he said, "Though I doubt there's much easy about this one."

Eli shook his head quickly, trying to suss out what Macallroy was really after. "I was under the impression you were prepared to discontinue the representation agreement between the firm and Macallroy Oil tonight. Was I mistaken?"

"No. I intended to see if you were brave enough to bring your balls to the table. You did, so I'm going to give you a chance to convince me you have the same sense of possessive pride in Macallroy Oil's interests as you do your bed partner's. Still, she has to go. Neither my rules nor my standards change."

Reagan sat up straighter in her seat.

If Eli could secure this account, if he could save this line of income for the firm, it would mean much larger bonuses and a faster recovery for the Bar C. But to make his client happy, he'd have to delve into a few gray areas he wasn't proud of, parts of being a lawyer he didn't want Reagan exposed to. His mind flashed to his first meeting with Cade in the sand hills last week. His middle brother hadn't thought he'd cared about anyone but himself. He had to prove to his brothers what they meant to him. It wouldn't be easy, but he was going to get this done for the ranch, for them and, in the end, to afford him the chance at a life with Reagan.

Digging out his wallet, he handed her several fifties. "If you want to grab a table downstairs, baby, I'll be there within the hour. We'll have dinner then."

Reagan glanced between the proffered money and Eli. "You want me to wait. Downstairs."

"I'll have him back to you with plenty of life left in him," Macallroy chuckled, shaking his empty glass at the waiter. "Then the evening's all yours, darling."

Eli stood and helped Reagan out of her chair, his hand at the base of her spine, hastily ushering her toward the staircase. Her heels issued sharp clips across ancient wood floors. "Give me thirty minutes to salvage this account and I'll be out of here. An hour at the most."

She took his cash, tucked it in her clutch and started down the stairs. He saw her pause as he began to return to his client, so he signaled to Macallroy he'd only be a moment. "Reagan? This is important."

She opened her mouth to say something, then closed it, smiling ruefully.

"What?" he pressed, exasperation sneaking into his voice against his better judgment.

"You're right. It *is* important. I just thought...nothing. I finally get it."

And with that, she took off her shoes and skipped down the dangerous treads with far less caution than she'd used climbing up them.

TURBINE ENGINES SPUN UP to a deafening roar as the plane gathered speed down the runway, forcing Reagan deeper into her seat.

She'd left with only the clothes she'd worn to dinner. She'd intended to retrieve her belongings, but when the cab pulled up to The Canyons' gated entry, Reagan had realized she'd never been given the code. He'd escorted her into his life, but it had become very clear he'd never let her in as a person he respected and loved.

She'd said to Eli that she finally got it. And she did. When he'd left her as a teenager, he'd had to go—staying would have destroyed him. So she'd let him go. And when he'd come back, when he'd insisted she should have begged him to stay, she'd told him the truth. Love should never be reduced to begging.

Tonight she'd left because she wasn't willing to beg him to find a way to fit her into a life she clearly didn't belong in. There was no place for her in Austin because if she couldn't fit organically, she'd never fit at all. But the trip hadn't been a total failure. The missing piece of herself she'd never thought to find had snapped into place. Reagan had finally realized she had to have more respect for herself if she demanded her partner offer her the same. That meant she couldn't go back to allowing Eli to be her sole reason for living. She knew herself better now, knew what she was truly worth, and what he'd handed her in cash hadn't been enough to buy her pride. What it came down to was simple, but it didn't assuage the hurt of his loss.

Eli might have her heart, but her life was her own.

20

STANDING IN THE middle of Peché, Eli listened to the maître d' explain he'd called a cab for Dr. Matthews at her request. She'd left through the front doors, alone, more than two hours ago.

Eli realized right then that terror had a definitive taste. Bitter but light, like a mouthful of horribly charred sesame seeds. The foulness coated the inside of his mouth and made it impossible to expunge the flavor. He couldn't breathe without aspirating the charred bits.

He'd known sending Reagan away had been the wrong choice the moment she'd kicked her shoes off and skipped down the steps. Never had he been so divided about what to do—go after her and save their relationship or go back to the table to salvage the client relationship that would allow him to earn enough to fund the ranch's recovery, thus saving his family. Who should garner his loyalty? At that very moment, how was he supposed to determine who came first? He loved both sides fiercely and had no idea how to decide who to see to first. So he'd remained at the table, his immobility making the decision for him.

His cell phone rang and he fumbled with it in his haste to answer. "Hello?" he shouted above the din. "Hold on. Don't hang up. I've got to get outside. Just—don't hang up!" Shoving his way through the crowd, he stepped into the ever-active warehouse district. "Reagan?"

"It's Stephen."

Eli's shoulders sagged. "I'm a little busy at the moment, Stephen."

"It can wait. Macallroy called and said you brought your stainless steel balls to the table tonight. All he wanted, apparently, was to know you still had them." Stephen chuckled, the cat-who-ate-the-canary sound grating inside Eli's skull. "He also said you brought your girlfriend but managed to shut her down effectively before kicking her to the curb so the men could get down to the kind of talk women weren't created to understand."

Eli stared at the phone's screen, stunned. Without a word, he disconnected the call, opened the Recorder app on his phone and redialed Stephen. The man answered immediately. "Call dropped," Eli said through numb lips. "I only caught part of that. Could you repeat it for me?"

Stephen launched into a repeat of his earlier words, complete with over-the-top embellishments. He openly laughed at the image of Eli standing Reagan up and walking her from the table to the spiral staircase in dismissal. "Did you really shove a wad of cash at her?" Stephen asked, making no effort to disguise the smile in his voice.

Eli's stomach pitched hard enough he braced one hand on his thigh for support. "I did."

"Wouldn't have thought you had it in you, Covington." Stephen chuckled. "Was she pissed?"

"That would be an understatement."

Stephen hooted with laughter. "Good thing you never bother to fall in love with your bed partners. What color was her hair?"

"Light brown." He blinked. "Why?"

"You just need a different color next weekend. Find a blonde, take her to bed. You'll be over this one in no time."

Rage, far too long suppressed, straightened Eli's spine. The guy nearest him took one look at Eli's face, tapped his buddies on their respective shoulders, and the group moved off to give Eli plenty of room. "Shut up, Stephen. For once in your damn life? Shut. Up."

Glass clinked against a stone countertop with a sharp crack. "What did you just say?"

"For fourteen years I've busted my ass, given up almost all of my life for you, attended every social function and toed company policy, reciting the firm's fustian rhetoric to anyone within hearing distance."

"I get you're a little stressed—"

"Stressed?" Eli said softly. "Screw 'stressed,' Smithy. You put me in a position tonight where I had to choose between love and love—for my girlfriend and my family—and there was no right decision to make. If I did right by her, my brothers lost out. If I did right by them, she lost out. But either way? The firm won. Well, congratulations. Your firm managed to retain the biggest asshole in corporate America, but you lost your best lawyer in the process."

Stephen breathed heavily across the line. "Are you threatening me?"

"No, Stephen." Eli grinned. "Threats usually come with demands. I'm simply quitting."

"You're not so stupid as to quit over a piece of ass."

"Refer to her that way one more time, and I swear to you on my mother's grave that I will haul you out of your office and show you how I was taught to handle problems where I grew up."

"You *are* threatening me," Stephen spat.

"No, I'm not. I'm just telling you how it works where I come from."

"You're done here."

"This is why you needed me so bad, Smithy. You were always two steps behind." Eli spun toward the valet desk and started toward the first vested man he saw. "I already told you. I quit."

REAGAN'S RETURN TO her little place was anticlimactic. She'd shed the trim black suit and hung it up, draping it in a garbage bag to keep dust off the fabric. Then she'd put the expensive heels in a brown grocery bag. Tucked in the top of her closet, no one would ever assume the footwear inside cost more than the stud fee on an above-average quarter horse.

The one thing that remained of Eli's extravagance was the lingerie she still wore. She'd chosen it specifically for the fact that the bra did something to her breasts that made them undeniably lush. And the cut of the high-hipped thong emphasized the length of her legs but also made her torso look longer, even leaner. The underwear made her feel pretty, and she liked that. She'd keep it as a reminder of what they'd shared, the hurt they'd overcome and the choices they'd both made. She'd also never wear it again.

Flopping down on the bed, she missed Brisket. She'd have to go out to the Bar C tomorrow and pick him up. Of course, that meant facing the Covington brothers, who would, without a doubt, want to know why she'd come home early. She draped an arm over her eyes and sighed. Maybe she'd wait and go get her dog on Saturday. An extra day wouldn't hurt anyone—least of all her. And, just once, she deserved to catch a break in that particular department.

Pushing off the bed, she shed her underwear and pulled on her favorite boxers and T-shirt, shut the house up and cut off all the lights.

Making her way to the bedroom, she paused in the living room at the sound of a coyote calling somewhere nearby. She'd have to start keeping her rifle by the front door again if they were going to be coming this close to the house. They worked in packs and the group would take Brisket down if they caught him out alone somewhere, and that just wasn't going to happen. She protected what was hers. The universe could kiss her ass if it believed it had the right to keep taking away everything that meant something to her.

The vehemence of her last thought shocked her. Clearly she had some anger issues to work through.

Glancing out the big picture window in the living room, she looked at a night sky full of stars. "Anger issues. Ya think?" she asked the universe at large. Then she flipped it the bird and went to bed.

She didn't delude herself that things would sort themselves out overnight, but she also wasn't stupid enough to turn down the first night's sleep she'd had in years—*years*—where she was the only one in her bed. No husband. No ghost. No memories. No dog. No one but her.

Rolling over, she punched the pillow and fought against the way her throat tightened.

REAGAN SPENT THE next three weeks working her ass off at every ranch but the Bar C. One of the Bar C's cowboys had dropped Brisket off on a run to town, and she and the dog had been making the rounds, pressing forward aggressively in treating every case of Bovine Respiratory Disease that had been reported. She'd crossed paths with the state vet, Dr. Alvarez, as well as the other large animal vet in the area, Dr. Hollinsworth. Both had been spread pretty thin trying to treat the sick herds while isolating the source of the virus.

On the first day of her fourth week home she found herself back at the Jensen place. Some of the calves they'd treated on her last visit had recovered and been cleared to move to stalk fields; meanwhile the ranch continued to treat the few that weren't recovering well. She'd come out today to decide which could possibly be saved versus those for which euthanization would be most humane.

Reagan was on foot, using Brisket to push the yearlings forward into the loading chute, when she had a moment of inexplicable clarity. When she'd been here a couple of weeks ago, she'd been riding the pipe, inoculating animals as they went through the chute to load on the truck. A steer had turned back and pushed his way off the truck. She'd called Brisket in. The truck driver had been helpful in getting things moving again. She'd issued his hauling papers and moved on, thinking nothing of it. Days later, the first animal on the Jensen place had begun exhibiting symptoms.

"Oh, shit." She glanced at that same truck driver as he climbed around the semi's trailer, kicking dried and not-so-dried cow feces off ventilation ports so he could get the gates to latch. This particular trucking company was popular among local ranchers because it was locally owned. Most everyone used them. "Oh, *shit*," she hissed, regret almost choking her.

The drivers were supposed to spray their trucks down with an antiviral if they were working different ranches with the same trailers. But just looking at the condition of this trailer made it clear the trucking company was cutting corners.

The virus was spreading by *truck*. Every time they loaded healthy yearlings into a trailer where infected calves and yearlings had been, they were exposing the healthy calves to the disease. No wonder they hadn't been able to contain it! Every step they took forward had involved moving calves around via truck, thus perpetuating the infection.

The Bar C hadn't been responsible.

Standing on the top rung of the pipe fence, she let out a sharp whistle. Dr. Armando Alvarez and several of the men glanced up. She jerked her chin at Armando before scrambling down. A soft chirp had Brisket at her side. Then she waited, watching the truck driver.

The moment Dr. Alvarez was within earshot, she laid out her suspicions. The look of surprise on his face told her he hadn't considered it, hadn't thought the trucking company might not be following health regulations to the letter.

Armando shook his head, considering the truck driver. "Well done, Reagan. Once it's confirmed, we'll be able to finish treating the remaining sick cattle and lift the quarantine on Harding and Quay counties much faster. I'll call in the FDA and state DoT and we'll get them to take over, since this is their jurisdiction."

"They'll only claim it was their responsibility after we take the fecal samples," Reagan said. "You know they're not going to get their lily-whites dirty when they've got us out here hip deep already."

"Someone's got to be willing to play in the crap," Armando responded, his tone dry as dust. "And in timing that couldn't be more ironic, your lawyer and his posse just showed up."

Reagan forced herself to hold it together. Lifting one shoulder in an elegant shrug, she pasted every ounce of indifference she could summon all over her body. "The lawyer doesn't belong to me."

Armando smiled. "Given the look on his face, I believe he begs to differ. I'm just going to make a few calls from my truck while you deal with him."

"Coward," she whispered at his retreating form. Yanking her hat off her head, she squared her shoulders and rounded on the Covington brothers, her mouth already moving to save them any awkward silences. "We believe the source of the virus has been identified. The Bar C will be released from quarantine in the next thirty to sixty days, provided the disease plays out." Slapping her hat against her thigh, she forced herself to look at Eli. "Congratulations. Appears you won't have to entirely abandon your lifestyle in order to bail the ranch out of debt."

She spun on her heel and started across the corrals. If she could get to her truck, she'd be able to escape. Without distance, she was afraid of what she might say or do, the options running the gamut from emotionally embarrassing herself to finding herself charged with manslaughter brought on by temporary insanity.

"Reagan," Eli called out. "Stop."

She kept walking and would have kept right *on* walking, if he hadn't said just loud enough for her and everyone around them to hear his plea. "Don't make me beg."

21

ELI HELD HIS BREATH. He wasn't a fool. The odds of Reagan giving him a chance to fix this were slim to none. Hell, even if she gave him the chance, it didn't mean she'd let her heart rule her mind. It only meant she'd hear what he had to say before she left him standing in a cloud of dust.

When he'd arrived at the ranch yesterday at noon, Eli had been surprised at the quiet but respectful welcome he'd received from the cowboys in the pens. They'd directed him to his brothers, who'd been up at the house putting together lunch.

Cade and Ty had been happy to see him but wary, both well aware Reagan had returned within a day of leaving with him. It had taken some explaining, a copy of his bank statements and a few raised voices before they'd settled around the table to talk things out.

Eli explained he'd pulled all his available cash together and, in a move of absolute irony, hired an attorney to liquidate his estate and all assets. Eli could've done it himself, but he hadn't wanted to lose whatever hope remained with Reagan. The sooner he could get to her, the sooner he could start to make this right.

He'd made arrangements to pay off the revolving debt he held, from student loans to the balance on his credit card. The cash he held in hand plus what he expected from the sale of his physical property would fund the changes he intended to propose here at the ranch. At what would now be his permanent home. In the midst of all the work he'd been doing to come back for good, he'd come up with a very viable plan to save the Bar C—he wanted to turn the place into a fully operational dude ranch.

His father was gone. He had nothing left to prove to the old man. Eli was proud of the man he'd become, and he had a lot to offer a new business opportunity. He'd only had to convince his brothers.

At first, Eli believed Cade was going to pass out. He ranted and raved about tourists and initial investments and the liability of having kids around the place. But when Eli opened his laptop and shared the potential income figures for the first fully operational year? Cade had gone silent.

Ty had watched and listened, and then he'd nearly driven Eli to his knees. "If it means you're home to stay? I'm in."

They'd talked for hours, his brothers rallying around his idea with more enthusiasm than he could have hoped for. He was stunned by their support of his choice to call the ranch home once again. But it was more than that.

Eli realized for the first time in his life that these two men, his brothers, cared about his happiness. His well-being mattered to them, and their instinct was to put his needs before their own if it meant he got his shot at being happy. It had humbled him, rendering him speechless. It was Ty who'd first understood his dilemma and simply hugged him, thumping him on the back hard enough to knock loose the wedge of emotions between his shoulder blades.

Cade had stepped up to him and held out his hand, his gaze sliding temporarily to Ty and then back. "I'm not hugging you, but welcome home, man. It's been too long coming."

Eli had retrieved his bags, carrying only two suitcases of worldly goods that he'd deemed necessary from his old life. The rest was inconsequential, material stuff he had no emotional ties to. He dumped the bags in his childhood room and returned to the kitchen to find Cade twisting tops off Coors Light bottles and handing them around.

His middle brother took a long swallow and focused on Eli. "How'd you screw things up with Reagan?"

He felt the urge to lie, but he found himself spilling his guts like a teenage girl to her two BFFs. It was miserable. It was embarrassing. It was irritating. But above all? It was painful.

They'd argued about the best way to approach her, but in the end, Eli had put his foot down. "This isn't about you guys. It's about her. And me. And how bad I screwed up. I have to prove to her I'm not the man who shoved her out the door Thursday night and that I want her for who she is. If I can't do that—I don't deserve her."

They'd agreed and a plan had come together, a plan that would make it very clear to Reagan exactly who had possession of his heart.

ELI HADN'T SLEPT a single minute all night. Cade and Ty had hunted Reagan down this morning as planned and, brothers being brothers, had piled into Cade's truck with him and headed to the Jensen place for the emotional showdown.

Now he took a measured step toward her. "I'd like to talk to you," he said softly.

"Stop treating me like an animal that might spook," she snapped.

"Honey, I've never seen so much of the whites of your eyes," Ty called out.

"Shut up, Ty," Reagan and Eli said at the same time.

She looked at him with wary confusion. "What are you doing here?"

Eli shifted his weight from foot to foot. "I came home."

She coiled her hair on her head and pushed her hat on tight. "Well, enjoy your stay." She turned away from him and started for her truck.

"I'm here for good, Reagan."

She stumbled to a stop and wheezed out a single word. "What?"

"I quit my job. A legal firm is liquidating my Austin estate. I'm home. For good. Might practice a little law on the side here if we need the money, but that's another discussion. For now? You need to know I'm here to stay." He stepped forward. "But none of it means anything without you. First, though, I have to apologize. Hear me out. Please."

"You want to apologize?" she nearly shouted as she spun to face him. "Fine. Act like a normal man and pick up the phone. Don't orchestrate an ambush." She issued a sharp whistle and Brisket came to her side.

He'd rehearsed what he'd say to her. He'd planned his approach, practiced his lines, his tone, his delivery. But it hit him right then that this wasn't court. This was life, and he had one shot to plead his case.

"Reagan, stop," he snapped. "You can't run away from this. We *are* going to settle things between us."

"Oh, hell," he heard Cade mutter.

"It gets ugly, you get to pin her, Cade. I'd rather deal with him," Ty said just loud enough to be heard.

She slowly rounded on him, her surprise clear. "You want to do this here? Now? There are witnesses, Eli. The whole world will know everything you say and do. No way to hide it. Not in this county."

"I'll get the Watsons on speakerphone if it'll get you to give me five minutes."

"You keep the Watsons away from me," she bit out.

"Then who? Who do you want to hear this? Name them, and I'll make it happen."

"Why are you doing this?" she asked quietly. "Twice wasn't enough? You need a trifecta of hurts to make sure I'm clear on where you stand?" He saw a hard shiver raced through her before she whipped away from him.

"I want to stand beside you, as your lover, your partner, your husband. For the rest of our lives."

Reagan tripped to a stop. "Don't," she said, voice breaking.

"Look at me, Reagan."

She shook her head.

His shadow covered her first, then he moved around her. "You won't come to me, then I'll come to you. From now on, baby. Every time you leave, I'll come to you."

Reagan's heart stumbled in her chest as he took her hands in his. "I can't marry you," she said, voice breaking.

"That's only because I haven't officially asked yet." Pulling a ring from his pocket, Eli went down on both knees in front of her. "You told me love shouldn't have to beg. You were right. But it should be willing to. If begging's the only card a man's got up his sleeve, then it's the hand he plays and pride be damned. I'm not down on one knee, Reagan. You've taken me down to both. This is what I've got to offer you—a lifetime of humility, humor, honesty and…" He scratched his chin then grinned up at her. "Oh, yeah. That other thing. I love you, Reagan Matthews. The strong, proud woman in front of me in jeans, a hat and cowboy boots. I wasn't brave enough to say it before. I kept thinking I'd get around to it when the time was right. And then I almost missed my window altogether. Give me the honor and the privilege of loving you to the end of my days."

In all her years, she'd never expected to find Elijah Covington kneeling in cow crap with a whopper of a diamond ring in one hand, his hat in his other and his heart in his eyes. For her. Only her.

"And if I say no?" she asked quietly.

He swallowed hard. "That's your right. But it's my right to keep asking until you change your mind."

"You ought to know he's got a degree in arguing," Ty called out.

"Shut up," Cade whispered, wiping at his eyes.

"Bro, are you *crying*?" Ty asked loudly. "You're not the one he's asking to marry him."

Cade boxed Ty's ear. "Shut up before your face finds out how deep the sludge is in the stock tanks."

"Shutting up, you big weenie," Ty muttered.

Eli looked up at Reagan. "Don't make me chase you, Doc. I learned the hard way that with the horses these days, a man only gets three swings. This is my third."

"I never stopped loving you," she whispered.

Eli surged to his feet and wrapped her in a hard embrace. "Ditto that, baby. You were always the one. I've never loved another." He leaned away just enough to see her face. "I don't expect to replace Luke. I don't," he insisted when she opened her mouth to speak. "I'd rather honor his memory by taking the best care of you I know how."

"And how are you going to do that?" she asked, smiling up at him.

He kissed the tip of her nose. "By adding your name to the deed to the dude ranch."

"Dude ranch?" she asked, stunned.

"The Bar C will be undergoing major renovations and should be open for business come late spring. We'll be a fully operational dude ranch catering to people who want the true Wild West experience."

"You're insane."

"Based on his numbers, we're going to be making *bank*," Ty called out.

Eli grinned. "I'll have the means to support myself—it will support both of us, actually, if you want to work alongside me. Regardless, you say yes and you'll never be completely free of me again, Doc. Think long and hard on this."

But she didn't need to. "Ty?" she called out, gripping Eli's hand and backing toward the Jensens' barn. "Keep the Jensens out of their barn for a half hour."

She squealed when Eli hoisted her over his shoulder and

started for the truck. "To hell with that. We've got a barn of our own. Stay the hell out of it this afternoon, brothers."

"I love you, Elijah Covington," she said softly as he settled her into the passenger seat of her truck.

"And I love you..." he said, and grinned, "Doc Covington."

* * * * *

Texas Outlaws: Jesse

Kimberly Raye

ABOUT THE AUTHOR

USA TODAY bestselling author Kimberly Raye started her first novel in high school and has been writing ever since. To date, she's published more than fifty novels, two of them prestigious RITA® Award nominees. She's also been nominated by *RT Book Reviews* for several Reviewer's Choice awards, as well as a career achievement award. Currently she is writing a romantic vampire mystery series for Ballantine Books that is in development with ABC for a television pilot. She also writes steamy contemporary reads for Harlequin's Blaze line. Kim lives deep in the heart of the Texas Hill Country with her very own cowboy, Curt, and their young children. She's an avid reader who loves Diet Dr. Pepper, chocolate, Toby Keith, chocolate, alpha males (*especially* vampires) and chocolate. Kim also loves to hear from readers. You can visit her online at www.kimberlyraye.com.

Dear Reader,

What do you get when you combine one wild, wicked, dangerously handsome cowboy, a botched bank heist and a truckload of premium grade-A moonshine? The first book in my new The Texas Outlaws trilogy, featuring the hot, hunky Chisholm brothers.

Three-time pro bull rider Jesse James Chisholm is desperate to forget his past—particularly the sins of his outlaw father—and get the hell out of Lost Gun, Texas. The only trouble? He isn't all that anxious to leave the girl who once stole his heart.

Soon-to-be mayor Gracie Stone wants nothing more than to see her old flame leave Lost Gun and never look back. Maybe then she can forget Jesse's touch and his kiss and...oh, boy. Gracie has a town to run and she certainly doesn't need the resident bad boy tarnishing her good-girl reputation.

But Gracie isn't half the good girl she pretends to be. Even more, she can't seem to keep her distance when it comes to Jesse. Likewise, Jesse is having trouble keeping his boots on and his hands off where Gracie is concerned.

I hope you enjoy reading Jesse and Gracie's story as much as I enjoyed writing it! I would love to hear from you. You can visit me online at www.kimberlyraye.com or friend me on Facebook.

Much love from deep in the heart...

Kimberly Raye

This book is dedicated to Curt,
My loving husband and best friend,
You still know how to rock a pair of Wranglers!

1

THIS WAS TURNING into *the* worst ride of his life.

Jesse James Chisholm stared over the back of the meanest bull this side of the Rio Grande at the woman who parked herself just outside the railing of the Lost Gun Training Facility, located on a premium stretch of land a few miles outside the city limits.

His heart stalled and his hand slipped. The bull lurched and he nearly tumbled to the side.

No way was *she* here.

No frickin' *way.*

The bull twisted and Pro Bull Riding's newest champion wrenched to the right. He was seeing things. That had to be it. He'd hit the ground too many times going after that first buckle and now it was coming back to haunt him. His grip tightened and his breath caught. Just a few more seconds.

One thousand three. One thousand four.

"Jesse!" Her voice rang out, filling his ears with the undeniable truth that she was here, all right.

Shit.

The bull jerked and Jesse pitched forward. He flipped and went down. Hard.

Dust filled his mouth and pain gripped every nerve in his

already aching body. The buzzer sounded and voices echoed, but he was too fixated on catching his breath to notice the chaos that suddenly surrounded him. He shut his eyes as his heart pounded in his rib cage.

Come on, buddy. You got this. Just breathe.

In and out. In. Out. In—

"Jesse? Ohmigod! Are you all right? Is he all right?"

Her desperate voice slid into his ears and stalled his heart. His eyes snapped open and sure enough, he found himself staring into a gaze as pale and blue as a clear Texas sky at high noon.

And just as scorching.

Heat swamped him and for a split second, he found himself sucked back to the past, to those long, endless days at Lost Gun High School.

He'd been at the bottom of the food chain back then, the son of the town's most notorious criminal, and no one had ever let him forget it. The teachers had stared at him with pity-filled gazes. The other boys had treated him like a leper. And the girls… They'd looked at him as if he were a bona fide rock star. The bad boy who was going to save them from the monotony of their map-dot existence.

Every girl, that is, except for Gracie Stone.

She'd been a rock star in her own right. Buck wild and reckless. Constantly defying her strict adoptive parents and pushing them to the limits. They'd wanted a goody-goody daughter befitting the town's mayor and first lady, and Gracie had wanted to break out of the neat little box she'd been forced into after the tragic death of her real parents.

They'd both been seniors when they'd crossed paths at a party. It had been lust at first sight. They'd had three scorching weeks together before they'd graduated and she'd ditched him via voice mail.

We just don't belong together.

For all her wicked ways, she was still the mayor's daughter, and he was the son of the town's most hated man. Water and oil. And everyone knew the two didn't mix.

Not then, and certainly not now.

He tried to remember that all-important fact as he focused on the sweet-smelling woman leaning over him.

She looked so different compared to the wild and wicked girl who lived and breathed in his memories. She'd traded in too much makeup and too little clothes for a more conservative look. She wore a navy skirt and a white silk shell tucked in at the waist. Her long blond hair had been pulled back into a no-nonsense ponytail. Long thick lashes fringed her pale blue eyes. Her lips were full and pink and luscious.

Different, yet his gut ached just the same.

He stiffened and his mouth pressed into a tight line. "Civilians aren't allowed in the arena." He pushed himself to his feet, desperate to ignore the soft pink-tipped fingers on his arm. "Not without boots." Her touch burned through the material of his Western shirt and sent a fizzle of electricity up his arm. "And jeans," he blurted. "And a long-sleeve shirt, for Chrissake." Damn, but why did she have to keep touching him like that? "You're breaking about a dozen different rules."

"I'm sorry. You just hit the ground so hard and I thought you were hurt and…" Her words trailed off and she let her hand fall away.

He ignored the whisper of disappointment and concentrated on the anger roiling inside him. "You almost got me killed." That was what he said. But the only thing rolling over and over in his mind was that she'd put herself in danger by climbing over the railing with a mean sumbitch bull on the loose.

He pushed away the last thought because no way—no friggin' way—did Jesse care one way or the other when it came to Gracie Stone. He was over her.

Finished.

Done.

He held tight to the notion and focused on the fact that she'd ruined a perfectly good training session. "You don't yell at a man when he's in the middle of a ride. It's distracting. I damn near broke my neck." He dusted off his pants and reached for his hat a few feet away. "If you're looking for City Hall—" he shook off the dirt and parked the worn Stetson on top of his head "—I think you're way off the mark."

"Actually, I was looking for you." Unease flitted across her face as if she wasn't half as sure of herself as she pretended to be. She licked her pink lips and he tried not to follow the motion with his eyes. "I need to talk to you."

He had half a mind to tell her to kick her stilettos into high gear and start walking. He was smack-dab in the middle of a demonstration for a prospective buyer who'd flown in yesterday to purchase the black bull currently snorting in a nearby holding pen.

Because Jesse was selling his livestock and moving on.

Finally.

With the winnings and endorsements from his first championship last year, he'd been able to put in an offer for a three-hundred-acre spread just outside of Austin, complete with a top-notch practice arena. The seller had accepted and now it was just a matter of signing the papers and transferring the money.

"Yo, Jesse." David Burns, the buyer interested in his stock, signaled him from the sidelines and Jesse held up a hand that said hold up a minute.

David wanted to make a deal and Jesse needed to get a move on. He didn't have time for a woman who'd ditched him twelve years ago without so much as a face-to-face.

At the same time, he couldn't help but wonder what could be so almighty important that it had Lost Gun's newly elected mayor slumming it a full ten miles outside the city limits.

He shrugged. "So talk."

Her gaze shifted from the buyer to the group of cowboys working the saddle broncs in the next arena. Several of the men had shifted their attention to the duo standing center stage. "Maybe we could go someplace private."

The words stirred all sorts of possibilities, all treacherous to his peace of mind since they involved a very naked Gracie and a sizable hard-on. But Jesse had never been one to back down from a dangerous situation.

He summoned his infamous slide-off-your-panties drawl that had earned him the coveted title of Rodeo's Hottest Bachelor and an extra twenty thousand followers on Twitter and eyed her. "Sugar, the only place I'm going after this is straight into a hot shower." He gave her a sly grin he wasn't feeling at the moment and winked. "If you're inclined to follow, then by all means, let's go."

Her eyes darkened and for a crazy instant, he glimpsed the old Gracie. The wild free spirit who'd stripped off her clothes and gone skinny-dipping with him their first night together.

But then the air seemed to chill and her gaze narrowed. "We'll talk here," she said, her voice calm and controlled. A total contradiction to the slight tremble of her bottom lip. She drew a deep breath that lifted her ample chest and wreaked havoc with his self-control. "A fax came in from the production company that filmed *Famous Texas Outlaws.*"

The mention of the television documentary that had nearly cost him his livelihood all those years ago was like a douse of ice water. "And?"

"They sold rights to a major affiliate who plans to air the show again and film a live 'Where Are They Now?' segment. They're already running promos for it. Sheriff Hooker had to chase two fortune hunters off your place just yesterday."

His "place" amounted to the burned-down shack and ten overgrown acres on the south end of town that he'd once shared with his father and brothers. As for the fortune hunters, well, they were out of luck. There was nothing to find.

His lawyer had been advising him to sell the property for years now, but Jesse had too many bad memories to want to profit off that sad, miserable place. Ignoring it had been better. Easier.

He eyed her. "When?"

"It's airing next Tuesday." She squared her shoulders, as if trying to gather her courage. "I thought you deserved fair warning after what happened the last time."

His leg throbbed at the memory. "So that's why you're here?" He tamped down the sudden ache. "To give me a heads-up?"

She nodded and something softened inside him.

A crazy reaction since he knew that her sudden visit had nothing to do with any sense of loyalty to him. This was all about the town. She'd traded in her wild and wicked ways to become a model public servant like her uncle. Conservative. Responsible. Loyal.

He knew that, yet the knotted fist in his chest eased just a little anyway.

"I know you just got back yesterday," she went on, "but I really think it would be better to cut your visit short until it's all said and done." She pulled her shoulders back. The motion pressed her delicious breasts against the soft fabric of her blouse. He caught a glimpse of lace beneath the thin material and he knew then that she wasn't as conservative as she wanted everyone to think. "That would make things a lot easier."

"For me?" He eyed her. "Or for you?"

Her gaze narrowed. "I'm not the one they'll be after."

"No, you're just in charge of the town they'll be invading. After all the craziness the last time I think you're anxious to avoid another circus. Getting rid of me would certainly help." The words came out edged with challenge, as if he dared her to dispute them.

He did.

She caught her bottom lip as if she wanted to argue, but then her mouth pulled tight. "If the only eyewitness to the fire is MIA, the reporters won't have a reason to stick around. I really think it would be best for everyone." Her gaze caught and held his. "Especially you."

Ditto.

He sure as hell wasn't up to the pain he'd gone through the first time. The show had originally aired a few months after he'd graduated high school, five years to the day of his father's death. He'd been eighteen at the time and a damn sight more reckless.

He'd been ground zero in the middle of a training session with a young, jittery bull named Diamond Dust. A group of reporters had shown up, cameras blazing, and Diamond had gone berserk. More so than usual for a mean-as-all-get-out bucking bull. Jesse had hit the ground, and then the bull had hit him. Over and over, stomping and crushing until Jesse had suffered five broken ribs, a broken leg, a dislocated shoulder and a major concussion. Injuries that had landed him in a rehab facility for six months and nearly cost him everything.

Not that the same thing wouldn't have happened eventually. He'd been on a fast road to trouble back then, ignoring the rules and riding careless and loose. The reporters had simply sped up the inevitable, because Jesse hadn't been interested in a career back then so much as an escape.

From the guilt of watching his own father die and not doing a damned thing to stop it.

It wasn't your fault. The man made his own choice.

That was what Pete Gunner had told him time and time again after the fire. Pete was the pro bull rider who'd taken in thirteen-year-old Jesse and his brothers and saved them from being split up into different foster homes after their father had died. Pete had been little more than a kid himself back then—barely twenty—and had just won his first PBR title. The last thing he'd needed was the weight of three orphans distracting him from his career, but he'd taken on the responsibility anyway. The man had been orphaned himself as a kid and so he'd known how hard it was to make it in the world. Cowboying had saved him and so he'd taught Jesse and his brothers how to rope and ride and hold their own in a rodeo arena. He'd turned them into tough cowboys. The best in the state, as a matter of fact. Even more, he'd given them a roof over their heads and food in their stomachs, and hope.

And when Diamond had nearly killed Jesse, it had been Pete who'd paid for the best orthopedic surgeons in the state. Pete was family—as much a brother to Jesse as Billy and Cole—and he was about to marry the woman of his dreams this Saturday.

That was the real reason Jesse had come back to this godforsaken town. And the reason he had no intention of leaving until the vows were spoken, the cake was cut and the happy couple left for two weeks in the Australian outback.

Then Jesse would pack up what little he had left here and head for Austin to make a real life. Far away from the memories. From her.

He stiffened against a sudden wiggle of regret. "Trust me, there's nothing I'd like better than to haul ass out of here right now."

"Good. Then we're on the same page—"

"But I won't," he cut in. "I can't."

A knowing light gleamed in her eyes. "I'm sure Pete would understand."

"I'm sure he would, but that's beside the point." Jesse shook his head. "I'm not missing his wedding."

"But—"

"You'll just have to figure out some other way to defuse the situation and keep the peace."

And then he did what she'd done to him on that one night forever burned into his memory—he turned and walked away without so much as a goodbye.

2

WAIT A SECOND.

Wait just a friggin' *second.*

That was what Gracie wanted to say. She'd envisioned this meeting about a zillion times on the way over, and this wasn't the way it had played out. Where was the gratitude? The appreciation? The desperate embrace followed by one whopper of a kiss?

She ditched the last thought and focused on the righteous indignation that came with violating about ten different city ordinances on someone else's behalf. Leaking private city business to civilians was an unforgivable sin and the memo from the production company had been marked strictly confidential.

But this was Jesse, and while she'd made it a point to avoid him for the past twelve years, she couldn't in good conscience sit idly by and let him be broadsided by the news crew currently on its way to Lost Gun.

Not because she cared about him.

Lust. That was all she'd ever felt for him. The breath-stealing, bone-melting, desperate lust of a hormone-driven sixteen-year-old. A girl who'd dreamed of a world beyond her desperately small town, a world filled with bright lights and big cities and a career in photojournalism.

She'd wanted out so bad back then. To the point that she'd been wild and reckless, eager to fill the humdrum days until her eighteenth birthday with whatever excitement she could find.

But then she'd received the special-delivery letter announcing that her older brother had been killed in the line of duty and she'd realized it was time to grow up, step up and start playing it safe right here in Lost Gun.

For her sister.

Charlotte Stone was ten years younger than Gracie. And while she'd been too young—four years old, to be exact—to remember the devastation when their parents had died in a tragic car accident, she'd been plenty old enough at nine to feel the earthquake caused by the death of their older brother. She'd morphed from a happy, outgoing little girl, into a needy, scared introvert who'd been terrified to let her older sister out of her sight.

Gracie had known then that she could never leave Lost Gun. Even more, she'd vowed not only to stay but to settle down, play it safe and make a real home for her sister.

She'd traded her beloved photography lessons for finance classes at the local junior college and ditched everything that was counterproductive to her new safe, settled life—from her favorite fat-filled French fries to Jesse Chisholm himself.

Especially Jesse.

He swiped a hand across his backside to dust off his jeans and her gaze snagged on the push-pull of soft faded denim. Her nerves started to hum and the air stalled in her lungs.

While time usually whittled away at people, making them worn around the edges, it had done the opposite with Jesse. The years had carved out thick muscles and a ripped bod. He looked even harder than she remembered, taller and more commanding. The fitted black-and-gray retro Western shirt framed broad shoulders and a narrow waist. Worn jeans topped with dusty brown leather chaps clung to trim hips and thighs and stretched the length of his long legs. Scuffed brown cowboy boots, the tips worn from one too many run-ins with a bull, completed the look of rodeo's hottest hunk. The title had been held by local legend Pete Gunner up until he'd proposed to the love of his life just two short years ago. Since then Jesse had been burning up the rodeo circuit, determined to take the man's place and gain even more notoriety for the Lost Boys, a local group of cowboy daredevils who were taking the rodeo circuit by storm, winning titles and charming fans all across the country.

Wild. Fearless. Careless.

He was all three and then some.

Her gaze shifted to the face hidden beneath the brim of a worn Stetson. While she couldn't see his eyes thanks to the shadow, she knew they were a deep, mesmerizing violet framed by thick sable lashes. A few days' growth of beard covered his jaw and crept down his neck. Dark brown hair brushed his collar and made her fingers itch to reach out and touch.

"If I were you, I'd stop staring and put my tongue back in my mouth before somebody stomps on it."

The voice startled her, and she turned to see the ancient cowboy who came up beside her.

Eli McGinnis was an old-school wrangler in his late seventies with a head full of snow-white hair that had been slicked back with pomade. His handlebar mustache twitched and she knew he was smiling even though she couldn't actually see the expression beneath the elaborate do on his top lip.

"You'd do well to stop droolin', too," he added. "We got enough mud puddles around here already. A few shit piles, too."

"I wasn't—"

"Drooling?" he cut in. "While I ain't the brightest bulb in the tanning bed, I know drooling when I see it and, lemme tell ya, it ain't attractive on a fine upstanding public servant like yourself. Then again, you ain't actually the mayor yet, so I guess I should be talking to your uncle when it comes to serious public-health issues."

"Uncle E.J. already left for Port Aransas. He and my aunt just bought a house there." Her brow wrinkled as the impact of his words hit. "A public-health issue?" The notion killed the lingering image of Jesse and snagged her complete attention. "What health issue?" A dozen possibilities raced through her mind, from a city-wide epidemic of salmonella to a flesh-eating zombie virus.

Okay, so she spent her evenings watching a little too much cable TV since Charlie had moved into the dorms at the University of Texas last year. A girl had to have *some* fun.

Anxiety raced up her spine. "It's mercury in the water, isn't it?" Fear coiled and tightened in the pit of her stomach. "E. coli in the lettuce crops? Don't tell me Big Earl Jessup is making moonshine in his garage again." At ninety-one, Big Earl was the town's oldest resident, and the most dangerous. He came from a time when the entrepreneurial spirit meant whipping up black diamond whiskey in the backyard and hand-selling it at the annual peach festival. Those days were long gone but that hadn't stopped Big Earl from firing up last year to cook a batch to give away for Christmas. And then again at Easter. And for the Fourth of July.

"You got bigger problems than an old man cooking up moonshine in his deer blind, that's for damn sure."

"Big Earl's cooking in his deer blind?"

Eli frowned. "Stop trying to change the subject. We've got a crisis on our hands."

"Which is?"

"Fake cheese on the nachos. Why, the diner used to put a cup of real whole-milk cheddar on all the nacho platters, but now they're tryin' to cut costs, so they switched to the artificial stuff."

"Fake cheese," she repeated, relief sweeping through her. "That's the major health concern?"

"Damn straight. Why, I was up all night with indigestion. As the leader of this fine community—" he wagged a finger at her "—it's your job to clean it up."

O-kay.

"I'll, um, stop by the diner and see what I can do."

He threw up his hands. "That's all I'm askin', little lady."

Her gaze shifted back to Jesse, who now stood on the other side of the arena talking to two men she didn't recognize. They weren't real working cowboys but rather the slick, wealthy types who flew in every now and then to buy or sell livestock. With their designer boots and high-dollar hats, they probably intimidated most men, but not Jesse. He held his own, a serious look on his face as he motioned to the black bull thrashing around a nearby stall.

"That boy's too damned big for his britches sometimes," Eli muttered.

Her gaze dropped and her breath caught. Actually, he filled out said britches just right.

She watched as he untied his chaps and tossed them over a nearby railing, leaving nothing but a tight pair of faded denims that clung to him like a second skin, outlining his sinewy thighs and trim waist and tight, round butt—

"It's mighty nice of you to come out and warn him." Her gaze snapped up and she glanced at the old man next to her. "Even if he don't realize it."

"It's fine." She shrugged. "It's not like I stop by every day."

Not anymore.

But for those blissful three weeks before they'd graduated, she'd been a permanent fixture on the corral fence, watching him every afternoon after school. Snapping pictures of him. Dreaming of the day when she could leave Lost Gun behind and turn her hobby into a passion.

She'd wanted out of this map dot just as bad as he had. Then.

And now.

She stiffened against the sudden thought. She was happy with her life here. Content.

And even if she wasn't, it didn't matter. She was here. She was staying. End of story.

"Still, you didn't have to go to so much trouble," Eli went on.

"Just looking out for my soon-to-be constituents." No way

did Gracie want to admit that she'd come because she still cared about Jesse. Because she still dreamed of him. Because she still *wanted* him.

No, this was about doing the right thing to make up for the wrong she'd done so long ago. She'd had her chance to warn him the first time, and she'd chickened out for fear that seeing him would crumble her resolve and resurrect the wild child she'd been so desperate to bury.

She'd lived with the guilt every day since.

"Tell him to be careful." She took one last look at Jesse, fought against the emotion that churned down deep and walked away.

"THAT MAGAZINE ARTICLE was right about you. You sure put on one helluva show." The words were followed by a steady *clap-clap-clap* as Billy Chisholm, Jesse's youngest brother, walked toward him. Billy was four years younger and eagerly chasing the buckle Jesse had won just last year. "I particularly liked that little twist you did when you flew into the air." He grinned. "Right before you busted your tail."

Jesse glared. "I'm not in the mood."

"I wouldn't be either if I'd just ate it in front of everyone and the horse they rode in on."

But Jesse wasn't concerned about everyone. Just a certain buttoned-up city official with incredible blue eyes.

He barely resisted the urge to steal one last look at her. Not that he hadn't seen her over the years when he'd happened into town—across a crowded main street, through the dingy windows of the local feed store. It was just that those times had been few and far between because Jesse hated Lost Gun as much as the town hated him, and so he'd kept his distance.

But this was different.

She'd been right in front of him. Close enough to touch. To feel. He could still smell her—the warm, luscious scent of vanilla cupcakes topped with a mountain of frosting.

Sweet.

Decadent.

Enough to make him want to cross the dusty arena separating them, pull her into his arms and see if she tasted half as good as he remembered.

Want.

Yep, he still wanted her, all right. The thing was, he didn't *want* to want her, because she sure as hell didn't want him.

He'd thought so at one time. She'd smiled and flirted and rubbed up against him, and he'd foolishly thought she was into him. He'd been a hormone-driven eighteen-year-old back then and he'd fallen hard and fast.

He was a grown-ass man now and a damn sight more experienced. Enough to know that Gracie Stone was nothing special in the big scheme of things. There were dozens of women out there, and Jesse indulged in more than his fair share. And while they all tasted as sweet as could be at first, the sweetness always faded. The sex soon lost its edge. And then Jesse cut ties and moved on to the next.

"…can't remember the last time you bit the bullet like that," Billy went on. "What the hell happened? Did someone slap you with a ten-pound bag of stupid?"

Okay, maybe Gracie was a little special. She'd been the only woman in his past to break things off with him first, *before* he'd had a chance to lose interest.

He would have, he reminded himself.

Guaran-damn-teed.

From the corner of his eye, he watched her disappear around the holding pens. The air rushed back into his lungs, but his muscles didn't ease.

He was still uptight. Hot. Bothered.

Stupid.

He stiffened and focused on untying the gloves from his hands.

"Alls I can say is thanks, bro," Billy went on. "I bet a wad of cash on your ride just now. My truck payment, as a matter of fact."

Jesse arched an eyebrow. "And you're thanking me for losing your shirt?"

Billy clapped him on the shoulder and sent an ache through his bruised body. "I didn't bet *on* you, bro. I bet *against* you." He winked. "Saw that little gal come round the corner and I knew things were going to get mighty interesting."

Forget stupid. He was pissed.

"She came to warn me," Jesse bit out, his mouth tight. "They're shooting a 'Where Are They Now?' special next week," he told his brother. "A follow-up to *Famous Texas Outlaws.*"

Billy's grin faltered for a split second. "You okay with that?"

Jesse shrugged. "I can handle my fair share of reporters. You know that."

"True enough." Billy nodded before sliding him a sideways glance. "But if you want a little peace and quiet, you can always send them my way." He winked and his grin was back. "I like getting my picture taken."

Billy had been fourteen at the time and excited about being in the limelight. He hadn't been the least bit unnerved by the endless questions about their father's death six years prior, because he'd been too young to really comprehend the gravity of what Silas Chisholm had done. Too young to remember the police and the accusations and the desperate search to recover the money that their father had stolen. Rather, he'd seen the media circus as a welcome distraction from an otherwise shitty life.

"Gracie wants me to lie low," Jesse added. "She thinks it'll help the town."

"And here I thought she came all the way out here because she wanted a piece of PBR's reigning champion."

If only.

Jesse stuffed his gloves into his pocket and fought the longing that coiled inside of him.

Gracie Stone was off-limits.

She'd broken his heart and while it was all water under the bridge now, he had no intention of paddling upstream ever again.

Then again, it wasn't his heart that had stirred the moment he'd come face-to-face with her again. Despite the years that had passed, the chemistry was still as strong as ever.

Stronger, in fact.

And damned if that realization didn't bother him even more than the fact that he'd just landed on his ass in front of an arena full of cowboys. Since Tater Tot had been the ornery bull responsible, he'd just become that much more valuable to the two buyers now waiting inside Jesse's office in a nearby building.

So maybe Gracie's visit wasn't a complete bust after all.

"I've got papers to sign." He motioned to the glass-walled office that overlooked the corral. "Get your gear and get in the chute if you want a turn on Tater Tot before they pack him up and ship him out. And you'd better make it quick because we've got a tuxedo fitting in a half hour and the clock's ticking."

"Sure thing, bro." A grin cut loose from ear to ear. "After that piss-poor display, somebody's gotta show you how it's done."

3

IT TOOK EVERY ounce of willpower Gracie had to bypass the one and only bakery in Lost Gun and head for the town square.

Sure, she eased up on the gas pedal and powered down her window to take in the delicious scent of fresh-baked goodies as she rolled past Sarah's Sweets, but still. She didn't slam on the brakes and make a beeline for the overflowing counter inside. No red velvet cupcakes or buttercream-frosted sugar cookies for this girl. And no—repeat *no*—Double-Fudge Fantasy Brownies rich in trans fat and high in cholesterol.

Which explained why her hands still trembled and her stomach fluttered when she walked into City Hall.

"How's my favorite mayor-elect?" asked the thirtysomething bleached blonde sitting behind the desk in the outer office with a chocolate Danish in front of her.

Longing clawed down deep inside of Gracie, but she tamped it back down. "Fine."

"Methinks you are one terrible liar." Trina Lovett popped a bite of pastry into her mouth and washed it down with a sip of black coffee.

Trina had been working for Gracie's uncle—the current mayor—since she'd graduated high school sixteen years ago—

four years before Gracie. Trina had been part of a rise-above-your-environment program that helped young people from impoverished homes—a trailer on the south end of town in Trina's case—find jobs.

He'd hit the jackpot with Trina, who was not only a hard worker but knew everything about everybody. She'd been instrumental in the past few elections—particularly in a too-close-for-comfort runoff with the local sheriff a few years back. E.J. had won, of course, due to his compassionate nature and Trina's connections down at the local honky-tonk. The young woman had bought five rounds of beers the day of the election and earned the forty-two votes needed to win.

Trina had also been instrumental in the most recent campaign, which had seen Gracie take the mayoral race by a landslide.

In exactly two weeks to the day, Gracie Elizabeth Stone would take the sacred oath and step up as the town's first female mayor.

Two weeks, three hours and forty-eight minutes.

Not that she was counting.

"You saw Jesse, didn't you?" When Gracie nodded, Trina's bright red lips parted in a smile. "Tell me *everything.* I caught him on the ESPN channel a few weeks back, but all I could see was a distant view of him straddling a bull for dear life." She wiggled her eyebrows. "What I wouldn't have given to be that bull."

"You work for a public official. You know that, right?"

"Don't get your granny panties in a wad. It's not like I'm tweeting it or posting to my Facebook status. This is a private conversation." She beamed. "*So?* What's he really like up close? Does he still have those broad shoulders? That great ass?"

Yes and *yes.*

She stiffened and focused on leafing through the stack of mail on Trina's desk. "I'd, um, say he's aged well."

"Seriously? I suppose you look ready to scarf an entire box of cupcakes because of some cowboy who's *aged well?*"

"I suppose he's still hot, if you're into that sort of thing."

"I am." Trina beamed. "I most definitely am."

Gracie frowned. "Not that it makes a difference. I went there strictly in an official capacity. I went. I spoke. He heard. End of story."

Trina regarded her for a long, assessing moment. "He told you to get lost, didn't he?"

"No." The brave face she'd put on faltered. "Yes. I mean, he didn't say it outright—there were no distinct verbs or colorful nouns—but he might as well have."

"Ouch." Her gaze swept Gracie from head to toe and she pursed her bright red lips. "But I can't say as I blame him. You look like you're going to Old Man Winthrow's wake."

"I do black for funerals. This is navy."

"Same thing." She gave Gracie another visual sweep with her assessing blue eyes. "Listen here, girlfriend, men don't take time out of their day to notice navy. It takes a hot color to keep a man from tossing you out on your keister. Red. Neon pink. Even a print—like cheetah or zebra. Something that says you've got a sex drive and you know how to use it. And the skimpier, the better, too. Show a little leg. Some cleavage. Men like cleavage. It gets their full attention every time."

"For the last time—this wasn't a social visit." Gracie eyed Trina's black leather miniskirt. "I'm a public figure. I can't prance around looking like an extra from *Jersey Shore*. Besides, he hates me, and a dress—skimpy or not—isn't going to change that."

"I'm telling you, a good dress is like magic. Slip it on and it'll transform you from a stuffy politician into a major slut. You do remember how much fun being a little slutty can be, don't you?"

As if she could ever forget.

She'd been the baddest girl in high school with the worst reputation, and she'd liked it. She'd liked doing the unexpected and following her gut and having some fun. And she'd *really* liked Jesse James Chisholm.

So much so that she'd been ready to put off attending the University of Texas—her uncle's alma mater—to follow Jesse onto the rodeo circuit. To continue their wild ride together, cheer him on and take enough live-action shots to launch her dream career as a photographer.

But then Jackson had been killed, and Charlie had stopped talking for six months. She'd realized then that she couldn't just turn her back on her little sister and go her own way as her brother had done after their parents had died. Charlie needed her.

And she needed Charlie.

So she'd packed up her camera and her dreams and started playing it safe. She'd followed in her uncle's footsteps, securing a business degree before taking a position as city planner.

Meanwhile, Jesse had ridden every bull from here to Mexico.

They were worlds apart now, and when they did happen to land within a mile radius of each other, the animosity was enough to keep the wall between them thick. Impenetrable.

Animosity because not only had Gracie stood him up on the night they were supposed to leave, but she'd refused to talk to him about it, terrified that if she heard his voice or saw him up close, her determination would crumble. Fearful that the bad girl inside of her would rear her ugly head and lust would get the better of her.

Lust, not love.

She hadn't been able to leave with Jesse, and she'd refused to ask him to give up his life's dream to stay with her in a town that had caused him nothing but pain, and so she'd done the best thing for both of them—she'd broken off all contact.

And her silence had nearly cost him his career.

Not this time.

She'd given him fair warning about the inevitable influx of reporters and now she could get back to work and, more important, forget how good he smelled and how his eyes darkened to a deep, fathomless shade of purple whenever he looked at her.

She fought down the sudden yearning that coiled inside of her. "I don't do slut anymore," she told her assistant.

"Duh." Trina shrugged. "You've been wearing those Spanx so long, you've forgotten how to peel them off and cut loose."

If only.

But that was the trouble in a nutshell. She'd never really forgotten. Deep in her heart, in the dead of night, she remembered what it felt like to live for the moment, to feel the rush of excitement, to walk on the wild side. It felt good—so freakin' *good*—and she couldn't help but want to feel that way again.

Just once.

Not that she was acting on that want. No way. No how. No sirree. Charlie needed a home and the people of Lost Gun needed a mayor, and Gracie needed to keep her head on straight and her thoughts out of the gutter.

"So what's on the agenda today?" she blurted, eager to get them back onto a safer subject. "City council meeting? Urgent political strategy session? Constituent meet and greet?" She needed something—anything—to get her mind off Jesse James Chisholm and the fact that he'd looked every bit as good as she remembered. And then some. "Surely Uncle E.J. left a big pile of work before he headed for Port Aransas to close on the new house?"

"Let's see." Trina punched a few buttons on her computer. "You're in luck. You've got a meeting with Mildred Jackson from the women's sewing circle—she wants the city to commission a quilt for your new office."

"That's it?"

"That and a trip to the animal shelter." When Gracie arched an eyebrow, Trina added, "I've been reading this article online about politicians and their canine friends. Do you know that a dog ups your favorability rating by five percent?"

"I already have a dog."

"A ball of fluff who humps everything in sight doesn't count." When Gracie gave her a sharp look, she shrugged. "Not that I have anything against humping, but you've got a reputation to think of. A horny mutt actually takes away poll points."

"Sugar Lips isn't a mutt. She's a maltipom. Half Maltese. Half Pomeranian." Trina gave her a *girlfriend, pu-leeze* look and she added, "I've got papers to prove it."

"Labs and collies polled at the top with voters, and the local shelter just happens to have one of each," Trina pressed. "Just think how awesome it will look when the new mayor-elect waltzes in on Adopt-a-Pet Day and picks out her new Champ or Spot."

"Don't tell me—Champ and Spot were top-polling animal names?"

"Now you're catching on."

Gracie shook her head. "I can't just bring home another dog. Sugar will freak. She has control issues."

"Think of the message it will send to voters. Image is everything."

As if she didn't know that. She'd spent years trying to shake her own bad image, to bury it down deep, to make people forget, and she'd finally succeeded. Twelve long years later, she'd managed to earn the town's loyalty. Their trust.

Now it was just a matter of keeping it.

She shrugged. "Okay, I'll get another dog."

"And a date," Trina added. "That way people can also envision you as the better half of a couple, i.e., family oriented."

"Where do you get this stuff?"

"PerfectPolitician.com. They say if you want to project a stable, reliable image, you need to be in a stable, reliable relationship. I was thinking we should call Chase Carter. He's president of the bank, not to mention a huge campaign contributor. He's also president of the chamber of commerce and vice president of the zoning commission."

And about as exciting as the 215-page car-wash proposition just submitted by the president of the Ladies' Auxiliary for next year's fundraiser.

Gracie eyed her assistant. "Isn't Chase gay?"

"A small technicality." Trina waved a hand. "This is about image, not getting naked on the kitchen table. I know he isn't exactly a panty dropper like Jesse James Chisholm, but—"

"Call him." Chase *wasn't* Jesse, which made him perfect dating material. He wouldn't be interested in getting her naked and she wouldn't be interested in getting him naked. And she certainly wouldn't sit around fantasizing about the way his thigh muscles bunched when he crossed a rodeo arena.

She ignored the faint scent of dust and leather that still lingered on her clothes and shifted her attention to something safe. "Do you know anything about Big Earl Jessup?" She voiced the one thing besides Jesse Chisholm and his scent that had been bothering her since she'd left the training arena.

"I know he's too old to be your date. That and he's got hemorrhoids the size of boulders." Gracie's eyes widened and Trina shrugged. "News travels fast in a small town. Bad news travels even faster."

"I don't want to go out with him. I heard through the grapevine that he might be cooking moonshine in his deer blind."

Trina's eyebrow shot up. "The really good kind he used to make for the annual peach festival?"

"Maybe."

"Hot damn." When Gracie cut her a stare, she added, "I mean, *damn.* What a shame."

"Exactly. He barely got off by the skin of his teeth the last time he was brought up on charges. Judge Ellis is going to throw the book at him if he even thinks that Big Earl is violating his parole."

"Isn't Big Earl like a hundred?"

"He's in his nineties."

"What kind of dipshit would throw a ninetysomething in prison?"

"The dipshit whose car got blown up the last time Big Earl was cooking. Judge Ellis had a case of the stuff in his trunk at the annual Fourth of July picnic. A Roman candle got too close and bam, his Cadillac went up in flames."

"Isn't that his own fault for buying the stuff?"

"That's what Uncle E.J. said, which was why Big Earl got off on probation. But Judge Ellis isn't going to be swayed again. He'll nail him to the wall." And stir another whirlwind of publicity when Lost Gun became home to the oldest prison inmate. At least that was what Uncle E.J. had said when he'd done his best to keep the uproar to a minimum.

"I need to find out for sure," Gracie told Trina.

"If you go nosying around Big Earl's place, you're liable to get shot. Tell you what—I'll drop by his place after I get my nails done. My daddy used to buy from him all the time when I was a little girl. I'll tell him I just stopped by for old times' sake. So what do you think?" She held up two-inch talons. "Should I go with wicked red or passionate pink this time?"

"Don't you usually get your nails done on Friday?"

"Hazel over at the motel called and said two reporters from Houston are checking in this afternoon and I want to look my best before the feeding frenzy starts."

"Reporters?" Alarm bells sounded in Gracie's head and a rush of adrenaline shot through her. "Already?"

Trina nodded. "She's got three more checking in tomorrow. And twenty-two members of the Southwest chapter of the Treasure Hunters Alliance. Not to mention, Lyle over at the diner called and said the folks from the Whispering Winds Senior Home stopped by for lunch today. They usually go straight through to Austin for their weekly shopping trip, but one of them read a preview about the documentary in the TV listings and now everybody wants to check out Silas Chisholm's old stomping grounds. A few of them even brought their gardening trowels for a little digging after lunch."

"But there's nothing to find." According to police reports, the wad of cash from Silas Chisholm's bank heist had gone up in flames with the man himself.

"That's what Lyle told them, but you know folks don't listen. They'd rather think there's some big windfall just waiting to be discovered." Which was exactly what the documentary's host had been banking on when he'd brought up the missing money and stirred a whirlwind of doubt all those years ago.

Maybe the money hadn't gone up in flames.

Maybe, just maybe, it was still out there waiting to be discovered. To make someone rich.

"I should head over to the diner and set them all straight."

"Forget it. I saved you a trip and stopped by myself on my way in." Trina waved a hand. "Bought them all a complimentary round of tapioca, and just like that, they forgot all about treasure hunting. Say, why don't you come with me to the salon?"

"I can't. The remodeling crew will be here first thing tomorrow and I promised I'd have everything picked out by then."

It was a lame excuse, but the last thing she needed was to sit in the middle of a nail salon and endure twenty questions about her impromptu visit with Jesse Chisholm and the impending media circus.

"That and I still need to unpack all the boxes from my old office."

"Suit yourself, but I'd take advantage of the light schedule between now and inauguration time. You'll be up to your neck in city business soon enough once you take your oath."

A girl could only hope.

Trina glanced at her watch and pushed up from her desk. "I'm outta here." Her gaze snagged on the phone and she smiled. "Right after I hook you up with Mr. Wrong, that is."

She punched in a number on the phone. "Hey, Sally. It's Trina over at the mayor's office. Is Chase in?… The mayor-elect would like to invite him to be her escort for the inauguration ceremony…. What? He's hosting a pottery class right now?… No, no, don't interrupt him. Just tell him the mayor-elect called and wants to sweep him off his feet…. Yeah, yeah, she loves pottery, too…."

Gracie balled her fingers to keep from pressing the disconnect button, turned and headed for the closed door. A date with Chase was just what she needed. He was perfect. Upstanding. Respectable. Boring.

She ignored the last thought and picked up her steps. Hinges creaked and she found herself in the massive office space that would soon be the headquarters of Lost Gun's new mayor.

Under normal circumstances, the new mayor moved into the old mayor's office, but just last week the city had approved budget changes allocating a huge amount to renovate the east wing of City Hall, including the massive space that had once served as a courtroom. Gracie was the first new face they'd elected in years and change was long overdue. She was getting a brand-new office and reception area, as well as her own private bathroom.

Everything had been cleared out and the floors stripped down to the concrete slab. A card table sat off to one side. Her laptop and a spare phone sat on top, along with a stack of paint colors and flooring samples and furniture selections all awaiting her approval. A stack of boxes from her old office filled a nearby corner.

She drew a deep steadying breath and headed for the boxes to decide what to keep and what to toss.

A half hour later she was halfway through the third box when she unearthed a stack of framed pictures. She stared at the first. The last rays of a hot summer's day reflected on the calm water of Lost Gun Lake and a smile tugged at her lips. She could still remember sitting on the riverbank, the grass tickling her toes as she waited for the perfect moment when the lighting would be just right. She'd taken the photograph her freshman year in high school for a local competition. She hadn't won. The prize—a new Minolta camera—had gone to the nephew of one of the judges, who'd done an artsy shot of a rainy day in black-and-white film.

A lesson, she reminded herself. Photography was a crapshoot.

Some people made it. Some didn't. And so she'd given it up for something steady. Reliable.

If only her brother had done the same.

But instead, he'd enlisted in the army on his eighteenth birthday, just weeks after their parents had died. He'd gone on to spend four years on the front lines in Iraq while she and Charlie had tried to make a new life in Lost Gun with Uncle E.J. and Aunt Cheryl. But it had never felt quite right.

It had never felt like home.

Her aunt and uncle had been older and set in their ways—acting out of duty rather than love—and so living with them had felt like living in a hotel.

Cold.

Impersonal.

And so Gracie had made up her mind to leave right after graduation, to make her own way and forget the tragedy that had destroyed her family. She'd snapped picture after picture and dreamed of bigger and better things far away from Lost Gun. But then Jackson had died and Charlie had become clingy and fearful. She'd followed Gracie everywhere, even into bed at night, terrified that fate would take her older sister the way it had snatched up their brother.

Gracie couldn't blame her. She'd felt the same crippling fear when their parents had died. She'd reached out for Jackson, but he'd left and so she'd had no one to soothe the uncertainty, to give her hope.

She stuffed the framed picture back inside the box, along with a dozen others that had lined the walls of her city planner's office, and reached for a Sharpie. Once upon a time, she'd hated the idea of tossing them when they could easily serve as cheap decoration, and so she'd kept them.

No more.

With trembling fingers, she scribbled Storage on the outside and moved on to the next box loaded with old files.

She rifled through manila folders for a full thirty minutes before she found herself thinking about Jesse and how good he'd looked and the way he'd smelled and—

Ugh. She needed something to get her mind back on track.

Maybe a brownie or a cupcake or a frosted cookie—

She killed the dangerous thought, grabbed her purse and headed out the door. Forget waiting on Trina. She would head out and check on Big Earl herself, and she wouldn't—repeat, *would not*—stop at the bakery on the way. She'd cleaned up her eating habits right along with everything else when she'd decided to play it safe and stop being so wild and reckless.

And *safe* meant looking both ways when she crossed the street and wearing her seat belt when she climbed behind the wheel and eating right. She had her health to think of and so she followed a strict low-carb, low-sugar, low-fat diet high in protein and fiber. That meant no brownies, no matter how desperate the craving.

No sirree, she wasn't falling off the wagon.

Not even if Jesse himself stripped naked right in front of her and she desperately needed something—anything—to sate her hunger and keep her hands off of him.

Okay, so maybe if he stripped *naked.*

A very vivid image of Jesse pushed into her thoughts and she saw him standing on the creek bed, the moonlight playing off his naked body. Her lips tingled and her nipples tightened and she picked up her steps.

No *naked* and no brownies.

4

GRACIE PULLED TO a stop in front of the bakery over an hour later and killed the engine.

She wasn't going to blow her diet with a brownie. She was headed straight for the health food store next door and a carob cookie with tofu frosting or a bran muffin with yogurt filling or *something.* A healthy alternative with just a teeny tiny ounce of sweetness to help steady her frantic heartbeat after the visit to Big Earl's place.

She hadn't actually had a face-to-face with the man himself, but she had come this close to being ripped to shreds by his dogs.

Charlie would freak fifty ways till Sunday if she found out. Luckily, she'd moved into the dorms at the University of Texas last year and so Gracie didn't have to worry about explaining the ripped hem of her skirt or the dirt smears on her blouse. At least not until this weekend when her little sis came home for her weekly visit and caught wind of the gossip.

If she came home.

She'd canceled the past three weeks in a row with one excuse after the other—she was studying; she had a date; she wanted to hit the latest party.

Not that Gracie was counting. She knew Charlie would much

rather go out with friends than make homemade pizza with her older sister. Charlie was growing up, pulling away, and that was good. Still, when her little sister finally did make it home, Gracie would be here.

She would always be here.

Because that's what home meant. It was permanent. Steady. Reliable.

Her gaze swiveled to the two old men nursing a game of dominoes in front of the hardware store directly across the street.

At ninety-three, Willard and Jacob Amberjack were the oldest living twins in the county. And the nosiest.

She debated making a quick trip home to change, but that would put her back at the health food store after hours and she needed something now—even something disgustingly healthy.

She drew a deep breath, braced herself for the impending encounter and climbed out of her car.

"Don't you look like something the dog just dragged in," Jacob called out the moment her feet touched pavement. "What in tarnation happened to you?"

"Was it a hit-and-run?" Willard leaned forward in his rocking chair. "Was it a car? A truck? Or maybe you got molested." He pointed a bony finger at his brother. "I been tellin' Jacob here that the world's goin' to hell in a handbasket."

"It wasn't a hit-and-run. And I wasn't molested," she rushed on, eager to set the record straight before their tongues started wagging. "I was just cleaning out my office and I snagged my skirt on a loose nail."

"You sure? 'Cause there's no shame if'n' you was molested. Things happen. Why, old Myrtle Nell over at the VFW hall accosted me just last night on account of I'm the best dancer in the place and she really wanted to waltz. Had to let her down easy and I can tell you, she was none too happy about it. Poor thing headed straight home, into a bottle of Metamucil. Ain't heard from her since."

"That's terrible."

"Damn straight. Everybody knows there ain't no substitute for good ole-fashioned prune juice."

O-kay. "Enjoy your game, fellas." Before they could launch into any more speculation, Gracie put her back to the curious old men and stepped up onto the curb.

"Afternoon, Miss Gracie."

"Hey there, Miss Gracie."

"See you at the church bake sale tomorrow, Miss Gracie."

"I wouldn't miss it for the world," she told the trio of women who exited the bake shop, glossy pink boxes clutched in their manicured hands.

The youngest one, a thirtyish soccer mom by the name of Carleen Harwell, held up two of the boxes that emanated a yummy smell. "Sarah donated ten dozen Rice Krispies Treats."

"Excellent." She waved as the women headed down the street and said hello to a few more people passing by before turning her attention to the display case that filled the massive storefront window. Dozens of pies lined the space, along with a sign that read It's Pick Your Pie Tuesday!

Not that she was going to pick a pie. Or a cake. Or anything else tempting her from the other side of the glass. But looking… There suddenly seemed nothing wrong with that.

"Go for the chocolate meringue."

The deep, familiar voice vibrated along her nerve endings. Heat whispered along her senses. Her stomach hollowed out.

"Or the Fudge Ecstasy. That's one of my personal favorites."

Excitement rippled up her spine, followed by a wave of *oh, no* because Jesse James Chisholm was the last person she needed to see right now.

He was the reason she was so worked up in the first place. So anxious. And desperate. And hungry.

Really, really hungry.

Run! her gut screamed. *Before you do something stupid like turn around and talk to him.*

"If memory serves—" the words slid past her lips as she

turned "—you were always partial to cherry." So much for listening to her instincts. "In fact, I seem to recall you wolfing down an entire cherry cobbler at the Travis County Fair and Rodeo." She didn't mean to bring up their first date, but her mouth seemed to have a mind all its own. "With two scoops of ice cream on the side."

"Miss Hazel's prizewinning cobbler," he said, a grin tugging at his lips as the memory surfaced. "That woman sure can bake."

"So can Sarah." Gracie motioned to the display case and the golden lattice-topped cherry pie sitting center stage. Inside gold certificates and blue ribbons lined a nearby wall, along with an autographed picture of Tom Cruise in his *Risky Business* heyday. "So why the switch to chocolate?"

"When I was laid up after Diamond Dust, Billy thought he'd cheer me up with some fresh-picked cherries from Old Man Winthrow's tree. I ate the entire basket in one sitting and made myself sick. I've been boycotting ever since."

"I don't do chocolate," she announced. She didn't mean to keep the conversation going. She had a strict no-talk policy where Jesse was concerned. And a no-closeness policy, too. Because when she got too close, she couldn't help but talk.

Which explained why she'd avoided him altogether for the past twelve years.

No talking. No touching. No kissing. No—

"I mean, I like chocolate—brownies, in particular," she blurted, eager to do something with her mouth that didn't involve planting a great big one smack-dab on his lips, "but I don't actually eat any."

"What happened to the Hershey's-bar-a-day habit?"

"I kicked it. I'm into healthy eating now. No Hershey's bars or brownies or anything else with processed sugar. I'm headed to the health food store." She motioned to the sign shaped like a giant celery stalk just to her left. "They make an all-natural apple tart. It has a cornflake crust. It's really delicious."

"Cornflakes, huh?" He didn't look convinced.

She couldn't blame him. She remembered the small sample she'd tasted the last time she'd been inside the Green Machine and her throat tightened. "Delicious might be pushing it. But it's decent." She shrugged. "Besides, deprivation is good for the soul. It builds character."

"It also makes you more likely to blow at the first sign of temptation."

And how.

Twelve years and counting.

"Everything all right, Miss Gracie?" Jacob Amberjack's voice carried across the street and drew her attention.

"It's fine." She waved at the old man and his brother.

"'Cause if that there feller's the one what assaulted you, Willard here would be happy to come over there and defend your honor."

"I didn't assault her," Jesse told the two men.

The old man glared. "Tell it to the judge, Chisholm."

"No one's telling anything to anyone, because nothing happened," Gracie said.

"That ain't the way we see it," the two men said in unison.

"I'd give it a rest if I were you," Jesse advised.

"We ain't afraid of you, Chisholm. There might be snow on the roof, but there's plenty of fire in the cookstove. Willard here—" Jacob motioned next to him "—will rip you a new one—"

"How come I'm the one who always has to do the rippin'?" Willard cut in. "Hell's bells, I can barely move as it is. You know I got a bad back."

"Well, I got bunions."

"So? You ain't fightin' with your feet…"

The two men turned their focus to each other and Gracie's gaze shifted back to Jesse. She expected the anger. The hatred. He'd been big on both way back when, particularly when it came to the citizens of Lost Gun. He'd hated them as much as they'd hated him, and he'd never been shy about showing it.

Instead of hard, glittering anger, she saw a flash of pain, a glimmer of regret, and she had the startling thought that while he looked every bit the hard, bulletproof cowboy she remembered so well, there was a softening in his gaze. His heart.

As if Jesse actually cared what the two old men had said to him.

As if.

No, Jesse James Chisholm didn't give two shakes what the fine people of Lost Gun thought about him. He hated the town and he always would.

Meanwhile, she was stuck smack-dab in the middle of it.

She ignored the depressing thought and searched for her voice. "So, um, what are you doing here?"

He motioned to the bridal salon just two doors down. "I have to see a man about a tux. I'm Pete's right hand."

"I didn't mean here as in this location. I meant—" she motioned between them "—*here.* You couldn't wait to get away from me earlier. Now you're standing here having a conversation. Because?"

He frowned, as if he didn't quite understand it any more than she did. "You caught me at a bad time, I suppose."

"I didn't mean to. I just wanted to warn you before the reporters beat me to it."

"You did the right thing."

"I just thought you should know..." Her gaze snapped up. "What did you just say?"

"It's not about what I just said. It's about what I *should* have said earlier." His gaze caught and held hers. "Thanks for giving me the heads-up." Where she'd missed the gratitude that morning, there was no mistaking the sentiment now. "Motives aside, you warned me and I am grateful."

"Me, too." When he gave her a questioning look, she added, "For the flowers that you sent when my brother died. I should have said thank you back then. I didn't."

"I'm really sorry about what happened to him."

"It was his choice." She shrugged. "He enlisted. He knew the risks, but he took them anyway."

"Seems to me," he said after a long moment, "he died doing something he believed in. I can't think of a better way to go myself."

Neither could she at that moment and oddly enough, the tightness in her chest eased just a fraction. "If you're not careful, you'll be following in his footsteps. That was a hard fall you took back at the arena."

A wicked grin tugged at the corner of his lips. "The harder, the better."

"I'm talking about riding."

"So am I, sugar." The grin turned into a full-blown smile. "So am I." The words were like a chisel chipping away at the wall she'd erected between them. Even more, he stared deep into her eyes and for a long moment, she forgot everything.

The nosy men sitting across the street. The endless stream of people walking past. The all-important fact that she needed to get a move on if she meant to get inside the health food store before they closed.

He made her feel like the only woman in the world.

Which was crazy with a big fat *C*.

He was flirting, for heaven's sake. Just the kind of sexy, seductive innuendo she would expect from one of the hottest bachelors on the PBR circuit.

It wasn't as if he wanted to sweep her up and ride off into the sunset. This wasn't about her personally. She was simply one of many in a long, long line of women who lusted after him, and he was simply living up to his reputation.

Just as she should be living up to hers.

She stiffened. "It was nice to see you, but I really should get going. I've got a ton of work back at City Hall."

"Duty calls, right?"

Her gaze collided with his and she could have sworn she saw

a glimmer of disappointment before it disappeared into the vivid violet depths. "Always."

And then she turned and hurried toward the Green Machine before she did the unthinkable—like wrap her arms around him, hop on and ride him for a scorching eight seconds in front of God and the Amberjack twins.

She would have done just that prior to her brother's death, but she was no longer the rebellious teenager desperate to flee the confines of her small town.

She was mature.

Responsible.

Safe.

If only that thought didn't depress her almost as much as the skinny treats that waited for her inside the health food store.

5

"THIS IS JUST plain wrong." Cole Unger Chisholm frowned as he stood on the raised dais in the middle of the mirrored dressing room of Lost Gun's one and only bridal salon. "Tell me again why I have to wear this."

"For Pete." Jesse ignored the prickly fabric of his own tuxedo and tried to forget the sugary scent of vanilla cupcakes that still teased his nostrils. Of all the people he could possibly run into—the local police chief, the busybodies from the Ladies' Auxiliary, the gossipy Amberjack brothers—it had to be Gracie. Talk about rotten luck.

"Stop your bellyaching," he told Cole. "You're wearing it and that's that."

"Pete don't give two licks about a freakin' tuxedo with a girly purple cummerbund and matching tie, so why should I?"

"Because he's marrying Wendy and she does give two licks." Jesse lifted one arm so Mr. McGinnis, the shop's owner and tailor, could adjust the hem on his sleeve.

Cole eyed his reflection. "But the cummerbund looks almost pink."

"It's actually lavender." The comment came from the petite

blonde who appeared in the curtained doorway. Her blue eyes narrowed as she eyed Cole. "And you're right. It's all wrong."

"See?" Cole pushed back a strand of unruly brown hair and stared defiantly at Jesse. "That's what I've been saying all along."

"You've got it hooked in the front," Wendy announced. "It's supposed to hook in the back. Isn't that right, Mr. McGinnis?"

"Sure enough, Miss Wendy." The older man slipped the last pin into Jesse's hem and turned to work on Cole's tux. In a matter of seconds, he readjusted the shiny taffeta material and stepped back. "There. Now it's perfect."

"Perfect?" Cole frowned. "But I look like a—"

"Where's Pete?" Jesse cut in, drawing Wendy's attention before Cole could say something he would later regret.

And Jesse had no doubt his middle brother would do just that. Cole had zero filters when it came to running his mouth, which explained why he ended up in more than his fair share of bar fights.

"He's trying on his tuxedo in the next room," Wendy replied. "He'll be out in a second." She turned a grateful smile on Cole. "Listen, I know you don't feel comfortable all dressed up like this, but I really appreciate it."

"It's our pleasure," Jesse cut in before Cole could open his mouth again.

"Damn straight it is." The comment came from Billy, who waltzed in wearing the same tuxedo.

Wendy turned on the youngest Chisholm and her eyes went misty. "You look wonderful!"

Billy winked. "Anything for you and Pete." He stepped up on the dais next to Cole so that Mr. McGinnis could work on the hem of his pants. "Ain't that right, bro?" He clapped Cole on the shoulder.

The middle Chisholm shrugged free. "I guess so."

"I was hoping you'd feel that way." Another smile touched Wendy's pink lips and Jesse knew she had something up her sleeve even before she added, "I've been meaning to talk to you,

Cole. See, one of my friends is flying in from Houston and I need someone to pick her up at the airport. I would get Red to do it, but Hannah—that's her name—comes in smack-dab during his soap opera time, and you know how that goes."

Red owned the only cab in Lost Gun. He was also a die-hard soap opera fan. Since he was as old as dirt, he hadn't yet discovered TiVo or a DVR, which meant he was completely out of commission between the hours of 11:00 a.m. and 2:00 p.m. on any given weekday.

"She tried to get a different flight," Wendy went on, "but it's the only one that will put her here in time for the rehearsal dinner."

"No problem," Jesse said. "Cole here would be happy to pick her up for you." He clapped his brother on the shoulder, his hand lingering. "Isn't that right?"

"But I've got a training session—" the younger Chisholm started. Jesse dug his fingers into muscle and Cole bit out, "All right, already. I'll do it."

"You will?" Excitement lit Wendy's eyes.

Jesse dug his fingers even deeper and the younger man blurted, "Sure thing. Family's family," he muttered. "We stick together."

"Great, because I told her all about you and she's dying to meet you."

"Who's dying to meet who?" Pete Gunner walked into the fitting area and slid an arm around his wife-to-be.

"Hannah," Wendy told him. "Ever since she moved to Houston from New York, she's been dying to meet a real cowboy. I told her all about Cole and she's super hyped."

"Wait a second." Cole shrugged loose from Jesse's warning grasp. "Picking her up is one thing, but this sounds like a setup."

"Don't be silly. You don't have to be her date for the wedding."

"That's a relief." Cole tugged at the tie around his neck as if he couldn't quite breathe. "For a second there, I thought you wanted me to babysit her the entire night."

"Of course not." Wendy smiled. "Just sit with her during the reception. And maybe ask her to dance once or twice. Oh, and make sure she gets back to the motel that night and—"

"Pretty much babysit her the whole danged night," Cole cut in. His mouth pulled into a tight line. "Hell's bells. I knew it. It *is* a setup."

"Okay, maybe it is." Wendy shrugged. "But it'll be fun. And speaking of fun, I've got to decide on the actual centerpiece so the florist can finalize the order." She planted a kiss on her groom's lips and headed for a nearby doorway and the endless array of floral arrangements spread out on a table in the next room.

Cole opened his mouth, but Pete held up a hand. "Don't fight it, bro. It'll only make things worse."

"But I can get my own date."

"True, but Wendy doesn't want you bringing one of your usual buckle bunnies to the wedding."

"He's talking about the Barbie triplets," Billy chimed in.

"They're not triplets," Cole said. "They're just sisters who are close in age. And I wasn't going to bring all three. Just Crystal. She's the oldest and the prettiest."

"And the wildest," Pete added, "which is why she's off-limits for the wedding. Wendy thinks you need to meet a nice girl."

"I meet plenty of nice girls." Cole unhooked the cummerbund and handed it to Mr. McGinnis.

"Nice and easy," Billy added.

"What's wrong with easy?"

"Nothing if you're sixteen and horny as hell," the youngest Chisholm pointed out. "You're twenty-nine. You should be thinking about your future."

"Like you?"

"Damn straight." Billy nodded. "As a matter of fact, I've got my own date already lined up for the wedding and I can guarantee her last name isn't Barbie."

"Big Earl Jessup's great-granddaughter is not a date," Cole

pointed out. "She's a death wish. She's liable to challenge you to an arm-wrestling match."

"So she's a little rough around the edges," Billy admitted. "She's a tomboy, and that just means we've got a shitload in common. She's interesting."

"And safe," Jesse offered.

"Exactly." Billy unhooked his own tie and handed it to the tailor. "I'm not looking to settle down, which makes Casey Jessup the perfect date for this wedding. I don't have to worry about her sitting around getting bright ideas from all this hoopla. She's as far from wife material as a woman can get."

"Casey's got a cousin." Cole's gaze shifted to Pete. "I could ask her to the wedding."

"Too late. Wendy got the draw on you and now you've got to man up."

"But I hate fix-ups." He shrugged off his jacket.

"Look on the bright side," Billy added, "Wendy's friend *could* turn out to have a smoking-hot body and zero morals."

Cole shook his head. "You know the odds of that are slim to none."

"True, but it can't hurt to fantasize." Jesse motioned to Billy. "Just like this one outriding me in Vegas in a few weeks."

"That buckle is mine," Billy vowed, trying to wrestle free when Jesse grabbed him in a headlock.

"Keep thinking that and maybe one day you'll knock me out of the running." But not this time. Jesse had been working too long and too hard to go down with just one buckle to his credit. He wanted a second. And a third. Hell, maybe even a fourth.

And then?

He let go of his brother and shifted his attention to the next room and a dreamy-eyed Wendy, who moved from arrangement to arrangement eyeing the various flowers.

For a split second, he saw Gracie leaning over a bouquet of lilies, her eyes sparkling, her full, luscious lips curved into a smile. Fast-forward to another vision of the two of them standing at the altar saying "I do," living happily ever after.

Crazy.

Not the "I do" part, mind you. Jesse wasn't opposed to settling down and having a family. It was the notion of living happily ever after with Gracie Stone that was just plumb loco.

She represented everything he wanted desperately to forget—his past, this town.

He wanted to escape them both. That was why he'd kept his distance all these years.

Why he needed to keep his distance now.

Jesse stiffened and peeled off the tuxedo jacket. "I need to head out." The back way this time. No way was he going to risk another run-in with her out front. She'd smelled so good and looked even more luscious than anything in the front window of the bakery.

And damned if he'd been able to think straight with her right in front of him.

That was why he'd talked to her. Flirted with her.

Crazy.

"Why don't you come back to the house with me and Wendy?" Pete's voice drew his attention. "Eli's got the cook working on a big spread for supper. The twins are visiting from El Paso. We could make it a family dinner."

The twins were Jimmy and Jake Barber, fast-rising stars on the team-roping circuit and the last two members of the notorious Lost Boys. They'd lived out at Pete's ranch with Jesse and his brothers up until Pete had proposed to Wendy last year. Jesse and the others had gotten together then and decided with Pete settling down and retiring, it was time for the rest of them to spread their wings. The twins had moved up to El Paso. Cole was in Houston. Billy had just bought a few hundred acres outside of Lost Gun and was making plans to build a house of his own. And Jesse had finally bought a spread in Austin.

Now it was just a matter of tying up all the loose ends here—namely selling his stock at the training facility—and moving on.

"Come on," Pete prompted. "It's been forever since we've all sat down together. Maybe Eli will pull out his guitar."

"Sounds tempting, but the drive out will put me back at the motel close to midnight and I need to be up early."

"So stay over at the ranch house. Hell, I don't know why you're cooped up at that motel in the first place."

"Because you're this close to tying the knot, bro. You and Wendy deserve a little privacy." Pete arched an eyebrow and Jesse added, "That way if you guys want to get naked in the dining room or the front parlor, there's nobody stopping you."

Pete looked ready to protest, but then he shrugged. "I suppose a man can't argue with getting naked. So what about you?" He eyed Jesse. "You got a date for the wedding? If not, I'm sure Wendy could rustle up a friend."

"I've got a few possibilities."

"Just make sure none of them work down at Luscious Longhorns—otherwise she'll blow a gasket." Pete grinned for a long moment before his look faded into one of serious intent. "Eli mentioned that Gracie came to see you today."

Jesse nodded. "They're going to re-air the television show."

"When?"

"Tuesday a week."

"Maybe you ought to leave early, then. Head up to Austin and get some extra practice time in before your next rodeo."

"I can practice here just fine. Besides, I've got another buyer coming in to look at a few more bulls in the morning. I want to get them all sold off before I leave. That and there's a little something called a wedding I need to be here for."

"You could always miss it."

Jesse shook his head. "Like hell. I'm your best man."

"And I'm the guy who watched you nurse a few dozen broken bones thanks to a she-devil named Diamond Dust. I have no desire to do it again."

"I was eighteen and gun-shy when it came to the press. I can handle it now. You just worry about getting your sorry hide to the church on Saturday." Jesse grinned. "Because I plan to keep you out plenty late the night before for the bachelor party."

"Thanks, man." Pete clapped him on the back. "I owe you one."

But it was Jesse who owed Pete. The man had saved him and his brothers all those years ago, and no way was Jesse jumping ship on the most important day of Pete's life. He was here and he was staying until the festivities were over.

Even more, he wasn't the same kid who'd been blindsided all those years ago. He dealt with reporters all the time now, not to mention overzealous fans and even the occasional critic. It was just a matter of staying one step ahead.

And he was, thanks to Gracie.

Because she wanted to keep the peace in her small town.

That was the only reason she'd gone to the trouble of warning him. He *knew* that. At the same time, he couldn't shake the crazy hope that maybe, just maybe, she'd wanted to see him.

As much as he'd wanted to see her.

There was no denying the chemistry that still sizzled between them. He'd felt the charge in the air, and so had she. There'd been no mistaking the tremble of her full bottom lip or the glimmer in her eyes. He knew the look even after all these years.

Yep, the chemistry was still there.

Not that it meant anything.

She was still determined to keep her distance—her quick retreat into the health food store proved that—and so was he.

He tamped down a sudden rush of disappointment. "I'd better get going. I want to get in another ride or two before I call it a night." He shed the tie and cummerbund and headed back to the dressing room to retrieve his clothes.

And then Jesse snuck out the back way and turned his attention to the one thing that wasn't beyond his reach—another PBR championship.

6

THIS WAS THE last place he needed to be.

The thought struck later that evening as Jesse pulled into the dirt driveway of the three-acre lot that sat just a few blocks over from City Hall.

He was supposed to be back at the motel, eating takeout and icing his shoulder after a hellacious training session. Or nursing a few beers at the local honky-tonk with his brothers. Or playing a few rounds of pool at one of the beer joints out on the interstate.

Anywhere but here, smack-dab in the middle of the town he so desperately hated.

His gaze pushed through the settling darkness and scanned the area. Once upon a time, reporters had walked every inch of this sad, miserable stretch, picking through the burned ruins that had once been the two-room shack that Jesse and his brothers had shared with their dad. The small single-car garage still sat in the far back corner, the paint peeling, the roof rusted out. His dad's broken-down 1970 Buick sat next to the shell of a building, the doors missing, the frame rusted and rotting.

The shame of Lost Gun.

That was how the newspapers had referred to the Chisholm

place when *Famous Texas Outlaws* had aired for the first time on the Discovery Channel.

Not that his dad had been a famous Texas outlaw. Far from it. Silas Chisholm had been a wannabe with a lust for easy money and an aversion to hard work, which was why he'd moved his three young boys to Lost Gun in the first place.

The town had originated as a haven to criminals and gamblers back in the early 1800s. Lost Gun, so named because it was rumored to be home to a pearl-handled Colt once belonging to one of Texas's most notorious outlaws—John Wesley Hardin. The man had supposedly hidden the gun while on the run from Texas Rangers, but other than a colorful legend, there'd never been any actual proof of its existence.

Word of mouth had been enough for a recently widowed Silas to uproot his three sons from Beaumont, Texas, and travel across the state in search of the valuable Colt. When the gun hadn't panned out, Silas had started looking for another big-money opportunity.

Now, remember, son, when things look bad and it looks like you're not gonna make it, then you gotta get mean. I mean plumb mad-dog mean. 'Cause if you lose your head and you give up, then you neither live nor win.

His dad's words echoed in his head. As worthless as the man had been, he'd been just as determined when it came to finding an easy payday. After an endless string of dead-end schemes, he'd turned to the Lost Gun Savings & Loan.

Jesse still wasn't sure how he'd pulled it off, but he'd actually made off with a quarter of a million dollars. All pissed away when he'd drunk himself into a stupor later that same night. He'd passed out with a cigarette in his mouth that had resulted in a deadly blaze.

He'd died in that fire because Jesse, only thirteen at the time, hadn't been strong enough to drag him off the couch. Even more, the fortune Silas had been so anxious to get his hands on had gone up in flames.

Not that everybody believed the money had perished. Curt Calhoun, the reporter who'd aired the story five years later, had posed so many questions that folks had started to wonder if maybe, just maybe, the money might still be out there. Calhoun's speculation had pulled in every two-bit criminal this side of the Rio Grande, not to mention a shitload of fortune hunters. They'd descended on the small town like a pack of hungry coyotes.

Jesse stiffened against the sudden tightening in his chest. He hadn't been out here in a long, long time.

Try never.

No, the closest Jesse came was the rodeo arena that sat ten miles outside the city limits.

But this was it. His last trip to the town itself. He was moving on, settling down, living his dream, and that meant laying the past to rest once and for all.

"Sell it," he'd told his lawyer just yesterday.

The mountain of paperwork would be ready for Jesse's signature by the end of the week, which meant he had all of five days to go through what was left of the garage and the old car and salvage anything he might want to keep.

Of course, he'd have to get out of his truck first.

He would.

He was sure there was nothing of value left to keep. Vandals had made off with nearly everything. Old tools. Car parts. After so many years, there wasn't a single thing left.

Still, he'd promised Mr. Lambert he would do a walk-through, and that was what he intended to do.

Tomorrow.

He eyed the car and a memory pushed its way into his head. Of him and his three brothers sleeping on the backseat so many nights when his dad had been too drunk and too volatile for them to be in the house. That had been before the fire, before Pete Gunner had taken them under his wing.

They would have wound up in foster care if it hadn't been for Pete. They should have, but he'd stepped up and fought for them. Eli, too. It had taken three weeks for Pete to win custody. A speedy process compared to the red tape nowadays. But Pete had had money and fame on his side, and a decent lawyer. That, and the county had been underfunded and severely understaffed. They hadn't had the resources to worry over three more children.

Still, the threat of foster care had been real for those few weeks and so Jesse had taken his brothers and gone into hiding in the woods. They'd stayed at an old hunting camp until Pete had finally found them and taken them home.

A real home.

But that first night right after the fire, they'd had only the Buick.

He could still feel the cold upholstery seeping through his clothes, the frustration gripping his insides because he hadn't known what to do or where to go. The fear.

For his younger brothers.

Jesse hadn't given a shit about himself. His future. His life. He'd been angry with the world for dealing him such a shitty hand and so he'd spent his young life pushing fate to the limit. Backing her into a corner and daring her to lash out at him. He'd raced his beat-up motorcycle down Main Street every Saturday night and thumbed his nose at authority and climbed onto any and every bull he could find, to hell with rules and buzzers.

Then.

But there was nothing like a severe concussion and thirteen broken bones to make a guy realize that he actually cared if he lived or died. He'd turned his back on his wild and reckless ways and started taking his career seriously after the Diamond Dust incident. He'd trained smarter, harder, and it had paid off.

He'd finally made it to the top.

Even more, he'd made it out of Lost Gun. The purse he'd won at nationals had been more than enough for a down payment on the Austin spread. And the endorsements that came with being a PBR champion gave him an ongoing income that far surpassed his winnings. For the first time in his life, he was financially set.

And so were his brothers.

Billy and Cole were making their own way on the rodeo circuit, pocketing not only their winnings but endorsements, as well. They were the new faces of rodeo. Young. Good-looking. Lucrative.

A far cry from the scared snot-nosed kids they'd been way back when.

He eyed the dismal landscape one last time. It was time to let go. To move forward and stop looking back.

To move, period.

He'd just keyed the engine and revved the motor when he saw the flash of headlights in his rearview mirror. Gravel crunched as a black BMW pulled up behind him.

A car door opened and slammed shut. Heels crunched toward him. The sweet smell of cupcakes drifted through the open window and Jesse's heartbeat kicked up a notch.

He killed the engine, drew a deep breath and climbed out from behind the wheel.

Yep, it was her, all right. Up close and in person. Three times in the same friggin' day.

So much for keeping his distance.

His groin tightened and he stiffened. "Stalk much?" he asked when Gracie walked up to him.

Her carefully arched brows drew together. "I seem to recall, you were the one who snuck up on me outside the bakery. Besides, I'm not here for you. I'm just keeping an eye on things."

He spared a glance at the falling-down stretch of property. "Not much to see."

"Maybe not yet, but with Tuesday looming and the interest picking up, that's sure to change. Besides, it's right on my way home."

"Still living on Carpenter Street?"

She nodded. "Aunt Cheryl and Uncle E.J. bought a place down in Port Aransas and left the house to me and Charlie."

"How's she doing?"

A smile touched her lips and a softness edged her gaze. "She's in her second year at the University of Texas. She lives on campus, but she drives home on most weekends. Straight As. Beautiful. She's got a ton of boyfriends."

"What about you?"

"I'm too busy for a boyfriend."

Her words stirred a rush of joy followed by a flood of *What the hell are you thinking?* He didn't care if she did or did not have a significant other. He didn't care about her, period.

Ah, but he still wanted her.

There was no denying the heat that rippled through his body or the crazy way his palms tickled, eager to reach out and see if her skin felt as soft as he remembered.

"Running this city is a full-time job," she went on, "especially with the extra notoriety from *Famous Texas Outlaws.* In addition to the out-of-towners coming in to dig for treasure, Sheriff Hooker caught Myrtle Nell's grandsons trying to drive a forklift over the back fence of this place."

"There is no treasure."

"Which makes it all the more aggravating." Her finger hooked a strand of blond hair that had come loose from her ponytail and she tucked it behind the delicate shell of her ear. "At least if there *was* something left, someone would have already dug it up. The press would have broadcast it from here to kingdom come and all the fuss would have died down. Instead, the D.A. is gearing up for a mess of two-bit trespassing charges."

He wasn't going to touch her. That was what he told himself when the silky tendril of hair came loose again and dangled next to her cheek. No reaching out and sweeping the soft strands away from her face. *No.* "Speaking of charges—" he cleared his suddenly dry throat "—shouldn't Sheriff Hooker be the one keeping an eye on things?"

"He had an anniversary dinner with the missus. I had the time, so I figured I might as well do a quick drive-by." She shrugged. "What about you? What are you doing out here?"

"Just looking around." He forced his gaze away from her and studied his surroundings. His gut tightened.

"I wasn't here when it happened," he heard himself say. A crazy thing to say, but it was so quiet that he almost felt as if he were talking to himself. Except that he could hear her soft even breaths and feel the warmth of her body so close.

But not close enough.

"I was over at the rodeo arena helping out with the horses," he went on, the words slipping through the darkness. "Eli used to pay me to rake the stalls. It was enough to buy lunch for me and my brothers, but sometimes it put me home late. The fire was in full force by the time I got here."

"Where were your brothers that night?"

"They were at the rodeo arena with me. They used to hang out until I finished work so that we could go home together. Eli would let them do their homework in the office. He had a few toys in there, too. To keep them busy while I finished up my chores. Eli dropped us off just up the street that night so my dad wouldn't see him. Silas got mean when he drank and he was always itching for a fight. Not that night, though. We saw the blaze clear down the street. We just didn't know what was burning until we got here."

He could still feel the heat licking at his face long after he'd gone in to discover his father passed out on the couch. Immobile. Unmovable. He'd stood outside afterward, his brothers whimpering beside him. There had been no sound from inside. Just the crackle of flames and the popping of wood.

Because his dad had been dead by then.

That was what Jesse told himself. What he wanted so desperately to believe. Because he didn't want to think he'd left the man in there to die.

"It wasn't your fault," she said, concern edging her words.

As if he didn't know that. He did. He *knew.*

So why the hell did he think that maybe, just maybe, he could have done something more? That he would have? It wasn't as if he hadn't tried. He'd rushed in, his shirt covering his mouth and nose. He'd tugged at the man's lifeless body. He'd begged him to get up. He'd even prayed.

But Silas hadn't budged.

The smoke had gotten thicker and Jesse had had no choice but to retreat. To leave him.

So?

His father had been a selfish SOB and Jesse and his brothers had done a hell of a lot better after he'd passed on. No, Jesse wouldn't have done a damned thing to change that night. He wouldn't have stayed a second longer to try to get him out. He couldn't have stayed.

"It's not going to work," he blurted, eager to change the subject. His gaze slid from her face to her modest blouse and plain navy skirt. The getup wasn't the least bit revealing, but it didn't have to be. The soft material clung to her curves, tracing the voluptuous lines. His dick stirred and he stiffened.

"What are you talking about?"

He motioned to her. "The provocative clothing."

"You think this is provocative?" She glanced down. Her brows knitted with concern as her gaze swiveled back to him. "Did you see a doctor today? Because you took a really hard fall earlier—"

"I'm fine," he cut in, determined to ignore the warmth slip-sliding through him. The last thing he wanted was her concern.

No, he wanted something a lot more basic from Gracie Stone.

And that was the problem in a nutshell. He still wanted her. A desire that neither time nor distance had managed to kill.

Because he'd never had the chance to work her out of his system. To grow tired and bored. Rather, she'd given him a taste of something wonderful, and then she'd taken it away before he'd managed to sate his hunger.

Once he did, he would be done with her like every other woman he'd ever been with. Like the cherries. The first few bites had been heaven, but then he'd gotten really sick, really fast.

And although Jesse Chisholm had no intention of letting his emotions get involved where Gracie Stone was concerned, there suddenly seemed nothing wrong with a little physical contact.

One really hot night with her would be enough to give him some closure. At least that was what he was telling himself.

"I really think you should see a doctor." She eyed him. "Maybe you hit your head."

A grin tugged at his mouth and he couldn't help himself. "Darlin', it's not my head that's aching like a sonofabitch." He closed the distance between them. "At least not the one on my shoulders."

And then he kissed her.

7

HE WAS *KISSING* HER.

Here. Now.

Oh, boy.

His strong, purposeful mouth moved over hers. His tongue swept her bottom lip, licking and nibbling and coaxing and—

Earth to Gracie! This shouldn't be happening. Not here. Not with him. Especially not him.

Just as the denial registered in her shocked brain, he deepened the kiss. His tongue pushed inside, to tease and taunt and tangle with hers. All rational thought faded into a whirlwind of hunger that swirled through her, stirring every nerve. It had been so long since she'd kissed anyone. Since she'd kissed him.

She trembled and her stomach hollowed out.

He tasted even better than the most decadent brownie. Sweeter. Richer. More potent. More addictive.

Before she could stop herself, she leaned into him, melting from the sudden rise in body temperature. Her hand slid up his chest and her fingers caught the soft hair at the nape of his neck.

His arms closed around her. Strong hands pressed against the base of her spine, drawing her closer. She met him chest for chest, hip for hip, until she felt every incredible inch of him flush against her body—the hard planes of his chest, the solid muscles of his thighs, the growing erection beneath his zipper.

Uh-oh.

The warning sounded in her head, but damned if it didn't make her that much more excited. Heat spread from her cheeks, creeping south. The slow burn traveled inch by sweet, tantalizing inch until her nipples throbbed and wetness flooded between her thighs.

And all because of a kiss.

Because the man doing the kissing was wild and careless and completely inappropriate. He was all wrong for her, and damned if she didn't want him in spite of it.

Because of it.

Because Gracie Stone wasn't nearly the goody-goody she pretended to be.

The thought struck and she stiffened. Tearing her lips away, she stumbled backward.

Breathe, she told herself. *Just calm down and breathe.* She couldn't do this. She had responsibilities. "I… You…" She shook her head and tried to ignore the way her lips tingled. "You and I…" She shook her head. "We don't even like each other."

"True enough." He said the words, but the strange flicker in his gaze didn't mirror the sentiment. "But it's not about *like,* sugar. It's about *want.* I want you and you want me. The pull between us…" His gaze darkened as it touched her mouth and she felt the overwhelming chemistry that pulsed between them. "It's strong."

"I should get going," she went on, desperate to kill the tiny hope that he would pull her close and kiss her again.

Lust.

That was all this was.

That and deprivation.

Character, she reminded herself. Deprivation built character. It made her stronger. More resilient.

It also makes you more likely to blow at the first sign of temptation.

His words echoed and she knew he was right.

This was temptation. *He* was temptation in his faded jeans and fitted Western shirt. He practically dripped with sex appeal. He always had. It only stood to reason that her starving hormones would shift into overdrive with him so near.

Which was why she'd made it her business to steer clear of him all these years.

And why she needed to get as far away from him as possible right now.

She backed up, eager to put a few safe inches of distance between them. "I should—"

"I told you to bring the shovel!"

The frantic whisper carried on the warm evening breeze and killed Gracie's hasty retreat.

Jesse's head jerked around toward the old garage and Gracie's gaze followed in time to see a pair of shadows disappear behind the edge of the old structure.

"Call the sheriff." Jesse leaned in his open window and plucked a flashlight from the glove box.

"Wait—" she started, but he was already halfway up the driveway. "Jesse! Stop! You shouldn't be doing this. It's dangerous...."

Her words faded as he darted behind the old car sitting in front of the garage and disappeared into the darkness. Her heart pounded for the next few seconds as the night seemed to close in. Panic bolted through her.

She darted for her car and snatched her cell phone off the dash. With frantic fingers, she punched in 911 and gave the information to Maureen over at the sheriff's station.

She said a few choice words, all of them involving a headstrong cowboy who should have exercised at least a little bit of caution. But no, he'd run off into the darkness and now she was here. Waiting and worrying and— *Hell,* no.

She couldn't just stand here. She stuffed the phone into her pocket and stepped forward.

She was halfway around the falling-down garage when she heard the chilling voice directly behind her.

"Hold it right there, lady."

The air stalled in her chest and she became keenly aware of the barrel pressed between her shoulder blades. Her heartbeat lurched forward and her hands trembled.

"Take it easy." She held up her hands. "No reason to get upset. We should all just stay calm—"

"Quiet," came the deep, oddly familiar voice.

She knew that voice, which killed the hunch that this was an outsider lured into Lost Gun by all the hype. Her brain started rifling through memories, desperate to find a face to go with the distinctive Southern drawl that echoed in her ears. "Just keep your mouth shut and no one will get hurt. I swear it."

I do solemnly swear to uphold the rules of the Lost Gun Ranger Scouts...

The past echoed, rousing a memory of the Ranger Scouts initiation she'd attended on behalf of the city council.

Her brain started fitting the puzzle pieces together and she frowned. "Troy Warren?" Troy was now a fifteen-year-old sophomore at Lost Gun High and a frequent visitor to the sheriff's office, most memorably after spray-painting I Love Sheila Kimber on the back fence of the middle school. "Is that you?"

"Heck, no," came the voice, slightly frazzled this time. "Ain't nobody here by the name of Warren."

"I know it's you." Gracie summoned her most intimidating voice. "I was standing right behind you at the seventh-grade Scout ceremony." She couldn't help but wonder how a once-upon-a-time Scout ended up with a gun in his hands.

The same way a thirteen-year-old ended up being a provider for his two younger brothers. It was rotten luck. A crazy twist of fate. An accident.

Jesse's image rushed into her head and a wave of panic rolled through her. What if this boy had already shot him?

Even as the possibility rolled through her head, she fought it back down. She would have heard a gunshot. A struggle. *Something.* Anything besides the eerie quiet.

"I told you this was a bad idea," came a second voice. Same slow drawl. Same familiar tone. "She knows your name. She knows your friggin' *name.*"

"She does now," Troy growled to his partner. "You were supposed to keep your mouth shut."

"And let you get us locked up and sent all the way to Huntsville? I knew we shouldn't have come here. I *knew* it."

Gracie's memory stirred again. Same Scout meeting. Different boy. "Lonnie? Lonnie Sawyer? Is that you?"

"No, it ain't him," Troy said. "It's somebody you don't know. A stranger. You just shut up if you know what's good for you—" the barrel nudged between her shoulder blades "—or else."

"Or else what?" The words were out before she could stop them. As scared as she was, she was also getting a little angry. She was sick and tired of having circumstances dictated to her. Of being told what to do and when to do it. Of being stuck. And although she couldn't stand up to the world and change the path of her life, she could change this moment. "You really think you have what it takes to pull the trigger?"

"Heck, yeah."

"Heck, no."

The answers echoed simultaneously and Gracie realized that the three of them had company.

"He's not shooting anybody." Gracie heard Jesse's deep, familiar voice a split second before she heard a grunt and a yelp, and suddenly the gun fell away.

She whirled in time to see Jesse standing between the two teenage boys, hands gripping the backs of their collars. The gun lay forgotten on the ground.

Leaning down, she picked up the discarded weapon and her lips pulled into a frown.

"It's just a paintball gun, Miss Gracie," Lonnie blurted as she inspected the weapon. "Please don't tell my grandma. *Please.*"

"Troy Eugene Warren." She turned on the first boy. "You almost gave me a heart attack." She dangled the weapon. "I thought this was an actual gun."

"It *is* a gun." His stubborn gaze met hers. "It can even break the skin."

"Makes a nasty bruise, too," Lonnie offered. "I know 'cause Troy tested it out on me—"

"What are you boys doing out here?" Jesse cut in, giving them a little shake.

"We're after the money."

"There is no money."

"Says you." Lonnie tried to pull away, but Jesse tightened his grip and held the boy close. "The TV says different," Lonnie blurted. "There's sure to be people coming from as far away as Houston looking for that money. Might as well be somebody right here in town who finds it."

"The money was destroyed in the fire," Gracie said.

"Maybe. But maybe Silas Chisholm just did a damn fine job of hiding it."

"Silas Chisholm wasn't that smart," Jesse growled. "There is no money."

"But—"

"If I catch you trespassing out here again, I'll press charges."

"We're only kids." Troy tried to shrink away. "The cops won't do anything but call our parents."

"Maybe," Gracie added. "But maybe the D.A. will be so outraged when I tell her that you led me to believe you were holding a real gun on me that she'll want to try you both as adults."

"They don't do that."

"Heard it happened over in Magnolia just last week," Jesse

offered. "You boys should get at least five to ten for armed assault of a city official."

"Five to ten *years?*" Lonnie looked ready to throw up.

"At the very least," Jesse added. "But I'd bet on an even stiffer sentence since there's an eyewitness—yours truly—who saw you threaten the mayor and hold a gun on her."

"I'm not actually the mayor." The words were out before Gracie could stop them. "I mean, I practically am, but it's not official. Not yet."

Jesse gave her a "too much info" look. "She won by a landslide," Jesse growled in Troy's ear. "She's practically the mayor and you boys are both screwed."

"Please, Mr. Chisholm," Lonnie pleaded. "I can't go to prison. My grandma Lou will kill me."

"I know your grandma. She's a sweet lady. What about you?" Jesse eyed Troy. "How do you think your folks will react?"

"They won't." Troy shrugged. "My daddy don't give a shit. He's drunk most of the time since my ma died."

Gracie didn't miss the strange glimmer in Jesse's eyes before his expression hardened into an unreadable mask. He loosened his grip on both boys. "Go. Get on home. Both of you."

Lonnie's eyes widened. "You're letting us off?"

"Hardly." He pointed a finger. "I want you both at the rodeo arena first thing after school tomorrow."

"For what?"

"To work off the cost of repairing that fence you just cut." Jesse motioned to his left at the barbed wire that hung open.

"Yes, sir," Lonnie said, snatching up the discarded shovel that lay nearby. "I'll be there. We both will. Ain't that right, Troy?"

"What if we don't show?" Troy eyed Jesse as if trying to gauge just what he could get away with.

"Then I'll file an official complaint with the sheriff and he'll arrest you." Sirens stirred in the background and Gracie knew that Deputy Walker was on his way. Both boys stiffened.

"Come on, Troy," Lonnie pressed. "Just take the deal. Please."

"Okay," Troy grumbled. "But I ain't picking up no horse crap."

"Of course you're not." Jesse grinned. "We don't pick it up. We use a shovel." His expression faded into one of serious intent. "And trust me, I've got plenty of shovels." Troy stiffened and Gracie didn't miss the grin that played at Jesse's lips. She watched as he forced a frown and glanced from one boy to the other. "Now get lost before I change my mind."

The two boys scattered toward the cut fence and disappeared on the other side just as a beige squad car pulled up to the curb.

"Are you okay?" Jesse's gaze collided with hers and if she hadn't known better, she would have sworn she saw concern.

But this was Jesse James Chisholm. Wild. Reckless. Carefree. He didn't give a shit about anyone. That was why she'd been so drawn to him all those years ago. He'd been a kindred spirit. Just as wild as she'd been. As reckless. As carefree.

If only she could remember that when he looked at her.

"That was a really nice thing you did," she told him. "Giving those boys a chance."

"Shoveling isn't a chance. It's hard work. Trust me, they'll be begging for me to file charges before I'm through with them." That was what he said, but she didn't miss the softness in his eyes. While he played the same "I don't give a shit" Jesse he'd been way back when, something had changed. He'd changed.

Even if he didn't seem as if he wanted to admit it.

A rush of warmth went through her that had nothing to do with the fierce attraction between them and everything to do with the fact that she admired him almost as much as she lusted after him.

Before she could dwell on the unsettling thought, she turned her attention to the deputy who rushed up, gun drawn, gaze scouring the landscape.

"I came as soon as I got the call," he said in between huge gulps of air. "I was right in the middle of Wednesday-night bowling. Just threw a strike." He drank in a few more drafts of air. "So where are they? Where are the perpetrators?"

"False alarm, Dan."

"But I ran two blocks just to get to the squad car on account of mine is in the shop and my wife dropped me off at the bowling alley."

"Sorry."

"But you said we had trespassers. Two of them."

"They turned out to be just a couple of kids taking a shortcut on their way home," Jesse added. "No harm, no foul."

Dan glanced around a few more seconds before shoving his gun back in his holster. "Doggone it. I shoulda known it was too early for any real excitement. That TV show doesn't air until next week. It'll be the usual snoozefest until then."

"Not true. It's bingo night at the Ladies' Auxiliary tomorrow night. That should mean at least three catfights and maybe even an incarceration," Gracie reminded him.

"Stop trying to cheer me up. You need a ride home?"

"I've got my car but thanks."

"You folks take care, then." The deputy turned. "If I hurry, I should be able to get back before the game is over. Not that I'll win now, on account of I missed my turn...."

"So?" Jesse eyed her when Dan walked away. His gaze darkened and the temperature seemed to kick up a few degrees.

Every nerve in her body went on high alert because she knew something was about to happen between them. She knew and she couldn't make herself walk away. "So what?" she managed, her lips trembling.

"Are you going to finish what you started with that kiss or not?"

8

"I DISTINCTLY REMEMBER *you* kissed *me*."

A grin tugged at his lips, but the expression didn't quite touch the depths of his eyes, which were a deep, mesmerizing violet. "Then are you going to finish what I started?"

Yes. No. Maybe.

The answers raced through her mind and her heartbeat kicked up a notch. "I don't know what you mean," she said, despite the fact that she knew. She knew because she knew him. The wicked gleam in his eyes. The heat rolling off his body.

Even more, she knew herself. The bad girl buried deep inside who urged her to take the initiative and make the first move. And the second. And the third.

She swallowed against the sudden lump in her throat and tried to get a grip. "I think you're misreading the situation."

"You want me and I want you." He stared deep into her eyes. "We should do something about it."

"Not happening," she blurted, despite the *yeah, baby* echoing through her. "I'm the mayor."

"Soon-to-be mayor."

"I can't just go around hopping into bed with every cowboy

who propositions me. I mean, yes, I liked the kiss, but that's beside the point. We're all wrong for each other."

"You say that like it matters."

"It does."

Pure sin teased the corner of his sensual lips. "I don't want to date you, Gracie." His gaze collided with hers. "I want to have sex with you."

She wasn't sure why his words sent a wave of disappointment through her. It wasn't as if she *wanted* to date him. Sure, he'd changed from the wild, careless boy he'd once been, but he was still Jesse James Chisholm. Still off-limits. Still temporary.

And Gracie had sworn off temporary when she'd turned her life around.

"It's obvious there's something between us," he murmured, his deep voice vibrating along her nerve endings. "Something fierce."

"I think—"

"That's the problem," he cut in. "You do too much thinking. You ought to start feeling again. You might like it."

Before she could respond, he pressed a key card into her hand, kissed her roughly on the lips and walked to his truck.

The engine grumbled, the taillights flashed and just like that, he was gone.

She stared at the plastic card burning into her hand. The Lost Gun Motel. It was the only one in town. Right on Main Street, next to the diner, the parking lot in full view of anyone who happened by.

Not that she was thinking about taking him up on his offer. Having sex with Jesse Chisholm would be the worst idea ever.

Because?

Because they were polar opposites. He was wild and exciting and she wasn't. At least she was doing her damnedest to prove that she wasn't.

And that was the problem in a nutshell. Jesse called to the bad girl inside of her. He made her want to forget the past twelve years of walking the straight and narrow. Forget the pain of losing her brother. Forget the promise she'd made to Charlie.

To herself.

Not happening. She had an image to uphold. A reputation to protect. She was the mayor, for heaven's sake.

Sort of.

She hadn't actually taken the oath.

Anxiety rushed through her as she climbed into her car and started for home. As committed as she was to the path she'd chosen, she couldn't help but feel as if she'd missed out on something.

On life.

On lust.

Forget the slutty college years. She'd spent hers taking extra classes at the university so that she could graduate early and earn an apprenticeship with the city planner's office. She'd missed out on so much. That was why she was feeling so much anxiety about the upcoming inauguration. Once she took her oath, her life would be set, the commitment made, her chance lost.

She wanted one more night with Jesse. One more memory. Then she could stop fantasizing and go back to her nice conservative life and step up as the town's new mayor without any worries or regrets.

She *would.*

But not just yet.

She slammed on the brakes, swung the car around and headed for the motel.

"Okay," she blurted ten minutes later when Jesse opened the motel door to find her standing on his doorstep. "Let's do it."

And then *she* reached out and kissed *him.*

THE MOMENT GRACIE touched her lips to his, Jesse felt a wave of heat roll through him. The real thing was even better than he remembered. She felt warmer. Smelled sweeter. Tasted even more decadent.

Her tongue tangled with his and she slid her arms around his neck. Her small fingers played in his hair. Heat shimmered down his spine from the point of contact.

His gut tightened and his body throbbed. He steered her around, backed her up into the hotel room and kicked the door shut with his boot. Pulling her blouse free of her skirt, he shoved his hands beneath the soft material. She was warm and soft and oh so addictive against the rough pads of his fingertips. His body trembled with need and he urged her toward the bed.

He shoved aside the duffel bag sitting on top and guided her down. He pulled back, his hands going to the button on his jeans. He made quick work of them, shoving the denim down his legs so fast that it was a wonder he didn't fall and bust his ass. He'd spent so many nights fantasizing about her and now she was real.

Warm.

Soft.

A passing spray of headlights spilled through the windows and she seemed to stiffen. As if she feared someone would bust through the door any moment and see them together. Because as much as she wanted him, she still had her doubts. Her fears.

Jesse fought for his control and steeled himself against the delicious heat coming off her body. He could wipe away the doubt if he wanted to. All he had to do was speed up and push things along as fast and as furious as the heat that zipped up and down his spine. She would be so mindless that she wouldn't care if they were standing on the fifty-yard line of the local football stadium at half-time.

But he didn't want her mindless. He wanted her on the offensive. He wanted her to want this despite the consequences.

He wanted her to want him with the same passion she'd felt so long ago.

That meant slowing down and giving her the chance to think about what was happening, to feel each and every moment, to forget her fear and give in to the heat that raged between them.

He closed his hands over her shoulders and steered her down

onto the mattress. His fingers caressed the soft material of her blouse, molding the silk to her full breasts.

Easy, slick. Just take it easy.

The warning echoed in his head and he managed to move his hands away before he could stroke her perfectly outlined nipples.

He would. But not just yet.

He scooted down to pull off her heels and toss them to the floor. One hand lingered at her ankle and he couldn't help himself. He traced the curve of her calf up to her knee and smiled as he heard her breath catch. Then his fingers went to the button on her skirt. His heart pounded and his pulse raced and an ache gripped him from the inside out. He stiffened, fighting the lust that roared inside of him.

Easy...

He grabbed the waistband and helped her ease the navy material down her hips, her legs, revealing a pair of black lace panties that betrayed the prim-and-proper image she fought so hard to maintain.

He knew then that there was still a little of the old Gracie deep inside and his heartbeat kicked up a notch.

His fingertips brushed her bare skin, grazing and stirring the length of her legs as he worked the skirt free. The friction ripped through him, testing his control with each delicious inch.

Finally he reached her ankles. He stood near the foot of the bed and pulled the skirt completely off.

His gaze traveled from her calves up her lush thighs to the wispy lace barely covering the soft strip of silk between her legs. He grew harder, hotter, and anticipation zipped up and down his spine.

He swallowed, his mouth suddenly dry. With a sweep of his tongue he licked his lips. The urge to feel her pressed against his mouth nearly sent him over the edge. He wanted to part her with his tongue and taste her sweetness.

Need pounded, steady and demanding through his body, and sent the blood jolting through his veins at an alarming rate.

He dropped to the bed beside her and reached out. His fingers brushed the velvet of one hip and that was all it took. Suddenly his hands seemed to move of their own accord, skimming the length of her body to explore every curve, every dip. He lingered at the lace covering her moist heat and traced the pattern with his fingertip. He moved lower, feeling the pouty slit between her legs.

She gasped and her legs fell open.

He followed the scrap of lace, his fingertip brushing the sensitive flesh on either side. The urge to dip his finger beneath the scant covering and plunge deep into her lush body almost undid him.

Almost.

But he wouldn't.

Because it wasn't about what he wanted. It was all about her at that particular moment. About convincing her that this was right. That *he* was right.

About making sure that this moment exceeded her expectations and made it impossible for her to turn her back on him again.

Jesse forced his hand up over her flat belly. Her soft flesh quivered beneath his palm as he moved higher, pushing her blouse aside until he uncovered one creamy breast.

His fingertips circled the rose-colored nipple, and he inhaled sharply when the already turgid peak ripened ever more. Leaning over, he touched his lips to her navel, dipped his tongue inside and swirled. She whimpered, the sound urging him on. He licked a path up her fragrant skin, teased and nibbled, until he reached one full breast. He drew the swollen tip deep into his mouth and suckled her.

He swept his hands downward, cupping her heat through the scanty V of her panties. Wisps of silky hair brushed his palm like licks of fire and his groin throbbed.

She gasped and then it was as if the floodgates opened. She

grabbed his hand and guided him closer. Her pelvis lifted, coming up off the bed, searching, begging for his touch.

The sound of a car door outside pushed past the frantic beat of his heart and he noted the flash of headlights that spilled around the edges of the blinds.

"The door's unlocked," he pointed out.

"So?" she breathed and he knew she was beyond caring at the moment.

Satisfaction rolled through him, followed by a punch of lust as he slid a finger deep inside her warm, sweet body. And then he started to pleasure her.

9

GRACIE STARED UP at the man looming over her. His finger plunged deep and she closed her eyes for a long moment before he withdrew. Her eyelids fluttered open in time to feel him part her just a fraction before tracing her moist slit. He knew just how to turn her on.

He knew her.

Her heart.

Her soul.

Her.

Hardly.

If he'd been the least bit clued in to the real Gracie Stone, the one who wore sweats and ate healthy snacks and watched late-night reality TV, he would have dropped her just like that. That was who she was now. She was nothing like the wild and wicked girl who'd climbed into the bed of his pickup truck way back when.

Even if she had done something only a bona fide bad girl would do—she'd chased him down and now they were going at it.

Still…he'd been the one to issue the proposition, to make the first move.

She held tight to the notion. But then he pushed a finger deep inside and all thought fled.

She gasped, her lips parting, her eyes drifting closed at the intimate caress.

"Open your eyes," Jesse demanded, his voice raw with lust. "Look at me."

Gracie obeyed and he caught her gaze. He slipped another finger inside her.

Her legs turned to butter. Her knees fell open, giving him better access. But he didn't go deeper and give her more of what she wanted. Instead, he stared down at her, his gaze so compelling that she couldn't help herself. She arched her hips shamelessly, rising up to meet him, drawing him in.

The more she moved, the deeper he went. The pressure built.

"That's it, sugar. Just go with it."

She continued to move from side to side, creating the most delicious friction, her insides slick, sweltering from his invasion. She tried to breathe, to pull oxygen into her lungs, but she couldn't seem to get enough. Pleasure rippled from her head to her toes, and the room seemed to spin around her. Her hips rotated. Her nerves buzzed.

Incredible.

That was what this was.

What *he* was.

Her head fell back. Her lips parted. A low moan rumbled up her throat and spilled past her lips.

He leaned down and caught the sound with his mouth. His hand fell away from her as he thrust his tongue deep, mimicking the careful attention his purposeful fingers had given her only seconds before.

Straddling her, his knees trapped her thighs. He leaned back to gaze down at her.

She touched his bare chest, felt the wisps of dark silky hair beneath her palm, the ripple of hard, lean muscle as he sucked in a deep breath. Her attention shifted lower and she grasped him, trailing her hand up and down his hard, throbbing shaft. His flesh pulsed in her palm and a shiver danced up her spine. She wanted to feel him. She wanted it more than she'd ever wanted anything.

He thrust into her grip as she worked him for several long moments before he caught her wrist and forced her hand away.

And then he touched her.

His hands started on her rib cage, sliding over her skin, learning every nuance. He touched her anywhere, everywhere, as if he couldn't get enough of her. As if he wanted to burn the memory of her into his head because he knew they would have only this one night.

That was it. She knew it and so did he.

If only the truth didn't bother her so much.

Before she could dwell on that fact, he lowered his head and drew her nipple into the moist heat of his mouth. Suddenly the only thing on her mind was touching him. She slid her hands over his shoulders, feeling his warm skin and hard muscle, memorizing every bulge, every ripple.

He suckled her breast, his teeth grazing the soft skin, nipping and biting with just enough pressure to make her gasp. Her breast swelled and throbbed.

Jesse licked a path across her skin to coax the other breast in the same torturous manner. A decadent heat spiraled through her and she rubbed her pelvis against him.

"Please." She wanted him, surrounding her, inside of her.

"Not yet," he murmured. He slid down her slick body and left a blazing path with the teasing tip of his tongue. Strong, purposeful hands parted her thighs. Almost reverently, he stroked her quivering sex. "I've thought about doing this so many times. I never had the chance that first night."

Their only night.

They'd both been so crazy with excitement that it had been fast and furious, and pretty fantastic.

But this… This went way beyond that night.

The breath rushed from her lungs when she felt his damp mouth against the inside of one thigh. Then his lips danced across her skin to the part of her that burned the fiercest.

She gasped as his tongue parted her. He eased his hands under her buttocks, tilting her to fit more firmly against his mouth. His shoulders urged her legs apart until she lay completely open. He nuzzled her, drinking in her scent before he devoured her with his mouth. Every thrust of his tongue, every caress of his lips, felt like a raw act of possession. Complete. Powerful.

Mine.

As soon as the thought pushed its way into her head, she pushed it right back out. There was no hidden meaning behind his actions. It was all about pleasure. About instant gratification. Sex.

His fingers parted her slick folds and his tongue swept her. Up and down. Back and forth. This way and that.

Heat drenched her. She bucked and her body convulsed. A rush of moisture flooded between her thighs, and he lapped at her as if he'd never tasted anything so sweet.

When she calmed to a slight shudder, he left her on the bed to rummage in his pocket for a condom. A few seconds later he slid the latex down his rigid penis and followed her down onto the mattress. Pulling her close, he kissed her long and slow and deep. She tasted her own essence—wild and ripe, bitter and sweet—on his lips. Desire spurted through her. Her blood pounded. Her insides tensed and she clutched at his shoulders.

He wedged a thigh between her legs and positioned himself. Thrusting, he joined them in one swift complete motion. The air rushed from her lungs and she gasped.

He pulsed deep inside of her for a long decadent moment before he started to move. He withdrew, only to push back inside, burying himself deep.

Over and over and over.

She skimmed her hands along his back, wanting him harder and faster, racing toward the bubbling heat of another climax. She clutched at his shoulders. She cried out his name.

He buried himself one last time deep in her body and went rigid. A groan rumbled from his throat as he gave in to his own release. He stiffened, bucking once, twice, before collapsing atop her. He nuzzled her neck, his lips warm against her frantic pulse beat.

She cupped his cheek and felt the roughness of his skin. The faint hint of stubble tickled her palm and she had the sudden thought that this—this closeness—felt almost as good as everything leading up to it.

The notion sent a rush of panic through her because tonight wasn't about getting close to Jesse. She'd had that once before and it had been even more addictive than the most decadent brownie. No, this was all about sex. About hooking up with him this one last time and building another sweet memory to add to her store before she took the oath and said goodbye to her past once and for all.

Mission accomplished.

She barely resisted the urge to wrap her arms around his neck and kiss him again. Instead, she slid out from under him and started snatching up her clothes.

He leaned up on one elbow and eyed her. "What the hell are you doing?"

"Leaving. I need to be up early in the morning. Really early."

"Gracie—"

"That was nice." Nice? "I mean, great. Really great. Thanks," she blurted for lack of anything better to say.

And then she headed for the door before she gave in to the wild woman inside who urged her to turn around and jump his bones again.

And again.

And *again.*

She wanted to. She wanted it so bad that it scared her and so she moved faster, shrugging on her skirt and blouse in record time and stepping into her shoes.

It wasn't until she heard the voices from the walkway outside that she slowed down. Her hand stalled on the doorknob.

"This has to be the room. The maid said so."

"Knock, then, and we'll find out."

The wood rattled against her grip and Gracie jumped. Jesse was on his feet in that next instant. He peered past the edge of the drapes, a tight expression etching his face.

"Who is it?" Her voice was a breathless whisper.

"A couple of guys I've never seen before," he told her. "One of them has a camera."

"Reporters," she murmured. "Trina said there were a few checking in today." Her gaze locked with his. "What am I going to do?"

A dark look carved his face for a long moment, but then his expression softened. "Wait a sec." He grabbed his jeans and pulled them on just as another knock sounded. A third knock and he reached for the doorknob. "I'll distract them and you can slip out." He pressed his lips roughly to hers, urged her back behind the door and then hauled it open.

"What the hell, dude?" He glared at the two men before stepping outside. "I'm trying to sleep." The door closed behind him.

"We just have a few questions—"

"That you can damned well ask at a decent hour. I'm filing a complaint with management."

She peeked past the edge of the drapes in time to see Jesse start down the walkway and disappear inside the motel lobby a few doors down. The reporters trailed after him, snapping a few pictures along the way. In a matter of seconds, they'd piled inside after him, their attention fixated on Silas Chisholm's oldest son, and the coast was clear.

Gracie drew a deep, calming breath, but it didn't help. Her heart still pounded, her blood rushed and her nerves buzzed, and none of it had anything to do with the fact that she'd almost been caught red-handed by the press. She was worked up because, despite the damage it might do to her reputation, she wanted to rip off her clothes and hop back into bed to wait for another round of hot, mind-blowing sex.

Jesse was dangerous to her peace of mind because he made her forget all about what she *should* do and reminded her of what she *wanted* to do.

Of the girl she'd been so long ago and how she'd lusted after him with a passion she hadn't felt in the twelve years since.

A passion she would never feel again after tonight.

She ignored the depressing thought and held tight to the fact that she'd yet to start her acceptance speech and she still needed to come up with a strategy to get past Big Earl's dogs.

She drew a deep breath, pulled open the door and did a quick check to make sure the coast was still clear. And then she made a beeline for her car parked several spaces down.

Climbing behind the wheel, she gave one last look at the main lobby, hoping to catch a glimpse of Jesse through the glass doors. Instead, she saw Hazel Trevino, the motel's manager, gesturing wildly while on the phone and she knew the woman was calling the police to report the disruptive reporters.

Which meant Deputy Walker would be responding any second and the last thing Gracie needed was to be seen sitting outside the local motel, her hair mussed, her lips swollen, her cheeks pink.

Talk about fuel for gossip.

She fought down a wave of regret, shoved the key into the ignition and headed home.

"SHOW'S OVER, FOLKS." Deputy Walker waved a hand at the small crowd gathered in front of the check-in desk in the motel lobby. "You two, get out." He motioned to the reporters.

"But we're staying here."

"Then get back to your rooms and leave everyone alone."

"But we just have a few questions—"

"Which you'll be asking from jail if you don't get going right now." Deputy Walker pulled open the door and motioned the two men outside. "I'll see you back to your rooms myself."

"Sorry about that, Mr. Chisholm." Hazel Trevino was in her late forties with black eyes to match her dark hair. "Hope you won't hold the disturbance against us. We usually run a nice quiet place here. But with all the hoopla about this whole *Famous Texas Outlaws* episode, I guess it's to be expected."

"It's not your fault."

"It's not yours, either." Hazel smiled. "I know how folks treat you around here, but you ain't your pa. Some of us are smart enough to know that."

"Thanks, Miss Hazel."

"None necessary. You'd think folks could just let sleeping dogs lie."

"Not when they think money is involved."

Her eyes took on an eager light. "You really think all that money went up in flames?"

Jesse shrugged. "If not, someone would have surely found it by now."

"Probably. We had more than our share of treasure hunters the first time it aired. Why, I remember watching it on TV. Wilbur and I had just got married. Even thought about looking for the cash ourselves. Would have made a nice little nest egg to raise our boys, but then his daddy passed and left us this place and just like that, we had our hands full."

"It's a nice place."

"Lord knows we try to run a tight ship." She reached into a drawer. "I hope you won't let tonight spoil your visit. Here's a free voucher for the Rusty Pig. Your next plate of barbecue ribs is on us."

He nodded at the motel manager and headed back to his room. A wave of disappointment swept through him when he walked inside to find the room empty. Not that he'd expected Gracie to wait for him. The whole point of throwing himself to the wolves had been to give her a chance to escape.

Still, a part of him had held out a tiny sliver of hope. The part of him that had longed to fit in all those years ago. To belong to a town that had never given him the time of day, to befriend the very people who'd turned their backs on him.

Which was most people.

There were a few, like Pete and Hazel, who'd refused to hold him accountable for someone else's sins. They'd always treated him decent.

But Jesse had wanted more.

He'd wanted to walk into church every Sunday without half the congregation staring at him as if he'd forgotten to wipe his boots. He'd wanted to walk down Main Street without people whispering behind his back. He'd wanted to spread out a blanket at the town picnic and share a slice of apple pie with Gracie Stone in front of God and the Ladies' Auxiliary.

He'd wanted to fit in.

Like hell. Fitting in was just a pipe dream he'd come to terms with a long, long time ago. He never would and that was okay. *He* was okay. Healthy. Successful. Happy.

He didn't give a shit what anyone thought.

But she did, and damned if that didn't bother him even more than when he'd been the one eager to fit into a town that had long ago locked him out.

He fought down the feelings and debated climbing back into bed and trying for some shut-eye. That was what he would have done after a pretty incredible sexual encounter. What he needed to do right now. He had a busy day tomorrow. He had two more bulls to sell and then he needed to get the rest of his stock shipped off to Austin, and he needed to make plans for the bachelor party.

He didn't need to feel so on edge, his muscles tight, his mind racing. As if he still sat poised at the starting gate rather than at the top of the scoreboard after a wildly successful ride.

Crazy.

The whole point of sleeping with Gracie was to give him some relief. So that he could stop thinking about her. Stop wanting her. Stop fantasizing.

Stop!

He snatched up his keys and his gaze snagged on a scrap of black lace peeking from between the sheets. He leaned down and scooped up the forgotten lingerie. His fingers tightened as a detailed memory of the past few hours washed over him. Her body pressed to his, her hands touching him, her voice whispering through his head, each syllable softened with that honey-sweet drawl that had haunted his dreams too many times to count. She tried so hard to hide her passionate nature, but it was there, bubbling just below the surface, waiting for the chance to fire up and boil over.

She hadn't even come close tonight.

Sure, she'd exploded in his arms, but he couldn't shake the feeling that she'd still been holding back.

Below the surface, she'd still been controlled. Restrained. Caged.

Shoving the undies in his pocket, he grabbed a shirt and his keys. A few minutes later he left the motel behind and headed out to the rodeo arena for the kind of ride that could actually tire him out.

Otherwise it was going to be one hell of a long night.

IT WAS THE longest night of Gracie Stone's life.

She came to that conclusion several hours later as she tossed and turned and tried to forget Jesse and the all-important fact that she'd had *the* best orgasm of her life.

She'd known it would be great. That had been the point of going to his motel room in the first place. To experience a little greatness before she doomed herself to the monotony of small-town politics.

At the same time, she'd sort of secretly hoped that it might be disastrous so that maybe, just maybe, she would want to forget it. Him. The two of them.

Fat chance.

Instead of putting tonight behind her, she kept thinking how great it would be to head back over to the motel and do it again. And again.

Not that she would ever do such a thing. Instead, she was doing anything—everything—to keep her mind off of him and her hands away from the car keys.

She answered email and cleaned out her refrigerator and watched three back-to-back *Bridezillas* reruns on cable and even checked her voice mail. Three messages from Trina detailing tomorrow's schedule and one from her sister.

"I just wanted to give you a heads-up." Charlie's voice carried over the line. "I've got study sessions on Friday and Saturday for my economics test on Monday. So I won't be able to make it down this weekend. Call you later." *Beep.*

"So much for homemade pizzas," she told Sugar Lips, who wagged her tail frantically before racing for the back door. That made four weeks in a row that Charlie hadn't been able to make it home.

Not that Gracie was counting.

In the two years since her sister had gone away to school, she'd seen her less and less. Which was a good thing. It meant Charlie was growing up, becoming independent, relying on herself instead of clinging to Gracie.

At the same time, she couldn't help but feel a little lonely because Charlie was the one making the break, pulling away, getting out of Lost Gun. Meanwhile, Gracie was stuck here. That was the promise she'd made to her sister and she intended to keep it regardless of what direction Charlie took with her life. She wanted her sister to have a home base. A place to come back to when life kicked her a little too hard.

She wanted Charlie to have the home Gracie herself had never had.

She finished listening to one more message from Trina reminding her about a meeting with the local library committee and then headed to the kitchen for a chocolate cupcake.

Okay, so it wasn't a cupcake.

If only she'd had a cupcake or a cookie or a candy bar, then maybe, just maybe, she wouldn't feel so deprived.

Instead, she scarfed a handful of Wheat Thins and then went after a glass of ice water. Her hands trembled as she turned on the faucet and her gaze shifted to Sugar, who sat nearby, her ragged stuffed animal beneath her. The maltipom wrestled for a few seconds with the worn toy before whimpering when she couldn't seem to get it beneath her for a little humping action.

"I know the feeling." She downed half the glass, but it did nothing to ease the heat swamping her from the inside out.

She still felt nervous.

Frazzled.

Disappointed.

She ignored the last thought and took another drink. Disappointed? Because Jesse hadn't come running after her? Begging her for round two?

A one-night stand, she reminded herself. That was all tonight had been. All it could ever be, because Gracie had an image to protect. She was a leader now. A role model.

She'd made a promise to the town.

Just as she'd made a promise to her sister to be there when Charlie needed her.

Even if Charlie didn't seem to need her all that much anymore.

She ditched the thought along with the glass of water and headed back upstairs. She bypassed the bedroom and headed straight for the bathroom. Since a glass of ice water had failed to cool her down, maybe a cold shower would do the trick.

Hopefully.

Because the last thing, the very last thing, Gracie intended to do was to climb back into her car and head back over to Jesse's motel room.

No matter how much she suddenly wanted to.

10

"I KNEW YOU still had it in you," Trina declared when Gracie walked into City Hall a half hour late the next morning.

After an endless night spent tossing and turning and trying to forget all about Jesse Chisholm. "What are you talking about?"

"You and a certain PBR champion."

"How did you find out?" She had the sudden vision of her and Jesse spread across the front page of *Lost Gun Weekly,* all the important body parts blacked out to preserve the newspaper's reputation.

But still…

She fought down a sliver of excitement and held tight to the fear coiling inside her. "The newspaper?"

"I admit that you gallivanting with anyone is definitely worthy of front-page treatment, but no. Kathy Mulcany heard it from Laura Lou Spencer, who heard it from Mitchell Presley, who said he was just hanging out watching the domino game with the Amberjack twins when he saw you and Jesse in front of Sarah's Sweets."

"The bakery? That's what the 'attagirl' was all about?"

"I'll admit I would rather hear that you were getting a little action instead of talking, but a girl has to start somewhere, I s'pose."

"We weren't talking. I mean, we were, but not in a social capacity. Trespassers," Gracie blurted. "He was worried about trespassers and I told him I would have the sheriff keep an eye on his place."

"So he didn't invite you out?"

"Of course not."

"And you didn't invite him out?"

"No." Technically she'd invited him *in.* A wave of heat swept through her and she cleared her suddenly dry throat. "Are the, um, painters here yet?"

"They're taping up edges right now." She eyed the cupcake sitting on her desk. "Look what the church ladies dropped off. There were six, but I didn't have time for breakfast so I scarfed down a few and gave the receptionist next door some. I guess I'll just save this one for later since you're always on a diet—"

"I'll take it." She snatched the vanilla goody out of Trina's hand.

"Really?"

Yeah, really?

"Picking out paint colors can be taxing work." That and she'd worked up an appetite last night that she'd yet to satisfy, particularly after two pieces of whole wheat toast and a grapefruit for breakfast.

She needed carbs in the worst way.

That or another night with Jesse.

Since option number two was out of the question, she would have to settle for second best. Besides, it was just one teeny tiny cupcake.

"I'd be happy to get you a bran muffin." Trina eyed her. "I know how you hate to cheat."

"That's okay, I don't mind cheating a little. Besides, maybe they're sugar-free. With whole wheat flour and egg substitute.

I heard Myrtle Nell is experimenting with some new Weight Watchers recipes. This is probably the result."

"It's not," Trina said, snatching the cake out of her hand. "Trust me, I've had three. There's nothing weight conscious about it." She set the vanilla confection on the far side of her desk. "I'll get you a bran muffin."

Gracie thought about arguing, but Trina was already looking at her as if she'd grown a third eye. She swallowed against the rising hunger and focused on the stack of papers on the edge of her assistant's desk. "So what's on the agenda for today?" She rifled through the papers. "A city council meeting? A water commission hearing?"

Trina plucked the papers from her hands and returned them to their spot. "The Senior Ladies expect you for their weekly breakfast in the morning, and then there's the middle school car wash. Then there's the Daughters of the Republic of Texas bake sale. It's at three o'clock on Thursday. The local kindergarten is also having their fundraiser on Thursday afternoon. I've also got you scheduled to lead the Pledge of Allegiance at the quilting circle on Friday morning. In the meantime, when you're not playing the goodwill ambassador—" Trina smiled and motioned to the open doorway "—you get to redecorate your new office."

Forget getting out and about today to distract herself. She was going to be cooped up all afternoon in her shell of an office. With nothing but flooring samples and furniture catalogs and her own damnable thoughts. Gracie swallowed again. "Now I *really* need a cupcake."

"YOUR CONCENTRATION'S for shit," Eli told Jesse when he finally managed to catch his breath after taking a nosedive off the back of an ornery bull.

"Stop giving me grief and help me back up, old man." It was early in the afternoon and his fifth time in the dust in as many hours.

Eli held out a hand. "I think you've had your butt beat enough for one day. Yesterday I could understand. You had that pretty young thing to catch your eye. But today?"

Today was worse. Yesterday Gracie had just snagged his eye. Today she was under his skin, in his head.

Why, he couldn't rightly say.

Last night had gone just like any other night with any other woman. They'd gotten down to business and then bam, she'd walked away. No talking or cuddling or sleeping over.

That fact bothered him a helluva lot more than it should have considering he'd gone into last night knowing full well where he stood.

Sex.

That was all he'd been interested in. That was all she'd been interested in.

At the same time, he couldn't forget the way she'd pressed her lips against the side of his throat and hesitated. As if leaving wasn't as easy as she'd thought.

The possibility had eased the throbbing in his shoulders enough so he could close his eyes. Or maybe it had been the swig of whiskey he'd downed the minute he'd walked back into the empty room after causing enough of a distraction for her to slip out unnoticed.

To preserve his own reputation.

That was what he told himself. The last thing he needed was the two of them all over the local paper. The *Weekly* would have them committed and married within a few paragraphs and his image as rodeo's hottest bad boy would be blown to hell and back.

He surely hadn't done it because she'd looked so petrified that he'd wanted—no, *needed*—to do something to ease the fear.

So he'd waltzed out of the room for a run-in with a duo from a local news network out of Austin and given her a way out.

"...if you don't start paying attention, you're going to split your head open."

He ignored the disappointment churning inside him and focused on Eli and the brand-new bull kicking and spitting across the arena.

Shitkicker had been delivered first thing that morning from a breeder out of California. He would have had the bull shipped straight to Austin, but the breeder had been ahead of schedule and so he'd arrived in Lost Gun instead. A descendant of two of the most notorious rodeo bulls to ever buck a rider, Kicker was two thousand pounds of pure whup-ass and had cost him a load of money. Well spent, of course. Jesse hadn't gotten to be the best by training halfway. He went all out in the practice arena, just the way he went all out during any ride.

Because every ride meant something.

Every time he climbed onto the back of a bull, he was one step closer to the next championship.

Another step away from the scared, angry kid he'd been way back when.

He focused on dusting off and heading back to the bull pen, where Troy and Lonnie, the trespassing duo from the night before, were busy shoveling manure. And complaining every step of the way.

"Let me use the shovel and you hold the bucket."

"I'm on shovel duty for at least fifteen minutes. Stop bellyaching and just hold the bucket steady."

Shit plopped over the side and both boys cursed.

Jesse would have smiled, except he didn't feel much like smiling. He drank in a deep draft of hay and manure, but instead of smelling either, he smelled Gracie. The clean scent of her skin. The strawberry sweetness of her hair. The ripe, decadent aroma of her sex.

Gracie had been there for so long in his memories, taunting and teasing and tempting him. One brief encounter wouldn't be nearly enough to get her out of his system. He needed to overindulge, to satisfy himself over and over until he was sick of her. Gracie was like that overflowing basket of cherries. One night with her wouldn't be enough to make him swear off her completely.

He needed more.

A lot more.

He bypassed the boys and pushed open the corral gate.

"Where you going?" Eli called after him.

"I've got business in town."

Eli chuckled. "I'll just bet."

Jesse was going after Gracie Stone, all right, and they were going to put out this fire that burned between them once and for all.

But first…

First it was going to get hot.

Very hot.

"I CAN HARDLY BREATHE," Gracie told Trina as she stood in the middle of the mess that would soon be her new office. The painters had finished two of the walls, but the rest they'd left until tomorrow. She fanned herself with a circle of paint swatches and eyed her assistant. "Is it hot in here or is it just me?"

"The electrician had to kill the power to the air conditioner unit supplying this room in order to replace the old ducts."

"That explains it."

"That and him." Trina stared past Gracie. "He definitely kicks up the body temp a few degrees."

Gracie turned to see the man who filled her open doorway. Faded jeans clung to his muscular legs. A crisp white T-shirt stretched over his hard, broad chest. Stubble shadowed his strong jaw. Her gaze collided with a pair of violet eyes, as rich and lush as crushed velvet. The air stalled in her lungs.

"If it isn't the infamous Jesse James Chisholm," Trina said. "To what do we owe the honor of this visit?"

"I've got some unfinished business with our new mayor." Jesse closed the distance between them and stopped just scant inches away.

"I'm not the mayor," Gracie heard herself say. "Not yet." Trina gave her a knowing look and she shrugged. "So, um, what can I do for you?"

"Actually, it's about what I can do for you." He grinned and pulled her black undies from his pocket. The scrap of dark lace dangled from one tanned finger. "You forgot these."

Gracie's heart stopped beating.

Trina cleared her throat. "I, um, really should get going. It's ladies' night over at the saloon and I've got to pick up my dry cleaning and get my eyebrows waxed. I always knew you had it in you," Trina murmured a split second before she hightailed it for the door. "I'll be leaving now. For good. So you'll have plenty of privacy to, um, talk, or whatever." The click of a door punctuated the sentence and then she was gone.

"We've been painting," Gracie blurted, eager to drown out the thunder of her own traitorous heart. "Sahara Tan." She eyed one of the finished walls.

"Tan, huh?" Jesse rubbed the silky material of her underwear between his two fingers in a sensual caress she felt from her head clear to the tips of her toes.

Crazy. He wasn't even close to touching her.

Not now. But last night? He'd touched. And teased. And seduced. And damned if she didn't want him to do it all over again.

Heat uncoiled in her stomach, followed by a slow burning embarrassment that washed through her. She came so close to snatching the panties from his hand, but she wasn't about to give him the satisfaction of knowing that he was right about her. That she was different now. Stiff and uptight and *good.*

"I like tan."

"Seems to me like you've got a hankering for black." He eyed the panties. "Me, too." He stuffed them into his shirt pocket and glanced around. "Tan's a little boring. I'd go with something a little bolder. Maybe yellow. Brighten the place up."

"I don't need brighter. I need reliable." Her gaze narrowed. "Is that why you stopped by? To offer decorating advice?"

"Actually—" his voice took on a softer note "—I wanted to talk to you about last night."

"There's nothing to talk about. It's over and done with."

"That's the point." His mouth crooked in the faintest grin. "It's not."

"What makes you say that?"

"Because I want you and you still want me."

"Speak for yourself."

His gaze caught and held hers. "So you haven't been thinking about me kissing you or you touching me or me sliding deep, *deep* inside?" His eyes darkened as he reached out to finger the collar of her charcoal blouse. "One night isn't enough." His fingertip dipped beneath the neck and traced her collar bone. "We need to do it again. And again. However many times it takes."

"For what?"

"For me to stop thinking about me kissing you and you touching me and me sliding deep, *deep* inside. For you to forget, too."

"What makes you think I haven't already?"

"Because your cheeks are flushed and your pulse is erratic." He pressed a fingertip to the side of her neck in a slow sweeping gesture that sent goose bumps chasing up and down her arms. "And you look a little faint."

She felt a little faint. And flushed. And completely erratic.

"You're turned on."

He was right. Despite the fact that she'd cut loose last night, she was no closer to being free of the fantasies that haunted her night after night. If anything, she was even more worked up. Desperate. Hungry.

Still…she couldn't just hop back into bed with Jesse. She was the mayor, for heaven's sake. She had a town to run. Commitments. Car washes and bake sales and quilting circles.

Okay, so she wasn't actually running anything at the moment. Not until the day of the inauguration. Then her life would officially become a series of city council meetings, park dedications and press conferences.

Ugh.

She swallowed the sudden bitterness in her mouth and focused on the man standing in front of her. For now, the only thing she *had* to do was put in a few personal appearances, which meant she had a few precious days to forget about what she needed to do and simply do what she *wanted* to do—play out the bad-girl fantasies that had been driving her crazy for the past twelve years and store enough memories to last her the rest of her boring, predictable life as mayor.

"Okay." The word was out before she could stop it. Not that she would have. She was doing this. She *wanted* to do this. Her gaze met his and a ripple of excitement went through her. "Let's do it again."

A grin played at his lips. "And again." His expression faded and there was nothing teasing about his next words. "I've got until Sunday. Pete gets hitched Saturday night and I head for Austin on Sunday morning."

And she would take her oath of office a full week after that.

She licked her lips and trembled at the anticipation that rippled through her. "So, um, when should we start? I could meet you tonight after the Little League game. I'm throwing out the opening pitch—"

"Let's go," he cut in.

"Now?"

"Unless you need to practice for that pitch?" He arched an eyebrow, a grin playing at his lips.

"It's just ceremony. Accuracy isn't a big factor."

He motioned to the window and the jacked-up black pickup that sat out front. "Then what do you say we take a little ride?"

Meaning dripped from his words and for a split second, she hesitated. There was just something about the way he looked at her—as if he'd been waiting for this moment even longer than she had—that sent a spiral of fear through her. Because the last thing she wanted was to unlock any of her old feelings for Jesse.

This wasn't about the past. It was about this moment. He

wanted her and she wanted him and once they'd satisfied that want completely, it would all be over. It was Tuesday and he was leaving Sunday. That meant they had five days.

The realization stirred a wave of anxiety as she felt the precious seconds ticking away. "Let's go."

11

THEY ENDED UP on a dusty back road that wound its way up to a steep cliff overlooking the lake. Lucky's Point had once been the hottest make-out spot back in the day. The spot, in fact, where she'd made out with Jesse James Chisholm for the very first time. Times had changed and the kids now hung out down below on the banks of Lost Gun River, and so the Point was deserted when they rolled to a stop a few feet away from the edge.

Still…this wasn't what she'd signed up for.

"I thought we were going to the motel," she said as he swung the truck around and backed up to the edge of the cliff.

"And fight our way past the reporters camped out on my doorstep?" He spared her a glance before killing the engine. "I thought you wanted to keep this low-key."

"I do. That's why I thought we'd go someplace a little more private to do the deed."

"Sugar, there's not a soul up here." He climbed out and went to lower the tailgate.

"That's not altogether true," she said as she followed him around to the back of the truck.

The sharp drop-off overlooked a spectacular view of the canyon and the rippling water. A huge bonfire blazed on the riverbank below. Ice chests were scattered here and there and dozens of teenagers milled about. Trucks lined the edge of the dirt road leading up to the gathering. Jason Aldean blasted from one of the truck radios, his rich, deep voice telling the tale of a dirt road just like the one that wound its way to the river.

"They won't bother you if you don't bother them." He winked and patted the spot on the tailgate next to him. "Climb up."

She hesitated, but then he touched her hand and she couldn't help herself. She climbed up and settled next to him.

He shifted his attention to the scene spread out before them. "It's still just as pretty as ever up here."

Her gaze followed the direction of his and she drank in the scene. A strange sense of longing went through her. It really was beautiful. Picturesque.

She dodged the thought and focused on the frantic beat of her own heart and the six feet plus of warm, hard male camped out next to her. "I'm surprised you remember." She slid him a sideways glance. "If memory serves, you didn't spend much time enjoying the view."

A grin tugged at his lips. "Oh, I enjoyed it plenty. It just didn't have much to do with the canyon."

"You were pretty fixated on one thing back then."

"Yeah." His gaze caught and held hers. "You." The word hung between them for a long moment and she had the crazy thought that he wasn't just talking about the past.

That he still felt something for her despite the fact that she'd walked away from him and ruined all their plans.

Crazy.

This was about lust and nothing else. Sex.

Thankfully.

"Thirsty?" His deep voice distracted her from the dangerous path her thoughts were taking.

She nodded. The truck rocked as he slid off the tailgate to retrieve a cooler from the cab.

She drew several deep breaths and damned herself for not

insisting he take her to a motel. At the same time, she couldn't deny that he had a point. Last night had been fast and furious and much too fleeting. Maybe they did need to take their time and ease into things. Enjoy the moment.

The notion sent a burst of excitement through her almost as fierce as what she felt when he actually touched her. Her body tingled and her nipples pebbled and heat rippled along her nerve endings.

"It's awful hot." His deep voice drew her attention as he walked back, beers in hand.

And how.

She took the bottle he offered her and held tight to the ice-cold brew. The glass was hard and cold beneath her fingertips, a welcome relief against her blazing-hot skin.

He hefted himself back onto the tailgate. Metal shifted and rocked and his thigh brushed hers. A wave of heat sizzled through her. The urge to lean over and press her lips to his hit her hard and heavy and she leaned forward. Laughter drifted from below and her blood rushed that much faster before she caught herself.

She couldn't do this in front of an audience. She wouldn't. Even if the notion didn't bother her half as much as it should have.

Because it didn't bother her.

The old Gracie would have jumped at it.

She shifted her attention away from Jesse and focused straight ahead. The sun was just setting and the sky was a spray of oranges and reds. "The view really is something. I can see why they call it Lucky's Point. I'm sure many a girl gave it up just because of the ambiance."

"Actually, this spot was named for Lucky Wellsbee. He was an outlaw back in the late 1800s. He was on the run from Texas marshals after a stagecoach robbery when they cornered him right here. Legend says he took a nosedive off the edge of this cliff and was never seen or heard from again."

"Did he drown in the river?"

"Probably. Still, they never recovered a body and so no one really knows." He shrugged and twisted the cap off his own beer. "Anyhow, that's where the name really came from." He took a swig. "Though your version is a damned sight more fun." He grinned and the expression was infectious.

She felt a smile tug at her own lips. She took a pull on her beer and stared at the scene before her, her mind completely aware of the man sitting only inches away. As anxious as she was to get down to business, there was something oddly comforting about the silence that stretched between them, around them, twining tighter, pulling them closer. As if they were old friends who'd shared this exact moment time and time again.

They had.

The thought struck and she pushed it back out. Jesse wasn't her friend. Not now. Not ever again.

Even so, a strange sense of camaraderie settled between them as they sat there for the next few moments. She sipped her beer while he downed the rest of his. One last swig and he sat the bottle between them. It toppled onto its side with a clink, and suddenly a memory made her smile.

"Remember that time we played Truth or Dare?" The question was out before she could remind herself that the past was better left alone. "It was back before we started dating. Back when we were sophomores and you barely noticed me."

"Honey, any man with eyes noticed you. You didn't exactly go out of your way *not* to get noticed."

"I *did* wear my shirts a little too tight, didn't I? And my shorts a little too short." A smile tugged at her lips. "It used to drive my aunt and uncle nuts."

"Which is exactly why you did it."

"A fat lot of good it did." She shrugged. "I did my damnedest to fight destiny, but I guess in the end, she won anyway."

"Or you let her."

"What's that supposed to mean?"

"That sometimes it's a lot less work living up to people's expectations than it is changing their minds." He gave her a pointed look. "Nothing's written in stone. Take me for instance. I could have followed in my old man's footsteps, but I didn't. I made my own destiny. You gave in to yours."

"I didn't have a choice." The words were out before she could stop them. "When my brother passed away..." Her throat tightened. "I couldn't just run off and leave my sister when she needed me most." She blinked back the sudden stinging behind her eyes. "I couldn't."

She could still remember the funeral and her brother's closed casket. Charlie had held tight, clinging to Gracie, desperate for some stability.

And that was what Gracie had given her.

"I should have told you that instead of just cutting things off between us." She wasn't sure why she said the words, except that they'd been burning inside of her for so long that she couldn't help herself. "I'm sorry about that." The memories of those first few weeks after the funeral raced through her and her heart ached at the loss. Of her brother. Her freedom. Jesse. "You deserved an explanation when I bailed on you, not the cold shoulder." She stopped there because she couldn't tell him she'd been afraid to face him, to talk to him, so fearful she would change her mind the moment she saw him because she'd been hopelessly, madly in love with him.

Then.

Because they'd had so much in common. They'd shared the same hopes and dreams. The same desperation to escape the labels of a small town.

But now? She was different, even if she did feel the same flutter in the pit of her stomach when his deep voice slid into her ears.

"It was at one of Marilyn Marshall's parties, right? That time we played Truth or Dare?"

She nodded. "The one right after the homecoming dance." A

smile played at her lips as she remembered the short red Lycra dress she'd worn that night. She'd been crazy for that dress even though her aunt and uncle had hated it, just as she'd been crazy for a certain tall, sexy boy in faded jeans, scuffed boots and a T-shirt that said Save a Horse, Ride a Cowboy. "I can still remember her making us all sit in a circle. Kevin Baxter kept landing on me and daring me to play Seven Minutes in Heaven in Marilyn's closet."

"But you didn't."

"I didn't want to go into that closet with him. I wanted to go inside with you." She shrugged. "But when it was my turn, it kept landing on the wrong person."

He eyed the bottle and his eyes gleamed with challenge. "Maybe you'll have better luck now."

Reason told her to turn him down. Cutting loose behind closed doors was one thing, but this... This was different. This was talking and reminiscing and... *No.*

She didn't need a walk down memory lane with Jesse Chisholm.

But, oh, how she wanted one.

She met his gaze and reached for the bottle. A loud *thunk, thunk, thunk* echoed as she sent the glass spinning across the tailgate. Slowly it came to a stop, the mouth pointing directly at Jesse.

"Truth or dare?" she asked him.

His eyes twinkled. "Dare."

"I dare you to kiss me."

"Whatever happened to Seven Minutes in Heaven?"

"There's no closet, so I thought I'd adjust accordingly."

"We don't need a closet for heaven, sugar. We can do it right here." No sooner had the words slipped past his lips than the truck dipped and he pushed to his feet. "Right now."

Before she could take her next breath, he stood directly in front of her, pure sin twinkling in his violet eyes.

He nudged her knees apart and stepped between her legs.

Anticipation rippled through her as he leaned close. His warm breath tickled her bottom lip and her mouth opened.

"Relax," he murmured a split second before he touched her shoulders and urged her back down. The cold metal of the truck bed met her back and reality zapped her. There was no stifling darkness to hide her excitement. No closet walls to shield her from the rest of the world.

They were outside, in full view of God and at least a dozen teenagers partying on the riverbank below.

He reached for the waistband of her skirt. He tugged her zipper down, his gaze locked with hers.

"I think a kiss would be better," Gracie blurted, her anxiety getting the best of her. Jason Aldean had faded and Luke Bryan took his place, crooning about love and lust and leaving, and her heart beat that much faster.

"Oh, I'm going to kiss you, all right." He unfastened the skirt and pushed the material up around her waist, his fingers grazing the supersensitive skin of her stomach. "Just not on the lips. Not yet."

The sultry promise chased the oxygen from her lungs as he urged her legs apart and wedged himself between her knees. His fingertips swept her calves, up the outside of her knees until his hands came to rest on her thighs.

He touched his mouth to the inside of her thigh just a few inches shy of her panties. White cotton this time with tiny pink flowers. Sensible, or so she'd thought when she'd tugged them on that morning. But damned if she didn't feel just as sexy as when she'd worn the black lace the night before.

He nibbled and licked and worked his way slowly toward the heart of her. She found herself opening her legs even wider, begging him closer.

He trailed his tongue over the thin fabric covering her wet heat and pushed the material into her slit until her flesh plumped on either side. He licked and nibbled at her until her entire body wound so tight she thought she would shatter at any moment.

She didn't.

She couldn't.

Not until she felt him, skin to skin, flush against her body. No barriers between them. That was what she really wanted despite their location.

Because of it.

Being outside filled her with a sense of freedom she hadn't felt in a long, long time.

She ignored the thought as soon as it struck and focused on the large hands gripping her panties.

She lifted her hips to accommodate him. The cotton eased down her legs and landed on the truck bed next to her.

He caught her thighs and pulled her toward the end of the tailgate until her bottom was just shy of the edge. Grabbing her ankles, he urged her knees over his shoulders.

He slid his large hands beneath her buttocks and tilted her just enough. Dipping his head, he flicked his tongue along the seam between her slick folds in a long slow lick that sucked the air from her lungs.

His tongue parted her and he lapped at her sensitive clit. He tasted and savored, his tongue stroking, plunging, driving her mindless until she came apart beneath him. A cry vibrated from her throat and mingled with the sounds drifting from below.

Her heart beat a frantic pace for the next few moments as she tried to come to terms with what had just happened.

She'd had the mother of all orgasms. An orgasm worthy of the most erotic dream.

But as satisfied as she felt, it still wasn't enough.

She opened her eyes to find him staring down at her. A fierce look gleamed in his bright violet eyes, one that said he wanted to toss her over his shoulder, tote her home and never, ever let her go.

A spurt of warmth went through her.

Followed by a rush of panic because it was all just the heat of the moment.

He *would* let her go, and then he would leave. That was why she'd agreed to this in the first place. A few days of lust and then they both walked away. She headed for City Hall and he headed for Austin.

My turn.

That was what she wanted to say, but she wouldn't. While she'd agreed to indulge her lust for him, she had no intention of unleashing the bad girl that she'd locked down deep all those years ago. Giving in to him was one thing, but turning the tables and taking charge?

Not happening.

"Stand up," he murmured, killing the push-pull of emotion inside of her and taking the decision out of her hands, and she quickly obliged.

She slid to her feet to stand in front of him. Her skirt fell back down her thighs, covering the fact that her panties still hung on the edge of his tailgate.

A fact he was all too aware of, if the tense set to his jaw was any indication.

He stood in front of her, his eyes gleaming in the growing shadows that surrounded them. His muscles bunched beneath his T-shirt. Taut lines carved his face, making him seem harsh, fierce, *hungry.*

She knew the feeling.

She swallowed against the sudden hollowness in her throat and fought to keep from reaching for the top button on her blouse. But then he murmured "Undress," and she quickly obliged.

She slid the first button free, then the next and the next, until the silky material parted. A quick shrug and the blouse slid down her shoulders, her arms, to glide from her fingertips and pool at her feet.

Her fingers went to the clasp of her bra. A quick flick and the cups sagged. The lace fell away and his breath hitched.

His gaze darkened and his nostrils flared as if he couldn't get enough oxygen.

Her lips parted as she tried to drag some much-needed air into her own lungs. Her breasts heaved and his eyes sparkled, reflecting the last few rays of sunlight.

She touched the waistband of her skirt. Trembling fingers worked at the catch until the edges finally parted. She pushed the fabric down her legs and suddenly she was completely naked. Warm summer air slithered over her skin, amping up the heat already swamping her from the inside out.

"Damn, but you're beautiful, Gracie." The words were reverent and her heart beat that much faster, drowning out the sounds coming from below until the only thing she focused on was him and the way he was looking at her and the way it made her feel.

Sexy.

Alive.

Free.

"You're not done." His deep voice sent excitement rippling down her spine.

"I don't have any clothes left."

"I do. Take them off."

She stepped forward to grasp the hem of his T-shirt. Flesh grazed flesh as she obliged him, pushing the material up his ripped abdomen, over his shoulders and head, until it fell away and joined her discarded clothes. A brief hesitation and she reached for the waistband of his jeans.

A groan rumbled from his throat as her fingertips trailed over the denim-covered bulge. She worked the zipper down, tugging and pulling until the teeth finally parted. The jeans sagged on his hips, and his erection sprang hot and pulsing into her hands.

She traced the ripe purple head before sliding her hand down his length, stroking, exploring. His dark flesh throbbed against her palm and her own body shuddered in response. She licked her lips and fought the urge to drop to her knees and taste him.

Luckily, he wasn't nearly as restrained.

He drew her to him and kissed her roughly, his tongue delving deep into her mouth over and over until the ground seemed to tilt. And then he swept her up, laid her on the tailgate of his truck and plunged deep, deep inside.

12

SHE STILL HAD her panties.

Gracie held tight to the knowledge as she slipped inside her house later that night. The steady hum of a motor out front reminded her that Jesse still hadn't pulled away yet.

Which meant she could easily forget the fact that she had to crawl out of bed before the crack of dawn in order to make it to Wednesday Waffles, the Senior Ladies' weekly gathering. She was scheduled to recite the opening Pledge of Allegiance and serve the first waffle. Not a bad gig except half the group was diabetic and the other half had intestinal trouble. Forget stacks of fluffy golden squares topped with whipped cream and chocolate chips. The waffles were all-bran, served with sugar-free syrup and Myrtle Nell's infamous prune compote.

Which meant instead of counting down the hours until tomorrow morning, Gracie would much rather haul open the door, throw herself at the cowboy idling in her driveway and beg for round two.

And three.

An all-nighter, as a matter of fact.

The urge gripped her and her hands trembled, but then Sugar

Lips scrambled from the kitchen. Her claws slid across the hardwood floor in a frantic scrape as she rushed for the door.

Bran was good. Healthy.

Gracie latched onto that all-important fact and scooped up the white ball of fluff. The dog licked at her frantically for a few seconds before her high-pitched barks filled the air. Gracie set her on the floor and she danced in place for a few seconds before leading the way to the kitchen and the treat jar.

Gathering her control, Gracie forced herself away from the front door and followed Sugar Lips into the kitchen. She unearthed Sugar's favorite powdered donuts from the cabinet and fed one to the frantic animal.

The dog wolfed down the goody and barked and danced for another.

"One a day. You know the rule."

Rules. That was what life was all about. About respecting boundaries and walking the straight and narrow and playing it safe. That was who she was now, even if Jesse had made her forget that all-important fact for those few blissful moments at the river.

She was still the Gracie who ate granola for breakfast every morning and wore conservative shoes and spent her Saturday nights in front of the TV. She wasn't wild and wicked.

Even if she had worn a black lace thong to the office yesterday. Sexy lingerie was her one indulgence. Pretty undies and lacy bras. Even the white cotton bikini panties she'd worn tonight were on the risqué side.

Which explained her thoughts at the moment.

The underwear. She needed to tame it down in a major way, which meant that first thing tomorrow she was going to do some online shopping for some sensible lingerie. Some Spanx and granny panties and boxy bras.

You're still as out of control as ever.

He was wrong and he would see that soon enough.

She intended to make him see that, to keep the emotional

wall as strong as ever between them so that when Sunday rolled around, it would be that much easier to say goodbye.

Because Gracie Stone didn't want a forever with Jesse Chisholm. She wanted to get him out of her head. Her fantasies.

Once and for all.

That meant keeping her guard up, holding back and showing him she'd turned into a bona fide good girl.

He would gladly call it quits then and run the other way once he realized she truly had changed.

She just wished that fact didn't suddenly bother her so much.

HE WANTED MORE.

The thought echoed in Jesse's head as he sat outside the modest brick home a few blocks over from City Hall, his engine idling, his blood racing.

While they'd just gotten down and dirty in the bed of his pickup, they hadn't come close to burning up the lust that blazed between them. He still felt every bit as restless. As hungry.

Not that he intended to do anything more about it tonight. He had to be up early tomorrow morning for a training session and he had no intention of letting their agreement get in the way of his next championship.

His heartbeat kicked up a notch as the lights flipped on inside and he watched her shadow move across the first-floor window. A vision played in his head and he saw her pushed up against a nearby wall, her legs wrapped around his waist. Her hands clawed at his shoulders and her tits bounced as he pumped into her and—

Awww, *hell.*

His gut tensed and his dick throbbed. He tightened one hand on the steering wheel and shoved the truck into Reverse with his other. With a squeal of tires, he pulled out of her driveway and headed for the motel.

Five minutes later, he sat idling in the parking lot, his attention fixed on the photographer camped out on the doorstep of his room. He'd expected the two from last night, but this guy was new. And probably just another in a long line he was sure to encounter over the next few days.

He thought of calling the front desk but then changed his mind. He could have this guy escorted off the property, but there would just be another to take his place. Better to give them what they wanted, answer a few questions and let them have their photo op, which was what he fully intended to do.

Just not tonight.

He turned his pickup around and headed for the training facility that sat outside of town. Ten minutes later he pulled into the gravel parking lot and killed the engine. He headed for the exterior staircase that led to a small apartment over the main office. During rodeo time, the competing cowboys used the spot to unwind or catch a nap in between rides. With a window that overlooked the main arena, they could enjoy the other events while kicking back and conserving their strength.

The place sat dark and quiet now.

Jesse flipped on a switch and the overhead light chased away the dark shadows, revealing a large living space complete with a living room, a fully equipped kitchen and a bathroom. Jesse was just about to head for the bathroom and a nice cold shower when he saw a flicker of light beyond the wall of windows overlooking the dark arena.

He closed the distance to the glass and sure enough, a light bobbed in the far distance near the animal pens.

A few minutes later he rounded the first bull pen to find Troy spread out on a blanket, an iPod in one hand and a magazine in the other. The minute he saw Jesse, he snatched the headphones out of his ears. The magazine slapped together as he scrambled to his feet.

"What are you doing?"

"W-working late," Troy blurted. "Eli wants us to clean out the pens first thing tomorrow. I thought I'd get a jump on it tonight."

"So you're here this late to clean pens?"

"Actually, I thought I'd just crash here and get an early start."

"And your folks are okay with you sleeping here?"

"My mom is dead. A car wreck about eight years ago." He shrugged. "My dad doesn't care what I do. The only thing he cares about is getting drunk. He's on a bender right now." His gaze met Jesse's. "If you let me stay here tonight, I promise I'll be up before anyone gets here. I'll even shovel all the stalls myself."

"A car wreck, huh?"

Troy nodded. "She was on her way home from work."

"My mom died when I was four," Jesse murmured. "She had complications when she had my youngest brother. My dad was never much of a dad, either."

"A drunk?"

"Among other things." He eyed the blanket. "But you can't sleep here."

Troy's head snapped up and his gaze collided with Jesse's. "Please, Mr. Chisholm. I won't get in the way. I promise."

Jesse shook his head. "As much as I'd like to let you sleep right here, I'm afraid I can't. If you start snoring, you might spook the bulls." The kid actually looked ready to cry until Jesse added, "I'm bunking out in the small apartment upstairs, but there's a pullout couch in the main office. Clean sheets in the cabinet. You can sleep there."

"Really?"

Jesse nodded. "But only if you promise to get up five minutes early and put on a pot of coffee. If you're camping out in the office, you're in charge of the coffee machine."

"I promise."

"Get some sleep, then." Jesse motioned toward the office. "I'll see you tomorrow."

Troy snatched up his blanket and magazine and made a beeline for the office. A smile played at his lips and Jesse's chest tightened.

He knew exactly what Troy was feeling at the moment. He'd

felt it himself every night when his dad had been three sheets to the wind and he and his brothers had bedded down in the old Buick just to get away from the chaos.

Relief.

Bone-deep, soothing relief because he didn't have to worry about waking to a drunken rant or picking his dad up off the bathroom floor or winding up on the opposite end of his fist. For tonight, Troy was safe.

If only Jesse felt the same at the moment.

Instead, he was on edge. Wired. Desperate.

And all because of Gracie.

Yep, he wanted more, all right. And he had only four days to get it, because he was leaving first thing Sunday morning.

That meant he was going to have to spend a lot of time with her between now and then, more than just the proposed sneaking around after hours, that was for damned sure. No, Jesse needed to *overindulge* if he meant to get Gracie out of his system and lay the past to rest once and for all.

He had to.

Because Jesse was finally moving on with his life. But in order to move on, he needed to let go of the past.

Of Gracie.

He would.

But first he was going to haul her close and hold on tight.

13

WHEN GRACIE WALKED into City Hall on Wednesday morning, she was more than happy to find Trina ready and waiting with a full day's itinerary. After a sleepless night spent reliving her encounter with Jesse, she needed something—anything—to get her mind off what had happened and how much she'd liked it.

And how she couldn't wait until it happened again.

But she would wait because she had responsibilities. Places to go. People to see. Waffles to eat.

High-fiber bran waffles that looked like cardboard and tasted even more bland.

"These are interesting," she said to the blue-haired woman sitting across from her.

"Don't be silly, child. They taste terrible like that." Myrtle Nell, president of the Senior Ladies' Auxiliary and chairperson for the brunch, handed Gracie a bowl filled with a dark brown jellylike substance. "You need the prune compote on top to really bring out the flavor."

"Wow. This looks yummy." *Not.* Gracie watched as the woman heaped a few spoonfuls onto her plate and tried not to make a face.

"It's homemade." Myrtle motioned her to take another bite

and Gracie had the sudden urge to run. Away from the waffles and the gossip.

Straight to Jesse.

She ditched the thought, forced herself to take a bite and tuned in to the conversation flying back and forth across the table.

She learned all about Carl Simon's new hair plugs and Janet Green's collagen injections and Helen Culpepper's latest affair with some rancher from nearby Rusk County.

Carl had developed a massive infection from the plugs that no amount of antibiotic cream could touch. Janet had overdone the treatment and now looked like a blowfish. And Helen's latest fling was a huge *Brokeback Mountain* fan.

The only thing she didn't hear about was any mention of her run-in with Jesse in front of the bakery. Not that the entire town wasn't privy to the information. They were, but they'd obviously written it off as a friendly exchange between politician and constituent.

That should have been enough to ease Gracie's nerves. She was still worked up after a sleepless night spent replaying her evening with Jesse. Want gripped her, but she tamped it back down. She had obligations first. Responsibilities.

Which was why she forced down not one but two waffles before she headed over to the seventh-grade car wash.

"I'm ready to work," she told Shirley Buckner, the fortysomething English teacher and supervisor for the fundraising event. Shirley wore blue-jean capris, a Lost Gun Middle School T-shirt and a haggard expression that said she needed a giant margarita a lot more than a helping hand.

She handed Gracie a bucket and directed her over to a dust-covered Chevy four-door pickup truck with the familiar Cartwright Ranch logo on the side. "You can start on Lloyd Cartwright's truck. He brought in all six of them." She indicated the row of matching vehicles that spanned the length of the middle school parking lot.

"Oh, and smile." Shirley lifted the camera that hung around

her neck as an afterthought and clicked a picture. "Great. Now get moving."

"Shouldn't you take off the lens cap first?" Gracie pointed to the covering on the high-dollar camera similar to the one she'd had back in the day.

"A cap?" Shirley eyed the contraption as if seeing it for the first time. Her eyebrows drew together into a frown as she twisted the covering. The cap popped off into her hands. "Great. Just friggin' great. I've shot over forty pictures in the past hour. All for nothing." She grabbed the walkie-talkie from her belt. "Charlene? Is June still in the bathroom?"

"I sent her home. She's *really* sick."

"Great. Just friggin' *great*."

"June?" Gracie eyed the teacher. "June Silsbee? The reporter from the newspaper?"

Shirley nodded. "She was here covering the event for the paper, but then she upchucked in the parking lot on account of she's pregnant with triplets. She and Martin did that in vitro thing. Anyhow, she handed me her camera and made a beeline for the restroom. I haven't seen her since." She eyed the camera. "The kids are so excited. The paper promised us front-page coverage, which we're counting on because the car wash itself never brings in quite enough money. But then the paper comes out and we get a rush of donations from local businesses." She shook her head. "But none of that's going to happen, since I can't even work this blasted thing."

"I can." The words were out before Gracie could stop them. Not that she would have. Her gaze shifted to the dozens of kids piled around a nearby car. They worked diligently, scrubbing and laughing. She ignored the doubt that rippled deep inside and gave in to the grin tugging at her lips. "Hand it over and I'll see what I can do."

She spent the next hour taking picture after picture while the kids sprayed and washed and got each other wet. She was just about to snap a pic of the girls choir group serenading one of the customers when she caught sight of a familiar pair of Wranglers in her peripheral vision.

She turned in time to see Jesse slam the door shut on his jacked-up pickup truck. He wore a fitted white T-shirt and faded jeans that hugged his muscles to perfection and tugged at the seams as he started toward her.

What the hell?

He wasn't supposed to be here. Not now. They'd made arrangements to meet tonight at his motel room. He wasn't supposed to be here in full view of everyone. Especially not looking so downright sexy. Her stomach hollowed out and she had the sudden urge to throw herself into his arms and kiss him for all she was worth. In front of God and the entire Lost Gun seventh grade.

"Excuse me." She snatched the water hose out of a nearby girl's hand and before she could think better of it, she let loose a stream of water directly in Jesse's direction. He sputtered and frowned, and she put her back to him, giving herself a silent high five for marksmanship.

Now he would turn and head the other way.

That was what she told herself, but then she heard his deep voice directly behind her.

"What the hell are you doing?"

She whirled and tried to look surprised. "Oh, my. Did I get you wet? You must have walked into my line of fire."

"I didn't do any such thing. I was your line of fire."

"Don't be silly." She tried to laugh off the coincidence, but he wasn't buying it. She finally shrugged. "So I got you a little wet. Stop making such a big fuss."

"A little wet?" He arched an eyebrow at her, amusement dancing in his violet eyes before they darkened and the air stalled in her lungs. "I'm soaked to the bone, in case you haven't noticed."

She'd noticed, all right. His white T-shirt, now practically transparent, stuck to him like a second skin, showing off every bulge and ripple of his broad shoulders and sinewy chest. She could even see the shadow of hair that circled his nipples and funneled down his abdomen. "At least I'm in good company." He nodded at her.

She became acutely aware of the glide of water down her own neck, the sticky wetness of her silk blouse plastered against her chest. A glance down and she realized her aim hadn't been that great. Her own clothing was in no better shape than his, her shirt practically transparent, revealing the lacy bra she wore and the puckered tips of her breasts. Her only consolation? The high-dollar camera hanging around her neck, the strap plunging between her perky nipples, was waterproof.

"It's a car wash." She bristled. "People get wet. It's a hazard of the job." She grasped for a change of subject. "What are you doing here?"

"I thought I'd pick you up and we could have lunch."

"Here? In town?"

"Why not?"

"Because you hate this town."

He shrugged. "A man's gotta eat. So what do you say?"

"I'd say your timing sucks. As you can see, I'm busy."

"Oh, I see, all right." He eyed her wet blouse and his smile widened. "You look good wet." His deep voice stirred something even worse than the sudden panic beating at her senses. "But then I already knew that." Excitement flowered inside her, making her heart pound and her blood rush.

She felt herself melting beneath the warmth in his eyes, his smile, and so she did what any freedom-loving woman would have done. She squirted him again for good measure, ignored the urge to snatch a picture of him soaked to his skin, turned on her heel and walked away.

Walked being the key word when all she really wanted to do was run. Because as much as Jesse excited her, he scared the crap out of her, too. The way he smiled. The way he made her feel when he smiled.

This feeling was not part of her plan. Working him out of her system to gain some much-needed closure—definitely tops on her agenda. But this warm, achy feeling? The urge to shirk her duties, climb into the cab of his pickup truck and drive off into the sunset?

No.

No matter how hot the temperature, how hot his gaze or how hot the heat that burned between them. This was strictly sex.

Closure sex.

Unfortunately, she wasn't used to any kind of sex, which explained why she couldn't forget Jesse James Chisholm or his damnable grin the rest of the afternoon after she dropped off the camera to the newspaper office and headed back to City Hall.

She turned her attention to unpacking the boxes of books back at her office and sliding them onto the newly delivered shelves. Unfortunately, it wasn't enough to make her forget Jesse or the upcoming evening.

He was there in her head, teasing and tempting and reminding her of last night. Of how much she still wanted him.

She found herself counting down the seconds until she could see him again.

Because he'd awakened her long-deprived hormones and so, of course, he was starring in a few crazy fantasies. But that was all they were. No way did Gracie actually want to ride off into the sunset with Jesse. She wasn't riding anywhere. She was here in Lost Gun to stay.

And Jesse wasn't.

Sunday.

The word echoed in her head, fueling her resolve as she picked up the phone and dialed his number. His voice mail picked up.

"I'm afraid I've got a late meeting. I'll have to take a rain check tonight. Talk to you tomorrow."

There. No matter how much she might want him, she didn't need him.

That was what she told herself as she slid the books into place, one after the other, until the shelf was full.

Like her life. Full. Content. She didn't want for anything.

OKAY, SO MAYBE she wanted for one thing. A way past Big Earl's trio of pit bulls.

"I need the biggest steak you've got," she told the butcher the next morning after a night of tossing and turning and surfing late-night cable TV.

She'd ended up on Animal Planet watching a *K9 Cops* marathon. After twelve back-to-back episodes and four packs of Life Savers, she'd hit on an idea.

"Rib eye? New York strip? Filet?" asked Merle Higgam, the head butcher at the local Piggly Wiggly.

"Yes."

"Yes to which one?"

"All three." She wasn't sure which cut would go over best with the vicious trio, so she didn't want to take any chances. "Just make sure they're all really thick."

Ten minutes later she climbed into her car with the freezer-wrapped package and headed over to Big Earl's. Trina had reported back that Big Earl was even older and more decrepit than they remembered. No way could he actually be making moonshine again.

At the same time, Gracie needed to see for herself. To warn him what would happen if he violated his probation.

"Lookie here, big boy," Gracie said, summoning her sultriest "come and get me" voice as she held one of her purchases over the fence and did her best to entice the first animal that poked his head out of an oversize doghouse. "I've got something *really* special for you."

He barked once, twice, before making a mad dash for her. She tossed the steak to her far left and waited while the other two dogs joined the first. Summoning her courage, she climbed over the fence and made a beeline for the house. She hit the front steps two at a time and did a fast knock on the door.

"Big Earl? It's me. Mayor Stone. I need to talk to you."

"Who is it?"

"Mayor Stone."

"Mayor who?"

"Stone."

"Sorry, I ain't got no phone."

"I didn't say phone. I said Stone."

"The mayor?"

"That's me."

"Ain't got no key, either. 'Sides, you don't need a key. The door's unlocked."

Gracie's fingers closed over the doorknob just as she heard the barking behind her. She chanced a glance over her shoulder to see one of the dogs catch sight of her. She pushed open the door and slammed it shut behind her just as Ferocious Number One raced for the porch, his jaws wagging, his teeth flashing.

Heart pounding, she turned to drink in the interior of the double-wide trailer. Wood paneling covered the walls. An old movie poster from *The Outlaw Josey Wales* hung over an old lumpy beige couch piled high with old lumpy pillows. A scarred mahogany coffee table sat stacked with crossword puzzles. In the far corner sat an old lumpy recliner with an old lumpy man parked on top.

The last time she had seen Big Earl had been at a Fourth of July picnic six years ago. He'd been in attendance with his great-granddaughter, Casey, who'd been helping Frank Higgins, the owner of the local gas station, set off the fireworks. Casey had just graduated high school. She'd been working for Frank at the time, pumping gas and cleaning windshields, and so he'd brought her along to help tote the fourteen boxes of sparklers and Roman candles he'd donated. That had been the night that Judge Ellis had bought a case of moonshine off of Big Earl and stashed it in the trunk of his Lexus, which had turned out to be the finale of the fireworks show.

Big Earl had been wearing the same red-and-white-checked shirt he had on now. Except the colors had been a lot more vibrant and the fabric a lot less wrinkled.

The old man had a head full of snow-white hair that was slicked back with pomade. His eyes were pale blue and enormous behind a pair of thick round glasses.

"Well, I'll be." Big Earl peered at her. "Don't just stand there, come on in." He waved a hand for her to sit down next to him, only the nearest chair was a good five feet away.

She eased onto the edge of the sofa across from him. "So?" Her gaze skittered around the room, from an old cuckoo clock that ticked away in the kitchen to the ancient movie poster. "How have you been?"

"Fair to midland, I s'pose. Why, back in the day I was as spry as a young spring chicken. I was into everything back then. Knew everybody's business. Had plenty of business of my own, if you know what I mean."

"About that..." she started, but Big Earl wasn't quite finished yet.

"But time sure has a way of slowin' a man down. Why, my back's been achin' somethin' fierce and I got these bunions. I've been doin' Epsom salts in my bath and that helps some."

"That's good to hear. Speaking of hearing, I was just wondering..." Her words faded off as she noticed the way his eyes fixed on the spot just over her left shoulder. As if he couldn't quite focus on her. She noticed the magnifying glass on the tray table next to him. And the extra batteries for his hearing aid. And a tube of arthritis cream.

She realized then that the only thing Big Earl could possibly cook up in his condition was a piece of burnt toast. The man could hardly see. Or hear. Or walk, judging by the cane propped next to him and the nearby walker parked in the corner. He certainly wasn't in any condition to measure out ingredients or tiptoe around and keep one eye out for the cops while maintaining watch over a highly combustible still.

He wagged a bent finger in her general vicinity. "So what is it you needed to talk to me about?"

Gracie shrugged. "Just checking in to see how you're doing."

He grinned a toothless grin. "Mighty nice of you. Why, I ain't had visitors in years. Used to head into town once a week for bingo, but I cain't even do that anymore. Thank the good Lord for cable—otherwise I'd be bored out of my mind."

"You watch a lot of TV?"

"I mainly listen to it. Turn the volume up real loud on account of my hearin' ain't what it used to be. But I get by. Still catch my favorite shows. Never miss an episode of *The Rifleman* or *Bonanza.* I love those old Westerns."

Her gaze shifted to the movie poster. "You a Clint Eastwood fan?"

"I'm a Josey Wales fan. Eastwood ain't never done anything since that's worth a hill of beans."

"Now, remember, when things look bad and it looks like you're not gonna make it, then you gotta get mean." Gracie read the movie quote at the bottom of the poster. "Plumb mad-dog mean." There was something oddly familiar about the saying, but she couldn't quite place it.

"Words to live by." Big Earl grinned. "'Course, I ain't in much condition to get mean anymore, either. I leave that to my Casey. Girl's got a fiery streak that would make her mama proud. Why, she don't let nobody push her around. She ought to be back in a few minutes. Ran into town to pick up my foot cream."

"I'm sorry I missed her." Gracie pushed to her feet. "Maybe we can catch up next time."

"You sure you don't want to wait and say hello?"

"I really should get going." Her hand closed on the doorknob and she heard the growls coming from the other side. "On second thought—" she summoned a smile and sank back down onto the sofa "—I wouldn't want to be rude."

14

WHAT THE HELL was he doing here?

Gracie's hand faltered on the brownie she was stuffing into a plastic baggie. She stood behind one of the handful of tables set up on the lawn in front of City Hall. She set the treat aside, next to the dozen or so she'd just bagged for the annual Daughters of the Republic of Texas bake sale and did her best to calm her pounding heart.

Pounding, of all things. When she'd promised herself just last night after she'd cancelled on him that she wasn't going to get nervous. Or excited. Or turned on when she finally saw him again.

Especially turned on. She had a reputation to protect and salivating at the first sign of the town's hottest bad boy, particularly in front of the biggest busybodies in said town, was not in keeping with the conservative image of Lost Gun's newly elected mayor.

Tongues were already wagging about the car wash incident. Of course, they were all focused on the fact that Jesse James Chisholm had been wet and practically half-naked in front of every female teacher at the middle school rather than Gracie, who'd been the cause of it.

It was all Jesse's fault. He was too bold and much too sexy for his own good.

She forced an indifferent expression and tried to ignore the way his tight jeans hugged his muscular thighs as he approached her table. He wore a black T-shirt and a dusty cowboy hat that said he'd been in the middle of a training session not too long ago.

Yet here he was in the heart of Lost Gun.

"Brownie, cupcake or cheesecake bar?" she croaked when he reached her table.

"I'll take all three."

"Wow. Somebody's hungry."

"You have no idea."

She knew by the way his eyes darkened that he wasn't talking about the scrumptious goodies spread out on the table between them. She tamped down on her own growling stomach and reached for a white bakery bag. With trembling hands, she loaded his goodies inside and handed them over. "That'll be three dollars."

He pulled out his wallet and unfolded a ten. "Keep the change." Their hands brushed as she took the money and a jolt of electricity shot through her.

"Why did you cancel last night?"

"I was busy."

"Busy or scared?"

"Scared of what? Of you?" She shook her head. "I'm not scared of you."

"No." He eyed her for a silent moment. "You're scared of us," he finally said.

"There is no us. This isn't a long-term arrangement. You're leaving on Sunday." She didn't mean to sound so accusing. "Which is a good thing," she blurted. "A really good thing. Enjoy." She pushed the goodies in his direction and turned her attention to the next customer in line.

She glimpsed his handsome face in her peripheral vision,

his eyes trained on her, his lips set in a grim line. As if he was thinking real hard about some question and he wasn't too pleased with the answer.

As if he wasn't any more happy to be here than she was to see him here.

She pondered the notion for a few seconds as she served up several more baggies of goodies and tried to pretend for all she was worth that his presence didn't affect her.

Fat chance.

Every nerve in her body was keenly aware of him. She felt his warm gaze on her profile and a slow heat swept over her, from the tips of her toes clear to the top of her head, until she all but burned in the midday heat. She shifted her stance, her thighs pressing together, and an ache shot through her. Her nipples pebbled, rubbing against her bra, and her fingers faltered on the pie she was about to slice.

The pie splattered to the ground at her feet and her heart slammed against her rib cage. She shoveled the gooey mess back into the pie plate and headed for the building and the small kitchen situated at the rear of City Hall, next to a large conference room being used for the monthly Daughters of the Texas Republic meeting immediately following the bake sale.

Inside the kitchen, the ladies had stored all of their extra sweets. There were rows of pies and cakes and cookies.

She dumped the peach mess into a nearby trash can and went to the sink to wash her hands. Her fingers trembled and the soap slipped from her grasp. "Damn it," she muttered.

"Careful, sugar. You'll have the ladies dropping to their knees for an impromptu prayer meeting."

The deep voice froze her hands.

Worse, Jesse leaned in, his arms coming around her on either side, his hands closing over hers to steady her as she reached for the bar of soap.

His large tanned hands were a stark contrast against her white fingers. His warm palms cradled the tops of her hands. The rough pads of his fingertips rasped against her soft flesh and heat spiraled through her body. His nearness was like a fuzzy blanket smothering the cold panic that had rolled through her the moment she'd realized that he'd followed her inside.

"Easy, now." His voice rumbled over her bare shoulder and warm breath brushed her skin. Goose bumps chased up and down her arms and she came close to leaning back into him, closing her eyes and enjoying the delicious sensation. Just for a little while.

She stiffened and fought for her precious control. Twelve years of cloaking herself in it should have made it easy to find, but not with Jesse so close. Too close for her to breathe, much less think, much less pretend.

"You have to cradle the bar of soap and slide it through your fingers like this." He slid his fingers over the slick bar and suds lathered between their fingers. "You have to go easy and slow." As he said the words, she got the distinct impression that he was talking about more than just washing her hands.

"Thanks for the advice, but no thanks. I do not need to go slow and easy." To prove her point, she focused every ounce of energy she had on ignoring the delicious feelings assaulting her body. She held her breath and rolled the bar between her palms before shoving her hands under the spraying faucet.

His arms fell away as she turned off the water and reached for a dish towel. She scooted past him and headed for the large storage room that sat just behind the kitchen, eager to put as much distance as possible between them.

"What are you doing here?" she demanded when he followed her into the back room. She forced her face into the tightest frown she could manage, considering she wanted to kiss him more than she wanted her next breath.

"We made a deal. Sex," he murmured, the word rumbling up her spine.

"Not now. Not here." While she wanted Jesse, she wasn't

supposed to want him. That meant no blushing or trembling or kissing. "There are too many people here."

"Why, there isn't a soul in sight." He glanced around to prove his point. A bare bulb hung overhead, illuminating the small room that housed everything from gallon cans of chili and beans to five-gallon jars of tomato sauce for the Senior Ladies weekly spaghetti night. The place stocked all of the supplies for any of the functions held in the main conference room next to the kitchen. Boxes of paper goods, from plates to napkin packets to disposable cups, lined a metal shelf that ran the length of one wall.

"This isn't a good idea." She turned her back on him, determined to forget his presence and keep her mind on the task at hand. She made her way to a six-foot table that held the rest of the goodies that the Ladies' Auxiliary had donated for today's luncheon. There were dozens of pies and platters of brownies and a few cakes. She was busy reading the masking tape labels on the tops of the plastic-wrapped goodies when she heard Jesse step up behind her again.

"This really isn't a good idea." She snatched up a carrot cake and turned, the confection smack-dab between them.

"Actually, I think it's a pretty fine idea." Jesse's deep voice sent a jolt of adrenaline through her. His eyes glittered with a hungry light that sucked the oxygen from her lungs and made her hands tremble. He caught the edge of the door that adjoined the kitchen and shut it behind him, closing them off from the rest of the world.

The cake slid from her grasp, landing in a pile of smashed frosting and plastic wrap at her feet. Ugh. That made not one but two desserts she'd killed on account of Jesse James Chisholm.

"You'd better get your checkbook ready to make a nice big fat donation." She knelt to retrieve the mess, but he was right beside her, his hands bumping hers as they both reached for the cardboard base at the same time.

"I'm not the one that keeps dropping everything."

"Because of you."

"Because you like what I do to you. You just don't want to admit it."

His hand stalled on hers and heat whispered up her arm. "I can't do this here."

"You don't have to *do* a thing." He reached for her hands, which were now covered with frosting. Before she could draw her next breath, his tongue flicked out and he licked one finger. Once, twice, before sliding it deep in his mouth and suckling for a breath-stealing moment. "Just feel."

"I..." She swallowed and tried to think of something to say, but with his lips so firm and purposeful around her finger, his tongue rasping her skin, she couldn't seem to find any words. "Somebody might come looking for me," she managed to say several moments later after he'd licked her finger clean.

"You'll be back with more desserts in no time." He licked his lips, and she had the sudden image of him licking other parts of her body. Lapping at her neck and her nipples and her belly button and the wet heat between her legs. "But first I want my dessert."

Chatter drifted through the open doorway. The PA system crackled as it switched on and Myrtle's voice came over the loudspeaker as she tested the mic for the upcoming meeting. Even closer, the hum of the coffee machine drifted from inside the kitchen, along with the rush of water as someone flipped on a faucet. There were people just beyond the thin walls of the storage room. People starting to prep for the upcoming meeting. People who could walk in at any moment and find their mayor having dessert with the town's baddest bad boy.

She stiffened and forced aside the stirring images. "I really think we should wait until this evening. I'll meet you at the motel."

"You cancelled on me once. I won't take that chance again. Besides, I don't like to wait." He kissed her then, his lips wet and hungry, his tongue greedy as he devoured her.

"I don't think—" But then he fingered her nipple through the soft cotton of her shirt and she stopped thinking altogether.

He dropped to his knees in front of her, his hands going to her hips. He paused to knead her bottom through the fitted material of her skirt. Fabric brushed her legs as he slid it down over her thighs, her knees, until the skirt pooled on the floor.

He stood, then slid his hands around to her bottom and lifted her onto the counter. He paused only to grab one of the large wire racks filled with boxes and shove it in front of the door. It wasn't enough to keep anyone out should they really want to get in, but it was enough to buy them some time to grab their clothes should they be discovered.

Walking back to her, he wedged himself between her parted thighs. He urged her backward until her back met the countertop and then he slowly unbuttoned her shirt and unhooked the front clasp of her bra.

He fingered a dollop of frosting from the cake plate. "I really do like cream cheese," he murmured before touching the filling to one ripe nipple. He circled the tip, spreading the glaze until it covered her entire areola.

His gaze drilled into hers for a heart-stopping moment before he lowered his dark head. His tongue lapped at the side of her breast.

The licking grew stronger, more purposeful, as he gobbled up the white confection, starting at the outside and working his way toward the center. Sensation rippled up her spine.

The first leisurely rasp of his tongue against her ripe nipple wrung a cry from her throat. Her fingers threaded through his hair as he drew the quivering tip deep into his hot, hungry mouth. He suckled her long and hard and she barely caught the moan that tried to escape her throat.

She bit her lip as he licked and suckled and nipped. Her skin grew itchy and tight. Pressure started between her legs, heightened by the way he leaned into her, the hard ridge of his erection prominent beneath his jeans. She spread her legs wider and he settled more deeply between them. Grasping her hips, he rocked her.

Rubbed her.

Up and down and side to side and—

The shrill whistle of a tea kettle filled the air, penetrating the haze of pleasure that gripped her senses. Panic bolted through her and she went still.

"Wait." She grasped his muscled biceps to still his movements. "I need to go check the tea. If I don't, someone else will."

He leaned back, his gaze so deep and searching, as if he were doing his damnedest to see inside of her. "No," he finally murmured, his fingertip tracing the edge of her panties where elastic met the tender inside of her thigh. "You're not going anywhere. This isn't about going, sugar." His finger dipped into the steamy heat beneath. "It's about coming."

One touch of his callused fingertip against her swollen flesh and she arched up off the counter. She caught her bottom lip again and stifled a cry.

With a growl, he spread her wide with his thumb and forefinger and touched and rubbed as he dipped his head and drew on her nipple.

It was too much and not enough. She clamped her lips shut and forced her eyes open. But he was there, filling her line of vision, his fierce gaze drilling into hers. Searching and stirring and—

"Is somebody back there?" Lora Tremayne's voice echoed in the background, followed by the rattle of the doorknob as the president of the Daughters of the Republic of Texas tried to open the door to the storage room.

Gracie stiffened, her hands diving between them to stop the delicious stroke of his fingers.

As if he sensed her sudden resistance, his movements stilled. His chest heaved and his hair tickled her palms. Damp fingertips trailed over her cheek in a tender gesture that warmed her heart almost as much as her body.

"Come for me." His gaze was hot and bright and feverish as he stared down at her, into her. But there was something else, as well. A desperation that eased the panic beating at her senses and sent a rush of determination through her.

"Hello? Who's in there?"

It was Lora again, but it didn't matter. Gracie no longer cared if the entire Ladies' Auxiliary stood on the outside of the door, waiting and listening.

It wasn't about what everyone else thought about her. It was about him. What he thought about her. What he felt for her. What he wanted from her. What he *needed* from her.

And what she needed from him.

Her fingers dove into his front pocket and retrieved the small foil packet tucked there.

He answered her unspoken invitation by tugging at the button on his jeans, pulling his zipper down and freeing his hard length. He opened the condom and spread it on his throbbing penis before leaning in closer, until the head pushed just a fraction of an inch inside of her.

Pleasure pierced her brain for a split second, quickly shattering into a swell of sensation as he filled her with one deep, probing thrust.

Her muscles convulsed around him, clutching him as he gripped her bare bottom. He pumped into her, the pressure and the friction so sweet that it took her breath away.

She was vaguely aware of the voices on the other side of the door. But then he touched her nipple and trailed a hand down her stomach, his fingertips making contact with the place where they joined, and all thought faded in a rush of sweet desire. She met his thrusts in a wild rhythm that urged him faster and deeper and…there. Right. *There!*

Her lips parted and she screamed at the blinding force of the climax that picked her up and turned her inside out. He caught the sound with his mouth and buried himself deep inside her one last time. A shudder went through him as he followed her over the edge.

She wrapped her arms around him and held him. Oddly enough, the fact that she would have to walk out of here with Jesse, past whoever had knocked on the door, didn't bother her nearly as much as it should have.

The heat, she told herself. It was so hot outside that she'd obviously suffered a minor heatstroke and so she wasn't thinking clearly. Because no way would she want anyone to know that their respectable leader had hooked up with the most disrespectable man in town.

The very last thing she needed was to tarnish her image. Unfortunately, what she needed and what she wanted were two very different things, and at that moment, the only thing she really wanted was Jesse.

In her bed and her life.

Temporarily, of course.

She knew full well that he was leaving in a few days, and she was staying, and that was that.

There would be no long-distance texts, no late-night phone calls, no keeping in touch. Jesse meant to let go of the past, to erase it, and she meant to let him.

Cold turkey.

It worked.

She knew firsthand and where she'd turned her back once before, she intended to let him turn his now. He needed to forget this place.

He deserved to forget.

Which meant she would let him go. She had to.

But not yet. Not just yet.

"I'M TELLING YOU, James Lee, the door is locked from the inside." Lora Tremayne's voice penetrated the frantic beat of Jesse's heart.

"But this door ain't got no lock on the inside, Miss Lora," came the deep voice of City Hall's lead maintenance man. "Maybe you aren't pushing it hard enough."

Jesse felt Gracie's body go tense and he knew she'd heard the speculation outside the door. He leaned back and saw the worry that leapt into her bright blue eyes.

"I pushed on it plenty hard," James Lee went on. "It's not locked, but it might be barricaded. Someone's definitely in there."

"Maybe it's Mabel Green," said another female voice and Jesse knew the situation had attracted the attention of more than one of the women on hand for the monthly meeting and bake sale. "She's been on a no-carb diet for the past six months and it's made her batty. She probably saw all those goodies and went on a binge."

"Sarah Eckles is doing the same diet," another voice said. "It could be her."

"Maybe it's an animal. I get possums in my trash all the time. One of 'em could have crawled in a window."

"Maybe it's a raccoon."

"Maybe it's a zombie."

The voices joined in a loud back and forth as the doorknob jiggled and James Lee did his best to push open the door.

"We have to get out of here," Gracie started, but Jesse touched a finger to her lips.

"Wait here and don't come out until the coast is clear." He worked at the buttons on his jeans and then pulled on his shirt. A split second later, he kissed her quickly on the lips before turning toward the door.

He pulled open the door just as James Lee pushed. The man would have tumbled him backward, but Jesse was much younger and stronger. James Lee stumbled backward instead as Jesse stepped forward, slipped out the door and shut it firmly behind him.

"Afternoon, ladies," he said, giving Lora and the half dozen women that surrounded her a wink and a tip of his hat.

"Jesse Chisholm," Lora said, her face puckering up as if she'd just sucked on a lemon. "What in land's sake are you doing here?"

"I must have got lost on my way to the clerk's office."

"You mistook the kitchen for the clerk's office?" She didn't look convinced.

Meanwhile the whispers floated around the room.

"The clerk's office? Fat chance on that."

"Why, that man cain't be up to no good."

"The Chisholms don't know the meaning of the word *good*."

"Somebody better count the brownies and pies."

"I'm selling some property," Jesse announced, as if that would kill the speculation. It wouldn't. His last name was Chisholm and nothing would ever change that. He knew as much and he'd come to terms with it, but he explained anyway because this wasn't about him. It was about Gracie. She was stuck in the room behind him and he wanted to give her a way out that didn't involve waltzing past these gossips. "I must have taken a wrong turn."

"Likely story," Lora snorted in the condescending way that had earned her the reputation as the most stuck-up bitch in the county.

He ignored the urge to tell her which way to go and how fast to get there. Instead, his ears perked to the sound of footsteps behind him. So soft that no one else would have heard unless they were listening.

A slide and a faint thud and then all was quiet.

No jiggle of the knob behind him. No creak of hinges.

Nothing because Gracie was heeding his words and not coming out until the coast was clear.

He ignored the crazy disappointment that twisted at his insides. It wasn't as if he wanted her to waltz out in front of God and everybody and tarnish the image she'd fought so hard to build.

At the same time, he couldn't shake the sudden urge to feel her hand on his arm, her warmth beside him, as she stepped up and declared to the world that she was here with him. For him.

"I'll just be on my way."

"I'll show you to the clerk's office," James Lee offered. "It's just down the hall." The man started forward, but Jesse wasn't budging until he had the entire entourage behind him.

"You sure you don't want to escort me out yourself?" He eyed Lora. "Just to make sure I don't overpower James, here, and come back to steal a peach cobbler."

"A smart-ass just like your father," she muttered, but she started after him anyway. As expected, the women followed and soon they were moving down the hallway toward the county clerk's office. When they reached the doorway, James turned.

"Show's over, ladies. There's a bake sale still going on out on the lawn that could use all of you, not to mention y'all got your meeting to get to." He motioned back down the hall. "Just get on about your business. I'll take care of things here."

"Make sure you do," Lora said, giving Jesse one last scathing look. He grinned and her frown deepened before she turned on the women. She rattled off new duties to them and they all disappeared through a nearby door that led to the front lawn.

"Sorry about that, Mr. Chisholm," James said once the women had disappeared. "Those busybodies don't think before they start running their mouths." He winked. "Saw you ride in Houston last year. You were something."

"Thanks, James Lee."

"Had my granddaughters with me. Bought 'em each a shirt with your name on it. Tickled 'em pink, it did."

"That's mighty nice of you."

"Ain't nothing nice about it. I was hoping you might sign those shirts for me. It sure would mean a lot to the girls."

"Bring them by the training facility and I'd be happy to. In fact, bring the girls with you. They could watch a few sessions.

I might have some rodeo passes sitting around, too, for the next event if you think they might like that."

The maintenance man grinned from ear to ear. "Boy, would they ever."

THE COAST WAS CLEAR.

Gracie gathered her courage, slipped out of the storage room, hurried through the kitchen and moved down the hallway toward the ladies' room at the far end.

She needed a few minutes to herself before she headed back out to the bake sale and the curious faces and the hot gossip that Jesse James Chisholm had been shoplifting brownies and cakes.

As if.

Jesse would never do such a thing, even if he had destroyed a few goodies in the name of some really hot sex.

Heat swamped her as she remembered the frosting on her nipple, followed by his lips. And his tongue. And…

Sheesh, it was hot in here.

She pushed inside the restroom, hit the lock button on the door and made her way to the sink. A second later, she splashed cold water on her face and tried to understand what had just happened.

She'd hopped up onto the table and had sex with Jesse James Chisholm just inches away from a very nosy group of constituents.

Even more, she'd liked it.

She liked him.

She ditched the last thought and focused on grabbing a wad of paper towels to blot at her face.

She didn't *like* him. *Like* involved a connection that went beyond the physical. It involved shared interests and mutual respect and admiration. It meant understanding someone's hopes and dreams and—

Okay, so she liked him. A little.

He was a strong, compassionate man. A man who put family

first. Who went after what he wanted. A man with hopes and dreams and determination.

A man with a future that did not involve Lost Gun or her or what they'd just shared.

Before she could dwell on the suddenly depressing thought, her cell phone rang. She fished it out of her pocket and hit the Talk button.

"Hey, sis," Charlie's voice floated over the line. "What's up?"

"My sugar level." She reached for another paper towel and dabbed at the water running down her neck. "I'm up to my elbows in brownies and cookies."

"A bake sale?"

"Unfortunately."

"Sounds like a blast. Listen, I just wanted to make sure you got my message about this weekend. I hate to cancel on you, but I've got a lot going right now and—"

"Sure." Why the hell was it still so hot in here?

"—I really don't have time to drive all the way to Lost Gun just to make homemade pizzas, even though they're like *the* best pizzas in the world and you're the best and—what did you just say?"

"We can do it some other time." Gracie blew out a deep breath and made a mental note to ask Trina to have James Lee check the main air conditioning unit. "Don't worry about it." She tossed the used paper towels and tried to ignore the rush of heat as she stared into the mirror and noticed that she'd missed one of the buttons on her shirt.

"You're not mad, are you?"

"Of course not."

"Yes, you are," Charlie insisted, obviously startled when Gracie didn't launch into a ten-minute lecture about how she'd bought all the pizza ingredients and pulled out the Monopoly board.

She would have. She would have reminded her sister about all the details and how much fun they would have being together, but suddenly the only thing she could think of was how hot it was and how she desperately needed to calm down and how she really needed to forget Jesse Chisholm.

And the fact that she liked him.

"You're mad and worried," Charlie went on, "but I'm not a little girl anymore. I know how to take care of myself. I won't be out late and I'll be super careful and—"

"I know you will. Call me later." She killed the connection before her sister could ask another question.

And then she concentrated on redoing her shirt and returning to the real world without thinking about Jesse Chisholm and the all-important fact that she couldn't wait to see him again.

15

HE WAS FRIGGIN' CRAZY.

That was the only explanation for the fact that the more Jesse James Chisholm touched Gracie Stone, the more he kissed her and slid deep, deep inside, the more he wanted to do it again and again and again.

Crazy, all right.

While he managed to get himself up and out of bed the morning after, it wasn't getting easier the way he'd expected. The way he'd hoped.

He stood beside the bed early Friday morning—four days after he'd first gotten her into his bed—and stared down at her luscious body spread out on his plain cotton sheets. Instead of the motel, they'd been keeping company in his apartment at the training facility. Away from prying eyes and the horde of reporters camped out at the motel.

He left the tack room and headed for the main corral. He had to give her up. He told himself that as he checked the feeding troughs. He had to give her up and forget about their time together and start thinking about the future. About Austin and his next ride and—

"Jesse!"

The name rang out and scattered his thoughts the minute he spotted the woman on the opposite side of the railing.

"Hey there, Wendy." He climbed over the railing and headed around to where she stood. "Pete's not here. I dropped him off on your doorstep myself last night after the bachelor party."

"I know, and thanks for not getting too wild and crazy. He said you kept it low-key."

He hadn't meant to. He'd meant to take Pete over to Luscious Longhorns and get them both as drunk as skunks. But Pete had been more interested in texting Wendy and Jesse had been more interested in getting back to Gracie, and so they'd left Cole and Billy and Jimmy and Jake to tie one on and close the place down.

"I'm not looking for Pete," she went on. "I'm looking for you. I need a favor."

"I really need to get going. I promised Eli I'd—"

"It's my cousin. She's flying in for the wedding this afternoon and I need someone to pick her up."

"I'll get one of the boys to drive out—"

"And take her to the wedding. And keep her company."

"I'm sure Joe or Sam or—"

"I need you, Jesse. I was thinking you could be her date for the wedding."

"But I already have a date."

"You do?"

That's right, buddy. You do?

Okay, so he didn't actually have a date, but he wanted one. He wanted to ask Gracie to be his date. The thing was, he wasn't one hundred percent positive she would say yes. When it came to sex, he knew she couldn't resist him. But this was different. This wasn't about being lovers. It was about being companions. Friends. And to a man who'd been judged and shunned most of his life, those were much harder to come by. Gracie had called it quits and turned her back on him once before. He wasn't going to be blindsided again.

"It's not one of the Barbies, is it?" Wendy went on. "I know they're a lot of fun, but I thought you might want to meet some-one with a little substance. Someone more long term—"

"Okay, I'll do it." He planted a kiss on her cheek. "Text me the flight information and I'll see to it she gets to the motel in one piece. And the wedding." And then he turned and walked away before he did something really stupid—like change his mind.

Gracie wasn't dating material. What they had was purely physical and very, very temporary. She'd made that clear from the get-go. Not that he wanted anything more permanent. Hell, he was leaving in two days. No strings. No regrets.

That meant ignoring the feelings churning deep in his gut and laying the past to rest once and for all.

He wasn't falling for her all over again.

Not this time.

Never, ever again.

THE WOMAN WAS driving him to drink.

Jesse finished off the last of his second beer and reached for number three as he watched Gracie two-step around the dance floor with one of Pete's ranch hands. Even dressed in a plain beige skirt and a matching jacket that did nothing to accent the luscious curves hidden beneath, she looked good enough to eat. With every turn, the skirt pulled and tugged across her round ass. With every dip, the bodice of her jacket shifted and he glimpsed the full swells of her breasts. A thin line of perspi-ration dotted her forehead, making her face glow. Her lips were full and pink and parted in a smile—

Hell's bells, she was smiling at the two-bit cowboy. She wasn't supposed to be doing that. She wasn't even supposed to be here. Her name hadn't been anywhere near the guest list and so he'd been more than a little shocked when she'd waltzed up to him, flashed a press pass, snapped a picture and said, "June Silsbee, the about-town photographer for the newspaper, is sick. I'm fill-ing in for her."

Only she wasn't standing around on the fringes, snapping

pictures for the world to see. No, she was having fun. Dancing. Laughing. *Smiling.*

Jesse latched onto beer number four as the song played down and Gracie traded Pete's ranch hand and the two-step for Eli and a popular line dance.

She twirled and wiggled her ass and smiled—holy crap, there she was smiling again. And winking. And at a man old enough to be her father.

Not that Jesse had any room to talk. He'd let Wendy fix him up with the brunette sitting next to him. A mistake if he'd ever made one. While she was nice enough, she wasn't Gracie.

And the problem is?

No problem, he told himself for the umpteenth time, shifting his attention to the woman and trying to focus on whatever she was saying. Something about the bridesmaids' dresses and how pretty everything had been and what a great time she was having.

"Would you excuse me for just a second?" A few seconds later, he left Lisa or Lynette or whatever her name was staring after him as he headed for the bar and did his damnedest to ignore the sexy blonde who floated around the dance floor.

"Beer?" the bartender asked, but Jesse shook his head.

"I need something stronger." A split second later the man pulled a jar of clear liquid from behind the bar and held it up. Jesse nodded and reached for the homemade moonshine.

He was on swig number three when Billy cut in for a waltz with Gracie. Jesse's hands tightened on the jar and he fought the urge to rush over, pull Gracie into his arms and make her smile and wink at him. An urge he managed to resist until Billy closed the few inches that separated them. Jesse forgot all about his moonshine.

"Don't you have your own date?" He tapped his brother on the shoulder. "Shouldn't you be dancing with her?"

"Are you kidding?" He motioned to Casey Jessup, who sat

near the bar, her elbow planted on top, her entire focus on the man she was currently arm-wrestling. "She hates to dance."

"So go referee the match for her." He elbowed his way in between them, his gaze fixed on the surprised woman who stared back at him.

"Don't you have your own date?" Gracie arched an eyebrow as he pulled her close.

"It's not an official date. I'm just keeping her company for Wendy."

"You're doing a piss-poor job considering you're here with me."

"I want to dance." He slid a possessive arm around her waist and pulled her close.

"What's gotten into you?"

"A special batch of white lightning."

She pulled back. "Big Earl's white lightning?"

"Something like that." His gaze caught and held hers. "You look really nice."

"You're drunk."

"Not drunk enough. I don't like it when you dance with other men."

"Then you should have asked me to be your date instead of bringing someone else."

"It's not a date."

"It sure looks like a date."

"You're right. I'm sorry." He stared deep into her eyes. "I should have asked you to come with me, but I didn't. I thought I needed some distance. But it doesn't matter if you're clear across the room or right next to me, I still want you the same." He saw the flash of surprise in her gaze. "I need you." He pressed a kiss to her soft lips before pulling her close. She seemed stiff at first, as if she didn't believe him. But then just like that, her body seemed to relax. She inched closer. And the rest of the world faded and they started to dance.

GRACIE HAD WON the battle, but not the war, she realized later that night when she rolled over after several hours of Jesse's fast and furious lovemaking to find the bed next to her warm but empty. As usual. Instead of the motel, he'd taken her to the training facility and the comfy full-size bed that filled up the bedroom of the small apartment that sat over his office. She heard him moving around in the next room—the creak of the chair as he yanked on his boots, the slide of change as he loaded his pockets, the clink of a coffee cup as he finished his last swallow. He was leaving her again. It was still dark, still a long way until sunrise, and Jesse was heading out to practice the way he had last night and the night before.

Admiration crept through her, along with a surge of anxiety. This was it. It was well past midnight, which meant that Saturday had come and gone and it was officially Sunday morning. The wedding was over and there was nothing keeping Jesse in Lost Gun. He would pick up and head for Austin first thing tomorrow morning. Even more, she would take her oath of office and assume the role of mayor.

It was now or never. Otherwise, she would never really know if she'd meant more to him than just a casual fling. If after today he would at least think about her every now and then. Remember her. And she would remember him. She pulled on his tuxedo shirt, snatched up the camera she'd been using at the wedding and started for the adjoining room. She wanted, needed, a place in Jesse Chisholm's memory since she couldn't claim a place in his heart.

JESSE HAD JUST retrieved a blanket from the tack room and walked back to the corral when the gate creaked open and he heard the camera click.

His entire body went on high alert when he caught sight of her—her long blond hair tousled, her face soft and flushed from sleep, her lips swollen from his kisses. She clasped her camera in one hand and a pang of nostalgia went through him. She wore only his white tuxedo shirt and an old worn pair of his boots. The shirt stopped mid-thigh, revealing long, sexy-as-hell legs. He felt a stir in his groin despite the fact that he should have had his fill of her by now.

He was full. Sated. Sick.

That was what he told himself, but damned if he felt it as she walked into the barn. The tuxedo shirt, unbuttoned to reveal the swell of her luscious breasts, teased him with each step. She snapped a few more pictures of him, the *click, click, click* keeping time with the sudden beat of his heart.

Work, he told himself, forcing his gaze away, determined to get back to work. He headed for the mechanical bull sitting off to the side of the rodeo arena where he'd been adjusting the settings. He leaned down and reached up under the backside of the bull to change the speed and friction. Harder. Faster. That's what he needed right now.

Unfortunately, *harder* and *faster* weren't the two words to be thinking of at the moment. Not with her so close.

He felt her gaze and every nerve in his body cracked to attention. He frowned. He was in the homestretch. No more wanting what he couldn't have. No more Gracie.

As relieved as the thought should have made him, the only thing he felt at that moment was desperation. To get back to work, he reminded himself. He was desperate to get the hell out of Lost Gun and head to Austin. End of story.

"What are you doing out here?" he asked gruffly.

"Same as you." She hooked her camera over a nearby corral post. Boots crunched as she neared the mechanical bull. "I thought I'd take a ride."

The words drew his gaze and he found her standing on the opposite side of the bull. "I hate to break it to you, sugar, but you can't ride."

"Maybe not at this moment, but practice makes perfect." Her eyes glittered. Her full lips curved into a half smile that did funny things to his heartbeat. "This is a training facility, right?"

"Last time I looked."

"So train me." She gripped the saddle horn, swung a sexy leg over and mounted up. "I'm all yours."

If only.

He shook away the thought and swallowed against the sudden tightness in his throat. "You're serious?"

"As serious as Old Lady Mitchell's last heart attack."

He eyed her for a moment more before he shrugged. "All right, then." He motioned to the side. "Put your right hand in the grip."

She slid her fingers under the leather strap. "What next?"

"Put your left up in the air."

"Okay."

"Now arch your back."

She thrust her breasts forward and an invisible fist punched in right in the sternum. "What now?"

He drew in some much needed air and tried to keep his voice calm. "Hold on tight."

He flipped the switch and the bull started to rock back and forth, this way and that.

"Mmm…" She closed her eyes at the subtle motion and a smile touched her lips. "Now I know why you cowboys spend so much time doing this."

"I don't think it's the same for us cowboys. Different parts."

Her eyes snapped open then and her passion-filled gaze met his. "I know." The bull kept moving and her eyelids drifted shut again. She threw her head back, her eyes closed, her lips parted as she leaned back and rocked her lower body, following the motion of the bull.

A sight that shouldn't affect him. After a week together, she was out of his system. His head was on straight, his mind back on business, his future crystal clear.

A soft, familiar sigh quivered in the air and the sound sent a bolt of need through him. A wave of possessiveness rolled through him and burned away reason. He flipped the switch and the bull slowed to a halt. He closed the distance between them in a few quick steps.

At the first touch of his fingertips on her thigh, her eyes fluttered open.

She stared down at him, her eyes bright and feverish. "Is it over already?"

"It's just getting started." He reached across her lap and urged her other leg over the bull until she sat sideways, facing him, her lap level with his shoulders. "*I'm* just getting started." He shoved the shirt up and spread her legs wide, wedging his shoulders between her knees. "Ah, baby, you're a natural." Her slick folds were pink and swollen after her recent ride, and he knew she was close. "You've got perfect form." He touched her, trailed a fingertip over the hot, moist flesh and relished the moan that vibrated from her lips. "So damned perfect."

There were no more words after that. He hooked her booted ankles over his shoulders, tilted her body a fraction just to give him better access, dipped his head and tasted her sweetness.

She cried out at the first lap of his tongue and threaded her fingers through his hair to hold him close. But he wasn't going anywhere. This was her first time on the back of a mechanical bull and Jesse intended to make it the wildest, most memorable ride of her life.

He devoured her, licking and sucking and nibbling, pushing her higher and higher and, oddly enough, climbing right along with her. He took his own pleasure by pleasuring her and when she screamed his name and came apart in his arms, the feelings that rushed through him—the triumph and the satisfaction and the warmth—felt as good as any orgasm he'd ever had.

Chemistry, a voice whispered. They were simply good together. That explained her effect on him.

It wasn't because she was different.

Because she was his one and only.

That's what he wanted to think. But truthfully, he didn't just want to hoist her over his shoulder, take her back to the bed and drive deep, deep inside her deliciously hot body until he reached his own climax.

He wanted to curl up with her afterward, talk to her, laugh with her, hold her. He wanted to walk down Main Street, her hand in his, and let the world know that she was his. She always had been.

She always would be.

Need gripped him, fierce and demanding and intense. He gathered her in his arms and started for the office.

"What about your training?" she murmured against his neck.

"It'll wait."

THE MINUTE JESSE pressed her down on the bed, Gracie knew something had changed. There was an urgency, a fierceness about him that she'd never seen before. Tension held his body tight, every muscle taut. His hands felt strong and purposeful and desperate as he ripped off his clothes, spread her legs wide and slid home in one fierce thrust.

"You are the wildest woman," he growled, resting his forehead against hers for several fast, furious heartbeats. "My woman."

She didn't expect the declaration any more than the determination that glittered in his eyes as he stared down at her, into her. And she certainly didn't anticipate the pure joy that rushed through her.

Before she could dwell on the feeling, large hands gripped her buttocks and tilted. He slid a fraction deeper and all rational thought fled.

The next few moments passed in a frenzy of need as Jesse pumped into her over and over, as if his life depended on every deep, penetrating thrust. His mouth ate at hers, and his touch was greedy and hungry, as if he could no longer control his need for her. As if he'd stopped trying. They joined together on a basic, primitive level unlike anything she'd ever experienced before, and as she stared up into his face at his fierce, wild expression, she knew she'd driven him over the edge. Way, way over.

The realization sent a thrill coursing through her, followed by warning bells. But before she could worry over what the change meant, he slid his hand between them and touched her where they joined, and she went wild with him.

Seconds later she screamed his name for the second time that morning as her climax slammed into her and she shattered in his arms. Another fierce pounding thrust, and Jesse followed her into oblivion, her name bursting from his lips as he spilled himself deep.

"I love you," he groaned as he collapsed atop her, his arms solid and warm, his body pressing her into the mattress.

I love you.

The words echoed through her head and sent a swell of happiness through her for a full moment before Gracie remembered the last thing, the very last thing, she wanted from Jesse James Chisholm was his love.

Love? He couldn't… He wouldn't… No! This wasn't happening. Not him and her and *love.*

"I really have to go." She scrambled from the bed, her heart pounding furiously as she snatched up her clothes in record time. She retrieved her camera from the corral and then Gracie did what any responsible, dedicated community leader would do with a totally inappropriate, sexy cowboy who loved her right at her fingertips.

She ran for her life.

JESSE LISTENED TO Gracie's footsteps as she left the training facility and barely resisted the urge to go after her. He wanted to. He wanted to haul ass, toss her over his shoulder and keep her here forever. *She was his.*

Now and always.

But the thing was, she wasn't his. Not now. And, judging by the panicked expression on her face when he'd declared his feelings, *always* seemed pretty far out of the question, too.

Not that she didn't have feelings for him. She did. She felt the same chemistry. The undeniable attraction. Even the companionship that came with being friends at one time and sharing a history. But love?

Maybe.

But if she did, it wasn't going to matter. She'd learned to put her feelings second, behind everything and everyone else in her life. She had too many people depending on her, watching her, judging her.

He knew the feeling.

He'd spent a lifetime being the object of everyone's scrutiny. Hell, he still was. Being escorted out of a bake sale, of all things, proved as much. It testified to the fact that there were folks in town who had no intention of forgetting who he was or what his father had done.

And James Lee and his granddaughters proved there were a few who couldn't care less about Jesse's past. A few who accepted him for who he was and what he'd done with his own life. Like Wanda Loftis who worked at the local pizza parlor. Wanda always gave him extra cheese on his pepperoni. A celebrity perk, she'd told him time and time again when he'd offered to pay, only she'd always given him extra cheese even way back when he'd been barely able to scrape together enough money to pay for a small to share with his brothers. And there was Mason Connor, the local pharmacist who'd given him free antibiotic samples that one time when Billy had caught strep back in kindergarten. And Miss Laura, the head waitress at the diner, who had his coffee and a great big smile waiting for him the minute he walked in on Saturday mornings. She'd given him leftovers too many times to count back when his daddy had been alive and food had been scarce. She'd helped him then, and she still had a smile for him when she spotted him now.

The realization sent a rush of warmth through him even though he'd learned a long time ago that the only opinion that really mattered at the end of the day was his own. It was nice to know he had a few supporters in Lost Gun. Friends even.

Which explains why you're still running away.

The minute the thought struck, he tried to push it back out. He wasn't running from anything. He was burying the past. Making peace. Moving on.

Running.

The truth struck, sticking in his head as he pulled on his clothes, parked his hat on top of his head, and headed outside to his pickup truck.

It was just this side of seven a.m. and he needed to get a move on. He had a meeting with Eli to tie up all the loose ends at the training facility—he'd sold all of his stock except for his one new bull and he needed to make arrangements for the old cowboy to look after it until he made arrangements for transport. That, and he needed to pick up the last few boxes of his stuff still stashed at Pete's ranch. Afterwards, he was going to head back into Lost Gun and swing by the motel to say goodbye to his brothers. Then it was just a matter of pointing his truck toward the city limits, pressing on the gas and getting the hell out of Dodge.

Once and for all.

He climbed behind the wheel and gunned the engine. It was the first morning of the rest of his life free and clear of his past. His lawyer had several prospective buyers on the list for his dad's run-down property. Hell, one of them had even made an offer. A damned nice one. Plenty for him to take his share and invest in his very own training facility closer to his spread in Austin. Maybe even buy one clear and outright for himself. Then when his heyday ended as PBR's number one, he could stop riding and start coaching the up-and-comers. That, or breed his own bucking bulls. He'd entertained that possibility, as well.

Either way, he had a solid plan.

One that had kept him up thinking and planning and dreaming on so many lonely nights.

It just didn't fill him with the same sense of hope that it once had. There was no rush of excitement. No sense of accomplishment. No flash of impatience to haul ass and never look back.

Instead, Jesse spent the next half hour driving out to the Gunner spread at a slow crawl that had even Martin Keyhole—the ninety-five-year-old owner of a nearby turtle farm—lying on his horn. Sure, Jesse tried to oblige and pick up his speed, but damned if his boot would stay down. There was just too much going on his head.

Because as much as he wanted to, he couldn't stop thinking about Gracie and the town, and the undeniable truth that whether he went after his own training facility or started breeding his own bucking bulls, he could do either of them right here. Even more, he couldn't shake the feeling that if he did leave, he would be running away from the best thing that had ever happened to him.

16

GRACIE PULLED OUT onto Main Street and took a whopping bite of the extra large fudge brownie she'd just picked up at the local bakery. Her second in less than fifteen minutes. She'd scarfed number one after three cups of coffee and a carob-covered scone from The Green Machine which had done nothing to touch the hunger that ate away inside of her. So she'd caved and walked into the bakery where she'd spent fifteen minutes listening to the clerk, Marjorie Wilbur, complain yet again about the pothole on the corner of Main and Hill Country before taking the rest of her order to go.

She hung a left at the first corner and waited for the rush of satisfaction that always came with even the smallest nibble of her favorite dessert, and the guilt. Especially the guilt. Anything to escape the feelings still pushing and pulling inside of her thanks to Jesse and his declaration.

The heat of the moment.

That's all it had been. Guys were notorious for it and so it should have come as no surprise. Hell, it was a wonder he hadn't proposed after the way she'd rocked his world.

That's what she told herself as she stuffed another bite into her mouth and tried to lose herself in the rich taste of chocolate and the all-important fact that she'd fallen off the wagon in a major way. Not one, but two brownies. She was a loser. A slug. She should feel terrible.

Not excited.

Or happy.

Or anxious to head back to the training facility, throw herself into Jesse's arms and beg him to take her away with him.

Yeah, right.

She hung a left at the second stop sign and eased onto her street. She had a life here with potholes to fix and a town that depended on her and a sister who needed her.

The minute the thought struck, she noted the familiar red Prius parked in her driveway. Charlie was home.

And Gracie wasn't.

She stifled a wave of guilt and pulled into the driveway. Stuffing the bakery bag under her seat, she snagged the camera and her purse and climbed out of the car.

"I thought you weren't coming home this weekend," she said when she walked into the living room to find her younger sister sitting cross-legged on the couch, her laptop balanced on her knees. The petite blonde, hair pulled back in a loose ponytail, wore a Texas Longhorns T-shirt, a pair of sweats and an expression that said *you are so busted.* "I would have had the blueberry pancakes ready and waiting had I known—"

"I'm not eating pancakes anymore," Charlie cut in. "Too much processed flour. And I wasn't coming home this weekend. But you sounded funny when I last talked to you, so I got worried." She shrugged. "I drove in last night."

"*You* were worried about *me?*"

"You didn't sound like your usual neurotic self when I told you I wasn't coming home. No twenty questions about where I was going or what I was doing. No blasting me about being careful. I figured you were sick, but I'm starting to think it might be something else. Or someone else." A knowing light gleamed in her gaze. "You've been out all night."

"I was working late."

"I drove by City Hall. I didn't see your car."

"I wasn't at City Hall. I was at the Gunner ranch. I was helping out with the local newspaper. Their photographer is out, so I offered to take pictures at Pete's wedding for the About Town section."

Charlie didn't look convinced. "That would put you home at midnight."

"I wasn't tired so I drove over to the all-night movie festival in Milburn county."

"All-night movies, huh?" Charlie's fingers moved across the laptop keyboard for a few frantic heartbeats before her gaze narrowed. "The only all-night movie festival in Milburn is Kung Fu Movie Madness at the Palladium." She eyed Gracie. "Since when did you become a Bruce Lee fan?"

"Are you kidding? I love Bruce Lee." Gracie sat her purse aside and headed for the kitchen. "He's super athletic. Listen, I've got some fresh fruit if you're hungry...." Her words trailed off as she headed straight for the refrigerator and tried to ignore the rush of guilt.

"And since when do you take pictures?" Charlie shifted the subject back to the wedding as she followed Gracie into the kitchen. "You don't even own a camera anymore."

"Yes, I do. I just don't use it."

Charlie gave her a knowing look. "Something's up with you."

"Nothing's up." Gracie ignored the gleam in her sister's eyes and busied herself pulling several peaches and a crate of strawberries from the refrigerator. "I was just helping out. It's my job. I'm trying to beef up my public service presence before the inauguration. Speaking of which, I was planning on getting a new dress, so maybe we can go shopping next weekend—"

"It's okay, you know." Charlie leaned on the granite countertop and plucked a ripe strawberry from the container. "It's high time you got a life."

"I have a life, thank you very much." Gracie retrieved a container of yogurt.

"No, you don't." Charlie nibbled on the ripe red fruit. "You facilitate everyone else's life."

"I'm the mayor." Gracie set the yogurt on the counter and reached for two bowls in a nearby cabinet. "That's what I do."

"No, you're you." Charlie pointed the strawberry at her. "That's what *you* do. You make sure everyone else is happy and healthy, but you don't waste five minutes worrying over yourself." The words hung between them for a long moment before her sister added, "You deserve to be happy and healthy, too, you know."

"I am happy." And healthy. Or she had been before Jesse's impromptu declaration and the double dose of brownies. "I'm happy if you're happy."

"That's the thing." Charlie abandoned the half-eaten strawberry. "I have enough stress. Do you know how much pressure I deal with knowing that your well-being rests on my shoulders?"

Gracie thought of the past twelve years since her brother's death. "Actually, I do."

"Then you know it's not that much fun." A pleading note crept into her voice. "I was supposed to go with Aubry and Sue to Dallas to go club-hopping, but I bailed on them to drive here because I was worried about you."

"I wish you wouldn't have done that."

"I did it because I know you would do the same for me. I know you love me, Gracie. You don't have to keep trying to prove it."

"I just want you to feel it. Every second of every day. I want to be there for you—"

"That's the thing," she cut in, "you can't. Not all the time. Not because you don't love me, but because that's the way life is. It's a bitch sometimes and there are moments when things don't always pan out. I'm going to have to stand on my own two feet eventually. All by myself. Alone. That doesn't mean I'm lonely, but you are. Which is why I was thinking that we could sign you up for one of those online dating sites. A friend of mine's mother did it and she has a date every Saturday night—"

"Charlie, I'm not lonely."

"You went to an all-night Bruce Lee festival," Charlie pointed out. "You're beyond lonely. You're just this side of depraved. You need a man."

"Just because I don't have a man doesn't mean I'm lonely or depraved. I've got an entire town to keep me company." She eyed the dog wagging at her feet. "And Sugar, too."

Charlie bent down and picked up the ball of fluff. She gave the animal an affectionate scratch behind the ears. "You really think Sugar Lips, here, is a fitting substitute for a *man?*"

She thought of Jesse and the past few nights they'd spent together. She remembered the way he'd touched her and kissed her and laughed when she'd said something really funny. The way he'd looked at her when she'd talked about her past, as if he understood what she felt. As if he felt it, too.

And then she thought of the nights that lay ahead with Sugar curled up on her lap and the remote control in her hand and the latest reality show blaring on the TV.

"Which dating site was that?" she heard herself ask.

GRACIE SPENT SUNDAY morning trying not to think about Jesse. Or the all-important fact that he loved her and she loved him and he was still leaving. He hadn't said a word otherwise. No phone call. No text. Nothing but silence.

Not that it would have made a difference. She'd made her choice. Her life was here.

Which was why she'd dragged herself into City Hall to get a jump-start on her week. She had dozens of things to do before the inauguration in one week. Today alone she had to put in an appearance at the local tractor races, recite the Pledge of Allegiance at the weekly softball games and then dish up potato salad for the afternoon picnic at the Lost Gun Presbyterian Church. Even if she wasn't too keen on facing an entire town full of people at the moment. She would do it anyway—all of it—because it was her duty. Gracie had made a promise, and she always kept her promises. *Always.*

But first…

She focused on the lime-green Hula-Hoop in her hands and started to swirl her hips. A quick twist of the hoop and for the next few seconds, she moved in perfect synchronization with the plastic circle swirling around her waist. But then it fell and she found herself back at square one.

"Why are you doing this?" Trina asked when she walked into Gracie's office to find her huffing and puffing and sweating up a storm.

"Because I promised Sue Ann Miller that I would do the Hula-Hoop for Hope with the rest of her Brownie troop tomorrow afternoon. I won't buy much hope if I can't Hula-Hoop for more than ten seconds a pop. People pledge by the minute."

"I'm not talking about the Hula-Hoop. I'm talking about this." She motioned at the office surrounding them. "All of this. It's Sunday. A day of rest. You should be sitting in your backyard, sipping a mai tai and reading a romance novel or a glamour mag. Or traipsing through the woods with that camera you love so much."

"I don't use my camera anymore."

"Sure, you don't." Her eyes twinkled. "I saw you last night at the wedding. The entire town saw you."

"That's different." She remembered all of the pics of Jesse she'd snapped at the training facility after the festivities. Pics that had nothing to do with what was happening about town and everything to do with the fact that she'd wanted to keep him with her. Not that she was admitting as much to Trina. "I was filling in for June."

"You were enjoying yourself, which is what you should be doing right now. Instead, you're working. You're cooped up when you hate being cooped up. You hate going to city council meetings and old-lady breakfasts and monthly VFW luncheons."

"I don't hate it."

"You don't like it."

"I'm good at it."

"That's not the point. Aren't you tired of faking it?" Trina echoed the one question that had been nagging at her all morning.

She *did* hate playing the part of little Miss Perfect. Sure, she was good at it. She'd learned to be good at it, but she didn't actually *like* it.

She never had and she never would.

"It doesn't matter what I like or what I don't like. I'm still the mayor-elect."

"And as mayor-elect, you are more than capable of picking a replacement should you decide to retire early."

The meaning of Trina's words sank in and for the first time in a very long time, Gracie felt a flutter of excitement deep inside.

"I can't just give it all up." That was what she said, but where that statement had been true twelve years ago, it was no longer true now. Times had changed. *She'd* changed. She didn't have to keep playing the martyr. She knew that.

At the same time, she'd been doing it for so long that she wasn't so sure she could stop. Even if she desperately wanted to.

An image of Jesse pushed into her head and she remembered the possessive look on his face when he'd cut in to dance with her last night. He'd taken her into his arms and held her as if he never meant to let her go.

He'd also been tipsy thanks to the primo moonshine that had been circulating at last night's wedding.

She ignored the ache in her chest and focused on doing something—anything—to keep her mind off Jesse and the fact that he was leaving and she was letting him go. Without putting up a fight. Or telling him how she felt.

"Where are you going?" Trina asked when Gracie abandoned the Hula-Hoop and reached for her purse.

"I need to see a man about some moonshine."

"You really think Big Earl is cooking again?"

Gracie thought of the pint of white lightning she'd seen at the wedding the night before and then she thought of the way Casey Jessup had helped her great-grandfather into his chair. "I think it's his recipe, but I don't think he's the one doing the cooking."

Gracie's instincts were jumping and buzzing because she knew Casey had something to do with the case of white lightning at the wedding the night before. It was just a matter of proving it.

"MY GREAT-GRANDPA'S taking a nap. You'll have to come back later," Casey said when Gracie knocked on the door a half hour later, after another visit to the butcher.

"I'm not here to talk to him." She glanced behind her at the dogs busy devouring the raw meat before turning a pleading look on Casey. "I want to talk to you and I'd like to do it with all of my limbs intact."

Casey looked undecided for a split second before she shrugged and stepped aside.

Gracie retreated into the safety of the double-wide trailer. A faint snore drifted from a nearby bedroom, confirming that Casey, at least, wasn't lying about Big Earl's nap.

"I know you made the moonshine for him," Gracie said, turning on the young woman. "I also know that you aren't going to do it again—otherwise I'll be obliged to report you to the sheriff."

Casey looked as if she wanted to deny the accusation, but then she shrugged. "It's no big deal. It was just one batch."

"It's still illegal."

The girl glanced toward the open bedroom door. "But cooking makes him happy, and not much else does these days. He used to love his crosswords, but now he can't see the puzzle. And he used to love to watch his old Western flicks, but now he can't even do that because of his glaucoma. And he cain't cook either and enjoy a glass every night like he used to on account of he can't see or move around or do anything else like he used to. So I took his recipe and I did it myself so he wouldn't miss out on the one thing he can do, and that's drink. I just want him to be happy."

Enough to sacrifice her own freedom should she gt caught.

Gracie knew the feeling.

"I understand you did it for a good reason, but it's still highly illegal. You can't cook out here. He'll have to switch to beer or whiskey or something they actually sell in a store."

"And if he doesn't?"

"Then I'll have the sheriff arrest the both of you. Consider this your warning. No more cooking."

Casey nodded and Gracie knew she'd won this battle. But Big Earl was well over ninety years old and had acquired a taste for moonshine a long, long time ago. Even more, Casey was too devoted to deny the old man much of anything. And so Gracie wasn't so sure she was going to win this war.

Still, she intended to try.

"No cooking," she said again, and then she held her breath, darted out the door and raced for her car.

A HALF HOUR later Trina was on her fourth drink while Gracie worked on her second. They sat at a small table at a local sports bar that was all but deserted thanks to the softball game going on down at the ball field. Still, a few die-hard football fans sat in the far corner, as well as the entire ladies' sewing circle who were drinking peach schnapps and watching a rerun of *Bridezillas* on one of the monstrous TV screens.

Gracie's gaze swiveled away from a bitchy bride named Soleil just in time to see a pair of worn jeans moving toward her. Her gaze slid higher, over trim thighs and a lean waist, to a faded denim shirt covering a broad chest… Jesse. A straw Resistol sat atop his dark head, slanted at just the angle she remembered and making him look every bit the cowboy who'd stolen her heart.

"Shouldn't you be on the interstate by now?" she asked as he stopped next to her table.

"I forgot something." Jesse's gaze caught and held hers and his words echoed in her head.

"What?"

"You."

Joy erupted inside her, stirring a wave of panic that made her heart pound faster.

"I don't know what you mean."

"I want you to come with me." His gaze darkened. "Be with me. You don't belong here, Gracie. You and I both know that."

"You don't know anything. Sorry, Trina," she told her assistant as she pushed to her feet. "I need to get out of here." Before Jesse could reach for her, she started past him toward the nearest exit. Fear pushed her faster when she heard Jesse's voice behind her.

"Gracie, wait!"

But she couldn't. Not because he wanted her to go but because she wanted it. She wanted to chuck it all, throw herself into his arms, walk away and never look back. The knowledge sent a rush of anxiety through her and she picked up her steps. She slammed her palms against the exit door and stumbled out into the parking lot. Gravel crunched as her legs ate up the distance to the car.

"Gracie!" The name rang out a second before he caught her arm in a firm jerk that brought her whirling around to face him. "Gracie, I—"

"Don't say it!" She shook her head, blinking back the tears that suddenly threatened to overwhelm her. "Please don't say it again."

"I love you."

The tears spilled over and she shook her head, fighting the truth of his words and the emotion in her heart. "Let me go. I—I need to get back to the office. I've got work to do."

"Gracie?" Strong, warm hands cradled her face, his thumbs

smoothing her tears. "What is it, baby? Didn't you hear me? You know I love—"

"Don't!" Pleasure rushed through her, so fierce it stirred the fear and the panic and made her fight harder. She pushed at his hands. "Don't say those things to me. Don't make this situation any harder. You have to leave and I have to let you."

"If saying I love you makes it harder for you to let me go, then I love you, I love you, I will *always* love you." His eyes took on a determined light. "That's why I want you to come with me. I thought you'd be happy. I thought you wanted out of this town."

"You thought wrong."

"Did I?" His fierce violet gaze held hers, coaxing and tempting, and she came so close to throwing herself into his arms—to hell with Lost Gun.

Instead, she shook her head, clinging to her anger and her fear and the pain of hearing her sister cry herself to sleep every night after their brother passed away. Charlie had been so uncertain for so long, but Gracie had changed all of that. *She'd* changed.

While she wasn't the goody-goody she pretended to be and she was far from content, she still liked it here. She liked the people and the town and her house.

Her home.

"I'm not going with you. I made a commitment to the people of this town. I have a responsibility. I can't drop everything just because you say you love me."

"How about because *you* love *me?*"

She shook her head. "I don't. I can't."

No matter how much she wanted to.

She fought against the emotion that gripped her heart and made her want to throw all pride aside, wrap her arms around him and confess the feelings welling inside of her.

"It doesn't matter how we feel. It doesn't change the fact that you have to go and I have to stay. I *have* to." She yanked free and started for her car, steps echoing in her head like a death knell. Inside, she gunned the engine and took a deep, shaking breath.

Heaven help her, she'd done it. She'd done the right thing by giving Jesse the freedom he so desperately needed.

So why did it suddenly feel as if Gracie had turned her back on the one thing that mattered most?

Wiping frantically at a flood of hot tears, she chanced a glance in her mirror to see Jesse standing where she'd left him, staring after her, fists clenched, his body taut, as if it took all his strength not to go after her.

It was an image that haunted her all through the night and the rest of the week as Gracie wrote her acceptance speech and picked out a dress for the inauguration and prepared for the rest of her life.

Without Jesse Chisholm.

"LET HER LOOSE!" Jesse yelled, stuffing his hand beneath the rope and holding on for all he was worth. The two cowboys monitoring the chute threw open the doors. The bull reared and darted forward, nearly throwing Jesse, who held tight, riding the fledgling for the very first time.

He held on, his grip determined as the bull kicked and stomped and snorted against the feel of the weight on his back. Seconds ticked by as he bucked and twisted and made Jesse the proud papa of a brand-new bucking bull.

Cheers went up a few minutes later as he climbed off after a brief but exhilarating ride.

"You did good, boy," he murmured, wishing Pete could have been there. But he was off on his honeymoon with Wendy, making memories and babies.

A pang of envy shot through Jesse. While he'd achieved so much in his life, he was just getting started. He had years left on the circuit. Too long to be thinking about a future beyond.

A home. Kids. Gracie.

It was three days since he'd last seen her. Instead of hauling ass to Austin on Sunday, he'd gone back to the Gunner ranch to pick up some boxes and ended up staying the night. To think on things and try to get his head on straight. Then Monday had rolled around and his lawyer had called with two more buyers and Jesse had stayed to meet with the man and go over things later that day. And then Tuesday had rolled around and he'd had papers to sign. And Wednesday he'd had to accept delivery of the fledgling bull since Eli had made an appointment to get new glasses.

But tomorrow… Tomorrow was the day.

Jesse helped the hands get Ranger back into his chute. He'd just flipped the latch when he caught sight of a familiar car pulling into the parking lot.

He pulled off his gloves, exited the corral and started toward her. Gracie climbed out of the car and met him near the front entrance.

"You're here," he said, his heart pitching and shaking faster than a bull busting out of the chute.

"I heard you got delayed with the offers on your place and so I thought I'd stop by before you finally do hit the road." She handed him a box. "I made it for you. Something to remember me by."

As if he could forget her.

She'd lived and breathed in his memories for so long and now she'd taken up permanent residence in his heart, and there wasn't a damn thing he could do about it.

There was, a nagging voice whispered. He could hitch her over his shoulder, load her into his pickup truck and haul ass for Austin. And when he got there, he could love her until she changed her mind and stayed. The heat burned so fierce between them it would be hot enough to change her mind. For a little while, anyway.

But then she would leave. He knew it. She belonged here and he didn't, and there wasn't a damned thing he could do about it.

His fingers itched and he touched her hand. Her gaze met his and he read the fear in her eyes, the uncertainty. As much as she wanted him to stay, she wanted to go. But she was afraid.

Afraid to follow, to abandon the town that had embraced her when she'd needed them.

The same town that had shunned him.

He pulled his hand away even though every fiber of his being wanted to say to hell with Austin, to crush her in his arms and never let go.

He concentrated on opening the box.

A navy blue photo album lay inside, nestled in tissue paper. Jesse pulled the album free and turned to the first page to see several landscape shots of Lost Gun. The surrounding trees, the lush pasture, the historic buildings lining Main Street. He flipped through several more pages, saw more pictures of the town, including James Lee and the kids at the car wash and even one of each of his brothers. Billy two-stepped his way around the dance floor down at the local honky-tonk and Cole held tight to an ornery bronc.

"It's a memory book. I know you don't have good memories of your childhood, but these are new memories. Good ones to replace the old ones."

Jesse simply stared and flipped until he reached the last page, which held a full glossy of himself astride one of his training bulls. He swallowed the baseball-size lump in his throat. With stiff fingers he managed to close the book. "It's missing something."

She looked genuinely puzzled. "What?"

His gaze captured hers. "You."

"I don't think this is the right time—"

"Do you love me? Because if you do, I need to hear it."

Fear brightened her eyes, made her hands tremble, and for a split second, he thought she was going to turn and run without ever admitting the truth to him. To herself.

"Yes."

The word sang through his head, echoed through his heart. He wanted to hear her say it again and again, to feel the one syllable against his lips. "Then come with me. You don't have to stay here for your sister. She's all grown up now, living her own life. She doesn't need you here. The town doesn't need you."

"But I need it." Tears filled her voice, betraying the calm she always tried so hard to maintain. "All I could think about for so long was getting out. It's all I dreamed of. I wanted to hit the road, to find someplace where I felt at home. But once I stopped trying to run, I realized that I felt it here. This is home for me, Jesse. It'll always be home."

He stepped toward her and touched his mouth to hers. The photo album thudded to the ground. Jesse wrapped his arms around Gracie and held tight, as if he never meant to let go. He gave her a gentle, searing kiss that intensified the ache deep inside him and made him want to hold her forever.

She loved him, he loved her. This was crazy. They could have a life together starting now. Today. In Austin. Or here.

It didn't matter to him.

The realization hit just as she pulled away.

This was home. Gracie was home.

Her warmth. Her smile. Her love.

It was all right here, and that was why he'd been stalling. This was where he needed to be.

He needed to stay.

And she needed him to go.

Because he knew she would never forgive him if she thought that he'd changed his plans just for her. She would never forgive herself.

Maybe she would. Maybe she'd be happy he'd changed his mind and they'd live happily ever after.

It wasn't a chance he could take. He didn't want her feeling as though she'd destroyed his dreams. Trapped him.

He knew what it felt like to live with guilt. He wouldn't doom her to the hell he'd faced for so long. The doubt. The uncertainty.

"You know where to find me," he murmured against her soft, sweet lips. "If you change your mind." While he knew with dead certainty that they were meant to be together, Gracie had to discover it for herself.

And if she didn't?

Jesse shoved his greatest fear aside and did the hardest thing he'd ever had to do in his life. He walked away from Gracie Stone.

And then he left Lost Gun for good.

"FORGET THE PICS at the bouncy house!" Trina motioned Gracie toward the large tent set up at the far end of the fairgrounds. It was the first day of the town's infamous three-week-long rodeo and barbecue cook-off, a huge event that drew tourists and fans from all over the state. "Cletus Walker is this close to breaking the record for eating the most bread-and-butter pickles. He's already eaten four hundred and twenty. He'll either blow or land himself in the *Guinness Book of World Records.* Either way, you're going to want firsthand shots."

Gracie clicked off two more shots of three-year-old Sally Wheeler sitting midbounce with her big toe in her mouth and rushed after the town's new mayor.

Rushed. That described her life over the past three weeks since she'd resigned as mayor, handed over the office to the new mayor-elect—Trina—and bought out June Silsbee's photography studio. June was now awaiting the birth of her triplets in peace. Meanwhile, Gracie was up to her armpits in work.

Between babies and youth sports and local chili cook-offs, she barely had time to look through her viewfinder before she was hustling off to the next assignment.

Not that she minded the whirlwind. She welcomed it because it kept her busy. Too busy to think about Jesse and the all-important fact that she missed him terribly.

"Are you okay?" Trina asked as Gracie caught up to her at the entrance to the pickle-eating tent.

"Fine."

"Uh-huh." Trina gave her a quick once-over. "I'm the mayor, sugar. You can't put anything over on me."

"I think I might be coming down with something."

"Yeah, a bad case of the gimmes."

"What?"

"You know. The gimmes. It's when a woman's been getting some and then all of a sudden she's not getting any. She goes into withdrawal and her body is like, 'Gimme, gimme, gimme.'"

"That's ridiculous."

And all too true.

"I just need a little vitamin C and I'll be fine."

That was what she said, but she wasn't placing any bets. While she'd done the right thing and let him go, a part of her still wished that she had begged him to stay.

Not that it would have made any difference. He would have left anyway. He'd had to leave.

She understood that.

She just wished it didn't hurt so much.

She forced aside the depressing thought, made her way up to the front of the tent and focused on a red-faced Cletus, who eyed pickle number 421 as if it were a snake about to bite him.

She documented the momentous occasion as he devoured the last bite and lifted his arms in victory before making her way toward the corral set up at the far end of the fairgrounds. Dozens of rookie bull riders lined the metal fence, cheering on the wrangler atop the angry bull twisting and turning center stage. The preliminaries hadn't actually started, but the cowboys were giving it their all in a practice round that would pick the lineup for the main event.

She maneuvered between two button-down Western shirts and started snapping pictures.

She aimed for another picture and a strange awareness skittered over her skin, as if someone watched her.

As if…

She glanced around, her gaze searching the dozens of faces.

It was just her imagination, she finally concluded, turning her attention back to her camera. Because no way in heaven, hell or even Texas could Jesse Chisholm be here—

The thought scattered the minute she sighted the familiar face in her viewfinder.

He'd stepped from behind a group of wranglers. The crowd milled around him and the noise rose up, but her full attention fixated on him. She watched as he talked to some cowboy who stood next to him, obviously oblivious to his surroundings, and her hope took a nosedive. For a split second, she thought that he'd come for her, that he was going to sweep her up into his arms and whisk her away.

Right.

He was obviously here for the rodeo. To ride his way straight to another buckle.

Without her.

The thought sent a burst of panic through her because as happy as she was here in Lost Gun, she could never be truly happy without him. She loved him. She always had and she always would, and it was time she owned up to it.

She'd made the last move and ended things with him, and now it was time to make the first move and set things right.

She pushed her way through the crowd, working her way around the corral until she came up behind him. A tap on the shoulder and he turned to face her.

Where she'd expected surprise, she saw only relief. As if he'd been waiting for her for a very long time.

He had, she realized as he stared deep into her eyes and she saw the insecurity, the doubt, the guilt. He'd been waiting for twelve years for her to admit her feelings, to tell the world, and now it was time.

Her gaze snagged on the weariness in his eyes and her heart hitched. "You look like hell," she said as she noted the tight lines around his mouth, the shadows beneath his eyes, as if he hadn't slept in days. Weeks.

"Nice to see you, too."

"You here to compete?"

"That, and I thought you might want these back." Two fingers wiggled into his jeans pocket and he pulled a familiar scrap of black lace from inside. He grinned his infamous rodeo-bad-boy grin that made her insides jump as he dangled her undies from one tanned finger. "These do belong to you, don't they?"

A few weeks ago she would have snatched the undies from his hand and stuffed them in her purse, desperate to keep up appearances and avoid any scandal that would disappoint the good folks of Lost Gun. But things were different now. She was different. She loved Jesse and she didn't care who knew it. She gave in to the smile that tugged at her lips. "They are, but I don't see that I need them at the moment. I'm wearing new ones."

"I know. I thought maybe we could make a trade."

"So you're collecting women's lingerie?"

"Just yours, Gracie. Only yours. I was hoping to add every damn pair you possess to my stash." Determination lit his eyes. "Just so you know, I might have retreated, but I'm not giving up. I would never try to force you to do anything. I've been staying away to let you know that I respect your decisions, and I'll keep staying away if I have to. If that's what you want." His fingertips trailed along her cheek as if he couldn't quite believe she was real. "Because you're what I want and I don't care who knows it."

"What about Austin? It's your home."

"You're home." His hands cradled her face, his thumbs smoothing across her trembling bottom lip. "Wherever you are, that's where I'll hang my hat."

"You hate it here."

He glanced around at the multitude of faces surrounding them. "I hate my past and the people who refuse to let me forget it. But not everyone here is like that. Miss Hazel is the sweetest woman who ever walked the planet, and she's here." He shrugged. "This place isn't so bad."

"But Austin is your dream. I can't ask you to give up your dream. I won't ask it."

Anger flared deep in his eyes as his mouth tightened into a grim line. "So you don't love me. Is that what you're trying to say?"

"No! I do love you. With all my heart. It's just… I don't want you making all the sacrifices." She shook her head and turned to stare at the bull kicking up dust in a nearby chute. "That's not what love is all about. It's about give-and-take. An equal amount of both."

"Meaning?" He came up behind her, so close she could feel the heat from his body, hear his heart beating in her ears.

"I'm pretty good with this camera," she told him. "I was thinking I could take some time off and follow you out onto the road. If you could use a good action photographer, that is." Her gaze met his. "I do want to live here, but I know you have a job that you love, one that takes you away for weeks on end. I don't want to be away from you that long." She caught his arms when he started to reach for her and held him off, determined to resolve the unanswered questions between them. "I'm willing to follow you—I want to follow you—if you're willing to follow me right back here when it's all said and done. Give-and-take. Fifty-fifty. You and me."

"What about your sister?"

"She's a big girl. She doesn't need me."

"I'd be willing to bet she still needs you."

She shrugged. "True, but I'm just a text away. So that's it. That's my offer. You let me go with you and I'll let you come back here with me."

He grinned, the sight easing the anxiety that had been coiling inside her. "I could use a new head shot or two," he declared as he drew her into his arms and hugged her fiercely. "To keep the fans happy."

"Not too happy," she said, her heart swelling with the certainty that he loved her as much as she loved him. “I don’t share very well.”

“Neither do I.” His expression went from sheer happiness to serious desperation. “Marry me, Gracie, and we’ll make a home for ourselves right here in Lost Gun. You can take pictures to your heart’s content and do anything that makes you happy, as long as we’re together. I want you in my bed.” He touched one nipple and brought the tip to throbbing awareness. “In my heart.” His hand slid higher, over the pounding between her breasts. “In my life.” His thumb came to rest over the frantic jump of her pulse. “Everywhere.”

She smiled through a blurry haze of tears and pulled away from him to grab the hem of her sundress and run her hands up her bare legs.

His expression went from puzzled to hungry. “What are you doing?”

She smiled wider. “Giving you a deposit.”

She shimmied and wiggled until her hot pink panties pooled at her ankles. Stepping free, she dangled the scrap of silk in front of him before stuffing the undies into his pocket along with the other pair already in his possession.

“Just so you know, there’s more where those came from. A future of them. Forever.” And then she kissed him, surrendering her body to his roaming hands, her heart to his and her soul to whatever the future held.

Right here in Lost Gun.

Epilogue

"YOU SURE YOU WANT to do this?" Jesse asked Gracie as he braked to a stop near the fence that surrounded Big Earl Jessup's property. He killed the engine on the pickup and flicked off the headlights.

"No." Gracie tamped down on her anxiety when she heard the dogs start to bark and held tight to the hand of the man sitting next to her. "But Jackie Sue Patterson told Martin Skolnik who told Laura Lynn McKinney who just so happened to mention when she brought her twins into the studio for pics that she saw Casey Jessup at the hardware store yesterday. She bought two propane lanterns, some rope, a tarp and some tie-down stakes. That means she's cooking moonshine again and I'm the one responsible since I let her off with just a warning instead of turning her over to Sheriff Hooker."

He squeezed her hand reassuringly. "It could just mean she's going camping."

"Maybe, but maybe not. Either way, I need to find out. If something's up, we'll head back to town and I'll notify the sheriff." For Casey's own good.

While Gracie knew the girl was just helping out her grandfather the only way she knew how, cooking moonshine was still illegal. And dangerous. And Gracie wouldn't be able to live with herself if something bad happened and someone got hurt.

She eyed the small house that sat several yards away. A television flickered just beyond one of the windows, but otherwise everything seemed quiet.

She whipped out her binoculars and scoured the area, from the old toilet that had been turned into a planter near the front porch, to the stretch of pasture that extended beyond the house. Her heart stalled when she noted the small light that flickered in the far distance.

"See?" She pointed and handed Jesse the binoculars. "It's her."

"It's definitely someone." He gazed at the horizon before handing the binoculars back to her. "I don't know that it's Casey."

"Who else would it be?" Gracie watched as the figure lifted the pinpoint of light and suddenly Casey Jessup's face came into view. "It's her." The young woman turned and walked toward the tree line, lantern in one hand and what looked like a shovel in the other. "I told you she was up to something."

"She's walking."

"Exactly."

"And carrying a light."

"Even more incriminating."

"Babe, she could just be going for a walk."

"At half past midnight?"

"Maybe she's meeting someone."

"To sell a few cases."

"Or to hook up." He shrugged. "It *is* one hell of a nice night."

She abandoned the binoculars to slide him a glance. Her heart hitched as her gaze collided with his and she felt the familiar warmth that told her she was sitting next to her soul mate. A man who loved her as much as she loved him. A man who always would.

She noted the gleam in his rich, violet eyes. "Since when did you turn into the eternal optimist?"

A grin tugged at his lips. "Since a certain buttoned-up city official whipped off her panties in the middle of town and handed them to me in front of God and the Amberjack twins."

Her own lips twitched at the memory. "I did give them something to talk about, didn't I?"

"Enough fuel to keep things interesting for at least another year." He winked. "It was definitely one of my most favorite moments."

"Glad I could renew your hope in mankind."

"Sugar, you *are* my hope." He leaned across the seat and touched her lips with his own in a fierce kiss that made her stomach quiver.

It had been a week since she'd handed her panties to him in front of an arena full of people and declared her love. A busy week since Jesse had changed his mind about selling his dad's old place and decided to clear the spot and build a brand-new house smack-dab in the middle of Lost Gun.

Not that he'd made complete peace with his past.

We're talking a week.

The recent airing of *Famous Texas Outlaws* had, as expected, lured a ton of tourists to town and stirred a wave of fortune hunting. And speculation. About the money. About Jesse and his brothers and their integrity. According to the latest round of gossip, they not only knew what had happened to the money, but they'd gone on a spending spree that included everything from new cowboy boots to a private island in South America.

Crazy, but that was the rumor mill in a small town. And part of the reason Jesse had been so desperate to get out of Lost Gun for good.

But while he'd yet to forgive the townspeople who'd made his life a living hell while growing up—the same people who were wagging their tongues and feeding the frenzy right now—he had managed to acknowledge those people who did accept him. Even more, he'd found the strength to forgive himself.

And so even though it had only been a week, the past didn't

hurt quite so much. And when it eventually did, Gracie would be right there to soothe the ache.

She loved him and he loved her and they were now focused on the future. Lost Gun's infamous three-week-long rodeo extravaganza was in full swing. Jesse had swept the preliminaries and landed at the top of the leader board. Meanwhile Gracie had been named the official photographer by the board of directors of the Lost Gun Livestock Show and Rodeo. Her pictures had been featured on the front page of the weekly newspaper just yesterday and her photography studio was booked solid for the weeks to come.

Speaking of which, she had an early shoot tomorrow morning and the last thing she needed was to be traipsing around in the middle of the night.

At the same time, she would never forgive herself if something bad happened to Casey or Big Earl.

While she'd given up carrying the weight of the world, old habits were still hard to break.

Before she could pull back and tell Jesse as much, he ended the kiss, pulled his keys from the ignition and reached for the door. "Let's get this over with so that we can get on with our own hookup."

"Such a romantic."

"It will be, darlin'." He winked. "That much I can guarantee."

She tamped down the excitement the blatant promise stirred in her and reached for the door handle. A few minutes and a full stretch of pasture later, they reached a cluster of trees. They picked their way through the thick foliage, following the small light that glowed in the distance until they reached the line of trees that gave way to yet another pasture. The light grew brighter, illuminating Casey Jessup and the shovel in her hands.

Gracie watched as the young woman shoved the sharp edge into the ground, pushed it down with her foot and scooped a mound of dirt to the side.

"That doesn't look like a still to me," Jesse whispered against her ear.

"Maybe she's burying the evidence. People bury everything from money to time capsules. Why not moonshine?"

"Because the goal is to sell it, not bury it," he pointed out under his breath. "Something else is up."

He was right, Gracie realized as she watched Casey dig not one, but two holes. Then three. Four.

Forget burying something. The woman was looking. Desperately looking, her movements frantic, anxious, determined.

She finished another hole and let loose a loud cuss as she hit another dead end.

Still, she didn't give up. She went for yet another spot, her expression mad. *Mean*.

The minute the thought struck, something niggled at Gracie's subconscious. Her mind rifled back and she remembered the meeting with Big Earl and the Josey Wales poster on the wall. The quote echoed in her head, so familiar, as if she'd heard it somewhere before.

She had, she realized as she held Jesse's hand and watched Casey Jessup break ground at another spot.

When things look bad and it looks like you're not gonna make it, then you gotta get mean. I mean plumb, mad-dog mean. 'Cause if you lose your head and you give up then you neither live nor win.

It was the quote engraved on Silas Chisholm's headstone. It had been his favorite saying or so Jesse had told her when they'd visited his grave just a few short days ago.

He'd been a die-hard Josey Wales fan, just like Big Earl.

"They knew each other," she murmured, the words louder than she intended.

Casey's head snapped up and she turned. Her gaze locked with Gracie's and a dozen emotions rolled across her face. Surprise. Aggravation. Relief.

"He knew Silas, didn't he?" The words were out before Gracie could stop them.

Casey didn't look as if she meant to answer.

No, she looked ready to come at them, shovel swinging. But the anger quickly subsided as her gaze shifted to Jesse and something close to defeat filled her expression. She shook her head. "He didn't just know him. They were friends. Partners." She slung the shovel down and stuck a hand on her hip. "You said we couldn't cook anymore and we need that money." Her gaze met Gracie's. "I can't take care of Big Earl like I need to. He's got heart problems and he needs that money."

"What money?" Gracie asked, but she already knew.

And so did Jesse. "It wasn't lost in the fire," Jesse murmured after a long, drawn-out moment. "It's here."

Casey nodded. "Silas gave it to Great-granddaddy and he buried it out here for safekeeping."

"That's great." Gracie's heart pumped with the realization of what such a discovery meant. Recovering the money would put an end to the treasure hunting and the speculation. The money would mean real closure.

For the town, and for Jesse.

"Actually, it's not so great." Casey blew out a deep, exasperated breath and stared around her at the multitude of holes. "Great-granddaddy's memory isn't what it used to be. He buried the money out here, but the thing is, he can't remember exactly where." She glanced behind her at the endless expanse of land that seemed to stretch endlessly. "We've got fifty acres and the only thing he can remember for sure is that he buried it in some tall grass."

Gracie stared around, at the endless stretch of tall grass and trees and enough possibilities to keep Casey Jessup digging night after night for the rest of eternity.

"It could be anywhere," Jesse's deep voice echoed in the dark night, confirming what Gracie was already thinking.

That there would be no quick fix. No digging it up and giving it back, and laying the past to rest for Jesse and his brothers.

Not just yet, that is.

* * * * *

Keep reading for an excerpt of
Ways To Ruin A Royal Reputation
by Dani Collins.
Find it in the
Billion Dollar Temptation anthology,
out now!

CHAPTER ONE

"RUIN ME."

Amy Miller blinked, certain she'd misheard Luca Albizzi, the king of Vallia.

She'd been reeling since she'd walked into this VIP suite in London's toniest hotel and discovered who her potential client would be.

Her arrival here had been conducted under a cloak of mystery. A call had had her assistant frowning with perplexity as she relayed the request that Amy turn up for an immediate consultation, now or never.

Given the address, Amy had been confident it was worth pandering to the vague yet imperious invitation. It wasn't unheard-of for managers of celebrities to conceal a client's identity while they brought Amy and her team into a crisis situation.

Amy had snatched up her bag and hurried across the city, expecting to meet an outed MP's son or an heiress being blackmailed with revenge porn.

The hotel manager had brought her to the Royal Suite, a title Amy had not taken seriously despite the pair of men guarding the door, both wearing dark suits and inscrutable expressions. One had searched through her satchel while the other inspected the jacket she had nervously removed in the lift.

When they opened the door for her, Amy had warily entered an empty lounge.

As she set her bag and jacket on a bar stool, the sound of the main door closing had brought a pensive man from one of the bedrooms.

He wore a bone-colored business shirt over dark gray trousers, no tie, and had such an air of authority, he nearly knocked her over with it. He was thirtyish, swarthy, his hair light brown, his blue eyes piercing enough to score lines into her.

Before she had fully recognized him, a hot, bright pull twisted within her. A sensual vine that wound through her limbs slithered to encase her, and yanked.

It was inexplicable and disconcerting—even more so when her brain caught up to realize exactly who was provoking this reaction.

The headlines had been screaming for weeks that the Golden Prince, recently crowned the king of Vallia, would be coming to London on a state visit. King Luca had always been notorious for the fact he was powerful, privileged and sinfully good-looking. Everything else about him was above reproach. According to reports, he'd dined at Buckingham Palace last night where the only misstep had been a smoky look of admiration from a married duchess that he had ignored.

"Call me Luca," he said by way of introduction, and invited her to sit.

Gratefully, Amy had sunk onto the sofa, suffering the worst case of starstruck bedazzlement she'd ever experienced. She spoke to wealthy and elite people all the time and never lost her tongue. Or her hearing. Or her senses. She refused to let this man be anything different, but he was. He just was.

She saw his mouth move again. The words he'd just spoken were floating in her consciousness, but his gorgeously deep voice with that Italian accent evoked hot humid nights in narrow cobblestone alleys while romantic strains of a violin drifted from open windows. She could practically smell the fragrance of exotic blossoms weighting the air. He would draw her into a shadowed alcove and that full-lipped, hot mouth would smother—

"Will you?" he prodded.

Amy yanked herself back from the kind of fantasy that could, indeed, ruin him. *And* her. He was a potential client, for heaven's sake!

A cold tightness arrived behind her breastbone as she made the connection that she was, once again, lusting for someone off-limits. Oh, God. She wouldn't say the king of Vallia reminded her of *him.* That would be a hideous insult. Few men were as reprehensible as *him*, but a clammy blanket of apprehension settled on her as she realized she was suffering a particularly strong case of the butterflies for someone who potentially had power over her.

She forcibly cocooned those butterflies and reminded herself she was not without power of her own. She could turn down this man or this job. In fact, based on this off-the-rails attraction she was suffering, she should do both.

She would, once she politely heard him out. At the very least, she could recommend one of her colleagues.

Why did *that* thought make this weird ache in her diaphragm pang even harder?

She shook it off.

"I'm sorry," she said, managing to dredge the words from her dry throat. "Did you say someone is trying to ruin you? London Connection can definitely help you defuse that." There. She almost sounded like the savvy, confident, cofounder of a public relations firm that her business card said she was.

"I said I want *you* to ruin me."

You. Her heart swerved. *Did he know?* Her ears grew so hot, she feared they'd set her hair on fire. He couldn't know what had happened, she assured herself even as snakes of guilt and shame writhed in her stomach. Her parents and the school's headmistress had scrubbed out that little mess with all the alacrity of a government cleanup team in a blockbuster movie. That's how Amy had learned mistakes could be mitigated so well they disappeared from the collective consciousness, even if the stain remained on your conscience forever.

Nevertheless, her hands clenched in her lap as though she had to physically hang on to all she'd managed to gain after losing everything except the two best friends who remained her staunchest supporters to this day.

"Our firm is in the business of *building* reputations." Muscle memory came to her rescue, allowing her voice to steady and strengthen. She said this sort of thing a million times a week. "Using various tools like media channels and online networking, we protect and enhance our clients' profiles. When a brand or image has been impacted, we take control of the narrative. Build a story." Blah, blah, blah.

She smiled while she spoke, hands now stacked palm up in her lap, ankles crossed. Her blood still sizzled because, seriously, he was positively magnetic even when he scowled with impatience. This was what a chiseled jaw looked like—as though a block of marble named "naked gold" or "autumn tan" had been chipped and worked and shaped to become this physical manifestation of strength and tenacity. Command.

"I know what you do. That's why I called you." Luca rose abruptly from the armchair he'd taken when she'd sat.

He paced across the spacious lounge. His restless movement ruffled the sheer drapes that were partially drawn over the wall of windows overlooking the Thames.

She'd barely taken in the decor of grays and silver-blue, the fine art pieces and the arrangements of fresh flowers. It all became a monochrome backdrop to a man who radiated a dynamic aura. He moved like an athlete with his smooth, deliberate motions. His beautifully tailored clothes only emphasized how well made he was.

He paused where the spring sun was streaming through the

break in the curtains and shoved his hands into his pockets. The action strained his trousers across his firm behind.

Amy was not an ogler. Men of all shapes, sizes and levels of wealth paraded through her world every day. They were employees and clients and couriers. Nothing more. She hadn't completely sworn off emotional entanglements, but she was exceptionally careful. Occasionally she dated, but even the very nice men who paid for dinner and asked politely before trying to kiss her had failed to move her.

Truthfully, she didn't allow anyone to move her. She preferred to keep her focus on her career. She'd been taught by an actual, bona-fide teacher that following her heart, or her libido, or that needy thing inside her that yearned for someone to make her feel special, would only leave her open to being used and thrown away like last week's rubbish.

But here she was acting like a sixth-former biting her fist because a particularly nice backside was in her line of sight. Luca wasn't even coming on to her. He was just oozing sex appeal from his swarthy pores in a passive and oblivious way.

That was ninja-level seduction and it had to stop.

"I'm asking you to reverse the build," Luca said. "Give me a scandal instead of making one go away."

She dragged her attention up to find him looking over his shoulder at her.

He cocked his brow to let her know he had totally and completely caught her drooling over his butt.

She briefly considered claiming he had sat in chewing gum and gave her hair a flick, aware she was as red as an Amsterdam sex district light. She cleared her throat and suggested gamely, "You're in the wrong part of London for cheap disgrace. Possibly hire a woman with a different profession?"

He didn't crack a smile.

She bit the inside of her lip.

"A *controlled* scandal." He turned to face her, hands still in his pockets. He braced his feet apart like a sailor on a yacht, and his all-seeing gaze flickered across her blushing features. "I've done my research. I came to *you* because you're ideal for the job."

Whatever color had risen to her cheeks must have drained out of her because she went absolutely ice cold.

"Why do you say that?" she asked tautly.

His brows tugged in faint puzzlement. "The way you countered the defamation of that woman who was suing the sports league. It was a difficult situation, given how they'd rallied their fans to attack her."

Amy released a subtle breath. He wasn't talking about *her* past.

"It was very challenging," she agreed with a muted nod.

She and her colleagues-slash-best friends, Bea and Clare, had taken on the case for a single pound sterling. They'd all been horrified by the injustice of a woman being vilified because she'd called out some players who had accosted her in a club.

"I'm compelled to point out though—" she lifted a blithe expression to hide the riot going on inside her "—if you wish to be ruined, the firm we were up against in that case specializes in pillorying people."

"Yet they failed with your client because of *your* efforts. How could I even trust them?" He swept a dismissive hand through the air. "They happily billed an obscene amount of money to injure a woman who'd already been harmed. Meanwhile, despite winning, your company lost money with her. Didn't you?"

His piercing look felt like a barbed hook that dug deep into her middle.

Amy licked her lips and crossed her legs. It was another muscle memory move, one she trotted out with men in an almost reflexive way when she felt put on the spot and needed a brief moment of deflection.

It was a power move and it would have worked, buying her precious seconds to choose her words, if she hadn't watched his gaze take note of the way the unbuttoned bottom of her skirt fell open to reveal her shin. His gaze slid down to her ankle and leisurely climbed its way back up, hovering briefly on the open collar of her maxi shirtdress, then arrived at her mouth with the sting of a bee.

As his gaze hit hers, his mouth pulled slightly to one side in a silent, *Thank you for that, but let's stay on task.*

It was completely unnerving and made her stomach wobble. She swallowed, mentally screaming at herself to get her head in the game.

"I would never discuss another client's financial situation." She would, however, send a note to Bea advising her they had some confidentiality holes to plug. "Can you tell me how you came by that impression, though?"

"Your client was quoted in an interview saying that winning in the court of public opinion doesn't pay the way a win in a real court would have done, but thanks to *Amy* at London Connection, she remains hopeful she'll be awarded a settlement that will allow her to pay you what you deserve."

Every nerve ending in Amy's body sparked as he approached. He still seemed edgy beneath his air of restraint. He dropped a slip of paper onto the coffee table in front of her.

"I want to cover her costs as well as my own. Will that amount do?"

The number on the slip nearly had her doing a spit take with the air in her lungs. Whether it was in pounds sterling, euros, or Russian rubles didn't matter. A sum with that many zeroes would have Bea and Clare sending her for a cranial MRI if she turned it down.

"It's…very generous. But what you're asking us to do is the complete opposite of London Connection's mission statement. I'll have to discuss this with my colleagues before accepting." Why did Clare have to be overseas right now? Starting London Connection had been her idea. She'd brought Amy on board to get it off the ground, and they usually made big decisions together. Their latest had been to pry Bea from slow suffocation at a law firm to work for them. Bea might have specific legal concerns about a campaign of this nature.

"I don't want your colleagues," Luca said. "The fewer people who know what I'm asking, the better. I want *you*."

His words and the intensity of his blue eyes were charging into her like a shock of electricity, leaving her trying to catch her breath without revealing he'd knocked it out of her.

"I don't understand." It was common knowledge that the new king of Vallia was nothing like the previous one. Luca's father had been... Well, he'd been dubbed "the Kinky King" by the tabloids, so that said it all.

Amy's distant assumption when she had recognized Luca was that she would be tasked with finessing some remnant of Luca's father's libidinous reputation. Or perhaps shore up the cracks in the new king's image since there were rumors he was struggling under the weight of his new position.

Even so... "To the best of my knowledge, your image is spotless. Why would you *want* a scandal?"

"Have I hired you?" Luca demanded, pointing at the slip of paper. "Am I fully protected under client confidentiality agreements?"

She opened her mouth, struggling to articulate a response as her mind leaped to her five-year plan. If she accepted this assignment, she could reject the trust fund that was supposed to come to her when she turned thirty in eighteen months. Childish, perhaps, but her parents had very ruthlessly withheld it twice in the past. Having learned so harshly that she must rely only on herself, Amy would love to tell them she had no use for the remnants of the family fortune they constantly held out like a carrot on a stick.

Bea and Clare would love a similar guarantee of security. They all wanted London Connection to thrive so they could help people. They most definitely didn't want to tear people down the way some of their competitors did. Amy had no doubt Bea and Clare would have the same reservations she did with

Luca's request, but something told her this wasn't a playboy's silly whim. He looked far too grim and resolute.

Coiled through all of this contemplation was an infernal curiosity. Luca intrigued her. If he became a client… Well, if he became a client, he was absolutely forbidden! There was a strange comfort in that. Rules were rules, and Amy would hide behind them if she had to.

"I'll have to tell my partners something," she warned, her gaze landing again on the exorbitant sum he was offering.

"Say you're raising the profile of my charity foundation. It's a legitimate organization that funds mental health programs. We have a gala in a week. I've already used it as an excuse when I asked my staff to arrange this meeting."

"Goodness, if you're that adept at lying, why do you need me?"

Still no glint of amusement.

"It's not a lie. The woman who has been running it since my mother's time fell and broke her hip. The entire organization needs new blood and a boost into this century. You'll meet with the team, double-check the final arrangements and suggest new fundraising programs. The full scope of work I'm asking of you will remain confidential, between the two of us."

His offer was an obscene amount for a few press releases, but Amy could come up with a better explanation for her friends later. Right now, the decision was hers alone as to whether to take the job, and there was no way she could turn down this kind of money.

She licked her dry lips and nodded.

"Very well. If you wish to hire me to promote your charity and fabricate a scandal, I would be happy to be of assistance." She stood to offer her hand for a shake.

His warm, strong hand closed over hers in a firm clasp and gave it a strong pump. The satisfaction that flared in his expression made all sorts of things in her shiver. He was so gorgeous and perfect and unscathed. Regal.

"Now tell me why on *earth* you would ask me to ruin you," she asked, trying to keep her voice even.

"It's the only way I can give the crown to my sister."